SILICON EMBRACE

SILICON EMBRACE
JOHN SHIRLEY

MARK V. ZIESING BOOKS
SHINGLETOWN, CA • 1996

Silicon Embrace © 1996 by John Shirley
Dustjacket Art © 1996 by Paul Mavrides

Published by
Mark V. Ziesing
Post Office Box 76
Shingletown, CA 96088

All rights reserved. No part of this book may be reproduced
or transmitted in any form or by any means,
electronic or mechanical, including photocopying,
recording or by any information storage and
retrieval system, without the written
permission of the Publisher.

Manufactured in the
United States of America

FIRST EDITION

Limited Edition ISBN 0-929480-44-7
Trade Edition ISBN 0-929480-44-9
Library of Congress 96-060878

For my wife, Michelina aka Micky aka St. Dominique Stigmata

I'd like to thank the following poisons I mean persons and THINGS:

Mark Ziesing and his nearly infinite patience (which is probably not as much patience as his wife Cindy needs with him).

Greg Bishop and his magazine *The Excluded Middle*.

Glenn Campbell and his *Desert Rat Newsletter*.

Richard Smoley and *Gnosis Magazine*.

Micky Shirley for editorial assistance above and beyond and behind and below and to the side and in the middle of the call of duty.

Martha Millard for catching the ball thrown from way out in left field.

Byron Shirley, Julian Shirley and Perry Shirley for being cool dudes.

Ivan Stang for demonstrating that non-human creatures can thrive in the squirming hive of humanity.

Harry S. Robins (entomology and etymology consultant).

If I could think of something to thank you for, Mavrides, I would. Oh wait. I just thought of something. Thanks for the great art-from-hell.

AND...

All the people I swiped ideas from and all the people (even more) who swiped ideas from me.

SILICON EMBRACE

PROLOGUE

Peter, James and John followed Jesus of Nazareth, whom they called Yeshua, up the mountain trail and into the gathering dusk. To one side the legions of night, all the shadows that had waited for the day to end, gathered in the laps of the mountains; in the far distance, smoke twisted upward from the settlements near the inland sea of salt. Was that an olive grove far below, on the slopes of the mountain, the color of jade and beaten iron?

Peter alone had been so high up before, had in fact once been to a mountain that had snow on it, and he was not afraid here. Was there not a trail?

"A trail for goats alone," said James, the brother of Jesus, who was often dour.

"Master," John asked, tentatively, "might we stop, and eat? I hunger, and I have brought some bread and cheese."

Yeshua seemed not to have heard him, but strode confidently on, just as if he'd been here before, though Peter thought it likely that he had not.

They rounded a crag, and the trail became even thinner, and steeper, and rougher, and a ground mist trailed here, and a permanent dew glittered like a shed snakeskin on the dull red and gray stones.

Peter's feet hurt where he'd struck them on stones, and his sandals were coming apart. But he would have followed Yeshua across a plain of fire if the Master had asked it. And somehow, in the presence of Yeshua, all discomforts seemed like just so much natural sound, like the night-calls that the animals of the mountains were beginning to make among the twisted little trees. With Yeshua, one found another center of gravity, a detached place within, that was like the austere perspective of this mountaintop itself. Or so it was for Peter.

But James, though he seemed drawn after his brother Yeshua like a leaf in a wind, looked at Yeshua differently from the others, and could not forget the child that he had known before the awakening of the Man.

"Yeshua," said James, "I'm tired and it grows cold; the night is coming. Surely we..."

But James said no more, for they'd come to a shoulder of the mountain, a flattened place, and a great light was gathering here, seeming to coalesce in the air itself, a light that had been waiting for them. It was as if stars could come down like the rain; and that rain of light fell onto Yeshua, and he was transfigured.

Yeshua turned toward them, and he was still the same man, the same craggy black eyes and beaky nose, the same bristling black beard, the back a little hunched from childhood rickets; yet in that moment he seemed to take another meaning into himself, like the meaning in numbers and astronomy; like a figure in the jade tablets used by the practitioners of the Egyptian mysteries.

And his face - it blazed like the sun! And his clothing became as light!

And then the light above him gave birth somehow, so that something that had been there, unseen, was now visible: a cloud, perhaps, but a cloud solid as a ship, and made of the finest silver; or so it seemed to Peter. And from this cloud, descending, came two men, in white robes and flowing white beards.

These two, Yeshua said to Peter, with the tongue of his mind, *are but Elijah, and Moses, come to bring light.*

And beside the Prophets came what must be imps, or

child-angels, for these smaller beings were no larger than a child, and their eyes were ovals of onyx, and their raiment was silver that changed color as they turned, like mica. Their heads were larger than the heads of men; their bodies smaller; their fingers numbered only four, on each hand. When Peter looked into their eyes he thought he saw something there that, if it was not evil, was just as hard and unyielding as evil. Were these fallen angels, given to Elijah and Moses for servants?

Yeshua spoke with the two men in white, in voices inaudible, and Peter thought he heard one of them laugh softly, as he turned to look at the small black-eyed ones; and Peter saw Elijah slap Yeshua upon the shoulder, as if they were drunken comrades. Then Yeshua turned toward Peter; his face still bright, though the light was bearable now.

James and John fell to their knees, weeping with fear. Though his mouth was so dry it was hard to speak, and though his knees trembled, Peter remained standing and said, in a croak, "Master...Lord...it is good that we are here. If you wish...I...I will make three shelters here...tabernacles of wood, one for you and one for Moses and one for Elijah..."

He heard his own voice as if in the distance, and he thought: Why am I babbling so?

And then came another cloud of light, another kind of chariot above the silvery chariot of the little black-eyed ones and the light of this Higher chariot seemed to spill out like a weightless luminous liquid, washing over them, carrying with it logos, as on a wave: *Behold, this is my son whom I love, and in whom I am well pleased. Listen to him. Listen to him....*

The words rippled through the disciples like the shimmy of an earthquake; the words threw them to the ground; they lay trembling on their faces, and never had Peter been so afraid: it is not given for man to hear the voice of God, and lesser visitations have left men raving and broken.

And the light - it seemed to search through them, so that every unworthy thought was brought out of its noisome cubby and examined.

Peter squeezed his eyes shut, as if that would block this painful scrutiny, but only after he prayed for release did it ebb away...

And he felt Yeshua's hand on his shoulder; he knew

without looking, from the nourishment in the touch, whose hand it was.

Peter opened his eyes, his head aching, his vision swimming, and saw that the cloud-that-was-solid was gone, and the Higher cloud chariot was gone, and gone also were Elijah and Moses and the little black-eyed angels.

"Rise up and do not fear," Yeshua said. "Our purpose here has been fulfilled. Let us return to the village."

Numbly, Peter and John and James started down the mountain. They glanced at one another, as if looking for answers, and there were none.

Walking beside Peter, Yeshua said softly, "Do not speak of the vision you have seen until the Son of Man is raised from the dead..."

James asked Jesus a question about Elijah, but Peter was not listening to the question or the reply, his mind was still full of the voice and the light; and the onyx eyes of the little angels, if angels they were.

After a time, John and James, eager for food and rest, were hurrying ahead of Peter and Yeshua, and Peter thought it safe to ask, "Master - you and I, we are friends, are we not?"

Yeshua looked at him with mild surprise. "Yes."

"And if I ask you to tell me something, and promise to reveal the answer to no one, will you trust me, Yeshua rabbi?"

"I trust you, and would trust you even as you sundered my heart with a knife."

Peter decided not to let himself be deflected by paradox and parable. He spoke softly, so that the others would not hear. "Then Yeshua, friend and Master, tell me this: the small ones with Moses and Elijah - were they angels, or demons?"

"Demons? Not as you mean it. They are those who think they control my power, only because they released it in me. And they suppose they are the fathers of Elijah and Moses, and they are not. They released a power, and they suppose that they created it; they are those who live on the shores of Heaven and see it not. They are those whom God has chosen as his instruments and who yet believe that God is their instrument, that God is a dream of their own creation. They are those in whom Knowledge has outweighed Being as the moon outweighs the temple in Jerusalem. But I say to you that they have their own amazement coming, as surely as Spring follows Winter; though it will take two thousand years and more, their amazement is coming."

Peter sighed; it was one of those sayings of Yeshua, who was also called Christos Jesus, which he would never recount to others, for he did not understand it himself. And he set himself to forget it.

PART THE FOIST

Watch me face me
    dress me baby me
    phone me wire me
house me bug me fire me
    people: are the mainspring
        spinning the world around
        people, they're the mainspring
    turning this world inside out
        –King Crimson,
        from the album "Thrak"

There's UFOs over New York
    And I ain't too surprised
    Nobody told me
    there'd be days like these

    Strange days indeed
        --John Lennon

CHAPTER ONE

HIS HEAD, HIS HEAD

Only about, what, two thousand years after Yeshua's chat with Peter on the mountain. About when you'd think it would be: the 21st century is still a teenager. Can you feel that? You can almost hear it if you go outside.

In the old Volvo, 20th century vintage, gasoline motor, were the whitebread young man Quinn Helden, gaunt and stringy blond; the woman Zizz; the black dude Qarma and the fortyish, black-bearded, German-Irish Mahler, and no one else. Quinn Helden was driving South down the California coastal highway, slowing now for the roadblock.
    Up ahead were two jeeps parked sideways across the road. The dented and dirty green military jeeps were back to back, and mounted in the rear of one of them was a 16MM machinegun. Looked functional.
    There was a shaggy haired guy in a US Army uniform sitting at the machinegun, squinting at them in the slant of the afternoon sun off the gunmetal sea. One side of the Pacific Coast Highway was cliff down to rocks and ocean; the other side was

a steep muddy hill. There was no way around. And Quinn figured, looking at these guys, that there was no going back North. These guys would follow. These guys looked too interested. When people were interested in you, now, along the fractal frontiers of the Second American Civil War, they hunted you.

There were guns in the trunk of the Volvo, of course, but Mahler had insisted they carry only the one pistol in the car. For a guy who styled himself a revolutionary, Mahler could be a candyass, Quinn thought.

With his beard and shaggy brows and eyes with all the warmth of digital readouts, Mahler looked the part of the modern Bolshevik; the apotheosis of the early 21st century's smalltime, doomed revival of Communism. Quinn thought his face should go on a postage stamp under a red star.

Zizz, now, was a cultural chimera. She was with them only because her Dad was one of the directors of the Alternative Media Channel; Zizz with her neopunk animated tattoos - one of them with smirking dancers and the threedee words:

BORN TO BE IRONIC

Zizz: with her crossgender bodystylings, prettything poodle skirt and heels, sex parts polymorphously pierced; but she had tits and a pussy and the soldiers would want them. Whether or not they were really soldiers. Whatever the fuck they were.

Qarma was a black dude who'd deserted from the Muslim Militia. He'd claimed to have worked "side by side" with Black Betty the so-called Media Terrorist, but Quinn thought he was full of shit. He had the tatters of a Farrakhan suit, and he had gone from grateful that Mahler had talked them into taking him along when they left the South San Francisco Muslim Nation Refugee Camp, to sulky and increasingly imperious in his demands as they'd traveled together. It was he, he kept reminding them, who got them the car. Who stole it.

And Quinn...Quinn used to have some kind of media-franchised cultural identity, thought of himself as a child of film-making, the arts, since his Mom had been a moderately successful leftist movie actress, his Dad a flame-out rock star. And now it seemed ridiculous. Now he was just trying not to get killed crossing the Bosnia-Herzegovina that California had become outside the FedControl umbrella of the Sovereign United States. Trying to survive and keep his smudgy dignity, was all that defined him now. He had a small beard and long hair only by default, and he had the leathers, but he was just trying not to grovel to his fear of being beaten to death or set on fire or something, trying to be some kind of mensch for Zizz and trying not to hate Mahler and right now trying not to whip the car into a U-turn in panic because the guys at the roadblock would start shooting, they'd open up the car and blood and gas would mingle -

Quinn stopped at the roadblock. "Hey fellas," he said.

He thought about the fact that the car was stolen. But these guys - seven of them, looked like, seven scraggly ass half starved soldiers in grimy uniforms - these guys, they were not going to be online to any law enforcement computer in the first place and in the second place there *was* no real law enforcement South of Sacramento in 2017, with the Famine and the new American Civil War, Separatists tearing California into shifting shreds along racial and religious lines - the Christian Funs and the Islamic Funs and the Hispanic Nation ripping at each other's scrotums and in between all the warlords gnawing on the leavings - and law was open to armed interpretation, and -

"Get out th' car, sir," said the guy in the officer's outfit. He had red eyes and a pint of something in his coat pocket. The wind snapped at his beard.

Were they really military, Quinn wondered again, or were they scraggers who'd ambushed some military patrol and taken their gear? Probably didn't matter; most of the supposed military peacekeeping forces in California had devolved into gangs. It was probably all the same.

Qarma muttered, "Gonna have to shoot some motherfuckers, Zizz..."

Zizz reached into her purse for the pistol.

"Don't be stupid," Mahler, in the back seat, muttered to her. And he glared at Qarma.

Her hand froze on the gun. "Quinn?" she asked.

Here it was again. He was supposed to be the mast for their sail; he was supposed to stand up and catch the wind and get them through this.

He felt like he wasn't *there* enough to stand up to it anymore. It was all unreal except for the fear. After the massacre in the shopping mall after the San Francisco Food Riots; the bodies folded into the shopping carts, bleeding through the silvery metal mesh. Since then, he'd felt like he was caught up in some inexorable, unconquerable current...

"You going to get out of that car, *sir*?" the officer asked. Quinn decided this dude probably had been real military, once. The shell of the behavior was there.

"What we wanted to do," Quinn said, having trouble talking with his mouth so suddenly dry, "is go to Long Beach, find some friends of ours, get some transportation for back East. We're journalists."

"Journalists," snorted the guy at the machine gun. "Who the fuck cares."

Quinn swallowed. Should he tell the officer-type more? Sometimes it was better to tell a hostile interrogator at least some of the truth.

And the truth was mostly innocuous: He and Mahler and Zizz had been up in Portland, for the Alternative Media Channel, and from there gone down to the Northern California warzone ostensibly to try and interview some refugees from San Francisco, actually to find out if the rumor was true that the activist "Black Betty", a black woman of potent charisma, had been kidnapped by CIAD for FedControl; that Central Intelligence Agency Domestic had taken her for some kind of closed-door prosecution out of the public eye...

...And then a push from the Christian Fundamentalist Army had cut them off, trapped them outside the refugee camp, and there was no place north or East to go - not without getting shot - and the only way out had been South of the Bay Area, and they'd picked up some Beamed Internet sources who said the roads to Los Angeles were open along the coast. The Internet sources had apparently been totally full of shit. Or they'd been carefully mis-led by cadres like this one.

He decided against trying to explain how they'd actually come here. For one thing, these guys, if they had any residual loyalty to the Pentagon, might well be hostile to the AltMed channel.

"We heard PCH was unsecured," Quinn said, "but I

guess that was wrong, so I figure we...we oughta turn around, head back to, uh, Monterey..."

"Yank it and U-turn us *now*, Quinn," Qarma hissed.

"What's that he said?" the officer asked, looked sharply at Qarma.

"I dunno, he's kinda out of his head from being tired," Quinn said. He turned and mouthed "Shut up" at Qarma.

"How come these weasels here ain't in the Army?" said a red-faced soldier, shuffling up beside the officer; guy who looked like he'd scraped his beard off with a pocketknife. His hair was short but patchy, like he'd hand-cut that too. His eyes were flat as prison paint. "Got a federal crisis, young able bodied fuckers like this supposed to be in the Service."

"Just get out the car," said the guy at the machinegun. "All of you. Hey - Lowry?" The guy at the machine was talking to the officer now. "Me first. You said I could be first next time."

He was looking at Zizz.

"Big fucking deal," said the officer, shrugging wearily.

Now some of the soldiers had moved up from the jeeps, sort of drifted around the car, were looking through the windows at Zizz, leering mossy teeth. "What we got here, we got one recruit," the machinegunner said, "and one comfort girl for the barracks - if we pull out all that piercing shit so we don't get caught on it - " They laughed at that. "And - " He looked at Mahler. "One hard-labor draftee to help build walls over at the base."

"Fuck this shit," Qarma said.

At this point, Quinn had to agree.

Quinn had the car in reverse; he didn't remember putting it in reverse. "Go ahead, Zizz," he said.

She pulled the gun and fired point-blank through the windshield at a leering pseudosoldier. Same moment, he hit the accelerator. Blood and broken glass and screams followed them backwards down the road...

Then the machine gun...Qarma's head...Qarma's head...

Don't look. Drive, turn the car around, head north, just *go*.

The jeeps followed them north a ways, but they were slow, and the soldiers couldn't get a good shot after that, and finally they gave it up because of the gasoline. It was so hard to get fuel in California now, they didn't want to waste it just for a rape and a few indentured workers.

But after the Volvo had lost the jeep, they were down to about an eighth tank themselves, and they had blood all over the car, and pieces of Qarma's skull on their clothes and they didn't know what they were going to do or where they were going to go. They couldn't go south, there was no getting through that roadblock...

They stopped to bury Qarma's body, and to clean out the car, and that's when Quinn spotted the camouflaged entrance to the private road. He didn't know the road was there, for certain. But he could feel it: *hidden access*, the feeling said. *Hidden access*...

• • •

Farraday suspected it was important to give the appearance of not being scared.

He was being escorted by two immaculately uniformed Marines with patent-leather shoes, each one carrying an M18, probably a loaded M18, through an underground base that Congress didn't know about; through a series of high security checkpoints where he was required to offer up first his thumbprint, then his retinal pattern, finally his quavering voice-ID, to match the identity-fixes Derrick had taken earlier and sent on ahead.

Farraday's every step was videotaped; his heartbeat monitored and his breathing analyzed.

Was all this necessary for security? Perhaps, he thought, its real purpose was to do just what it had succeeded in doing: to make him afraid. To scare him into...not divulging something, presumably, which was absurd, since his only skill, really, his whole *raison d'etre* was divulging, exposing. But then again, his trade also involved downplaying things, even concealment, at times.

Farraday was a PR man. He was a fortyfive year old Public Relations man, hired from the glass towers of Chicago by the United States government under the auspices of the Chief of Staff; brought by a USMC chopper to Wright-Patterson, from there flown on a surprisingly comfortable troopjet to Nevada. Brought to a Top Secret base so he could plan a promotional campaign, which made no sense, none at all.

Well. The military was famous for its flat-eyed, deadpan absurdities; its five hundred dollar toilet seats, its friendly fire and its massive invasions of Grenadas.

He was aware that, marching along between the two Marines, (not asked to march, but finding himself doing it), he was trying to thread together some kind of pattern of familiarity in all this, to ease his fears.

He thought about his wife, Lyn, and the application for child-bearing in the offing; he thought about his home on the Lake, in Chicago. He tried not to panic.

They passed sliding steel doors, thick as a bank vault, and strode out into a vast hangar nearly the size of a coliseum, and Farraday had to wonder again how they fit all this into a Nevada mountainside without the vast majority of the government catching on.

Derrick, anyway, claimed that most of the government didn't know about this place: Dale Derrick, Colonel, USMC, the older black guy who'd recruited him. The guy who knew too much about him, and let him know it.

• • •

"You've been married eighteen years, got one kid in college, her name's Della, named after some black nanny you had as a kid," Derrick had said, the day Farraday had been recruited. "Your kid Della, she's a Liberal Arts major. Your other kid, your son, died of a drug overdose five years ago. You've got an application in to have a new baby, maybe because of the one you lost to drugs."

Derrick had reeled off all this, over lunch, a month before. And at the same lunch, somewhere between entre and dessert, Derrick had blithely reminded Farraday about the secretary he'd gotten pregnant and all the behind-the-scenes hassle he'd had in keeping Lyn from finding out, and getting the baby illegally adopted out, and paying off the girl.

Derrick recounted everything with an unnervingly jovial cynicism. He was a white-haired black man of maybe sixty, maybe sixty five, vigorous, trim, his eyes yellowing but his teeth like ivory, his uniform spit and polish, a big gold fraternity ring on his thick pinky.

Lunch had been no-expense-spared, paid for by Washington, at Supermodel, a hightone restaurant in Chicago - one of the few luxury restaurants to survive the economic downturn that followed in the wake of the Second American Civil War.

"Your knowing all that is pretty impressive," Farraday had said blandly, trying to seem unimpressed. That was the first time they'd made him afraid, and he tried not to show it then either.

"I could talk about your psyche profiles all the way back to the third grade."

"Only third grade?"

"We didn't get much on the first and second grade, except for the report cards and the basic records, a few interviews. Congratulations, by the way, on getting two gold stars on that second grade oral report about Thanksgiving."

"Thanks very much. I couldn't be prouder."

"As for the psyche profiles.....Did you know they decided you were a 'seven-point expulsive' - you hide some things by exposing others. Sort of like a magician distracting with one hand while palming the coin with the other. Makes your motivation for your choice of professions kind of obvious, doesn't it?"

"I didn't know all that." He'd known he had that tendency - but he hadn't known the school authorities had known it. "Is it really necessary to do this much research into tired, discouraged, slightly overweight tax-paying Mike Farraday?"

"You *do* pay your taxes - except for that money that Georgie Harris paid you so you'd drop out of the DeathMonkey Vodka account. You never did declare that nine grand."

"You trying to scare me?"

"Trying to let you know out front where you stand with us," Colonel Derrick said, taking a cigar from a jacket pocket, and looking at it longingly. Not a chance they'd let him smoke in here.

Man's been showing me how powerful he is, Farraday thought, but he doesn't dare smoke a cigar in here.

"You know what?" Farraday said, testing his boundaries, "All Americans know where they stand with Big Brother. Especially with 'provisional martial law in ten states'."

"Really? You know where you stand?" Derrick smiled warmly at him. "I don't think you do, not at all. You see, you've been singled out. And once Majestic15 - we call it MJ15 - once it singles you out, your life is in their hands, totally and completely. Now, understanding that, it's a situation not without its rewards. You'll get paid ten times what you've ever been paid for any one commission. And that's just for starts. You'll get all kinds of special dispensation, and longterm protection. You'll be secure. But at the price...the price of knowing where you stand, my man..."

In that moment, Derrick had signaled the waiter for the check, and the restaurant noises seemed to dim away, and all Farraday could hear was the classical music playing, a string quartet by Bruckner that he'd never heard before, but he would always remember; a light tune, for a composer like Bruckner, but for Farraday it had the reverberation of a dirge.

Now...

• • •

Now. In hangar 18 of their favorite, shiniest underground base. Derrick had been the white rabbit checking its watch, luring him down the rabbit hole. And Farraday stood in this echoing amphitheatre of a building, with men scurrying everywhere, techies looking in their yellow jumpsuits like Goldfinger's minions, and around the edges were the armed Marines, two stationed at each door, another in front of each of the giant toy tops...

Tops? They looked like tops to Farraday, three-story children's tops for a giant child to spin, brushed chrome, forty yards wide in the central bulge, two yards wide where it stood on its "spinner" on the floor. Stationary but waiting to be spun...

"Yeah," Derrick said, shaking his hand, "the simulators do grab the eye, don't they though?"

"Simulators?"

"Yeah. These aren't the real thing. What you see there are just training devices. One thing at a time, my man. Good to see you again. Let's grab a cup of coffee. I want you to meet one of The Boys."

We've had the iron hand, Farraday thought, it's back to the velvet glove. Or anyway, simulated velvet.

They walked off through a lot of technical activity that looked as staged as anything else, and maybe it was staged, or maybe it was real.

It had dawned on Farraday that all this might be one big mind control test; some kind of elaborate disinformation ploy to push the public's buttons. The civil crisis had gone on for two years and the bastards were getting desperate. And what Derrick had told him about The Boys might be pure bullshit. He might meet a couple of guys with Hollywood special effects contact lenses that he was supposed to believe were -

The alien was suddenly there, standing in front of him. He'd come out of the "simulator", walked down the metal stairs, was looking gravely - if that's what that look on his face meant - up at Farraday.

He? Was it a *he*? Farraday thought of it that way because they called the aliens "the Boys". But who knew if this creature had gender at all?

This was not special effects. This was not a costume. If it was, it was the greatest cosmetic robotics, the greatest costume ever created, and - but no, he knew it wasn't: he could feel the otherworldly life of the thing, the way you can feel a powerful electromagnetic field if you stand next to a Tesla generator.

It was a Grey, the classic Grey described in close encounters, an alien in ordinary human clothing: Calvin Klein jeans, short sleeved white Arrow shirt, slippers; it was an alien with improportionately big oval eyes of whiteless onyx, and something that might have been a nose, and the slit of a mouth, and no hair, and holes for ears, and its hands...

He stared at its hands. Four fingers, one hand moving restlessly, the other eerily still.

There was flexibility in the thing's face, but the meaning of its expression wouldn't resolve in his mind.

He felt a ripple of disorientation go through him. But not so much disorientation as all that, really: they'd been prepared for this. By Steven Spielberg; by Roswell and perhaps by calculated leaks.

Derrick's voice spoke to him, but not from Derrick. "How do you feel? Are you adjusted to me?"

The thing's mouth didn't move; the voice came from its throat; he could see it vibrate.

Derrick grinned. "Just when you think you're used to the idea, Jaron here talks to you in my voice." He shrugged. "That's just how they do it. Some kind of ancient survival strategy they evolved, send another creature's voice back at them, they don't attack. Something like that."

"Something like that," the alien said, in Derrick's voice.

"Some of them are scholars of our ancient languages," Derrick said. "Others only learned English in the 50s, when the real face-to-face communication first happened, between MJ15 and the Zetans. They communicate with one another with graduated telepathy. Or...it's closer to biological radio, I guess. They can be very selective about what they transmit or receive, talking to one another."

"Uhhhh..." Farraday said.

"Would you like some chocolate?" the alien asked.

Twenty minutes later, they were sitting in an otherwise empty cafeteria, under bright fluorescent lights, drinking hot chocolate. The alien never blinked; it had no eyelids. But there was a sort of iris, a darker place in the blackness, which shrank under brighter lights.

"The Boys can eat only very select human food, and it has to be all in liquid form. They have some other way of eating, some kind of skin osmosis thing, for their own food, there's a membrane under the neck..."

"Ummm..." Farraday said.

"But they do like chocolate. Chocolate's their favorite Earth food. And they know about all our foods. They've been surveying us for two hundred thousand years."

Farraday was gazing frankly at the alien; it was dabbing leftover drips of chocolate into its mouth with a forefinger. If that rubbery digit was a finger. Somehow, the humanlike motion, like a kid with a treat, put Farraday more at his ease. The clothes hadn't done that; to Farraday it looked more alien in human clothes than it would have in, say a skintight silver spacesuit. Maybe because he had difficulty separating it, otherwise, from the Media Extraterrestrials. It was as if the Media ETs, from the *X-Files* of his boyhood, were so familiar that in the popular mind they were just a blacksheep member of the human family. And after all...maybe...

"They're related to us, aren't they," Farraday blurted, though some instinct told him he wasn't supposed to know that.

He was right. It was all in the sullen blankness of Derrick's look, just then.

"This is not good security," the alien said, to Derrick - in Farraday's voice.

Farraday shivered.

"Where'd you hear that?" Derrick asked.

"Nobody told me," Farraday said. "It's just...obvious. What're the chances of another biped developing on another world, two eyes, skull like ours, mouth, breathes our air, can eat some of our food..."

Derrick started to interrupt him, "Well actually -"

"Oh I know the theory. Only a limited number of utilitarian forms and the humanoid biped is high probability. I don't buy it. We're related...How?"

"You know, we don't have to tell you *any* damn thing," Derrick said softly, looking flatly at him, "except what you need to know. And that's not need-to-know."

"Sure it is. Because you want me to break all this to the public, right? Isn't that why I'm here? And we're going to have to explain why the aliens look like us."

"The utilitarian-humanoid explanation will float," said Derrick.

"So does shit."

"Shit?" said the alien.

"They won't buy it -" Farraday persisted.

"We just are *not* going to tell the public every damn thing we know," Derrick said with finality. "In fact we might not tell them anything - we might decide this whole public relations Embrace project is not going to happen at all. And then you'd be sworn to life-or-death secrecy, my man. And frankly I'm beginning to be alarmed by your attitude."

"I'm sorry...you must know I refused to work for the cigarette companies because they insisted on lying...nineteen years ago I refused to do PR for Nike and Adidas because they were subcontracting to Asian child-labor sweat shops - slave labor really...Knowing all that, why'd you hire me?"

"Because we thought that meant we could trust you. A perverse interpretation of the facts, I agree, but I personally didn't pick you."

Farraday didn't like the look on Derrick's face. Like he was considering options.

Farraday knew instinctively what one of the options would be. Mike Farraday turning up dead, from an "apparent suicide".

"Look - I'm just testing the envelope here," Farraday said, hoping it wasn't too hastily, "to see what's, uh, for distribution and what's not."

"You'd have been briefed."

"I'm a civilian, Colonel. I'm not used to your procedures. I've never been in the service."

"No, no you haven't. Very true. Well. We'll take this step by step. We're not going to be telling you what our overall objective is right away...Generally, of course, you're going to find a gentle way to break the Zetans to the public. But more specifically...Well, we'll see. We'll see."

Derrick reached into his coat, took out a large Cuban cigar, and a single cigarette.

"Okay if I smoke, Jaron?" Derrick asked. And he offered the alien the extra smoke.

"You won't tell General Wescomb?" the alien asked, in Derrick's voice, his tone ingratiating.

"No, no, just between you and me."

The alien reached for the cigarette; Derrick lit it for him with an antique Zippo, then lit his own cigar.

A young Marine, with *Cpl. Collins* on his shirtpocket, looked through the door, frowning.

"There is absolutely no smoking in this facility -" Then he recognized Derrick. "I'm sorry, Colonel, I didn't realize it was you."

"Look before you leap, son. Now go away."

"Yes sir." Collins said, going away.

"The Greys smoke?" Farraday asked, not a bit ashamed of asking the obvious.

"A few of them experimented with it, over the years, out of curiosity. They're not supposed to smoke. They're a precious resource, the Boys, and General Wescomb - head of our Non-Department here - he doesn't approve. The nicotine has a more powerful effect on them." He puffed on the cigar; the alien sucked at his without moving its mouth; its eyes moved, as it looked from face to face; its chest moved slowly, in and out, like a man's. It made a loud sucking sound. It was like a little boy trying to smoke his first cigarette, though evidently it wasn't the first. "By the way, we don't call them Greys. You can call them The Boys or you can call them Zetans. They are from a planet around the star Zeta Reticuli."

"Zeta Reticuli....The Betty Hill star-map."

"Betty Hill," Derrick echoed, musing aloud, to Jaron. "The first 'abductee'. She wrote a book, *Interrupted Journey* about her and Barney Hill being abducted - did you ever see the book, Jaron?"

"Yes," said Jaron, in Farraday's voice. "Very amusing."

So they can be amused, Farraday noted. Or perhaps it's only pretending it can be amused.

"But you know - " the alien added, "we don't like the word 'abductee'. We prefer 'guest'."

"Right - you should make a note of that, Farraday. We may as well get into this abduction thing right now. 99.9% of it is horseshit. Most of it never happened - and just between you and me that's the absolute truth, that's not the 'public truth'. Nobody ever got anything rammed up them, either. But there have been a few abductions - like the Betty Hill thing - and they were specifically carried out by the Zetans so that the word would get out. They rigged up the starmap for her, the whole thing. She and her husband were *supposed* to tell the public."

"And the cattle mutilations?"

Derrick glanced toward the door, lowered his voice. "The cattle mutilations were supposed to remain secret. But they needed fresh parts...some sort of genetic experiment. The Zetans tried to keep that under cover. They didn't want to be associated with the cattle thing. See, they've been thinking Public Relations right along. Hell, they've been getting us ready for the Embrace for about seventyfive years now."

"The 'Embrace'?"

"Codename for the hypothetical occasion when we finally tell the public about the Zetans. We've only known about them for sure since 1947. The alien bodies at Roswell...And we've geared up to tell people about it three or four times and it keeps getting vetoed by the CIA or the NSA. They're afraid we haven't got the technology in control enough and some foreign power's gonna get in touch with the Zetans and get a jump on the technology and all that...power. But this time...this time I think they're ready..."

"The time has come," Jaron said, in Derrick's voice. He stubbed out his cigarette in the dregs of his cocoa. "Enough years."

"Years..." Farraday murmured. "How old is...Jaron? How long do they live?"

"They won't tell us either thing," Derrick admitted.

"It is a need-to-know question," Jaron said, in Derrick's voice. "There is no need-to-know."

So the aliens kept the government in the dark about some things, Farraday thought. Maybe it was just intelligent caution. Or maybe there was some other reason.

CHAPTER TWO

THAT DISTASTEFUL ALIEN AUTOPSY FILM

"I keep seeing Qarma getting shot," Zizz said, her voice lifeless.

Mahler made one of his infamous cold-comfort reassurances. "It's better than being tortured to death, like Johnny Castro."

"I'm sorry Qarma got killed, but we're better off without him," Quinn said, as he climbed the rubble pile beside the road. "To me, seemed obvious Qarma never knew Black Betty, he never got anywhere near her Media Terrorism Project. He was just hustling a ride to L.A. from us. Or thought he was."

"I kind of liked him when he wasn't bitching," Zizz said, lazily making a cross with her foot on the shallow grave they'd dug in the ditch.

Hidden access... Quinn felt it again. *Hidden access...*

When the intuitions came, they came on strong, and they were almost always right.

Working from the intuition, Quinn had climbed to the top of the high mound of rubble and disintegrating trash to get a look around, and, balanced atop a rusted, overturned gas-pump, he saw the road.

The wreck of an old service station, complete with the Shell sign, had been pushed up to the junction with some sort of earthmover, probably to camouflage the road from the Warlords and the Crips' "road boys". The cracked open, cheese-yellow sign now hosted a wasp nest.

He looked at the wasps' nest inside the sign and began to get another one of his feelings: he could read the nest's peculiar orderliness in the chaos around him: its patterns spoke to him. *People with guns were near* - then he lost it.

He looked back at the road. "Definitely a road back here, and it looks like it's more or less maintained."

"Probably some Warlord base," Mahler said.

"Maybe. But they have a way of slapping their graffiti all over everything...And I don't see any."

The other two clambered clumsily up the rubble after him, and looked. Zizz spotted an old plywood sign lying face down in the dirt by the road. She climbed down the cracked concrete slabs, and ran to the sign like an excited kid. She turned it over, squatted beside it, brushing red dirt away.

WESTWARD CONDOPLEX
High Comfort, High Security

Quinn walked up to her and looked the sign over. And found himself looking down Zizz's dress-front, at her cleavage.

Nearly getting killed is an aphrodisiac, he thought. For me, anyway. Maybe for her it makes her want to close her legs and roll up like a potato bug.

She'd never offered herself to him and he'd never asked; he'd taken her for one of those girls who freely and knowingly radiate sexiness, who enjoy male attention enormously, and have no intention of putting out.

Okay, he told himself firmly, you can respect that. Don't be a sexist asshole.

Aloud he said, "There are some settlements around where people either couldn't get out or didn't want to. Heavily defended but, you know, civilized. Maybe it's one of those. Maybe we can get some help there..."

"Or it's Warlords and they rape me again and again, and they kill you guys, and I of course eventually become the queen of their gang," said Zizz cheerfully, standing and kicking an old plastic Shell Motor Oil can. Born to be ironic.

Quinn turned to look at the road. "We're gonna have to take the chance. You know? And I got a good feeling about this place."

Something fluttered in the debris pile; a yellowed piece of print-out newspaper, seeming to beckon to Quinn in the breeze. He strolled to it, pulled it out from under a dirty chunk of asphalt. There was a headline.

MEDIA TERRORIST INDICTED *IN ABSENTIA*.

Picture of Black Betty. Synchronicity.

He remembered the first time he'd become sharply aware of Black Betty. A few years earlier, at a Mono-Rave. A dance where they played the same song all night. They'd been playing a Jerome-X acidhouse dancemix version of an old Iggy Pop song, *Raw Power*.

...Dance to the beat of the livin' dead
lose sleep baby, stay away from bed
RAW POWER is sho to come runnin to you...

And on one of the ravehouse's the ubiquitous, translucent, multi-image, wafer thin rave-video monitors, each one big as a billboard, was an image of Black Betty, from one of her video incursions: she had overlaid her image on a live C-SPAN transmission from Congress. There was Black Betty's video performance art, so-called media terrorism, really a kind of Frank Capra character she'd created: just a superimposition of Betty, tall and slim and black and robed like a bedouin; Betty dancing among the oblivious Congressmen, a spirit unseen to them and, significantly, visible to the rest of humanity; Betty doing a kind of urban voudoun conjuration, putting a "spell of honesty" on them. You couldn't hear it during the rave but later he'd downloaded a recording of the transmission online.

"I call you in the name of all your inner demons, I call you to become real, become real: you are only half real; you are men and women, Senators and Representatives, living in one corner of yourselves; you are incapable of self honesty and hence incapable of honesty with the people you were elected to represent. I conjure you to exorcise your lies; to give birth to the underlying

truths; to tell us how you are bought and sold and who owns you and who you'd really like to belong to, if you dared: how you secretly yearn to belong to your higher selves; to God and to the People...How you have betrayed, through FedControl, all your ideals in your panic; how you have looked the other way as racial and religious scapegoats were led into these chambers for the slaughter...You are the living dead; you are trapped in sleep; your desks are your beds; I conjure you with the raw power that God gave the People: awaken! Awaken and speak the truth!"

Quinn remembered; and remembered why he'd come here, after all. Looking for Black Betty.

He folded the paper up; he put it in his pocket.

• • •

The five acres of grounds around the Westward Condoplex were wooded with graying palm trees, great droopy eucalyptus, and small purple ornamental plums grown wild. Among the trees were the dagger-clusters of yucca; mossy, lichen-painted outcrops of sandstone; dusty red clay, fallen palm boles and stiff yellow grass.

It'd be a natural playground for a thirteen year old boy like Anatole - if not for the constant adumbration of invasion and death.

Anatole was a kid with hair the color of the grass, and almost as thatchy, and cobalt blue eyes. He was wearing cut-off jeans; his t-shirt asked the world to

WATCH FOR BLACK BETTY

His tennis shoes had been wrapped in duct tape to keep them from falling apart. His hands were red from the dirt.

Just now he was moving in a crouch through the brush, trying not to be seen or heard.

He came to a place where the tree cover parted for the sky. He looked up. You never knew: once or twice he saw RPVs fly over, robot reconnaissance drones looking for Separatist troops. Other times he thought he'd seen silvery flecks, high up in the sky, that might be manmade vehicles. And might be UFOs; might be a damn flying saucer. You really never knew. Someday he'd see a for-real UFO.

He vaulted over a high, fallen log, dived for cover,

listened, looked...Then moved on, bent over...

And stopped at a series of electric wires half-hidden in the brush. He rolled deftly under the wire, came up running, sprinting toward the nearest terrace of the condoplex -

"Shit!"

He thought he felt the laser sensing device, though that was probably his imagination; you couldn't usually feel them. But immediately he broke the beam he heard the recording, the woman's scratchy voice:

"INTRUDER! THE LINE HAS BEEN CROSSED. THE LINE HAS BEEN CROSSED. LOCATION, YARD SEVENTYTWO E-SIX. ALL INTRUDERS ARE WARNED TO TURN BACK BEFORE..."

The voice shut off, and Jack Sullivan stepped out of the brush, assault rifle in his hands. "All intruders are warned to turn back before I turn your ass into hamburger," he said, grinning at the boy.

Sullivan was a big, effortlessly buff guy, who would have had movie-star good looks if not for ragged hole that remained where his right ear had been shot away, and the scar that bisected his mouth under his right eye. He wore a sleeveless khaki shirt, jeans, workboots; his long, thinning, white-streaked hair tied back; cobalt eyes like Anatole's crinkled with amusement at the face the boy was making.

"Ok," Anatole said, "blah goddam blah, so the beam works. What about the video surveillance? I don't think that's worth the maintenance, Dad."

"Not much, no. You found the blind angle, I couldn't see you - but maybe the cams we got'll spook people into thinking they're watched everywhere."

"If we had some roving cameras, maybe."

"Yeah well - if I ever get a supply corridor reopened..."

He saw the look of fear flicker over the boy's face. He'd said *if*. And his son knew that if they didn't reopen the corridor, they would likely be dead in under a year.

As Sullivan put his arm around his son and walked back to the 'plex, he thought about just plain making a run for it, cross country. The odds, though - not even fifty-fifty...

Eventually, if he waited, Federal troops would get here. Some days it sounded as if the fighting, the shelling, was getting closer.

If it got close enough that might mean help - or it might mean death.

"We still have some vibration sensors we haven't put in," Anatole said, as he moved away from his father to tight-rope-walk a fallen treetrunk.

"Those vibers, squirrels set 'em off. I don't want to waste ammunition on an animal...Not that kind of animal..."

They emerged into the open area Sullivan had cleared with the road grader. The U-shaped condoplex, fifty yards on the other side of the exposed red soil, was cordially falling apart, a little more each season. Only a handful of people remained in the whole 'plex. It was a big place, three stories, thirty units in each building; three buildings originally, two of them remaining more or less intact.

"Anyway," Anatole said, "we've got a roomful of ammunition."

"Yeah. We still have to conserve it." Sullivan looked up at the roof as they trudged across the rutted dirt.

"Pretty soon, we've gotta teach Kian to shoot."

"I hate to do it. His grandma wanted him kept away from guns. But I guess I'll have to, yeah."

Anatole thought about Kian with a gun. Kian was young, was half Korean, half Mexican, was entirely a sweet kid, if impatient and pushy, like all little kids. They took care of him. Anatole couldn't imagine him with a gun...

They glanced up, at a flare of light.

The solar power panels on the roof flashed with the late afternoon sun.

• • •

Quinn drove the car around the hill of rubble, and down the road, and around a curve - and stopped at another sign. This one was six feet by four feet, still standing, made of a big piece of sheet rock on two by fours planted right in the dirt at the end of the road, the words stenciled in slightly runny red letters.

DANGER!
TRESPASSERS WILL BE SHOT!
WE CAN TAKE NO CHANCES
Westward Condoplex

Quinn got out of the car and looked at the sign, and at the condoplex just slightly visible through the grove of trees up ahead. The original tarmac road was pocked with shell-holes, from some earlier Second Civil War engagement, and basically not passable. There was a crude dirt road, leading through the trees, looked like it was made by the same earthmover that had piled up the rubble. To either side was brush-tangled hillside; in one of the hillsides was a graffiti'd culvert.

"There's your graffiti," Mahler said, getting out of the car and pointing at the culvert, fifty feet away.

"That's all faded, 20th century stuff," Quinn said. "And the way this sign is worded...*We can take no chances...Westward condoplex*...seems to me these are real citizens...if they're still there, and it's not just squatters now or something..."

"Or they want you to think they're legitimate."

"Or, right, they want us to think that. Even if they're legit they'd probably shoot us if we got too close - but maybe if we get to shouting distance we could get a dialog going, talk 'em into letting us in. And we can plan our next move from there."

"Sounds like a plan," said a stranger, stepping out of the culvert, pointing an M18 at Quinn.

"Oh shit," Quinn said. "Not again."

"Oh God, what a bore," Zizz said.

But the break in her voice said something different, to Quinn. *Is this when I die?*

The guy was wearing a cammie uniform. Army, it looked like. Two more came out of the culvert, guns at ready. Was it the same ragtag gang of runaway soldiers who'd shot Qarma?

Looking them over, Mahler murmured, "They look like they might be the real thing...uniform's together, hair's cut, they look a bit starved, but..."

The three soldiers came toward them, the one in the lead was about thirty, a white guy with a crew cut, helmet hanging from his backpack, sergeant's patch on his shoulder. The name on his shirt pocket was METZGER. Behind him was a black guy, BUFORD, early 20s. Then a younger, red-haired white kid, HUXLEY.

Huxley looked scared. The other two looked suspicious, but interested. Metzger kept glancing at Zizz.

Quinn thought: I'm a jerk for not getting the guns out of the trunk.

"Hey fellas," Zizz said, smiling, her voice shaking just a little. "What's up? You don't have to point guns at us."

"We got to point guns at anybody we don't know," Buford said. "We had five of us, after the Looter ambush, and some lady and her kid stabbed the other two when they was asleep. And that's the way it is, this part of the country. Now what business ya'll got here?"

"We're just passing through," Mahler said. "We're...journalists."

"Journalists?" Metzger said. "The whole fighting zone is way, way out of Media Access."

"We know," Zizz said, "we got lost, we got cut off up North-"

"You're not with the people in that building?" Huxley asked, disappointed.

"Nope," said Quinn. "You neither, huh?"

"No, we're -"

"Huxley," Metzger snapped, "shut up."

"Metzger, shit, lighten up," Buford said, "we got to trust somebody sometime or we not going to get out of this mess. These people here, they got a car."

"And we're authorized to take the damn car if we have to," Metzger said.

"So you guys are real Army?" Quinn asked. "We just ran into some used-to-be-military down the road to the South. Up North it's all Warlords and the war."

"We're the real thing, with the 210th," Buford said. "We're the only survivors we know about from our Div...Lost our uplink, out of touch with the mainframe..."

"Haven't eaten in two days neither," Buford said. "Hey, scan this, I joined the Army so's I could eat regularly. An' the Army's done run short of food, too. We was on half rations."

"Now we're down to nothin'," Huxley added, glancing at the car. "You got anything to eat?"

"Nope, we seriously don't," Quinn said. He'd been trying not to think about food all day.

"So you guys are basically lost too, huh?" Zizz asked.

Metzger hesitated, then admitted, "Yeah. We sure as hell are. Cut off and lost."

"Here's a thought, Quinn," Zizz said. "These guys are,

like, real Army, we're journalists, maybe that'll give us credibility when we ask at the Condoplex there if they'll let us in."

"Yeah," Quinn said. "If they're into it."

Buford lowered his rifle. "You mean, we go over there together." He looked at Metzger.

Metzger's rifle wavered. Then the muzzle went down, and he nodded. "We can say we're escorting the journalists..."

Something about that way of putting it made Quinn uncomfortable. But at least they weren't pointing the guns at him anymore.

• • •

Sullivan was sitting with his back to the wall between two of the boarded-over windows, watching Anatole and the boy Kian. Sometimes Sullivan glanced at the framed photo atop the Home Computer System console: Anatole, still a toddler, on his Mother's lap. Jenny had died in the first riots and Sullivan was glad Anatole couldn't remember it.

Anatole was setting up a small videocam on a tripod, cabled into the home computer console, and Kian was trying to help and getting in the way.

Kian was Sullivan's unofficially adopted son; his parents had died in the riot that had taken Jenny.

"Kian - *wait!*" Anatole was saying, trying to be patient, as the little boy tried to jam the videocam onto the tripod. "You're gonna *drop* it!"

Yamahira came in, with his daughter Lila, a young AmerAsian woman, pretty and centered, who was much in Sullivan's thoughts.

Yamahira was thin, dour, his hair speckled gray; he wore dark glasses even inside because of the painful sensitivity of his eyes.

Lila smiled at Sullivan; he nodded, and, with an effort of will, looked away from her clinging black shift and short-shorts...

I'm too old for her, Sullivan thought, and I had an ear shot off and my face looks like...Just forget it.

"I haven't heard from them, Yamahira," Sullivan said.

"Maybe I'm here for something else," Yamahira said, a little pettishly.

"You want to check for messages - go ahead. I'd have told you if we'd heard from the Feds."

"I have to see for myself," the older man admitted sourly. "I don't know why." He went to the console, tapped the keypad for satellite uplink.

Sullivan couldn't see the screen from here but he could read the console's response in a frustrated bob of Yamahira's head:

> THIS 24 HOURS NO RESPONSE

Yamahira cursed softly in Japanese. "Why don't they..."

His daughter went to him, put her arms around his waist from behind, perched a chin on his shoulder. "There are hundreds of thousands of people in the same situation, Father."

"We are as important as anyone else! They abandon us to *die!*" He broke from her, strode angrily from the room, fists clenched at his sides.

Kian and Anatole looked up, at that. Kian's mouth quivered. "Kian!" Anatole said hastily, "I think I got it working, let's try it!"

"Umm...'kay."

Smiling apologetically, Lila went to Sullivan, said softly, "I'm sorry, Jack. He didn't mean to scare the kids..."

She knew how Sullivan felt about staying positive in front of the kids.

"It's okay. Everybody gets frustrated."

She nodded and sat beside him. He thought her perfume was probably gardenia.

Anatole stood back from the camera with the air of a director. "We're going to try to send a transmission to my school, Lila - you want to send video anywhere?"

"No, no thanks."

"I wanta send something," Kian said, dancing around the camera.

"You will, you've got a book report to do. We'll do your school next."

Anatole tapped a button activating the link to the console, then tapped the console keyboard, to uplink to the satellite that would transmit to his school.

Everyone at his school knew, of course, that he was trapped here, behind the lines; the Feds knew they were there.

But there were costs to consider; and guerilla surface to air missiles to consider...

Anatole threw a switch; a cone of light formed in front of the videocam. He stepped into the light and the videocam began to record. Kian watched him, looking awestruck. Anatole was his hero.

Anatole's image in video appeared on one of the four console monitors; under his picture the computer confirmed in green lettering:

RECORDING FOR TRANSMIT.

Anatole cleared his throat. "My Video Essay on Our Situation, for Civics Two, Remote Network School 7, by Anatole Sullivan." He looked down at the paper in his hand and read, "The problem comes down to too many mouths and not enough food to put into them. That is the original cause of our situation at Westward Condoplex. The world population has increased sharply in the last two decades and the food shortage was aggravated by..." He paused to squint at the words. "...by the plutonium spill in the Pacific, that effect...effectively killed most life in that ocean, and by the pesticide build-up in the groundwater that has been killing crops and interfering with the ecological cycle. Along with PCBs it's been damaging the immune systems of the animals, especially sea animals, so they die of ex...extant viruses. Global warming also had a disastrous effect on food production...And..." He wet his lips. "...the struggle for the remaining resources has created extensive political and social faction..." He struggled with the word. "...factionalization, um, often based on religious and ethnic differences, so that in our part of the country we are now in Civil War. A pre-famine trend toward religious and ethnic fanaticism was the..." He struggled with this one too. "...arm...armature...of the struggle for resources -"

Sullivan frowned, thinking, *Armature of the struggle for resources...?* Where's he getting this stuff?

"...which was particularly harsh on the West Coast and in the New York and Louisiana areas...Certain elements of the Hispanic population in California banded together into the North American Hispanic Nation."

Sullivan was frowning, increasingly, as the boy went on.

"...Feeling threatened by the Hispanic power base, the Muslim immigrants started their own paramilitary ethnic armies...Unwilling to struggle for local power with these ethnic forces, the Christian Fundamentalist Army, as it called itself, was the first to declare its control of California's Sacramento Valley, and from there it was a short jump to declaring secession.

"More ethnic and religious groups, beginning with the new Muslim Fundamentalists, declared themselves separatist nations in a series of contradictory declarations beginning in 2010 - attempts at ethnic cleansing in Orange County led to open fighting - Federal Troops were largely occupied with similar problems in Washington DC and New York City...the drug trade was eclipsed by the trade in weapons, especially heatseeking hand-held missile launchers. California military bases were captured by surprise attacks of..." He pronounced it very slowly and carefully: "...*ethnic/religious* power bases - in response the Sovereign United States established FedControl, a partial state of martial law, in much of the country, including government control of most media - "

"Anatole -?"

Anatole looked up, startled. Surprised his father had interrupted the recording.

"What?"

"Switch it off."

Anatole stared at him. Sullivan went to the camera, switched it off himself.

"Son - you were supposed to do research, and write the piece in your own words. You've taken someone's article, or maybe two articles, and lifted whole sentences and paragraphs out verbatim. You didn't write the 'trend to religious and ethnic fanaticism being the armature of the struggle for resources'. You don't even know what an armature is."

"I do too."

"So what is it?"

"..."

"That's what I thought. Anatole, the way you did it is cheating -"

"I don't *want* to put it in my own words, Dad." His voice was breaking.

"Why not?"

"I don't want to *think* about it that much!" He was close

to tears. "Why'd you give me this stupid assignment! *Shit!*"

He threw the papers at his father; they fluttered like confused doves in the air between them, and the boy walked out of the room.

"Everybody's walking out today," Kian said.

"Yeah," Sullivan said, picking Kian up in his arms. He wanted to go to his son, just then, but he knew he had to give him time.

He'd thought writing a report on the historical basis of their situation would give Anatole perspective, give him a mature outlook, so that he would cope with the whole thing better. But he'd been trying to force maturity on a boy. He should have let him write the report he'd wanted to write, on the mutated seaweed in the Pacific, or even on flying saucers. Kid's room was covered with pictures of flying saucers.

"He'll be okay," Lila said, picking up the papers.

Sullivan hugged Kian, and wished he could look out the windows.

That's when the siren went off, and the scratchy recorded voice said, "INTRUDER! THE LINE HAS BEEN CROSSED..."

Sullivan went to get his gun.

• • •

Quinn and Buford stood frozen, uncertain which way to run as the sirens blared and the warning rang out.

Quinn started to bolt - Buford grabbed his arms, spoke loud enough for the others behind to hear: "Might be mines! Don't be running!"

"- THE LINE HAS BEEN -"

The voice cut off. Another, non-recorded, replaced it, from the same scratchily amplified PA.

"WHO ARE YOU AND WHAT IS YOUR BUSINESS?"

"Journalists and Federal troops!" Quinn shouted. "Six of us! Can we come in! We will leave our arms where you can retrieve them -!"

"Now wait a minute!" Metzger hissed.

"Man's right," Buford told Metzger. "They never let us in we don't give up the weapons."

"Anything," Huxley said, "I'm so hungry."

There was no reply from the house. It occurred to Quinn that the unknowns in the house might be setting up hand-held heatseekers; they could be using this lag to home in on them. Kill them rather than take a chance. It's what a lot of sensible people would do.

He might have done it himself, if he lived out here.

• • •

The Condoplex was situated on a low ridge; to one side was the woods, on ground gently sloping up to the 'plex, on the other was the parking lot - now occupied with a halfdozen vehicular hulks, pitted metal debris in various parking slots. A charred Saturn Electric still had a skeleton in it. The doors had been fused shut by the incendiary bomb that had made the tarmac into a puddle, and the skeleton was glued by remnant flesh to the seat's melted Naugahyde, so Sullivan had "buried" the skeleton by covering the car with a plastic tarp.

Sensors and wires crisscrossed the parking lot and the contiguous mortar-pocked ground.

Beyond the parking lot was a sheer drop-off to a now-disused highway, rubbled from a fallen overpass, cratered by artillery; beyond that: scrubland, tangled with razor wire Sullivan had strung himself. The scrubland had once been park, and was still scabbed with the half melted toystore-colored remains of what had been a hard-plastic playground climb-on. And beyond that, the wreckage of the Westward Mall.

On the second floor of the 'plex, the wooded side, was the observation bunker. It was made up of cemented sandbags, cinder blocks filled in with concrete, and layers of sheet metal; inside were gunports, fire extinguishers, ammo boxes, and the handheld heatseeker launcher for which they had exactly four shells.

Sullivan was looking into a cantilevered mirror he'd set up in the gunport chute so he didn't have to look directly into the slit to see who was out there. People aimed at gunports.

He could see the group of strangers but not clearly. He decided to chance a more direct look with the binoculars.

Okay, yeah. The ones in cammies looked like real Army. They didn't look too ragtag. But so what - they could be recent deserters, and it would be better to trust no one. The soldiers should have used a radio to contact him, and they apparently didn't even have that.

He was aware that Yamahira was standing behind him.

"What?" Sullivan asked, looking through the binoculars.

"These people are our contact to the outside world; they are a chance to get out of here," Yamahira said.

"Chance is the word," Sullivan said. "We'd be better off driving them off - or cutting them down. We've got kids here, we shouldn't take a chance with something this doubtful, man."

"It's now or never, Jack."

Sullivan turned to look at him. He had no authority over Yamahira. "You got your mind made up?"

Yamahira said, "I'll get their weapons."

• • •

Yamahira held the old M16 steadily on Quinn and the others as Lila gathered up the weapons they'd piled on the edge of the open ground between the woods and the 'plex.

Lila herself carried an uzi, slung on a strap over one shoulder. Her face was as grim as her father's. They both understood the risk they were taking. She didn't even return Zizz's smile. She couldn't smile back till the stranger was disarmed and under control.

Sullivan was covering them from the bunker. He'd fired a shot overhead to make sure the strangers knew he was there.

"Let's go, hands on your heads," Yamahira said.

"I hope you know what you've gotten us into, Quinn," Mahler said, putting his hands on his head.

What he'd gotten Mahler into! Quinn thought, ruefully putting his own hands on his head and marching along in front of the old Japanese guy with the automatic weapon. That was a good one. It was Mahler who'd recruited him from film-school in Orlando, promising him he'd make a documentary about Black Betty, and while the Alternative Media Channel couldn't pay him, it'd cover his basic expenses.

But from the start the project had no real center of gravity. They'd been saddled with Zizz, supposedly a journalism student, daughter of some AltMedia mucketymuck. He had mixed feelings about Zizz.

And there was Mahler; he and Quinn were hemispheres apart politically. Quinn was closer to an anarchist than a communist - but he admired Mahler's ideological doggedness. Maybe Mahler was dogmatic, but his dogmatism wasn't flaky like some of the fly-by-night politicos Quinn had known. Yet it was

Quinn who ended up in the leadership role, when it came to the crunch.

Quinn was no physical coward. Before moving to Orlando, deciding to use film-making as his weapon, he'd fought with 9mm hardware against the Neofascists, the post-Buchanan New Right militias, on the streets of Brooklyn and in New Orleans.

They'd lost New Orleans - it was only nominally a state, now. It was still grudgingly part of the Union. But the Louisiana Christian Funs, even the ones who hadn't gone totally Separatist, routinely flouted the Constitution, banning abortion, requiring not only school prayer but Christian prayer, pressuring Muslims and Hindus out of the state by denying them business licenses. Most of the Mormons had left to join the secession of Utah...

Quinn was young, but he'd pulled the trigger on a few people, and he believed in armed struggle.

But here? Here it was all meaningless. He was caught between warring factions and bands of criminals and he had no sympathy or loyalty for any of them. His death would have no political significance. Trying to get closer to the legendary Black Betty he'd gotten, instead, too close to the chaos and madness at the core of the new social reality.

Black Betty had been trying to organize some political heft for the NorthernCal refugees. Quinn and Zizz and Mahler had tried to peer past the Civil War media blackout and promote what Black Betty was doing and somehow had become refugees themselves.

And now he'd turned himself over to armed strangers who might just execute him on general principle. A meaningless death...

But an hour later they had not been executed. They were waiting to eat in the basement the condoplex used for a dining room. The windows were blocked off with cemented cinder blocks.

The disarmed soldiers, and Quinn's party, sat around the long folding metal table, hungrily watching Lila putting canned stew into a big microwave oven.

"You always make her cook?" Zizz asked.

Quinn winced. "Zizz...Let's not get into politics..."

"It's okay," Lila said, smiling, getting plates. "I like to cook...if this counts as cooking. Maybe it's my Asian Female heritage or something. Really I think I just like to feed people. Sullivan and Dad cook as often as I do. Sullivan makes a pretty mean macaroni and cheese..."

"*Mean* is right," Anatole murmured. "It'll kick a hole in your stomach."

Sullivan smiled. He was standing against the wall with Yamahira, both of them with weapons on straps over their shoulders; a shrug away from shooting.

Anatole sat at the table with the soldiers, Kian close beside him; but out of the newcomer's reach.

"So, uh, tell me," Metzger asked, "how'd you manage to have food when everyone else in this sector is basically starving?"

Anatole blurted, "My Dad was ready when the famines started. He already had the solar power and a big stock of guns and ammo and food -"

"Anatole!" Sullivan barked. He shook his head at the boy.

"Your dad don't trust us yet," Metzger said.

"I don't blame him," Huxley said. "He don't know anything about us. People tryin' to break in here all the time probably..."

"It happened twice," Kian said, suddenly. "Warlord platoons. We hada kill 'em."

Sullivan winced.

The six newcomers turned their heads as one when the microwave *dinged*. Lila spooned stew onto their plastic plates. "If you haven't eaten in a couple of days," she said, "you might want to go slowly."

The newcomers ate ravenously, ignoring her advice.

She smiled. "It's been in the can for about two years, it might taste like tin..."

"It tastes *great*," Huxley enthused. "Tin and all. I sure am grateful to you people."

"That's right," Buford said, "folks just don't *do* this no more."

Sullivan snorted at Yamahira. "*Sane* people don't."

"My Dad's not like other people," Kian said simply, proudly.

"That's true," Lila said, with a softer smile, pouring instant coffee.

His voice carefully modulated, Metzger asked, "You

going to keep those guns of ours, Mr. Sullivan?"

"For the time being. Any idea why I haven't been able to raise the military on the radio?"

Huxley answered through a mouthful of food. "They changed frequencies. We had a convoy of supplies, mostly weapons, and the Looters used the old frequency, set us up and jumped us...Just us and the two officers survived..."

"Chickenshit officers," Metzger growled, "left in a minicopter to 'get help'."

Buford snorted. "What a joke. Help their own asses is all."

"We haven't been able to raise the military or the government in a while," Yamahira said. "They must know we're here. We've thought of taking our chances cross-country..."

Buford shook his head. "If you don't run into Warlords or road Crips, you probably get picked up by the Moslem Militia, and they'll decide ya'll are spies and shoot ya. You oughta be able to get airlifted out, sometime." He drank some coffee. "Deal is, our uplinks to Computer Command stopped working. And calls from civilians, they're running into endless red tape, because of the fake ones."

"Fake ones?" Lila asked.

"Sure. The Separatists - all three groups - they put out false calls for help, and lay traps. Terrorist bullshit but there it is."

"So that's why we're being ignored..." A note of despair crept into Lila's voice. She busied herself cleaning a bowl.

"That," Metzger said, "and the EMP bombs."

"That for real?" Sullivan asked.

"You betcha. Separatists know that this man's Army nowadays, it's organized around computers and remote control. Most of the budget went into long-range stuff, right? Remote control, Remote Piloted Vehicles, your smart missiles, EP7s, all that. But you set off an electromagnetic pulse bomb, it scrambles all that shit for miles, sometimes it fries the works for good. Dipshits in the military reduced the ground troops to minimum - thinking they were gonna rely on remote controlled gear, computerized long-range, and all that tech turns out to be bigtime vulnerable and so now we can't use more'n half of it without wasting it and we don't have enough trained men and...and there you go. Country ain't strong enough to prevent a damn Civil War..."

"The Remote Control military seemed like a good idea at the time," Lila said. "Less risk to our troops..."

"Truth is, Pentagon currently ain't got a clue," Metzger said.

"Includes us," Huxley muttered.

"This is all great to hear," Quinn said, "just great. More confusion means more mayhem, more refugees, more suffering."

Zizz looked at him. "I was doing great at feeling sorry for myself till you said that."

"Sorry to rain on your...rain."

"Suffering is part of the struggle," Mahler observed.

"And suffering is succotash," Zizz muttered obscurely, eating peas and carrots before Lila was done spooning them out for her. Her flippancy hid bitterness, Quinn thought.

"I don't know what the hell we're gonna do, tell you the truth," Huxley was saying.

Sullivan read disappointment in Yamahira's downcast eyes: These men weren't going to be able to help them.

But then, he thought, maybe it is a help, having some strangers here: for the kids. Because it's civilized. Because it teaches society. Sure, it'd be good.

If the newcomers didn't kill them in their sleep and take their supplies, that is.

• • •

Farraday didn't want to enter the saucer.

At first sight, the saucer might have been faked-up by a Hollywood special effects man. It was seamless, so far as he could tell, but that could be an effect too. It was about a hundred feet in diameter, a dull aluminum-colored oval, from where he stood, and it was standing on something he couldn't make out yet. It really wasn't anything...scary.

He didn't want to enter the damn thing. The alien, Jaron, was somewhere in the background talking to a technician in the technician's voice, and Colonel Derrick was there, at Farraday's elbow, urging him on, but he didn't want to go in.

There was a frightening smell about the saucer, though Farraday could smell nothing but the burnt coffee in the pot at the technician's worktable. It was as if the saucer gave out an irritating sound, though it was soundless; it was as if it glared a painful light into his eyes, but it glowed not at all.

"Oh wait," Colonel Derrick said suddenly, "I feel it too now. Sorry, I forgot about that...Some people I guess are more sensitive to it than others. Jaron!"

"Yes?" The alien said, coming over, speaking Derrick's voice back at him.

"The field is still on."

"I will turn it down," the alien said, walking to the saucer. A small moveable metal stairway, just the sort pushed up against passenger jets, rose to the oval doorway of the saucer. Jaron climbed up it; his movements were very natural, most of the time, but climbing stairs looked strange on him - it was as if his joints didn't like bending that way.

He entered the saucer, and almost immediately most of the undefinable sense of dread fell away from Farraday.

"There's a field that psychoactively repels human beings," Derrick said, as they approached the saucer. "That's what you were feeling. Goes right to some particular area of the brain. Lot of strange ambient fields with this thing."

On impulse, Farraday bent and looked under the saucer to see what was holding it up and, as he half expected and half dreaded, he saw that...nothing was holding it up. It was apparently levitating.

"That's right," Derrick said, "the ground field is permanent."

Could it be hanging from wires? Supported by rods extended from the wall? When he was a kid he saw the magician David Copperfield "levitate" a small car. Of course it was a trick, but it had fooled an audience of thousands watching in person. Could this, he wondered again, be some great disinformation scam?

He'd heard a story on the Internet, once, that the military had fabricated the whole flying saucer scare as a cover-up for their own experimental aircraft and SDI activity. Could they have a reason to want the public to believe aliens were among us? And were they using him to spread that belief?

But again, as he entered the saucer and looked at Jaron, the doubts refused to stick; they slipped away from him, and he felt himself in the presence of the otherworldly. Some unfamiliar sixth sense confirmed that Jaron was alien to his world.

The interior of the saucer was roughly circular, the seamless walls pebbly like cobblestone but all of one piece; they were a faintly iridescent metallic color, and there were recesses in which were shelves that might be consoles, but he could see no instruments on them. In fact there were no seats...and no windows.

There was a faintly luminous irregular section of the smooth floor where the metallic deck seemed to graduate seamlessly into something like waxy crystal. When he approached the yard-wide patch of flat crystal floor, he began to hear voices in his head, with hallucinatory clarity: his mother's voice, chiding him, "I don't know where your mind goes - as soon as you walk into the bathroom you scatter towels and dirty clothes all over the floor..." He heard his dead son's voice, wheedling, "But if you buy it for me now I won't ask for anything else for -" His ex-boss's voice, weeping softly, saying, "I can't believe it, can't believe they'd do this to me..."

He stepped hastily back from the panel. The voices ceased.

Derrick laughed. Jaron "laughed", too, in Derricks' voice. Probably just to be sociable.

"The field that comes from the drive-force, as we call it, also has psychoactive properties for human beings," Derrick said.

"Your brains are not well shielded," Jaron said.

Suddenly Farraday was angry, though he wasn't sure why. "Are you naturally shielded, Jaron, or - artificially?"

"What's that mean?" Derrick asked.

"I mean...they hide things from you, right? How do you know...it sounds stupid when I actually say it but...how do you know that's his head? How do you know it's not a kind of...of biological helmet?"

"You've been reading too much science fiction," Derrick said.

"You're saying that to me while I'm standing in a flying saucer? How do you know that's his head? I mean - they could have some kind of shielding technology they're not giving us...There was that alien autopsy, when I was a kid - that thing they showed on Fox. If the alien autopsy film was real, then the eyes -"

"*That*," Jaron interrupted, raising Derrick's borrowed voice for emphasis, perhaps even anger, "was not real. We would *never* have permitted such a thing."

"Santilli - the guy who sold the alien autopsy thing to the Fox Channel - he got the 'alien autopsy film' made," Derrick said, shrugging. "The Black Project, he called it. Underground special effects team. CIA funded it, of course. It was part of a long tradition of UFO disinformation - there was old Donald Menzel, there was Keyhoe... It was preparation for the Embrace - "

"It was a *bad* preparation," Jaron said. "It was wrong. It was a mis-step. They intended to show human power over my people so your humanity would feel...reassured. But your humanity - it was only confused."

The alien really did seem ticked off, somehow: the hint of a shout in the voice and a certain twitching of his digits. The alien autopsy film had apparently been a human *faux pas* as far as the "space brothers" were concerned.

Twice, Farraday noted, the alien had referred to Earth people as "your humanity". Interesting way to put it.

Farraday went to the place he'd picked out as being the likeliest control consoles. "There must be instruments somewhere."

"They are in front of you," Jaron said, in Farraday's voice. "Put your hand over the console."

Farraday reached out, held it over the long, iridescent-gray shelf that followed the curve of the wall, in one of the slight recesses. His hand tingled - and he felt a pressure against it though he was touching nothing visible. Was there something invisible there? But as he pushed his palm down over the console he felt no physical resistance - only a sense of *thereness* pushing back, and that faint tingle. Running his hand up and down the console he felt the tingles only in certain areas.

"More ambient fields - " Derrick said. "They react to your body's bioelectric fields, transmit very precise control to the mechanism...whatever the mechanism is. If our techboys have figured it out, or had it figured out for 'em, they didn't tell me about it. I'm subject to the need-to-know thing myself." He cleared his throat and added, "...I hope those controls are disengaged from the drive, Jaron."

"Of course," Jaron said. "He can do nothing. I have taken the keys out of the car. But I will give you seats."

Farraday turned to watch as Jaron went to another console, made a single dexterous, curving pass over it, his digits an inch over the surface, and instantly the floor between Derrick and Farraday buckled, then shrugged itself up, flowing into the rough shapes of chairs.

"Holy shit," Farraday said.

"Always gets me too," Derrick said, sitting down.

Farraday made himself sit down. He almost leapt up again when the chair seemed to shift under him - until he realized it was adjusting itself to his contours. Suddenly, it was the most comfortable chair he'd ever sat in.

He found himself looking out a window that hadn't been there a moment before, a window big as the windshield of a bus - the same sort of waxy crystal in the center of the floor had appeared in the midst of the wall panel in front of him, and as he looked it became perfectly transparent, and he was seeing a new view of the hangar: men in jumpsuits working on the frame of a human-made copy of the saucer, the manmade version flat on the cement floor.

That thing, he thought, looking at the copy, *can't be any kind of real duplicate of this. It's like a Cargo Cult construction.*

He stood up, and the seat shrank into the floor, as into the "animation fundament", the primal stuff from which Gumby and Poky sprang.

He turned to Jaron. "You've really given them...us...the power that moves this thing? Faster than light travel?"

"We have given the beginnings. Enough for this world."

"That's a need-to-know issue, Jaron," Derrick warned him.

"It's one of the first things people are going to ask, and ask again and again till it's answered, Colonel. *Will the Zetans give us access to the stars.*"

"People are going to be preoccupied with other issues," Derrick said, taking out a cigar - then putting it away again.

"What issues are those?"

"The Meta," Derrick said. "The Meta are going to present a challenge."

"The Meta? Who are the Meta?"

Derrick stood, and stretched; the chair melted into the floor. "The Meta are the other aliens, my man. The hostile aliens."

In the same dead retail complex as the partly ruined Mall,

across the scrubland and the broken highway and a vast mall parking lot from the condoplex, was the shell of a looted surplus discount store. A Costco. It was an hour after dawn, in the huge store-space, vacant but for broken-down empty shelves, ankledeep trash, some of it turned into mush by old rains and a leaky ceiling.

A few broken-open cash registers lay on their sides amid the rubbish; a yellowed, mummified human foot; a puddle of oil; the wreckage of a laser bar-code reader.

A haggard man, Caucasian, long hair matted, bearded, wearing unraveling mechanic's overalls and no shirt, came poking through the refuse with a stick. He carried a shotgun under one arm. A rat moved through the trash, exciting not disgust in the man but hunger; it was too fast for him, scuttled into a drain.

The man spotted a tin can, snatched it up - it was empty. He threw it aside - and spotted another, three yards away. And this one looked intact!

Licking his lips, he hurried toward it. A single unopened can of tuna fish. And then he knew he wasn't alone.

The other man looked like he was maybe Pakistani, also bearded and longhaired and grimy. He stepped out from behind one of the few standing empty shelf-racks. This Pakistani had a .45 automatic in his hand.

He was staring at the tuna fish can too.

"I'm first come," said the Caucasian. "Back off."

He pumped a round into the 12 gauge.

"I have a family," the Pakistani replied.

"You were warned."

He aimed the shotgun - the Pakistani guy dived to one side, firing the pistol. Missing. Both men took cover, the Pakistani behind the metal shelves, the Caucasian behind an overturned cash register.

The Pakistani fired again and the bullet struck a fiberglass counter beside the computer-cash-register. The Caucasian ducked down, began bellycrawling through debris, trying to outflank his competition. He could see the tuna fish can between them. Three running strides from where he lay: but he'd be shot before he got to it.

The Pakistani decided to just go for it. He zigged around

the corner of the shelf, zagged for the tuna fish can, firing his pistol toward the trash heap the Caucasian was crawling through.

The Caucasian got to his feet and lunged, firing the shotgun from the hip, almost point blank, as the Pakistani fired the pistol, the two of them equidistant from the tuna fish can -

The Pakistani spun, and fell, wailing, spouting blood from a fist sized hole in his belly. He writhed and died in a tangle of grocery receipt paper.

The Caucasian bent, very slowly, and picked up the tuna fish can, and looked at it. Then his fingers wouldn't hold onto it anymore, they ignored his demands, they let the can fall, and then he fell, too, and all the strength in him drained out through the bullet hole between his lungs, and he gasped like a landed fish and he died.

Thirtyseven seconds of silence.

Then the crunch of boots in the rubbish. Austin stepped into the little clearing in the debris where the two men lay, bodies still steaming the heat of life away.

Austin's pistol was smoking; he'd fired at the same time the Pakistani had, because he had been able to see, with a kind of polished instinct, that the Pakistani would miss. And he'd shot the Caucasian between the lungs.

Austin was a "lieutenant", as he styled it, in the "Public Militia", a wolfish white guy with exactly half of his upper row of teeth missing, all on one side of his mouth. His beard was carved into three distinct spikes, his hair carved into a precise grid of barbs. He wore a pieced-together paramilitary uniform, with a black and red armband, the initials PM spraypainted on the back of his appropriated army jacket.

He picked up the tuna fish can, admired it, put it in his coat. He retrieved the shotgun and the .45, looked through the pockets of the dead men, found some ammo, pocketed that, and strolled off, whistling, kicking cans. He walked out the hole where the glass doors had been.

Fiftyfive seconds of silence.

Then a woman named Anja stepped out from hiding, and looked around the ravaged discount store. Her head was shaved, her scalp itself tattooed: images of angels wrestling with devils. She was pretty, but her expression was bitterly tough. Her lower lip was doubly pierced. She wore a tattered bomber jacket, cammie fatigues, heavy boots. There were two knives and guns strapped to her: those were the visible weapons.

She squatted beside the dead men, inspected them, leaned over the Caucasian, taking a serrated hunting knife from her boot sheath, and cut the cloth away from the leg; then she began cutting away at the Caucasian's thigh. She cut off eight long strips of stringy flesh, four from each leg. She also cut away his biceps.

Anja's expression, all this time, was distracted; she was thinking of something else entirely.

As she cut away the guy's flesh, her expression never changed.

• • •

The Mezzanine level of the Mall was mostly intact. It included a Balcony Terrace, where the Dining Court customers had once eaten their chimichangas and curries and gyros and plates of shrimp-fried-rice.

All that remained of the Dining Court was broken glass from the glass-topped tables; around the bent, overturned table frames was a mulch of styrofoam crockery and paper napkins and the droppings of men and feral dogs.

Bremer, the Warlord - or the Chief of Staff, as he preferred it - of the Public Militia, stood at the faux-wrought-iron railing edging the Terrace, gazing out over the wasteland of the parking lot to the scrubland, the highway, the buckled overpass, and finally the condoplex.

Nearly a head shorter, Austin stood beside him; eight other oilers - looters, stood about, complaining under their breaths, cradling their stolen assault rifles.

Bremer's head was shaved. There was a rose-twined crucifix tattooed on his scalp, atop his cranium. He was a tall man, with broad shoulders, but narrow of chest, long of arm. Like the others Bremer wore a mismatched military outfit, *PM* spray-painted across the back; Bremer's outfit was supplemented with a General's billed cap which had been looted from a costume shop. On one shoulder an M18 hung from a strap. Around his neck hung digital binoculars.

Austin was saying, in his Texas accent, "They've got juice. It's either an underground line from the city or -"

"Solar power," Bremer said. His own accent was British.

"Open your fucking eyes. The panels are right there on the bloody roof."

"If it's like the scout says, they're stocked, they can last for months. The fuckin Marines'll be here by then."

Bremer took his M18 from his shoulder, aiming the rifle as he mused aloud. His voice was melodious as an oboe. "This part of California, the Marines will be kept very, very busy..."

He fired a short burst with his auto-rifle at the condos, then looked through the binoculars to survey the damage, see what the reaction would be.

Dexie, the skinny Arkansas speedfreak whose mouth was never quite closed, but whose right eye was infected shut, chattered, "You trying to hit the solar panels, Brem? Can't hit em from here, too much range, not enough impact, they hardened glass prolly. We could, like, blow the fucker up..."

"I want the place more or less intact," Bremer murmured.

Austin shook his head. "Tip 'em we're out here, shootin' at the solars that way."

"They assume we're out here whether we are or not," Bremer said. "That bastard in there killed our scouts, not two months ago, killed all but one, and he knows we'll be back."

"We're back," Dexie said, "we're back now. We're back. They's a girl in there too, you know that?"

"So I heard," Bremer murmured melodiously. "Let us just go see, shall we?"

He led the way off the Terrace, to the stairway, the parking lot, and the highway, heading for the woods around the condoplex.

The condoplex was not aware of him coming. But Anja, who'd stationed herself on a hill overlooking the mall, knew where the Militia would be going.

Throwing strips of fresh human meat to the thing that fed in the back of her battered van, she wondered at the opportunities.

See, she had some ideas she wanted to try out.

CHAPTER THREE

NOTHIN' UGLIER THAN A LAND OCTOPUS

The deserted Westward condo was carpeted with an old, stained synthetic rug, some shade of light blue once, now the color of an overcast sky. There was a sofa missing its legs, sitting on the floor against the wall, and a big-screen TV that was just a shell, long since gutted for parts, and there was a bathroom that "sort of" works, as Lila told it to them, using buckets of water from the well.

Trying to put Zizz at her ease, Quinn asked, "Lots of empty rooms here - any reason we can't all have separate ones?"

"There is a reason, yes. We prefer you stay together," Lila said, the uzi still on her shoulder. But she smiled. "I put some water in buckets in the bathroom, there's enough for a sponge bath. Better get some rest."

She left them, Mahler and Zizz and Quinn, alone in the apartment. It was about eleven at night. Nothing had been resolved, except their hunger pangs. But they had time, and a place, to think.

Mahler went into the bedroom, where he found a bare mattress on the floor, and nothing else. He lay down and was snoring almost instantly.

Quinn sank onto the couch, half sprawled; Zizz sat beside him, in the other corner, hugging her drawn-up knees. "I was in the kitchen downstairs, trying to clean Qarma's blood off my pants. I couldn't get it all off," she said, staring at the broken TV screen.

"Well. Tomorrow we'll get some clean clothes from the car."

"I'm such a dess," she said morosely, with a depth of feeling that surprised him.

"A dess?" Short for decimal; contemporary equivalent of a dweeb. "Why?"

"I just...I hate it when my Dad's right about something - he's all: there's no short cuts. And...he was right. I made him put me on this assignment so I could get a short cut to...to *something*. Some kind of career. I mean, I couldn't even make up my mind what my major was. And after the war started everything seemed so fucked up...All cracked...And I...I just want to be something solid, you know? But I'm just a dess."

"You know what I was thinking today, when we found this place? I was thinking how amazingly good you were about keeping yourself together. You didn't panic. You never screamed when the shooting started at the roadblock. Or when somebody got killed right next to you. You helped me bury him. Most..." He started to say most girls, but he stopped himself in time. "Most people would've tripped out, been totally useless."

She looked at him sidelong. "Serious?" She was so pleased she was getting goosebumps; he could see them on her arm.

He saw into her then: the way he could, sometimes. He could see into things, into situations; felt the pattern shaping out of chaos. And in her he saw a girl coming of age who wanted to be more than a media sylph. She kept up the born-to-be-ironic surface because she didn't know what else to do, but she wanted something palpable. She wanted all the things that everyone wanted...She was a suburban gamin who wanted to be a Joan of Arc. A Black Betty.

"Serious," Quinn went on. "I mean - I did, I lost it the first time I was in a fight. I never did get really used to people shooting at me. Or me at them."

"Was that in Brooklyn?"

"Yeah. My friend got gut-shot. It's not like in the movies. They don't die when they should; they don't hang on bravely and give you a thumbs up as you go out to revenge them. When your friends get gut-shot, they scream. Then they scream some more and they writhe around and they keep screaming and calling for help and begging and screaming and they don't stop -"

Seeing the expression on her face, he changed lanes. "My crowd in Orlando, it was, like, all the fashion to join the resistance to the neofascists, up in New York...It was - I think this was the fantasy - it was like Hemingway's pals in the early twentieth century going off to fight against Franco in Spain. So I went, and I about lost it, the first two weeks. I made two friends and both of 'em were killed about the time we got close. I rode in the truck all the way back to Florida with their bodies...Let me tell you, when the bodybags started coming back the fashion to go fight for freedom up North kind of deflated..."

"You're not from Orlando. You don't have an accent."

"I started out in upstate New York - before the shooting started bigtime...Went to film school in Orlando after it replaced Los Angeles as the film making hot-spot. Surprising how many lefty-types migrated there. But I remember my professor - when I got involved in the politics, was getting ready to get into the fighting - he said, 'If Jean Luc Godard hadn't gotten sucked into radical politics, he'd have made a lot more good movies...'"

She chuckled, with just enough diffidence he knew she was only pretending to know who Godard was. He wanted to tell her: relax, why should you know obscure 20th century lefty film makers? But that would make her feel busted. So instead, seeing her eyes droop with fatigue, he said, "So. If I can have one of those couch pillows, you can have the couch, I'll crash on the floor."

She looked at him with a strange flatness. Then she nodded. "Sure."

They turned out the light, and he lay down in front of the door. He didn't know why. Some instinct maybe.

He closed his eyes. He was in the midst of a societal no-man's land; he was behind the lines of a Civil War. He was asleep in seconds.

. . .

Jaron was waiting for Colonel Derrick in the cubbyhole they called an office. He could smell the faintly alien smell off the

Zetan, reminding Derrick of the way the water smelled in his son's little plastic turtle terrarium when it needed to be cleaned.

The alien was standing in a corner, crushing a cigarette in its digits, sniffing at the crushed tobacco, crushing it some more. It looked unblinkingly at him and spoke in Derrick's own voice.

"I am wondering, Colonel Derrick..."

Whenever he was alone with Jaron and it spoke with his borrowed voice, Derrick had to struggle with the feeling that he might, after all, be dreaming all this. And hadn't the Zetans said something about "the breakdown of your shared-reality paradigms" and the "troublesome intrusion of unwanted miracles"?

"...about the issue of the Metas and this man Farraday. Perhaps we should say no more to him about it. Indicate that the subject is closed."

"What? How can we do that?" Derrick perched on the edge of his desk, stared unseeing at a Jet Propulsion Lab calendar on the opposite wall. "I mean, we already brought it up number one, and number two we've gotta get the public ready for the Meta again."

"Yes but - it's better if we - I think the phrase is: agree on a story about the hostiles. We should not tell him anything more about the Meta themselves."

"You're suggesting we create a...a sort of designer hostile alien? We make one up? The Meta seem dangerous enough to me."

"Yes. To you. You have a military mind-set. You are part of the military mind, in fact. But Farraday, he is part of the Media mind. The damage may already be done."

"We haven't told him much -" He thought about it, aloud. What had they told Farraday? "Ummm...The Meta can be incorporeal. The Meta may be influencing some human beings and may have been mistaken for demons in the past. The Meta have a different relationship to time and space. When physicalized they may appear to be floating crystalline forms...That's about it."

"That is already too much. It may imply something about their relationship to universal absolutes that a superstitious mind could make too much of. He may lose sight of their danger...And he should not be told about the interdimensional connection."

"Yeah well - okay."

"And Colonel? Absolutely do not mention the C-Craft."

"The - oh yeah, right, sure, you got it." It'd taken him a moment to remember the term. It wasn't something he liked to think about: Camouflage Craft, as the AF called them. Most alien spacecraft that were flying saucers were made to be noticed. C-Craft were spacecraft that looked like, say, a Boeing 767, or a helicopter.

The alien dropped the remains of the cigarette in a trash can and walked out, without amenities.

Derrick went behind his desk and sank into his seat.

Had the alien just given him an order? Had he accepted its authority unquestioningly?

Not for the first time he wondered about telepathic influence.

He shook his head. Paranoia. He opened a drawer and took out the Glenfiddich, and poured himself a shot.

· · ·

Anatole lay in bed, too mad and nervous to sleep. He'd felt kind of strange, the last couple of days. Was he horny? But he'd already masturbated, as he usually did once Kian really got off to sleep, and still the strangeness hadn't gone away.

A little slat of light from a space atop the door fell on Black Betty's eyes. A poster of Black Betty. Her picture and a quote from her: IN EVERY SECOND IS A CHOICE.

He didn't really understand her, when he downloaded the recordings of her "acts of media terrorism"; the appearances on C-Span, at the old president's State of the Union address; he most remembered the one at the United Nations. He'd replayed it a dozen times. A session at the United Nations about refugees from the Second American Civil War asking for asylum in Canada. The Canadians deftly managing to say *no* without seeming heartless. Then Black Betty, in a brown African robe, appearing at the General Secretary's elbow, as the Canadian representative finished; Black Betty unseen by the United Nations, seen by everyone watching the scene on television. Billions around the world.

"You are all in the same room, here; you use the same equipment; you are on the same frequency; you eat in the same cafeterias; you use the same bathrooms; you are all in the same building..."

She just kept saying this over and over again. *You are all in the same room, here; you use the same equipment...*

Why couldn't the Canadians help them? They could if they wanted to. The Canadians cowered on the other side of the border...But they were really all in the same room...He wished he knew where Black Betty was...

The girl Zizz had noticed his t-shirt, told him she'd been looking for Black Betty, who'd disappeared, even from the underground.

He thought about the strangers and his Dad and the saucers and the strangers again. Zizz, that girl called herself. She showed a lot of her thighs and a tattoo that called attention to her cleavage. He'd fantasized about her, when he'd masturbated, but he knew she was too old for him.

Masturbation didn't leave him feeling guilty, the way it had a year or two ago when he'd first started. His Dad had never said anything about it. But his Dad *did* edit explicit sexual stuff out of the movies he let him put on the VCR, which implied that sex was something to hide. But then he'd read some books about it - clinical books his Dad had given him when he'd started to grow pubic hair - and they said masturbation was okay, it was no big deal, it was just a way of coping.

He never thought about Lila sexually - she was like a second Mom to him - but he guessed that his Dad thought about her. Sure as hell looked at her a lot.

Now he lay there, on the wet spot in his bed, letting his mind drift above the angry landscape that kept them prisoner, letting it drift to fantasies about the saucers, the other worlds. The sexy alien women.

• • •

Straddling an updraft, Seeking One let her perception spread exponentially out, and down: down, anyway, relative to the construct-mass, the planet, this world. She felt the mind of the young male she'd been watching. The male was casting about for her.

The male could not see her, not in the strictly physical sense, couldn't see the cluster of weightless crystal the color of blue steel; that appeared to disappear; that seemed to be in one configuration one moment, another the next.

But she was aware of his awareness, in his dim, indirect

way; he felt her as a pressure in spacetime itself.

Touch a sheet of silk held taut in a frame. Close your eyes. Someone else touches the silk, far from your touch. But you feel it, in the slight shift of tension in the silk.

He felt her there. But he thought he was imagining her.

She let her perception spread, like paint in water; she tasted the ripples at the quantum level, and they resonated with a critical mass of improbabilities: the place where improbabilities became possibilities.

Behold! The time was near. The fruition of vastly copulating unlikelinesses was near. The time of the miraculous was at hand.

• • •

Sullivan was about to tap on the door to the kids' room when Yamahira came around the hall corner.

"Jack? Someone has shot out one of our solar cells."

"Yeah? For sure shot out?"

"I just came from the roof. We only lost one. We're still functional but..."

"It might be just a random gunshot. We get 'em."

"Or it might be an omen of intent."

"Yeah...OK. Who's on watch now?"

"Lila. I just came off watch."

"I'll go on with Lila, till morning. We'll double the watch. If you want to get up and check the monitors now and then..."

"Yes. I will."

Brooding, Yamahira walked on. Sullivan tapped the bedroom door. No answer. But he felt sure that Anatole was awake.

He went in, quietly so as not to wake Kian, though it took a great deal to wake Kian. Anatole was lying on his side, motionless, his back to the door, on his lower bunk; Kian was curled up above, snoring.

"Anatole..."

No answer. He went to the desk chair and sat, looked around the room by the dull green night-light glow. Flying saucers everywhere.

There were collector's item *X-Files* posters, twentysome years old. There was a poster from New Year's Eve 1999. Sullivan remembered the event. The California event's sponsors had claimed that channelers had told them ETs would be landing in a certain stadium in the San Fernando Valley, for the first public contact with humanity. Of course, the aliens hadn't come, and the laser light show and sound effects couldn't conceal that. The poster proclaimed

"LOVE TO OUR SPACE BROTHERS"

And beneath the declaration was a fanciful Harry S. Robins painting of a smiling ET shaking hands with a little boy as the boy's proud parents watch, all tearful-cheerful - the artist *trying* to take the subject matter seriously and not succeeding. There were movie posters from *Independence Day* and AlienNation and the recent movie foggily based on Philip Dick's THE DIVINE INVASION. Hanging from the ceiling on fishing wire was a plastic replica of Bob Lazar's "sport model" flying saucer, the secret alien-tech antigrav antimatter-powered vehicle supposedly tested in Area 51. There were shelves of Grey Aliens models, books on UFOs, on Roswell, on abductions; there were flying saucer CD-Rom games and stacks of science fiction videos. Except for a battery-dead video poster of the media terrorist Black Betty, the room was a little museum of UFO myth and folklore.

There was a gift from Sullivan himself, on the unpainted pinewood chest of drawers: a silvery plastic model of a landed UFO on struts, from the old Roy Thinnes TV show THE INVADERS. Sullivan had watched re-runs of it as a small boy.

In fact, as a boy Sullivan had been a science fiction fan, and something of a UFO aficionado: both fragments of the past he kept to himself. They embarrassed him.

And four years in the Special Forces, fighting brushfire wars in Iran, Libya and Taiwan had left him with a bitter aftertaste, a disillusionment with anything fanciful, anything beyond the narrowest confines of hope and optimism. Life sucked and rioters beat your wife to death and then you died.

Except, of course, for the consolations. Like the two in the bunkbed. One's kids consoled. Moments in life consoled. Moments with children; moments with women; moments listening to music; moments of satisfaction in work.

And that's all there was. It was enough.

But Anatole needed something more. For him, Reality behind the lines was indigestible, otherwise.

"I was wrong, Anatole," Sullivan said. "I should have let you do the report you wanted. Flying saucers, sure, why not. Long as you thought it out well." What matter, he added silently to himself, if it was bullshit? Most essays were bullshit. "I guess I was trying to help you and getting in the way of you growing up on your own, again. If your Mom was here she'd have...it wouldn't have happened. I do the best I can without her. And sometimes I screw up. Okay?"

No answer. But a certain tension had gone out of Anatole's shoulders, and Sullivan knew he'd been heard.

He stood, bent, kissed the boy on the head, and went out.

He went for his rifle, and then climbed the crude wooden stairs he'd built to the roof.

• • •

"I'm just saying it's something to think about," Metzger said. "I mean, okay - we're stuck outside FedControl, so we might as well make the most of it." He and Huxley and Buford were bedded down on three mattresses spread across the floor of the otherwise-unfurnished condo; Huxley was asleep, snoring with his mouth open. Buford was lying on his back, hands behind his head, scowling at the ceiling. Metzger was propped up, smoking his last cigarette. Actually his last fourth of a cigarette. He'd smoke a little, put it out, save it, smoke another inch of tobacco later. He'd made it last two days that way.

"You notice anything on that guy Sullivan's arm?" Buford asked.

"You mean the tattoo?"

"That's right. That tattoo is Special Div Army Rangers. That's not just any old overtrained, half psycho Army Rangers. That's *Special Div*. You know? You try to steal anything from here, try to take over - that motherfucker would tear your head right off your shoulders."

"From behind, bro, they're all the same size."

Buford snorted in disgust.

Metzger went on, "Hey - don't get, like, lofty. Who was it said to me yesterday, *Tell you what, I'll do what I have to do to survive....?*"

"That's survive. I'm telling you, you wouldn't survive.

How you think that big hunk of spunk has survived here all this time almost alone? You think it's an old man, a girl and two little boys backing him up? He's prepped, man."

"He so prepped, why's he here? He must've seen it coming."

"He was in charge of the place. He didn't want to just leave in a panic like everyone else. He was supposed to get airlifted out so he waited - the airlift chopper came in. And they shot it down about quartermile off."

"That must have sucked bigtime."

"Ohhhhhh yeah. You want to take this place over, you're going to have to kill that man. Shoot him in the back. And he's got two kids, right here in front of me. And the man *fed me*. He sheltered me. He took a chance on me. No, uh uh. I do what I have to but I got to live with it too. Fuck that."

Buford turned over and tried to go to sleep.

Metzger stayed up for awhile, staring at his cigarette butt, then slowly crushing it in his fingers.

. . .

"What we gonna do, Brem, you got that worked out or we gonna just play it by ear and - "

"Shut up, Dexie," Austin said.

Brem, Dexie and Austin were in a position a bit forward of the others, flattened in the brush of the scrubland between the fallen-in overpass and the remains of the condoplex parking lot. The rest of the looter militia was waiting down below, encamped in the lee of the concrete wall, on the old highway.

Bremer was looking through his electronic binoculars, turning up the night-vision, as he scanned the rooftop of the condoplex. "I only see one guard up there...looks like a woman...I can't see much with all the stuff they've got piled up for defense..."

"A girl! Shit a girl!" Dexie breathed. "A girl a fuckin' girl!"

"Shut up, Dexie," Austin said again.

Austin was looking at the perimeter of the condoplex grounds, and saw something move, high up, out of the corner of his eye.

"Somebody on the hill over there, above the old culvert. You see em Brem? That one of ours?"

Bremer swung the binoculars around, 90 degrees south.

"Ummm...no. That's a girl too, by God."

"Another one!" Dexie gasped.

"Dexie - shut up," Bremer said. "A tall woman...I suppose she might be some kind of flanking guard from the 'plex but I don't think so...I think she's freelance...That hair...Shit, I think that's Anja!"

"Anja?" Austin said. "No shit? I thought she was dead or something."

"Or something. Last I knew she shot her boyfriend and he was braindead and the military cops gang-raped her...She was in a coma for awhile...I thought she was dead by now but by God...I think that's her...Yes indeed, that's the way she walks..."

"Can I see? Can I see how she walks?" Dexie asked.

They ignored him. "She a factor?" Austin asked.

Bremer shook his head. "Wouldn't think she would interfere with us. Not unless there's something in it for her. Well. Anja."

"What we gonna do about making a move on this place?" Austin asked, more thinking aloud than really asking a question.

"I think," Bremer said, lowering the binoculars and crawling backwards down the slope the way he'd come, "we wait till most of 'em are quite asleep. But not so much they get enough rest. And then we move in."

• • •

Farraday was aware that they were listening in on him. Let them. He wasn't going to talk about the assignment. He wanted to know how his wife was; if the childbearing permissions had been granted.

"Senator Cobbs talks about eliminating the permissions process," Lyn was telling him, her voice sounding so near over this connection. "And just going back to letting people have babies when they want and to hell with the Famine and the immigrants and the Population Explosion and - well it's not going to happen anytime soon. He knows that too. He's just trying to get on the air. Getting our hopes up for nothing."

"Yeah. Sounds like Cobbs. A hog for TV time."

He wondered if Derrick himself was listening in on the phone call, or if it was some paranoid intelligence drone from MJ15.

"I miss you," his wife told him.

"I miss you too."

"So...can you talk about it yet?"

"Not yet."

"Huh."

"That bothers you?"

"Sort of. Yeah."

It scares her, he thought. It scares me too. And suppose he never got the go-ahead to make any of this public...Would he ever tell her, in private?

Darling, I've been working closely with alien beings from the star system Zeta Reticuli. I'm not sure if they give health benefits but there's a good retirement package.

Yeah right. Try...

Darling, I was a public relations consult to the US Government. And that's where he'd have to leave it.

Lyn was talking about his daughter, about how Della couldn't make up her mind if she wanted to get a teaching degree and maybe Della might want to move to Canada which was so much more politically stable, so *very* many people they knew had been making arrangements to move to Canada...

"You listening?" she asked suddenly.

"Yeah. It's good to hear nothing's changed lately..."

When your paradigms were shattered, you clung to the whatever changed slowest, he thought.

"Jake called from the office, he wants to know if you're 'firm about not marketing *Street Punishers'*. What the hell is it anyway?"

"It's a syndicated Reality Programming show, we don't get it in Chicago. It's...basically cops beating people up, those places where they have a Judgement Call ruling like Louisiana and Florida. You catch Bad Guys in the act, you can beat the shit out of em - there's also the new deterrent rulings in some counties allowing sexual humiliation for its deterrence value –"

"You're kidding."

"No, I'm not. Live action gang-rape on TV, for your entertainment, carried out by those who Serve and Protect."

"God is it that bad?"

It could be worse, he thought. We could have interstellar invaders. "Anyway – " he said, "you can tell Jake I'm firm, I won't have anything to do with the show."

His wife was also his lawyer. A mixed blessing.

"Damn right...You really okay? You sound...I don't know...If this government gig is bothering you, just quit..."

Could I?

Aloud he said, "I'm okay babe. I miss you. I just...I don't like working away from home."

"They won't let me join you?"

"Nope."

What was really bothering him, he realized, was that he needed to warn her and was not allowed to. He wanted to warn her about the Meta...didn't he?

The Meta were the invaders. The Zetans were our Space Brothers, for Chris-sakes.

He shook his head. He didn't know what was real anymore. And who he could trust.

Except Lyn. "Hey - I love you. I've got a meeting I should go to, but...did I mention I love you?"

"I don't think you did more than once or twice. I love you too..."

There was more she wanted to say, he could feel it. But she apparently decided against it. "OK. Call me soon..."

"I will."

"Bye hon."

"Bye."

And she hung up. Into the dial tone, in case someone was still recording, he said, "Was that okay, Colonel Derrick?"

And instantly regretted it.

Don't fuck around with these people...

He left the cubby they'd given him, went down the hall, asked a Marine for directions. The Marine - young Collins again - checked his ID with unnecessary punctilio, then escorted him down a maze of hallways and a concrete back stairs.

They emerged into a featureless hallway with only one door. GENLAB, it said on the door. The Marine unlocked the door for him and Farraday went in. Collins stayed outside; was careful to not even glance through the door in the second it was open.

Inside there were banks of Gates-Wangchen computers, various devices, looking like mutated microwave ovens, and cages. Farraday looked around with a real foreboding. He didn't want to be here. Whatever this was, he knew instinctively he'd rather not know about it.

Jaron and Derrick came around the corner of a bank of computers, accompanied by the ugliest creature Farraday had ever seen. The creature shuffled across the floor and gazed at Farraday with a disquieting intelligence. It looked like an independently motile scrotum with human eyes and the legs of a human toddler interspersed with octopal tentacles.

Derrick grinned at the look on Farraday's face.

"What the fuck *is* it?" Somehow he knew it wasn't...from offworld. But...

"It's the result of an experiment by our friends the Zetans. It's a land octopus."

"I prefer the term *cephaloped*," the land octopus said, in a sweet, ingratiating tone.

"Cephalopod..." Farraday said numbly.

"No, no, my friend: Cephalo-*ped*. Get it?" And it waved one of its horrible little limbs at him.

• • •

The roof of the condoplex was a quirky combination of fortress, bunker and garden.

The broad, tar-roof areas between the walls of concreted sandbags and sheet metal, and around the solar power panels, was lush with potted plants and flowers, tended as much by Yamahira as Lila. Some of the roses, Sullivan thought, would have won awards, if there were flower shows in California anymore.

A civilization without garden clubs and flower shows, Yamahira had said, is a civilization with too many morbid concerns. A society in trouble.

Sullivan had never been interested in gardening, until he realized that every day here, whether they were under attack or not, was a day of siege. He had begun to be afraid, trapped here, that the trained side of him would emerge, would dominate, and he would become a paranoid animal fixated on nothing but survival - and his kids would suffer, and sicken, by his example.

So now he stopped and, in the moonlight, tried to appreciate the roses, the hyacinths. Sometimes he was able to get on that particular wavelength. But now he found himself squinting up at the solar power panels. Yeah. A bullet-hole. A shattered cell.

Lila joined him; the Uzi over her shoulder. "I think it was a rifle shot, from over at the mall somewhere."

He nodded. "How you holding up?"

"I'm okay."

He looked at her, and had to look away. He wanted her even more than usual tonight. He gazed out over the woods. Nothing moved. "Well - I just checked all the sensors, the screens, everything. Nobody's anywhere near us. I figure the local Warlords just fired a shot in passing to let us know they're here. I don't expect 'em to come around anytime soon."

"You think we're all right?"

"I do, yeah." In one sense, they were always under siege here: a short distance beyond their guarded perimeters, they were in great jeopardy. They couldn't leave without great risk. But in another way he was pretty sure they were as safe, tonight, as they'd ever be...

"So," he added, "You can go to bed. I'll take over."

He looked at her - and wanted to find some way to compare her to the flowers, the moonlight. Something that didn't sound grasping, corny, stupid. "You look...great."

"Yeah? This uzi, it goes with my shoes?"

He laughed, to cover his embarrassment, and went to the gun emplacement, moved the barrel of the machinegun aside and looked out the gunport.

He felt her touch on his arm. He turned to her and she looked up at him. The moonlight reflecting off the machinegun lined her cheek. Even here...

He thought about his missing ear, his scarred face. Did it sicken her? Was she touching him out of pity?

She still had her hand on his upper arm. It was a very...*conscious* touch.

"I'm tired of waiting for you to make a move," she said. "You going to make me do it?"

His face, even in the dimness, must have shown his surprise. It was major, high voltage surprise.

"I...uhh...Do you mean -"

"I guess you are going to make me, aren't you."

Moving with confidence and calm, she took off the uzi, hung it on a hook, and pulled his face to hers.

His dick jumped like a salmon up a waterfall.

• • •

Anatole sat up in bed. At least he thought he was sitting up. Maybe he was dreaming it, some part of him thought, because he was floating up the wall now, feeling like he was too buoyant for the air, like a balloon released underwater. Then he saw wood and insulation and nails and spiders. Then a room with the strangers sleeping in it. Huxley was fondling himself in his sleep and whimpering. Then more wood and nails and spiders.

Then he was passing the roof, had a glimpse of his Dad - it looked like someone was taking off his shirt - was that Lila? Cool! - then stars, stars and the full moon. There were some men in the woods. Were they enemies? Somehow, here, he didn't feel afraid.

A star was coming to meet him. It was a solid star, that made him think of a picture he'd once seen of a particle of airborne pollen magnified millions of times. It had blood circulating in it: its blood was illumination.

It spoke to him.

"Are you a UFO?" he asked it.

"Sure, isn't everyone?" it replied.

"What you mean by that?"

"Aren't you a UFO? You're flying and you're unidentified, aren't you?"

He had to admit she had him there. He could feel the star was female. And he realized happily she could be more than one shape.

• • •

Quinn jerked awake, coming out of it so hard he hurt himself sitting up.

He felt that there'd been...what? An earthquake tremor?

He wasn't sure. The air...the air around him was charged. It was - he looked at his watch - about four in the morning, a little before...

Something was going to happen.

• • •

Lila was still amazing. She was so self contained, normally. She hadn't given him a chance to lie down with her - she'd pulled him against her, standing, and wrapped her legs around the back of his thighs and drew him into her and he had to use every erg of self control to keep from coming too soon, from exploding in her wet tight warmth, on the first thrust. It had been so long and she was so...

Her skin was amazing under his fingers; her mouth was amazing on his. Her eagerness, her need. Amazing.

When he drove himself to the deepest part of her he thought he could feel an electrical arc jump from his dick to the base of her spine.

She cried out and squeezed him harder to her with her muscular legs, hard enough to hurt him a little, and he laughed with more amazement, and kissed her throat and her jawline and her eyes.

"Don't hold back," she gasped, "come in me, do it now. We have all night..."

The trained part of him thought: We should be watching our perimeters, not screwing.

But months of cabin fever, months of anxiety converting to sexual energy, months of sublimated desire; it all twisted together, like a pillar of hungry wind, and protesting it was like shouting into a tornado.

The twister carried the waters of the earth up into the sky. Somewhere a mirror shattered, a box car jumped the tracks, a meteor struck a satellite, a dolphin leapt farther from the water than it ever leapt before or ever would again; a bottle, on the other side of the world, rolled off a table and spilled; and Sullivan came. He gushed, he filled her with his miracle: he shot cum into her like a son of a bitch.

It was a good five minutes before they lay down on the blankets she used for sunning, and he found, another amazement, that he was hard again. Her back was bleeding, a little, scraped where he'd fucked her against the wall. "So I'll get on top, this time," she said.

It was twentyseven minutes after that, when they were lying in one another's arms, the sweat drying on them in the cool night air, the moon grinning at their nakedness, when Sullivan noticed the star moving far overhead.

His body still resonating, his mind drunk with release, he watched the star, thinking about it abstractedly, not really caring.

A plane, way up, or maybe a satellite. But it moved so erratically. Updrafts creating the impression of that improbable zigzagging...

He rolled over to look at her.

"Lila," he said suddenly. "Why tonight? Why did you choose to...to let me know you wanted me like this."

"I feel...I don't know. Something's going to happen. And..."

She broke off, rolled onto her side, frowning gently. Then continued dreamily, "My uncle, he was always so nice to me when I was a kid...and he...he went into virtual reality. I mean, he just...went in, one day, moved into the helmet, and wouldn't leave. And he..."

"He starved?"

"Yes."

"Happened to someone I knew..."

"Dad found him...My uncle, he was like a mummy, by then, in the helmet. His wife sprayed him with permaset to preserve him, but he didn't keep very well, so finally she buried him."

He traced his fingers over the lines of a tattoo on her left breast, Japanese characters surrounded by a geometrical shape he didn't recognize. "What's this mean? This tattoo - what's it say?"

"It says 'the escape from a bad dream is to wake up'. From one of my father's books. I was rather dramatically into philosophy when I was younger..."

"Younger than *now*? Christ."

She laughed. She put her hand over his, pressing his fingers onto the tattoo.

She murmured: "A dream...virtual reality...it isn't real enough for me, Jack. Someone out there...someone wants to kill us. Maybe not right away, but eventually. Someone. I don't know who or when..."

He nodded.

She went on, "I think about it a lot more than anyone knows. I try to hide it." She shrugged. "I think about it so much I'm only half alive. Part of me is always in the place where I've already been killed...I want to be completely alive, for awhile."

Then she put his hand on his dick again.

He smiled. "You're gonna kill this poor old dude."

She chuckled, squeezed. He groaned softly.

Then she became serious, stroking him.

"I want you to see me, Jack...while you make love to me. Eyes open. I want you to see me. I want you to see that I'm alive and when I react to you it means you're alive...we're really alive...alive and awake..."

He rolled onto her, and was about to enter her...

That's when the first mortar shell hit the roof, fired from beyond their sensor perimeter. Lila screamed.

CHAPTER FOUR

A GAS ABOVE, SLOW BELOW

Loose your compassion on them; they are only flickers of life, only guttering consciousnesses, soap bubbles of Being: Let the quality of mercy fall on them like Billy S's gentle rains; like the light that comes in a cloud and seems to fall in dripping stars.

• • •

Anatole in the sky. Anatole, way up, almost a quartermile over the condoplex. Anatole, above it all, in the place where the wind is indistinguishable from a ghost; where invisible wheels interlock and turn and then fly asunder; where the impossible rides a horse with hooves of thunder.

Below, with Anatole's father, there was only the evidence of the senses. And who could blame them? Who could fault them their porous, half crumbled belief? Yamahira had already been nicked by a bullet and he knew he wouldn't be so lucky the next time and he didn't know where Lila was and he was looking desperately for her and he had to go to the bathroom but he couldn't and his own sweat made him sick and he was emptying a clip through the gunport and fumbling around for another clip and there was the angry wasp sound of bullets hitting the sandbags and all the sensors and alarms were going off, why couldn't someone shut them off, they were pointless now and where's that other clip...

Here below, Kian, alone in the bedroom with Anatole - Anatole's sleeping body. Anatole who refused to wake up; Kian, shouting for his father and getting no response.

Yamahira, who dropped a clip as he tried to ram it into a rifle and when he tried again his fingers were caught in the slide and the skin tore and he thought: *my panic will kill us -*

Just as he had told Lila: *panic kills; panic kills, Lila.*

As another fusillade of bullets tore into the sandbags and slapped into the walls.

Who could blame them, Kian and Yamahira and the others below, truly who could blame them for believing only in the evidence of the senses?

Above, with Anatole, the senseless was in evidence.

Anatole, floating apposite Seeking One, thought: I want to float higher.

And he floated higher.

"Will it happen that anything I imagine will come true, here?" Anatole asked.

"No," she said. "Only some things. There are laws everywhere. Natural laws. But laws are also opportunities."

"Give us a gun, give us our guns dammit!" Huxley shouted.

"We've got to be armed, we've got to work collectively or we're dead!" Mahler was yelling. "You must open the weapons locker!"

"Look, man," Quinn was shouting, "we surrendered in good faith - no weapons - but the goddamn time has come -"

"Laws are..." Anatole grappled with the idea.

"Opportunities, chances: avenues. Laws are media. A natural law is a medium for relating to the universe."

"Are you something that used to be a human being? I mean, you speak English..."

"I've simply taking the words and the...grammar... from minds like yours...and from the Collective Mind..."

Anatole wasn't going to let himself be sidetracked. "Then you're an alien?"

"You're an alien *to me,* of course -"

"Oh I know that. Sure."

"And me, from your point of view...well, I'm not the sort

of 'alien' you're thinking of, Anatole."

"Aren't you from another planet?"

"Some questions are only answered like this: yes and no. With some questions, the only honest answer is the ambiguous answer. Is 'both yes and no'. Have you ever noticed that?"

"Yes...yeah sure..."

"So that's how I must answer that question...yes and no."

Suddenly Anatole felt a tugging - and with it a nausea, a sense of going down a drain...

"I feel...I don't feel good..."

"Yes: you're going back to your body. I've tried to keep you out of what's happening down there. But they won't let you - they're trying to reach you, down below. You'll have to go."

"I don't want to..."

"I'll -"

But he couldn't hear the rest of what she said. He was going down the drain.

Draining into:

Weight and anxiety. "Anatole!" His father shouting at him, shaking him.

There was blood on his father's face. There were gunshots, somewhere beyond the walls.

"You're hit -" Anatole said.

His father crushed him in a hug, almost sobbing. It was the closest his father ever got to sobbing. That he knew of.

"Oh Christ...I thought you'd caught a stray round or something..." Sullivan muttered.

"I just..." Could he tell him?

Anatole knew it had been more than a dream; it had such a different quality. And he remembered it as he did any normal waketime event. But he knew his father would regard it as a dream.

"I was sleeping so deep...Dad - what happened to you, what's the shooting about?"

"We're under attack. I just caught a graze on the side of the head, I'm not hurt. Lila was hit by shrapnel but she's alive...Son - you've got to get to the bunker. We need every gun we can get."

• • •

Quinn and Mahler looked around the roof and both of

them saw the hole at the same time. A gaping mortar hole. There was blood nearby, in a small pool. The building vibrated as it took another hit; the blood quivered, reflecting the sky: and in it, for a moment, Quinn saw treachery and burning and a coruscating light; he felt a Something move through the air around him - calling to him - the spirit of this place, spontaneously organized around a principle -

"Quinn?" Mahler sounded worried. "You okay?"

Whatever it had been...one of those flashes...dissipated, and Quinn was left with the gritty residue that was his usual subjective reality. He was back in the fight.

He looked around. The solars had been hit again too, big time. They were shot to pieces. The satellite dish was a twisted wreckage, looking like a giant gray fungus in the dull dawn light.

"Oh shit," Quinn said, for both of them.

Yamahira had given them both M18s and a sack full of 16 shot magazines. A patter of gunfire came from the woods; one of the few remaining solar power panels spat broken glass.

Quinn realized he was now lying flat on his stomach - and so was Mahler, beside him. They'd flattened at the gunfire without even knowing it. Quinn laughed miserably and shook his head.

"Let's get into the bunker," Mahler said.

• • •

Sullivan looked out a hallway gunport and wished, for a moment, that a bullet would come through it, and hit him right between the eyes. Because surely Lila would die, and it was his fault, he hadn't been watching, he had assumed the shot-out solar panel was just harassment, he had gotten slipshod and he had let down his guard and when he should have been on watch he'd been fucking Lila and now they were all likely to die, because he'd let the assholes get close enough to pound them, let them get within reach of those who counted on him -

Anatole and Kian and Yamahira and Lila.

Lila.

It was his fault, it was -

You go this way, he told himself, *you'll fold up, and the kids are going to get killed for sure. Put it behind you.*

Take charge of yourself. Don't make it worse.

Do what you have to.

He turned away from the gunport and went to get the launcher.

Lila...!

• • •

Zizz was scared this woman would die on her. She'd had a year of nurse training from when she had fantasized herself a sort of hip, left-wing Florence Nightengale to the resistance fighters, but her practical experience consisted of some minor ER assistance work.

Lila was lying on the bed, maybe seeing the ceiling through her slightly-open eyes; maybe seeing nothing. She was breathing shallowly, was pale as a lily, might be in a coma and might not. Had stopped bleeding on the outside but inside she might be crumbling.

Kian was lying on the floor, on a pad of foam rubber, curled up, hands pressed to his ears, trying to muffle the sounds from outside the building.

Zizz sat next to Lila, with a handful of the emergency medicines Sullivan had given her on the nightstand, and thought: *This is for real, a real chance to help, and I don't think I can do a damn thing.*

She'd given Lila a little water; she'd washed her; she'd checked her pulse, her temperature, both were low. Beyond that...

She looked around the room. There were water colors, well rendered in the classical Japanese manner, probably by Lila; there were numerous books on Zen, all in English. There was a poster photo of a Buddhist monk, in silhouette against the sky, meditating on a hillside, looking like part of the hill himself.

Seemed like Lila had been trying to get in touch with her heritage, or something.

A rattle of gunfire came from outside. Could the rounds penetrate to this inner, basement bedroom? Zizz wondered.

Maybe.

Zizz took Lila's hand and squeezed it. There was no response. "Lila?"

No answer.

Zizz kept Lila's hand in hers, and hummed a song. She didn't know what else to do.

• • •

Anatole was loading his rifle with sure movements. He felt strange. Not scared. And it felt strange to be unafraid, now. Something from the Seeking One was lingering with him.

Sullivan came in carrying a handheld missile launcher, came glaring at Metzger and Buford and Huxley, who had their backs to him; who were aiming rifles out gunports of the lower bunker. The bunker churned with gunsmoke; but just now it was quiet.

He wished he knew how to tell the others. *It only matters up to a point.*

There was no gunfire from out in the woods but Huxley opened up at a shadow, firing two bursts.

"You wastin ammo," Buford said.

"There's maybe thirty crates more ammo in the store room," Huxley replied.

Anatole saw his father's glower deepen at that.

"They haven't shot no more mortars, I notice," Metzger said. "They musta used what they had or what they're willin' to use up."

"Made a big damn hole downstairs," Buford said.

"Sullivan's got that part of the building walled off, long before we got here. That hole don't matter much."

Yamahira came in, his face drawn, his hands bloody and shaking.

"How is she?" Sullivan asked.

Yamahira's voice was like sandpaper. "I can't tell how much shrapnel is in her. She drifts in and out of consciousness. I think she's stopped bleeding but...inside, I don't know. Probably she's bleeding internally."

"We've got to get her out of here, get her to a surgeon, a hospital..." Sullivan said; as if in confirmation a spatter of gunfire struck the building.

"Yes," Yamahira said. "Yes."

"But - they'll cut us down if we try to leave."

"We could...negotiate something."

"They'd lie, Yam. They'd kill us, no matter what they 'negotiated'."

"Yes to that too." He sank onto a plastic box in a corner. "Yes."

Anatole looked at Yamahira, wanting to ask if Lila was

going to live, but knowing that no one knew the answer. No one knew, and he knew no one knew, but he wanted badly to ask it anyway.

Instead he went to a gunport and sighted through it. He thought he saw someone moving in the brush. He exhaled to relax, steadying the rear gunsight over the muzzlesight, both on the vague shape he almost saw in the brush: he squeezed off a burst. There was movement in response: Something falling? He thought so.

It wouldn't be the first time he'd had to shoot someone.

I hope, if I killed someone, they have someplace to go, after death; I hope there's an afterlife for them to go to. And for Lila. And for me.

"Yamahira..." Sullivan was loading a handheld heatseeker. "You let three strangers into our supplies."

The three soldiers turned to look at them.

"We needed defense," Yamahira said. "I needed their help. I wasn't sure how badly hit you were. I'm afraid if these thugs outside get close enough to us, they may set the building on fire."

Sullivan nodded.

Anatole knew what that particular nod meant: *I understand but I think it was a mistake. But it's too late now.*

"I looked at the monitors -" Yamahira said morosely. "They've found most of the cameras, shot them all down. Cut most of our wires. Found our traps. They seem to know what they're doing."

Sullivan went to one of the larger gunports and put the small missile launcher through, balanced one end on his shoulder. "Where away?" he asked Buford.

"Down about three o'clock, in them fallen trees there. Last time I saw a muzzleflash."

Sullivan aimed in that direction and fired. The launcher went SHOOSH and strobed and left an acrid smoke that made Anatole cough.

They heard the rocket sh-sh-shivering nearly to its target, then whistling at a higher pitch as it changed course to pursue someone or some thing...

Then there was a scream and an explosion.

Buford laughed, "Whoa - you got at least two of em."

"Look like four or five to me," Huxley said.

"How many of those heatseeker rounds you got?" Metzger asked.

Sullivan looked at him expressionlessly. "Not many. But they don't know that."

Sullivan went to the PA system and hit the switch, spoke into the grid. His voice boomed scratchily out over the woods.

"AS YOU HAVE JUST SEEN, WE HAVE OUR HEATSEEKERS SET UP NOW. WE HAVE ALL WE NEED TO TAKE YOU APART. YOU ARE UNDER SURVEILLANCE. I'M NOT TALKING TO YOUR LEADER, I'M TALKING TO YOU: YOU'D BETTER KNOW WHAT YOU'RE IN FOR BEFORE YOU COME ANY CLOSER! MAYBE YOU DON'T KNOW WHAT YOU'RE GETTING INTO. THERE ARE PLENTY OF US UP HERE AND WE'VE GOT PLENTY OF AMMO...YOU COME ANY CLOSER AND WE'LL BE FORCED TO KILL ALL OF YOU!" He switched off the intercom and waited.

There was no reply.

• • •

A couple of hours after dawn, Anja heard a guttural cough, and turned to see a mountain lion poised on a boulder. She knew what the poise meant; she saw the fur risen along its spine, the twitching end of its tail, the tension in its haunches. A sleek, full grown cat, probably female, with green-golden eyes and fur the color of wheat touched with faded ruby.

Anja wanted the fur.

"You're beautiful," she told the mountain lion, as it prepared to kill her.

The cat wriggled in place, just slightly: she was about to spring, to rend.

Anja turned and opened the back door of the van and stepped aside as the cougar jumped; at the same moment Anja pressed the remote control, and Sol lunged out of the van to meet the cat, both of them snarling. Jacked up by the cerebro-implants, Sol was faster: he sidestepped and, howling with a sound that made the cougar seem civilized, he caught the cat about its middle, flung it down hard on its belly, smashed a knee down to crush its spine and sank fingers into those beautiful eyes.

• • •

It was ten o'clock in the morning before they had clear sign of the siegers.

"They're just sittin' out there. You can barely make out a few of 'em. And there's a campfire," Buford said, peering through a lower gunport. "Not a peep from 'em in hours..."

"Maybe send another one of those heatseekers, cook a few of those motherfuckers, they'll back off," Metzger said.

"Nope," Sullivan said decisively, passing out plastic cups of coffee and packages of saltines.

He wanted badly to check on Lila but he stayed where he was.

Sullivan and Anatole and the soldiers were sitting on the floor of the bunker; Yamahira was on the roof.

Anatole had fallen asleep. Sullivan glanced at him anxiously, from time to time. He'd been so hard to wake, before. Something strange in it.

Metzger was sipping his coffee; the sullen tiredness in his eyes was like a sort of tinder, waiting for ignition. "Sullivan - don't you think we got a say in all this? Like how the weapons are used, what have you?"

"No," Sullivan said.

"Our lives are on the line too."

Sullivan took a sip of coffee. Without even a hint of rancor, he said, "I can survive without you. You take your orders from me while you're here. Or you can take your chances out there."

Metzger stared at him. Then he snorted into his coffee cup.

• • •

"Whatcha gone do, Brem?" Dexie asked, coming to squat in front of him. "Whatcha gone whatcha gone whatcha gone do?" Dexie had his hands tucked in his armpits because they were shaking so much.

Bremer leaned back against the bole of a tree and kicked at the dying campfire to make sparks rise and flicker out. A sunbeam spotlit ghosts in the smoke.

He thought he recognized some of the ghosts.

"Well," Bremer said, "I'm thinking -" He drew his gun and shoved the muzzle up against Dexie's forehead. "Of just having a bit of a look to see if you have any brains left."

Dexie stared up at the gun in fascination till his eyes crossed and his mouth went into a twisted smile.

"Gowan ahead," Dexie said, "I wanta see that crystal light again that come. Last night I seen this crystal light awatchin us and I knew if I went to the Dead Land she'd be there and we could ride and ride on a fucking tesseract moebius dick in a pussy that was a dick that was a pussy that rolled up into a dick that turned inside out so it was a pussy -"

Bremer rolled his eyes and shoved with the gun so Dexie went sprawling backwards into the embers of the fire.

Dexie laughed and tossed ashes into the air, his pants catching fire.

Wearily Bremer waved Austin over. "Dexie's been up a week too long. Get him to sleep."

Austin nodded and turned to Dexie who was happy in the flame as a pig in mud, and cold-cocked him with the butt of his rifle. Dexie went over, out cold.

Austin pissed on him to put the fire out.

"We could just set the whole fuckin place on fire," Austin said. "Burn that condoplex."

"No," Bremer said, not for the first time. "I want the place as intact as I can get it. I want that girl, too. If she's alive."

He leaned back and stared at the light trembling in the leaves far overhead. A possum stared back at him. He raised his gun and sighted carefully and shot it through the neck and it fell almost on his lap. Some of the men laughed.

"Find me Anja," Bremer said. "I have this intuition she might know how we can crack this nut...Oh - and bring me a couple dozen of those refugees from the Mall. Send a team to herd 'em over here..."

. . .

"Okay, my man," Derrick said, "We've got a step more up the ladder of clearance. What you hear today's the second level - it's all I can give you right now, Farraday, so don't ask for more."

"All you can give me now? What a surprise." Farraday had long since given up worrying about the effect of his sarcasm on Derrick.

Farraday, the alien, Colonel Derrick. They were in the cafeteria, entirely alone except, of course, for the remote surveillance.

Two cups of cocoa, a cigarette, a cigar. Farraday sipped cocoa; the alien sipped cocoa, puffed the cigarette; Derrick puffed the cigar.

Farraday cleared his throat, chewed the eraser off a pencil, doodled with the pencil in a yellow tablet, where he was supposed to be jotting ideas for the campaign.

A wall clock said it was about 9:30 in the morning, but there was no sense of it being morning. No one was here eating breakfast - that had been hours before - and down here the days blended into a seamless maze of corridors and echoing hangars.

"It's about uniting the country," Derrick said, as Farraday always thought he would, eventually. Derrick blew a cigar-smoke flying saucer; there was a smell of whiskey on him. He went on, "The idea of cueing the public to the alien presence, in a highly controlled way for maximum benefit...well, it's been around MJ15 for awhile. Reagan wanted to do it during his tenure. That's what he kept saying, in his speeches." He did a Reagan impression which Farraday barely recognized from high school video-Civics: "'Why, if aliens were to visit our planet we'd be united damned fast around here'. Reagan, now, had a global vision of it. But at this point - we just want the country back together. Or the fucking Chinese are going to infiltrate the American Chinese League and try to pull off a coup, or the Socialist Arab Republics'll try to destabilize us, and they'll pry us all apart, and we won't fucking *have* even a sovereign United States anymore."

"I envy profanities," Jaron said, in Derrick's voice, sucking cocoa from a fore-digit. "I have been grappling with the linguistic function of profanities. They seem to have more often a psychological value than a purely information-transference value. I don't understand them but they are interesting...They make little explosions in your biofields."

Derrick turned a startled glance at the alien.

Farraday thought: *He didn't know they could see 'biofields'. The cigarettes make the alien looselipped; except it hasn't got lips.*

"The plan," Derrick said, recovering, "is to wait for the right moment in the negotiations - the President, unless she changes her mind again, will announce a new all-out FedControl attack on all insurgent fronts, and then, just as it looks like it'll be the holocaust we've been trying to avoid since this thing started, we'll announce the alien presence. Complete with the President meeting Jaron here on national TV, just like it's the first time. Keep in mind, it has to look as if she didn't know about this, and as if the presidency has been in the dark about all this. Of course, it'll still be pretty obvious we've been covering some stuff up -"

"God I *guess* - the Zetans look almost exactly like the aliens in that *Roswell* movie! In *any* of the Roswell movies!"

"That remark might be regarded as insulting," Jaron said, "but I will let it pass."

"Uh - sorry."

"Anyway," Derrick went on impatiently, "at that point it'll come as a big shock but also a kind of relief. The aliens are friendly - but they also announce that the Metas are after our asses. The Metas are difficult to spot, inscrutable, morphable, weird-beard critters and we all gotta unite if we're gonna protect ourselves against their Evil Empire. That's our basic line. We'll be locking down the rest of the media on this one - starting with the World Wide Web - "

What was it Chris Carter said, back when? Farraday thought. *'New World Wide Web Order'? Was that original with him? Carter's arrest, on the set of the "X-Files", during its final season, for something ostensibly unrelated to the show's mythos...was it connected with all this? He'd claimed he was framed - "I'm a patsy" he'd said, just like Oswald...*

" - and from there we do a major media campaign about our friends the Zetans and the dangers of the Meta, but we spoon-feed it to people." Derrick was warming to the subject. "See, we don't want panic about the Meta. Still, we've got to make sure that the various factions feel seriously threatened with respect to the Meta, so we'll be sending up -"

"Derrick," Jaron said.

Derrick looked at him.

"Derrick, you are indiscreet again. Perhaps I should not smoke cigarettes, and you should not drink Glenfiddich."

Derrick's own voice telling him that, like a cartoon conscience.

"Yeah well - " Derrick's eyes flicked to the cameras near the ceiling. "Anyway the basics you got, right Farraday?"

"I think so...The Zetans are friends, and the Meta are...enemies?"

"Yeah. *But* - it's very important to understand that the Meta threat is *not out of control*. We have a projected field that..." He glanced at the Zetan. "...Well, we've got a handle on it. We don't want people panicking, that's the main thing. It's sort of like the Communist threat in the Cold War, see - the Red Menace was dangerous, it was out there, but we were never *really* likely to have a nuclear war with the Reds, and, the same way, we're not likely to have alien saucers raygunning the White House anytime soon either. We give people enough sense of threat to unite them, but not enough to make em go over the top and start looting and shouting it's the end of the world."

"How do you know?"

"How do I know what? That it's not the end of the world?"

"More specifically, how do you know," Farraday said slowly, "that the Metas are not about to raygun the White House, like in *Independence Day*? I mean - shit - you yourself said they're mysterious -"

"Now you're crossing that line again, man," Derrick said in that low, very definitely threatening tone. "You got to get a feel for this and fast. You're asking questions outside need-to-know again."

Farraday felt his face flush, his heart race with suppressed anger. Were the surveillance monitors taking note of his heart-rate, somewhere?

Changing his tack, almost contradicting himself, Jaron said, "I think you need to consult your psychiatric specialists, Colonel Derrick, and they will tell you that our Mr. Farraday must *adjust* to the painfully intrusive revelations that he has been force-fed in the last few days. He must be allowed some flexibility for his psychological health. We have always observed it to be so. You yourself break some minor rules, and the authorities observe us break them, they must be aware of it: that you give me the occasional cigarette, for example. A little flexibility at the borders of reality is necessary for sanity." After a moment he added, "But only a little."

Derrick nodded. "You're right. A little...flexibility. Just a little."

Managing to keep the irony out of his voice, Farraday said, "I appreciate it, Jaron. Well...let's talk about what I can reveal about you: about our friends from Zeta Reticuli. People will want to know about your planet. Do you have oceans, for example;

what do you do for fun - harmless stuff like that. But stuff people here can relate to. Analogous stuff. Do you dance, do you have comedians, do you, I don't know, swim in the ocean?"

"I'm rather a good surfer, on my world, you know," Jaron said, "but surfing is slow and stately there, as the waves are what you would call gelatinous, and they move very slowly..." After a moment he added, "Very, very, *very* slowly."

"Good," said Farraday, scribbling, "charming. Now. People are gonna want to know about religion - do you have one, do you have many, are you 'sent by God', have you interfered with our own religions -"

"Why would you ask that?" Derrick said, sharply.

"What? About the interference with our religions? Because of, oh, *Chariots of the Gods*, all that crap."

"That book was a very amusing little fantasy," Jaron said, in Farraday's voice: Farraday's *amused* voice. As Jaron got to know you he picked up more and more of your inflections, vocal mannerisms, expressions. "But it was also very bad science, even very bad human science, very bad anthropology, and indeed it was rather 'racist', as your expression is. This von Daniken evidently believed that the...'the little brown people', so to speak, the Egyptians, the Picts, what have you, could not have built the pyramids, raised the dolmens, built Stonehenge, working it out all on their own. But of course they did. We watched them do it."

"So you didn't influence religion at all?"

Derrick interjected quickly: "As far as the public is concerned - no. The time may come when...more can be revealed, in that department. But for now - *no*."

"And as for our 'religion' on our own world - " Jaron said, crumbling the remainder of the cigarette in his digits. " - we have none. We are...atheists."

"Jaron - shit!" Derrick burst out.

"Shit. Shit," Jaron murmured appreciatively, in Derrick's voice. "'Shit'."

"Atheists..." Farraday felt his heart sink at that, without knowing why.

"It is not a problem, Colonel Derrick," Jaron said lightly in Derrick's voice. "This has all been worked out. We will not *say* atheists, to the public. We will say that we are 'universal pantheists'. That the universe is alive and we 'commune' with it. This is rather like the Great Spirit concept, with the American Indians. Something very vague and formulaic and all-inclusive. It will comfort people. We may want to play up this 'communing' more later...as if we are 'channeling', as the expression is, this universal intelligence. It may give us more...more aura of authority."

"But do you?" Farraday asked. "Do you believe the universe is alive and...intelligent?"

"Yes."

"But at the same time you are atheists?"

"Yes. The universe is alive but it is not 'God'. And...it is not friendly. Nor unfriendly. However, we do not wish to make these distinctions with the American public. Let them believe we are in 'communion' with this 'great, benevolent universal intelligence'. We are in nothing of the sort, but they need not know this."

"Speaking of which, we're getting past need-to-know again, with some of this," Derrick said.

"I disagree," Jaron said. "Sometimes it is necessary for Mr. Farraday to know what our thinking is, so we do not confuse one another."

Farraday was still mentally replaying something Jaron had said. *The universe is alive but it's not God...And it's not friendly.*

Disturbing. There was no moral compass for travel through that idea. Did the Zetans have any moral center at all? Just now Jaron sounded like an interstellar cynic. They'd shown their willingness to play God in creating the land octopus.

"Oh - " Farraday said, "I've been meaning to ask: can we talk about the...the cephalopeds? Things like that?"

"No," Derrick said firmly. "It was a mistake to show you that..."

"Actually," Jaron said, in Farraday's voice, "I have been meaning to ask you a favor, since you have been introduced to the creature. The cephaloped - 'land octopus', if you prefer - it liked you very much."

Jaron reached out and patted Farraday's knee. His boneless digits fluttered there.

The alien went on, "The cephaloped has been very depressed lately. We like to keep it happy as that increases its chances for survival, and we need it to survive, so we can observe its capacity for adaptation. Hence, we give it plenty to read and let it watch all the TV it wants. It loves to watch MTV and the

Discovery channel and *Global Entertainment Hourly.* Colonel Derrick even lets it watch the Alternative Media Channel. But it's lonely, the poor thing. It doesn't like the lab boys. It wanted me to ask if you would take it on, adopt it as...a pet?"

"Uhhhh...." Farraday said.

• • •

Sullivan stood up and slapped a magazine into the rifle, all in one motion.

Anatole woke at the sharp sound - sitting up, blinking. He looked up at the ceiling of the bunker, as if he could see through it to the sky.

"You okay, son?" Sullivan asked.

Anatole blinked, and licked his lips. "Sure. Yeah. Is there anything to drink?"

Sullivan squatted beside him, gave him some water and a protein bar. "Hang in there, pal."

"Is Lila...?"

"She's holding steady. Not much change."

"We've got to get her out of here."

"I'm workin' on it, son."

"I know."

Sullivan put a hand on his son's neck and pulled him close and kissed the top of his head, and thought: *We've got to get her out.*

Wasn't there. Wasn't there to get Jenny out. Wasn't there.

Looking out a gunport with binoculars, Huxley said, "There's a big buncha people, looks like...ragtag refugee types...they're coming up to the edge of the woods...Some are armed - can't tell if they all are. Looks like...like a couple of the militia types are sorta...sorta herdin' em here...I guess those bastards got some new recruits..."

• • •

Anja was still scraping the hide when the PM gunmen got the jump on her. She'd been so fascinated with the cougar hide she'd let her guard down.

Should have left Sol on watch, she thought, as she turned to face the rifles and the gun-eyed men.

"Drop your weapons and drop your pants," the noseless one said.

A militiaman with an old diagonal scar from a gouge that had taken most of his nose, he was approaching her with way too much confidence, not even pointing the muzzle of his carbine directly at her.

Two others approached, farther back in the waist-high grass of the slope just beneath the crown of the hill.

I've got a few seconds, she thought.

"What've you got there, a pussycat?" Noseless asked, grinning. He had a surprisingly nice smile in a face that otherwise looked like it had been worked over with an electric knife. "Now you drop that pistol there, girlfrenn," said Noseless. "And I mean now. And I mean very carefully, don't get anywhere near that trigger."

He was already undoing his trousers with one hand as he came up to her, thinking she'd be an easy rape now he had the drop on her.

She slowly drew her pistol, thumb and forefinger on the edge of the gunbutt, as if to surrender it - then she tossed it at him, so that he reflexively reached out to catch it with the hand that had been working the zipper. That distracted him, long enough: She snapped into the kick-boxing stance and sank a foot-jab into his gut.

He folded up, wheezing and she brought a knee up to meet his face, at the same time snatching the rifle away, turning it to fire at the other two.

Both the other Militiamen dropped into the high yellow grass. Her burst passed harmlessly over their heads. A tall thistle tipped over, shot in half.

Anja opened the back of the van, and, moving to keep it between her and the thugs in the grass, pressed channel 7 on the remote clipped to her jacket; responding instantly, Sol came roaring out and sank his teeth in Noseless's neck and shook him like a rat.

Noseless might have escaped, then, but his terror undid him: he shrieked and flapped his arms and flailed and fell and in a few minutes more Sol had pulled his head right off.

Anja patted her ex boyfriend on the head as Sol knelt over the body, shaking, mouth streaming blood.

"Good boy. Good boy."

But then she felt a small, cold metal circle on the back of

her neck. She knew what a gunmuzzle felt like.

"Hi Anja, girl, good to see ya'll again. Don't move your hands or feet okay?"

She turned her head enough to see. "Austin."

"Surely is. *My* you're lookin fine. Is that Sol there, playing with Ugly Mug's head?"

"What's left of Sol."

"I gotcha. Okay. Well. Can you control him so's I don't have to shoot him?"

"Sure."

She reached for the remote.

"Anja? Be *very* careful how you order that nutty little buddy of yours, okay? I got me a hair trigger on this motherfucker."

"You got it."

She pressed a button on the remote and Sol went to sleep, instantly.

"Whoa! I'd like to get that shit hooked up to Dexie. All right - Guess who's down in them woods?"

"I know. I saw him. That fuckhead Bremer."

"Brem, he wants to see you."

She shrugged. "Okay. Can I bring Sol. And my cat skin?"

"Why surely."

"Listen - I had to kill your pretty boy here."

"You think I give a fuck? One less eyesore. Just don't fuck around no more or we *will* have to kill you. Damn it's good to see you again."

CHAPTER FIVE

RUINED A PERFECTLY GOOD GUN

It was when the shadows were at their longest. That's when the charge came.

It was as much a rout as a charge, but Sullivan didn't know that at first. He saw several dozen ragged figures charging out of the woods, across the open space toward the condoplex. Men and women, rifles and pistols in their hands, shouting - in fear or fury? He couldn't tell. Some of them opened fire on the condoplex...

Yamahira and Buford opened up on this ragged company, and men and women fell like harvested wheat.

The looters. The woods. Dexie and Bremer watched from the brush. Forced into the charge, driven out into the open by the militia, the refugees spun and screamed and fell. Bremer had armed some of them, for appearance's sake, but they were given very little ammunition; and all the time his men had weapons trained on the refugees' backs.

"Dumb as a box of rocks," Dexie said, shaking his head in wonder.

"I only see one fire source...two, at most," Bremer mused.

"There's shootin' from the roof, too. There might in fact be less people in there than you brave soldiers thought, Dexie..."

"They got that heatseeker don't fergit that launcher they got don't fergit."

"Do they now? They only used it once. They may have no more, or not much. Ordnance is hard to come by."

Dexie snorted crystal from the back of his hand. "Could be. Could be could be could *beeeeeeeeee*."

"Dexie - take twenty of our men...probe the far side of the place. And tell Austin to bring me the girl now. Bring her to the camp."

"Sure sure sure -"

"Just bloody *go*."

Dexie went scrambling off. Bremer turned to watch the "battle". Ten or eleven shabby figures had gotten past the firing angle of the defenders, were prying at the planks and slats nailed over the lower windows.

As Bremer watched, one of the refugees pried back a wooden slat - and the window exploded outward, killing half a dozen men in the blast.

Bremer couldn't tell if the window had been mined, in some way, or if someone had fired a charge out the window from inside.

A smoking, twisted piece of rifle-breach and splintery gunbutt fell to the ground in front of Bremer, blown through the air from the explosion.

"Well shit," Bremer murmured. "Ruined a perfectly good gun."

Now he could see through the smoky gap where the boarded over window had been - beyond it was a cracked, blackened wall of cemented cinder blocks. So it had been booby trapped.

He strolled back through the brush, to the camp, where Austin was just bringing Anja. Parked a little ways off was her van.

"That van makes a fuckin' good target," Bremer observed. "Somebody better move it."

"Something in it I wanta show ya first, bro," Austin said.

Bremer was staring at Anja. She'd cut a ragged hole through the middle of the cougar skin, and thrust her head through it, so its head hung down in front - eyeless, boneless - and its tail hung in back - still dripping blood. She hadn't finished curing it.

She was dirty and flinty eyed, but she looked good to Bremer. She looked *hot*.

"Convince me not to kill you, Anja," Bremer said.

"*Bremer!* How sweet. I'm glad you remember me. It means you're not all brain damaged here," she said quietly. She didn't seem at all afraid. He could tell she'd changed. She'd always been tough but she'd gone that extra mile since last he'd seen her.

There was a kind of toughness that was almost indistinguishable from psychosis; Bremer valued it, and she had it.

"You haven't told me why I shouldn't kill you, Anja." Bremer turned to Austin, sensing it was necessary to establish absolute authority with Anja and only the threat of certain death could do it. "Sod it. Just kill her."

Austin raised a rifle and pointed it at her head -

She never twitched, her eyes never wavered. At the last possible moment she said:

"I've got something you need, Bremer."

Bremer raised a hand - Austin lowered the rifle. "What would that be, Anja dear?"

"Someone," she said, glancing at the van, "who won't be stopped." She pointed at the condoplex. "He can get you in there. With the minimum of losses."

"Really. And how's that?"

"Can I show you?"

A couple of minutes later, they stood a respectful distance from the van as she opened the back; the door opened partway, streaking light on a man's face: Sol.

His face was emaciated, scarred, tattooed, and the tattoos were all but indistinguishable from the scars. His eyelids were tattooed with grinning skulls. Every time he blinked the skulls flickered in his eyes and were gone and back again.

He giggled.

Anja pointed the adapted TV-remote at him. He jumped from the van in response, and waited. The ring of PM gunmen stepped back, as one, training their weapons on him.

She pressed another button and he took a spasmodic

step toward them.

Guns cocked.

"Hold your fire," Bremer said.

Sol was nearly nude; he wore only boots, the tatters of a shirt. He was big, nearly seven feet, all lean trembling muscularity, scarred like a map of the L.A. sewers. He looked soddenly angry, miserable, drooling, swaying slightly, sniffing the air. Anja pressed another button and he grinned in reaction; the grin almost like a dog snarling.

"You give him a pleasure jolt just now?" Austin asked.

She nodded.

Bremer took a step closer, looked closely at Sol.

"That's..."

She nodded. "Sol."

Bremer laughed, pleased. "The fucker you left me for!"

"Anyway," she said, "he used to be Sol. He's still *part* Sol. He got a little too heavy into pleasure-center stims...and then he had the hardware put directly in...Terminal electrostim addiction. Really classic."

"And then he left you."

"Wandered off is more like it. But fuck him, it amounted to the same thing. So I had him captured and made a deal with his surgeon..."

Bremer cackled, shaking his head in appreciation. "You evil little bitch!"

"Uh huh. Watch this."

She hit several buttons on the remote and in instantaneous response Sol leapt about idiotically.

Everyone laughed. Then she hit another series of buttons and Sol threw himself into the side of the van, banging his head on it with a dull metallic ringing, again and again. Bloodying himself.

"I can make him *like* what he's doing to himself," Anja said contentedly, hitting a remote control button that stimulated Sol's pleasure center as he bashed and bashed and bashed himself and he moaned with pleasure and bashed again...

"Yeah!" Sol roared. "YEAH!"

"That's pretty much all he can say," Anja murmured, hitting the remote again.

Sol suddenly sat down, blinking through blood streaming

from his scalp. He hummed tunelessly to himself.

"And what good's that to us, if you please?" Bremer asked.

"Who," she said musingly, "have you got here who's tough but expendable."

Bremer snorted. "Most of 'em." He looked around, called to a guy who was pissing against a tree trunk about fifty feet off. "Ginch!"

Ginch came toward them, shaking his dick as he came, tucking it back in, wiping pee from his fingers onto his khakis. He was a massive, barrel chested blond, long matted hair, surfer tats, stupid blue eyes and a sagging mouth. "Whassup?"

"Ginch," Bremer said, "I thought I told you not to piss close to camp. I don't like the smell."

"Well shit dude's gotta pee I mean shit -"

"I don't like to be disobeyed, even with respect to the disposition of your urine, Ginch." Bremer nodded to Anja.

She pressed a sequence of buttons on the remote.

Ginch turned just in time to catch Sol head-on. Ginch sprawled over backwards, jerking a pistol, but Sol moved snakestriking fast and in one snap bit three of Ginch's fingers off, his trigger finger with them; blood spurted and Ginch screamed. Sol sat on his chest, Ginch futilely bucking; Sol with several fingers and the pistol still clamped in his mouth, like a dog with a bone, giggling, his eyes way, way past insane, his hands twisting Ginch's head around on his neck, breaking the neck quickly, Ginch quivering, dying, but Sol kept on, twisting the head on the neck, all the way around to the front again, then toward the back, then toward the front, like a twist-top bottlecap, the neck wrung like a rag three more times around, fast, and *pop* -

"Fuck!" Austin said admiringly. "Right off his shoulders!"

The men murmured appreciatively. No one had particularly liked Ginch.

Sol was gnawing at Ginch's eyes. Then he started cracking the severed head on the ground like a monkey with a coconut.

Anja stepped up behind Sol, pointed the remote at his head; Sol went stiff, stood, dropping the head; Anja kicked it into the brush. She pressed another button on the remote.

Sol turned and marched back into the big van and sat

glassy-eyed in a corner.

"Well yes," Bremer said. "He might just be useful..."

Suddenly there was the cough of a missile launcher from the condoplex; a heatseeking round shivered toward them. The men scattered. Anja slammed the van doors and rolled under the vehicle, Bremer flattened and rolled in beside her.

Bremer shouted a warning but a cluster of four men, running for the cover of a fallen tree, failed to outrun the heatseeker, and sucked into a fireball.

"THAT'S FOUR MORE OF YOU ASSHOLES!" boomed the amplified voice from the condo. "WE'LL WHITTLE YOU DOWN TILL YOU'RE ALL GONE!"

"He's trying to psyche you out," Anja said. "I'll bet he hasn't got that many heatseeker rounds left or he'd have used 'em."

"Yeah," Bremer said, looking at the ring of smoke around the crater by the fallen tree. "He's figured out I don't want to burn the place. He's got some battery power and some ammo. But I've got more time than he does..."

"I don't think Sol's gonna live much longer...May as well use him good. But I wanta piece of whatever's in there."

Bremer chuckled. He wiped a drop of oil from his cheek; it was dripping from the oilpan over his head. He turned to Anja.

"Oh indeed."

"Yes. Indeed."

Bremer caught a drip of oil on his fingertip, traced it over her lips like lipstick. "Will you stay for dinner, my dear?"

Quinn and Mahler had come into the lower bunker. They'd put out a fire on a corner of the building; they'd shot two more stragglers trying to jimmy the back windows. They'd eaten lunch. Yamahira hadn't been able to keep his down.

And Sullivan made a suggestion that was more than a suggestion.

Quinn shook his head at Sullivan. "No man, that is just fucking nuts."

"The floor is open," Sullivan said. "Let's have your ideas, Quinn."

Quinn stared at him. "We...can wait it out."

Sullivan said, "You know what? This asshole isn't going

away. I know who he is. His name's Bremer. He's one of the worst. He's just not going to give up."

"But it's fucking *suicide* - "

"Don't underestimate my Dad," Anatole said, authoritatively.

"They've taken my vehicles," Sullivan said. "Yours is our only hope."

"But the roads that are passable are all over run with the same kind of scumbags -"

"I know a back road, heads East, mostly gravel, probably mostly intact. Eventually fetches up in Nevada. Where's the car exactly?"

"The car is..." Quinn looked at Mahler.

Mahler hesitated - then nodded.

Quinn let out a long breath. "It's in the culvert, the one on the south side. We piled a lot of brush on the car to hide it. If they haven't found it, go for it. But what's the point? There's just no way you're going to make it."

"I'll make it. Anatole's right," Sullivan said, peering out a gunport. "Don't underestimate his Dad." He looked down at the bodies swelling in the sun. "You see what they did? They took refugees, innocent people, they psyched them up, they threatened them, they launched them against us and we had to kill them..."

"*Did* we have to?" Mahler asked. "I don't think so. We should have done anything else. They were our people; our allies. They would have been if we'd had a chance to reach them."

"I don't have any allies, man," Sullivan said. "Except Anatole. But I'll tell you this: I don't ever want to have to do that again. And they'll make us do it again."

"And Lila..." Yamahira said.

Sullivan nodded. "And Lila. We can't wait. She needs help, and fast and if it won't come to us, we'll take her to it."

"Getting her to help might kill her too," Quinn said.

Sullivan nodded.

There was an explosion from the woods near the Southeast corner of the building.

They rushed to the gunports - and saw a tall eucalyptus tilting, falling with a creaking sound, pitching onto the condoplex - falling just right. The Looters had set off a charge on the treetrunk's half rotted base.

It was the closest tree, and Sullivan had often thought he ought to cut it down. But it was too late, respect for beauty might have killed them all, the tree had crashed down so its top fifteen feet hit the edge of the roof, about forty feet from the roof bunker, and men were already scrambling up the treetrunk at a 45 degree angle, swarming like soldier ants toward the roof, keeping low, under cover of the thick foliage.

Sullivan grabbed his only grenade from where he'd wedged it between two sandbags, and shouted as he ran: "Buford, Huxley, Metzger - man this bunker - keep the intercom on in case we have to reassign you - " He paused at the door to the stairs. "Anatole - you go the rear and side gunports, run to them consecutively, fire at anything that moves - "

"Oh no, oh no," Yamahira said, grabbing his weapon.

Yamahira and Quinn and Sullivan and Mahler were on the roof in thirty seconds, the four of them running toward the silvery green foliage quivering on the edge of the roof-corner, Sullivan firing an M18 in suppressive bursts. Eucalyptus leaves were clipped by bullets and drifted aromatically away; a man screamed and fell.

Sullivan reached the tree just as a militia thug leapt from the foliage onto the roof -

Quinn's stomach lurched with each shoulder-kick of his rifle as he shot one of the men coming around the aluminum ventilator chimney; the other ran toward Yamahira who was dragging the tripod machinegun out of the bunker and turning it toward the tree -

Seeing Yamahira's face, the rictus of the older man's mouth in that moment, Quinn realized that Lila's father had flipped out, he'd gone over some brink, was shrieking at the invaders and trying to fire the machinegun in his hands, the recoil much too heavy for him, the gun yanking him around, bullets flying randomly, the old man staggering, stumbling, bellowing, "Leave us alone leave us alone leave us ALO-O-O-NE!"

Sullivan knocked another tree-climber backward with a kick to the jaw, at the same moment firing a burst at two others.

Mahler turned to open up at the man who was rushing from cover toward Yamahira but the thug was already firing from the hip with a carbine and Yamahira's torso was ripped up in five places, spun to be ripped some more, the thug shouting, *"Suck it up suck it up suck it up suck it up hard motherfucker!"*

And then Mahler shot the looter in the spine and the guy went into a tumble, folded up into an unnatural shape, firing into the rooftop, then going limp.

Sullivan had dug the grenade from his pocket, thumbing its switch, dropping it onto the treetrunk halfway down, shattering the treetrunk, the tree falling with a WHUMP, the air thick with nitro smoke and eucalyptus menthol - Mahler firing -

And Quinn was firing; wanting to be a on a beach in Florida far from the sound of guns. Was Firing. Firing.

• • •

"Now's the time," Metzger was saying. "Now's the time. We get whatever we can carry from this place in that car - and we make a deal with these bastards out there, we trade 'em the building, we trade em the people, we trade 'em the goods -"

Buford shook his head. Bullets whisked and whined into the building. He hated the sound of them. "You can't do that, Metzger - "

I'm coming, each impacting bullet seemed to say, *I'm on my way, be there in a minute, no hurry, but don't go nowhere, I'll be right there, homes, here I fuckin come...*

"The fuck I can't -"

And as Huxley watched with his mouth gaping, Metzger opened up on Buford; he cut him in half with a long burst from his M18.

Here I fuckin am. Hi, how's that feel?

"Oh lord oh shit what'd you do," Huxley said.

Metzger turned the gun toward Huxley. "Well?"

Huxley looked at Buford, twitching, dying.

The spreading pool of blood.

Then at Metzger's gun.

Then he said, "I guess. I guess so. Sure. I mean, you know - Whatever."

• • •

"I'm sorry, Dad," Anatole said. He meant: Sorry he'd let them disarm him.

Sullivan had found them in the storage room behind the lower hallway that led to the barricaded front door. Metzger and Huxley were standing behind Anatole; Metzger had a gun pointing at Anatole's head.

"Move away from my kid," Sullivan said.

Metzger smiled wearily. "I'm not gonna drop the hammer on the kid unless you make me, man. But I'm willin' to do it and I'm ready to do it - or, you can drop your weapons, and open the storage rooms."

Sullivan shook his head. "You'll kill us anyway."

"No. Someone might, later on. Not me, if you don't make me, bro'."

"You're going to turn this boy and the women over to those sons of bitches out there?"

"They'll get us all anyway. They're not gonna give up. This way, with luck, I survive. Maybe even Huxley. And hey - they probably won't kill the girls, if they're cooperative. Some of 'em maybe like boys, you know? So he could survive. Sorta. Drop the guns or I kill the New Generation Kid here and then you. Three count, okay? One, two - "

Sullivan dropped his weapon.

There was a rumbling from outside. The sound of a diesel engine.

Quinn came down through the stairway door. Mahler, carrying the heatseeker launcher tube, came breathing hard close behind. "Sullivan," Quinn was saying, "somebody shot that black soldier -"

"Buford," Mahler said, scowling. "His name was Buford. He had a name."

"They shot Buford at close range," Quinn was saying, coming in. "Looks like from inside the...the..."

They stopped, staring, at the new dynamic: Metzger, the gun, Anatole; Sullivan disarmed. "Shit," Mahler said, feelingly.

"Yeah, you drop it too, fake journalists," Metzger said. "Make a nice neat pile with the weapons."

The rumbling outside was closer.

"Okay," Metzger said, "Huxley, tie 'em up. Then we go to the PA and we start the trade."

The rumbling...

"Metz..." Huxley began, staring at Sullivan. "If I get close to that guy -"

"*Do it*, dumbshit!"

Huxley licked his lips, then nodded -

97

Sullivan prepared to kill Huxley; the preparation was all internal. On the outside he didn't move, he didn't even get tense.

The barricade behind them boomed and shuddered and collapsed inward with a crack and a grinding thud and -

"What the fuck!" Metzger shouted.

Sullivan turned and saw his little Cat earthmover crunching through the walls and the door, with Dexie at the wheel, shouting, "Honey I'm home!" and the blade of the Cat pulling a chunk of the outer wall down with it as it came down the hall -

Startled, Metzger looked away from Anatole, who saw his chance, pulled the buck-knife from its hiding place under his shirt and in the same motion turned, slammed it hard into Metzger's gut with his right hand, twisting and digging with the blade the way his Dad had taught him, his left hand shoving Metzger's gun muzzle away.

Metzger screamed piercingly.

Huxley was already running for the stairs but he caught a round in the back, his spine shot clean through, as Dexie stood up on the back of the Cat and opened up -

"Fuckafuckafuckafuckafucka!" Dexie yelled, giggling, firing his piece - spinning and falling off the still-moving Cat as Quinn cut him down with his rifle. The Cat stalled and stopped.

So wired that the bullets in his gut vibrated harmonically with one another in his wounds, Dexie stood shakily up and shouted, "Dickinapussyan' pussyinnasky pretty jewelry innasky-y-y-yyyy why dontcha die-eeeee!" as he raised his weapon firing but firing crookedly now and Sullivan stepped up to him from the side and chopped the gun away, spun him and straight-armed Dexie's forehead so the back of his head splashed onto the wall and he went down muttering with ever diminishing volubility: "I'm a monkey I'm a mum-mum-munkey pretty pussy innna skyyyyy...." And died.

Metzger was writhing on the floor, intestines carved up, screaming like a small woman having a twelve pound baby. Anatole stared at him.

Sullivan scooped up his weapon. "Fuck you," Sullivan told the writhing soldier, pulling Anatole behind him and shooting the top of Metzger's head away. The screaming stopped.

Sullivan tossed Quinn his rifle, grabbed the heatseeker from him, just as a cluster of PM Looters came rushing up to the gap Dexie'd made in the front of the building. The heatseeker was already loaded.

"Tell Bremer we got some more of these," Sullivan yelled at the Looters, lying convincingly, as he fired his last heatseeker at the surprised faces in the opening.

The looters turned and ran and most of them didn't make it; the explosion took out half a dozen. Okay, maybe five.

Sullivan tossed the launcher tube aside, turned to Quinn and Mahler. "Can you and Zizz and Kian carry Lila down here - carefully?"

They nodded - Mahler was looking at the blank faced Anatole with something like awe - and ran up the stairs.

Sullivan gathered Anatole into his arms. Anatole started to shake. To sob. "I'm sorry you had to do that, son. Nobody should have to do that."

Seven minutes and seventeen seconds later...

Sullivan had gotten the Cat backed up and out into the cleared area when the mortar round came down, whistling merrily, blowing a cloud of dirt and dust and blood from the bloated corpses of the refugees.

Clods of Earth pattered down around the condoplex defenders; the cloud hid them for a moment. It was more opportunity than threat.

"You sure you're up for this?" Sullivan asked.

Quinn nodded.

Zizz and Kian were crouching next to the stretcher they'd brought Lila out on, just inside the ragged gap in the wall, Anatole on the other side, holding her hand. She was whitefaced but conscious. "Jack?" Lila said weakly. "Where's my Dad?"

Sullivan bent and kissed her. "He's taken care of."

(Lying in a pool of blood on the roof).

Sullivan nodded to Quinn who sprinted through the thinning smoke - toward the woods but away from the main body of the looters.

Sullivan went to the idling Cat, Mahler with him; Kian and Zizz crouched near the stretcher. Kian was crying, Zizz had her arm around him.

"What the hell is that?" Mahler asked, pointing.

Sullivan turned to see the figure of a man in the dustcloud, backlit by the lowering sun. A big man, bulked out with armor of some kind, giggling like a moron.

He came closer. His face emerged from the dust. It was Sol. Grinning. Sparks glimmering over his rotting, metal studded skull.

"YUUUHHHHHHHHHHHHHHHHHHHHH WAN PLAYYYYYYYYYYYYYYYYYYY YUHHHHHH!" The way he said it was almost a yodel. High pitched and ululating. "YUUUUUUHHHHH WANN PLAYYYYY?"

He stalked toward them; three bulletproof vests were strapped overlapping on his chest; pieces of others on his legs.

In his hands was a crowbar...with nails welded to it.

Mahler fired and then Sullivan; bullets rebounded from the armor, making Sol stagger a little as he rushed Sullivan, roaring with the delight of the already-dead, moving upstream against the outpouring of bullets.

Kian screamed.

"His head!" Anatole shouted, watching from the gap behind Sullivan. "Shoot his -"

Sullivan did, five rounds raking across Sol's face, one of them knocking out the pins of his jaws so the lower jaw sagged and rocked like a porch-swing and one of his eyes just vanished and the top of his head lifted away like, well like smashing pumpkins, and -

But it didn't stop him. He hardly used that part of his brain.

And Sol was on them then, smashing their guns aside with his crowbar, though he took three more rounds in his neck and coughed blood; he knocked Mahler aside with a swipe of one arm, with the other swinging the crowbar at Sullivan, knocking Sullivan onto his back, driving the crowbar down on Sullivan's throat...

In the woods Anja was pointing the remote at Sol's back, alternately pressing the *pleasure* and the *fight* buttons, muttering "Kill 'em and love it, kill em and love it you fucking shit-animal, kill em and love it..." She laughed to herself and added: "Happy-happy joy-joy."

Just managing to keep the crowbar from crushing his throat, Sullivan was staring up at Sol's face from ten inches away;

Sol's blazingly vacant eyes and foaming mouth. Looking into the murderous void. Spittle and blood and brains drooled into Sullivan's mouth.

(Kian screamed).

Anatole and Mahler were on Sol from behind, trying to pull him off...Shooting came from behind: Mahler was forced to turn and lay down suppressive fire on the Looter army coming across the open space - Quinn fired at the looters from the other side of the Cat. Sol began to crush the cartilage in Sullivan's throat.

Austin was leading a charge...

(Kian was screaming).

Anatole found Sullivan's rifle and shot away the back of Sol's head, from the side, but SOL DIDN'T STOP. He had the welded nails pressing down into Sullivan's neck now; Sullivan's blood began to runnel, mix with Sol's; his drool falling into Sullivan's eyes.

Anatole yelled and shot Sol again. Sol held on. "YAHHH SURE YAHHHH!" Only a small part of Sol's original brain remained. He shat himself and quivered but he didn't stop he - seriously, he: DIDN'T STOP.

Anatole could see metal-and-silicon hardware exposed in the cheesy red-grey wreck of Sol's brain.

Anatole screamed and shot again - from the side so as not to hit his Dad -

Austin had thrown himself flat in the crater left by the mortar and was firing past the Cat - Mahler lost part of an ear and a chunk of skin and a shallow ditch of flesh from a shoulder -

Sol collapsed onto Sullivan. Grunting, Sullivan rolled him off.

Sullivan got to his feet, took his weeping son by the wrists and dragged him to the Cat, put it in gear without getting into it -

They ran beside the vehicle, Sullivan and Mahler carrying the stretcher, Lila trying not to yell in pain with each step - a brick held the Cat's accelerator down and they followed it, used it for cover, toward the southwest side of the woods, away from the bulk of the PM looters -

Anatole fired over the Cat and two Looters went down -

Kian had been screaming for a long time now, since Sol had began to come at them, and normally if Kian screamed

Sullivan would have made him an instant priority but now Kian screaming seemed like it was way down the list, it was almost nothing, it was just a child screaming in horror.

So?

Welcome to the fucking planet Earth.

• • •

"Hold your fire!" Bremer shouted, from the cover of the woods. "They're moving away from the building - you can't hit them at this angle - "

"I'm gonna check out that building," Anja told Bremer. "See if it's wired."

"Good," Bremer said. "You might just be useful yet."

"You're sweet," Anja told him. "How about giving me a weapon?"

"Not a chance. Sprint like hell, is my advice."

She smiled coldly at him, and she sprinted like hell.

• • •

Sullivan reached the edge of the woods, turned the Cat so it was moving in another direction, toward the Looters. The decoy worked; the bunch Bremer sent to outflank him ran toward the noisy, smoking vehicle, assuming...

Assuming wrongly, getting there in time to see the cat was moving alone, no one with it; just in time to see the burning rag hanging from the gas tank door -

The Cat exploded; took four of 'em with it -

Okay, maybe three; the other didn't die till the next day.

Sullivan and Zizz and Mahler and Anatole and Kian, carrying Lila's stretcher, reached the farther edge of the wood just as Quinn drove up to them in the old Volvo.

"Hope you know where to go from here," Quinn said.

Mahler got in the front; Zizz crammed onto his lap; Sullivan and Anatole and Kian got in the back; they held Lila across their laps. She tried not to yell with pain when they hit bumps. They drove off to the East.

Kian had stopped screaming.

Sullivan asked him how he was. He didn't say anything.

So?

• • •

Anja waved from the smoldering gap in the condoplex outer wall. "It's deserted and it's safe!"

The Looters were up and running toward the condoplex at that - till Bremer fired his weapon into the air.

"Halt, you sodding nitwits!"

They turned and looked at him.

"I'm going in first - I don't trust you fuckers with whatever's in there - I don't want anybody looting my goods! You'll get a share after I've gone over it!"

He ran past them; past their glares; past Anja; into the building. Anja turned and walked decisively away from the building, stepped over Sol's body without even looking down; turned and waited. Smiling sweetly.

The explosives that Sullivan had set up - which Anja had carefully delayed - went off, with Bremer in the building. Firebombs reminisced about David Koresh, and the building was consumed.

"Oh dear," Anja said. "I guess it was wired after all."

"You timed that just right," Austin said, stepping up to her. Said it so the others wouldn't hear.

"Did I?" she said.

"It's all right - we're gonna need a new leader. Me, I never wanted that job - people like to shoot the leader in the back. Or blow The Leader up with fire bombs, say." He grinned. "But if you don't mind that kinda risk...you wanta give it a shot...It's lush with me, girlfriend...I mean, fuck it. You want the job?"

"The thought had occurred to me..."

She turned to watch the burning shell of the building. Pieces of it were still falling, like cheap imitations of fireworks, trailing smoke and sparks.

A sizzling ball fell about fifty feet away: might be Bremer's head. She wasn't sure. It was somebody's head, anyway.

It was a nice fire. Kind of a nice blue-violet color to the flame.

The next day they managed to salvage some of the more protected food from the smoking ruins, and the day after that she led them North, toward San Jose.

She had some ideas she wanted to try out.

• • •

Farraday felt like getting drunk, as he stared at the land octopus, but instead he said, "So - it's your move."

The cephaloped - 'Ceph', the lab boys called it - moved

its queen to put his king in check.

"I concede the damn game," Farraday said, sighing. They were in his dinky quarters, Farraday on the bunk, the genetic experiment on a metal stool, a TV tray between them for the chess board.

Just after dinner. The cephaloped, a vegetarian, had eaten here with Farraday; it'd eaten mostly raspberry-fruit-salad jello, with a beak on its underside. Farraday had seen all he wanted of *that*.

The land octopus extended several of its human-baby's arms, with skin that was partly pink and partly the color of a dead infant, and then two more limbs, and began to meticulously pick up the plastic chess pieces and put them into the box.

Ceph was propped up on a stool and several old phone books, its octopus-head shifting inside itself, lop-siding over a little to the right, then slopping restlessly to the left, changing color with its thoughts.

Farraday had more or less gotten used to the creature.

"So you don't need to be immersed in water?" Farraday asked.

"I told you - no." An unusual irritation in its voice. The land octopus was usually so mellifluous, so tender in its tonality.

"You sound a little irritated with that question."

"I'm sorry. You see, water...I have nightmares about it. I must occasionally bathe myself, of course, and it's an ordeal. The nightmares are so vivid - I so fear being immersed in water...and when I'm in the water, in the dreams, I'm choking, and dying, and then the...some hideous undersea creature comes after me...its jaws agape."

"'Jaws agape'?"

"I took the phrase from an old adventure book. I think it was by Robert E. Howard. I love reading books about magic and heroes and especially dragons, flying dragons - I adore the old adventure writers."

"Uh huh. And you imagine yourself - "

"The heroine of course! But then, I'm gay, perhaps. I'm male actually you see. . .I think."

Farraday decided to steer away from that whole area of discussion. He really didn't want to know about this thing's sexuality.

Still - he respected the creature. It lived with its uniqueness with a kind of Elephant Man dignity, and it deserved to be more than an *it*. Since Ceph was male, Farraday resolved to think of him as a *he*.

"What do you think, Ceph - are they listening to us here?"

"They would be; but I rerouted the wires. They hear random chit chat from the hangars instead."

"What do you mean, you rerouted...?"

"Well," the land octopus said sweetly, "I really have no gift with computers, I'm basically a point and click person. I use the old Windows 95 program, which was outdated in 97, but it's all they give me. Oh but wiring - I have a gift for the guts of machines. I can build things, rewire things, install chips -"

"Whoa, slow down. Why exactly did you decide to rewire my room?"

"And without even asking you."

Ceph oozed off the stool, his babylegs and octopal tentacles helping him down the side, making the stool rock only slightly. He lifted himself up onto the bunk next to Farraday; a climbing puddle of flesh, human and octopal.

Farraday was *mostly* used to the creature.

"I do apologize about the rewiring," Ceph went on. "It was presumptuous. But I do have some things I *must* talk to you about it in private."

"Do you now? Your agenda - or theirs?"

"Whose?"

"The military. The Zetans. I don't know who. All I know is I don't know. I don't know a whole hell of a lot about you - I've only...had you as a 'pet', if that's what it is -"

"I hardly think so, really, though I was quite sincere in swearing obedience to you."

" - whatever you call it. Adoption..." Farraday's stomach lurched at the term. Adoption. He thought about the baby he and Lyn wanted. The babyarmed thing in front of him seemed a grotesque mockery of that desire.

"True, you don't know me. You wonder, I'm guessing, if you *can* know me. Am I animal? Human? Are there alien genes in me? All three, yes. But let me assure you - my agenda is my own. Or...it is not, at any rate, something arranged by our Keepers."

Our Keepers...?

Am I as 'kept' as this thing is?

Farraday too was an experiment, after all, in some way: a public relations experiment.

And how could Ceph have any kind of agenda? Hadn't the cephaloped lived his whole short life here, on the base? Perhaps Ceph's agenda was escape; perhaps he simply craved freedom.

"Are you thinking about...breaking out, Mike?" Ceph asked softly.

Was the room really un-bugged? he wondered. Or was this creature trying to draw him out for Derrick, see if he'd betray their...Keepers.

He shuddered. And decided: the hell with it. I'm going to trust the goddam land octopus.

This living grotesquerie has a decent vibe about it; those around me I'd more naturally trust *don't* have that vibe. The untrustworthy are trustworthy; the trustworthy are likely back-stabbing sons of bitches.

He'd always trusted paradox...You could count on a paradox being there...

"No," Ceph was saying. "Not breaking out, exactly. Not right away. I am in fact...in touch with others. No one knows it, here. They don't realize that I've been contacted; that I'm a contactee. They don't realize. The Zetans, as they allow you to call them, do not know it; the military doesn't know; the CIA doesn't know. They don't have access to those media. They may think they do but they don't. They haven't the grace and they haven't the faith."

I'm not dreaming, Farraday told himself. A 'land octopus' made by aliens from Zeta Reticuli is talking to me about grace and faith.

He had a potent need, then, to be back home alone with his wife. Just lying beside her, like two spoons in a drawer, in bed, his kneecaps tucked into the hollow of her knees, his arm over her, one hand on her breast. He ached for it.

He got up and poured himself a shot from the bottle of Glenfiddich Derrick had given him.

"You want to be more specific, Ceph?" Farraday asked.

"No, if it's alright with you - I just can't be more specific now. What I want to tell you, just now, is this: tomorrow, if my information is correct, you will have a meeting with a Lieutenant Colonel named Dodge. This Dodge will tell you he's from Psyche Tech Division, which is basically responsible for the morale of the troops, and that he's going to work with you and Colonel Derrick and Jaron - but in fact..."

Colors were shifting across his fleshy sack of a body, murky primaries, one into the next. "...in fact, he's part of a longstanding CIA Mind Control division. And various other secret organizations; some of them going back many centuries. He plays the good-ole-boy part, but he's very much more than that, though he probably won't show himself to you as he really is. You can't trust him. You must be very, very careful what you agree to take part in, with him...."

"They don't give me a lot of choice, here."

"One way to get out of things...perhaps...is to say you're not trained for it or to imply you don't want the responsibility of that clearance. You can *try* it...They usually let you slide."

"Do they?"

"From what I've heard of peacetime military protocol and psychology. Just be very careful. For one thing - if you take part in certain experiments, Mind Control experiments involving abductions and saucers, the MK Ultra projects, and you don't like what you see - well, my friend, it's quite likely that they'll kill you. And that would be a great shame. You're a very nice man, really. And you'd miss out on the Silicon Embrace, and the waves of improbability and I like you, I'd be saddened if you missed out on those things...Of course, all that could fail, if that's any consolation: perhaps it won't come about, and you won't have missed anything if you die..."

He stared at the land octopus. Then he looked away. It was too much to absorb Ceph's presence and the things he was saying, both.

Something came home to him.

"Did you say - they'd kill me?" Farraday asked, his voice hoarse.

"Oh yes. Oh yes indeed. That's what happened to the last gentleman who was here from the Public Relations field. Or perhaps he killed himself - I'm not clear on that."

Ceph rippled himself from bluish to a kind of gruesome pink. And decided to change the subject.

"Do you like rocknroll, by the way? I always identified with the Panther Moderns although most of the Lab Boys seem to prefer Madonna's kid - what's her name, I've forgotten -"

"Hey Ceph? The PR guy you mentioned: He killed himself, for sure?"

"Or...appeared to kill himself. Or did kill himself but was manipulated into the suicide, or...well, it hardly matters."

Silence. Farraday laid his hand on the empty chessboard, as if searching for the chess pieces that had been taken away from him.

At last Farraday said, "I was thinking along those lines, Ceph - that my life might be in danger here. But I thought, chill: you watched too many episodes of *X Files* as a kid, you read too much Louis Pawels, too much Robert Anton Wilson, too much conspiracy theory stuff. Told myself I was just being paranoid."

"Welllll..."

Ceph seemed to consider. Then his body rippled and changed color, pinkish to grey-green; his version of a shrug.

"It is paranoid, Mike," Ceph said. "And paranoia is absolutely appropriate."

Paranoia: don't leave home without it.

PART THE SUCKUND

*Don't you see
when you're lookin at me
that I'll never end
transcend, transcend...
Ain't it strange?
A new...
a new direction
A new...
a new dimension
Ain't it strange?*
- Patti Smith,
from the album "Radio Ethiopia"

*Psst....C'mere!
I hear the music daylight disc
Three men in black said,
"Don't report this..."
...All praise:
he's found the awful truth...*
–Blue Oyster Cult,
from the LP, "Agents of Fortune"

CHAPTER SIX
THEY'RE JUST LIGHTS. JUST LIGHTS.

East on Highway 15. Sullivan driving, Mahler beside him; Zizz crammed half on Mahler's lap. Mahler too politically correct to get a hard-on.

Quinn in back; Anatole and Kian; Lila was lying across their laps, head pillowed on an old shirt folded over Quinn's arm.

Highway 15. East. It'd taken them so long to get here; the safest remaining highway route to Nevada: to the nearest clearly-defined border of the Sovereign United States.

Just get to Highway 15, East, Quinn had said, and we're home free.

But they'd been on Highway 15, East, a long time. So long. And they'd come only to the ruins of recently burned-out motels, burned-out restaurants, burned-out housing tracts, glimpses of burned out people; and through ruins and past them to desert; to the carcasses of overturned semitrucks; to ghost towns like Baker, with its erstwhile tourist attraction now a giant, cracked leaning-tower thermometer.

Where was the fucking Nevada state line?

The car was too crowded. The car was *way* too crowded.

The air rushed through the broken windshield, sucked over them, hot and dry, parching, etching every epidermal crevice with grit.

Quinn kept turning to look at the boy, Kian. *Forget it. It's not your kid.*

But there was something disturbing about the vacancy in Kian's eyes as he stared out over the noontime Mojave desert. It was as if he had taken the desert itself into his gaze; he had interfaced perfectly with its predatory near-emptiness; with its dusty, scarred tangles of cacti and desiccated, arthritic shrubs and its flickering lizards.

The air conditioner was meaningless behind the shattered windshield. They were so packed together it would have been a bitch under the best conditions. A miasma of their sweat and suffering skirled in the air blown through the windshield.

Sullivan was painfully but not seriously shot up; Mahler was grouchy when anyone bumped into his bandages; and Lila...

Lila had shrapnel in her gut and sometimes they had to check to see if she was alive. Her lips were blue around the edges. Her temperature ranged wildly. Her eyes fluttered and drooped.

The horizon seemed to jeeringly withdraw; seemed to suggest with a bleak Cheshire smile that they would never cross the Nevada border.

Sullivan's gas-cache, hidden in the hills east of the condoplex, was almost exhausted; they were down to about three gallons. There'd been a little dried food and water in the cache but it was mostly gone now too.

They rarely spoke. They were all sick of the car. Sick of each other.

Sometimes the radio worked and sometimes it didn't. It was the EMP, Sullivan said. They didn't hear anything of value; snatches of country music from Vegas. Static. The usual apocalyptic preachers. Someone, speaking in Farsi, presumably making the usual demands. Static. Static. But once someone on a pirate station out of San Francisco said, *"Where's Black Betty? Does anyone know? Does anyone know who to ask? We know who to ask. But we also know which answers we will not be given...if Black Betty has been..."*

Mahler was excited at that, but the signal withdrew behind a curtain of static and they heard no more about her.

Most of the time Quinn and Zizz and Mahler steered clear of talking about Black Betty. They felt they'd lost their original mission; their only mission now was to survive, to escape, to find the Sovereign States again.

"I can't believe it," Zizz said. "I'm gonna turn into my parents. I was bitching about FedControl and how they controlled the media in the Sovereign U.S. and how they relocated people when they felt like it and how they're so fucking awful...and now..."

"Now you can't wait to get back there," Sullivan said, nodding. "Back to all those laws. A little anarchy goes a long way."

Quinn had gotten annoyed with Mahler, when he'd muttered about all this fragmentation being the result of hegemony, imperialism, capitalism.

"Personally," Quinn said, "I think it's the result of people having kneejerk assumptions in general - communistic, capitalistic, racialist, whatever. Just not being tolerant and flexible. And you with this communist bullshit - I mean, how can anyone be a communist in the 21st Century? You may as well be Amish."

"Convenient point of view, glibly put together by someone who was educated thanks to the power elite -"

"Oh I feel *real* powerful right *now* -"

"And I'll tell you something my friend, Marxism has never been tried. Not as Marx intended it." He paused to cough from the dust. "The USSR, the Red Chinese, the Vietnamese, the Koreans - all false Marxisms, self serving political distortions -"

Sullivan broke in, "You assholes argue about this crap anymore, I'm going to put you out of your own stolen car and drive away. And don't fuckin imagine I'm kidding, either."

"Take it easy, Dad," Anatole said gently.

Mahler lapsed into resigned silence.

Sullivan glanced at Anatole, then at Kian. A lingering look at the silent, distant Kian.

Zizz reached into the back and held Lila's hand and, at times, silently wept.

Mahler tried to sleep; or pretended to.

Anatole sat with his arm around Kian. The older boy seemed be half sleeping, half thinking, his mouth sometimes curving into a smile, sometimes pinching with fear.

The road curved, now, which seemed impossible. Hadn't it been straight on forever? But gradually a ridge bulged from the flat desert and the road curved around its boulder strewn prow - and suddenly Sullivan ground to a halt, marking the road behind him with licorice stripes.

Up ahead an RV was burning.

It was a Winnebago, standing on its wheels but skewed to the side. Dirty-black and yellow flame licked from its windows and its engine. A man with a soot-blackened face - short hair, maybe fifty years old, grimy t-shirt and cammie pants - sat with his back to a boulder, staring dully at the Winnebago.

He had more or less the same look that was in Kian's eyes.

It's like they're pod people, Kian and the stranger, like the Body Snatchers got them, Quinn thought.

But they'd been taken over by the desert geometry, the crowded emptiness of despair.

Quinn stared. A burning Winnebago. A Recreational Vehicle funeral pyre. Black bubbles on its aluminum and fiberglass sides. It looked all wrong: You could picture a sports car burning, or an old Cadillac, even, and surely a hot rod: but a Winnebago, no, a burning Winnebago looked all discordant. It was like Dali's flaming giraffes.

Still, Quinn and Zizz and Mahler were glad to get out of the car, Quinn easing with excruciating care out from under Lila. Stretching, shaking the feeling back into the arm that had pillowed her head.

Sullivan, rifle in hand, approached the man on the roadside, glancing around.

Sullivan's thinking this could be a trap of some kind, a lure, Quinn thought.

The scarred ex-merc was staring up into the tumble of big red-gray boulders; the rocks were like a lumpy cow-catcher around the locomotive prow of the ridge.

"You got a pistol?" asked the man sitting with his back to the boulder, squinting up at them as they approached. Same tone a man used to ask a stranger for a match on a streetcorner.

"Are you hurt?" Zizz asked.

"Not...hurt," the man said.

"This your Winnebago?" Quinn asked.

The man nodded.

"What happened?" Sullivan asked.

"Family's in the RV," the man said. His voice, now, was cheerful but unnaturally high pitched.

Quinn could feel the heat from the burning RV on his face. "You shouldn't be so near the fire," Quinn told the stranger. "The gas tank..."

"It already blew," the man said, as if he was talking about the weather. "That's why it's burning. They shot an incendiary round into it."

He licked blistered lips and blinked up at them.

Zizz trotted back to the car, as Sullivan scanned the rocks above them. Nothing moved up there. She returned with a canteen and gave the stranger a drink.

He drank for a full minute, and poured water over his face, and lips, but made no move to get up. He let the canteen sink onto his lap, and stared at his boots.

"Your family was killed?" Mahler asked, gently.

The man nodded.

Quinn turned and looked at the car. Anatole was sitting with his arm around Kian. Anatole watched curiously but made no move to get out. He didn't want to leave Kian unless he had to.

"Who did it?" Sullivan asked, wearily. Something in his tone saying: *Not that it matters who. Not around here.*

"Fresno Freemen. They control...Fresno and East, to the state line...most of the way south..."

"Freemen." Sullivan seemed puzzled. "Stupid bastards. But they don't usually kill civilian types - "

"I left," the man said. "I wanted out of the Freemen...wanted to take my kids to Nevada...Join the USA again...Changed my mind, see...they just don't..." He gave a cracked little laugh. "They said I was a spy for the New World Order..."

"These Freemen around here?" Quinn asked nervously.

The man shrugged. "Dunno. They left me for dead - they thought I was in the RV. I panicked and got out a window and ran and...when I came back..." He looked at the burning RV.

He swallowed. He swallowed nothing. Then he swallowed more nothing.

"I just want to defend myself..." he said in a soft, almost inaudible voice.

No one spoke for a few moments. The RV crackled to itself as it burnt. Flames rattled. The wind twisted smoke and slapped it away and added its particulates to the fine murk of all the other things men burned.

Quinn thought he could smell flesh burning.

"East on this road," Sullivan said, "we going to run into these Freemen types?"

The man nodded. "Sure as hell will." Voice barely audible at all now. "And Ataska is out there too, somewhere..."

"Oh fuck..." Sullivan muttered. "Ataska."

"Who's Ataska?" Zizz asked.

"Godclone nomadic cult. Thinks he's Christ and Mohammed both, goes into religious ecstasies at the drop of a hat, froths at the mouth, comes out of it deciding who he's gonna murder for God today. Butchery. Thinks that dogs are 'ghosts'. Your standard organized religion gone psychotic."

"Any route around all this?" Mahler asked.

The man pointed at a dirt road branching off from the tarmac. He raised his hand, pointed, and left the finger pointing as if he'd forgotten about it.

"I think that dirt road, maybe it goes to a military base...the other side of the state line. I was headin' there...Surrender to the military..."

He finally let his hand drop into his lap.

"We'll have to get him into the car someway," Mahler said. "It's already too crowded...Maybe take out the seats?"

"We could maybe take the trunk lid off," Quinn said, "make the trunk into a sort of trundle seat...Let him ride in there."

Sullivan shrugged. "Take too much time. Got to get Lila to help. But he can ride in the trunk with the lid open if he wants, if he can stand to be that crammed..."

The man shook his head. "Staying here. Bury my family. I need a pistol, is all, just want to protect myself if..."

Mahler took a pistol from his back pocket and gave it to the stranger.

Sullivan said, "Whoa, wait –"

But on *wait* the guy pulled the trigger, with the gunmuzzle stuck in his mouth, and the top of his head popped off like a jack in the box lid.

Mahler gaped at the twitching body. "Lied to me to get the gun!" Shaking his head. "Fuck!" He turned away and said, "Lied to me! He -I didn't know he was..."

Zizz wailed and went back to the car, holding her stomach, and Quinn, feeling dizzy, went with her. It had been just too sudden. Jack in the box.

"He fucking lied - !" Mahler was saying, almost crying. "I didn't know -"

"All right, all right, man, it's not your fault," Sullivan said, retrieving the gun. His face was impassive. He put an arm around Mahler and walked him back to the car. "Forget it."

Anatole stared past them at the dead man and said, "Shit!"

Kian said nothing.

They all got back in the car, and Sullivan turned onto the dirt road, heading northeast in the dust-raw Mojave. Maybe toward a military base.

• • •

The alien took a bite out of a cigarette.

"I'm gonna buy you some legitimate smokeless tobacco, man," Farraday said.

"Smokeless? Is that possible?"

"Yeah you, like, chew it or something."

They were sitting in plastic chairs in the hall outside Colonel Dodge's office. Waiting. Jaron wanted a cigarette but apparently didn't dare smoke one here.

Farraday leaned back against the cold concrete wall, tired and nervous. He'd spent all morning taking psychology profile tests of some kind, which apparently were evaluated by a computer. Could a computer suss out his irrationality? Who better, perhaps?

I'm fucked, Farraday thought.

Get a grip, goddammit.

Farraday cleared his throat. "So - Jaron - about this guy Dodge...should I be nervous about him?"

Jaron turned Farraday his lidless stare. His eyes darkened in bright places, Farraday had noticed, like photosensitive sunglasses; and lightened, became translucent, in dimmer places, and it was then that you could see they were much like human eyes, under the natural film, but overgrown and with less color. "Why do you ask about being nervous around Colonel Dodge, Mike?"

"Well - I heard..." Then he thought better of it.

"From whom did you hear something about Lieutenant Colonel Dodge?" Jaron asked, in Farraday's voice.

"I..."

Farraday was saved from that one when the door to Dodge's office opened and Corporal Collins beckoned them in.

Collins always made a point of not staring at Jaron. He closed the door quickly behind them, waited in the hall.

The windowless little underground office contained only a desk with a desk-top-concealed PC, a couple of guest chairs, a few cheap seascapes on the walls, framed diplomas, a minifridge in one corner.

Dodge was a long-faced white guy with tapering white fingers, a sardonic mouth and deeply-receded hair which was otherwise as long as the military would allow. He wore a blue, neatly pressed short sleeved shirt and Gap slacks. No uniform, but the air of authority was there.

He smiled and shook hands with Farraday, "Thanks for coming in!" As if it hadn't been ordained from on High Command. He threw a mock-salute at Jaron who replied in kind. "Have a seat, Mr. Farraday -"

"Call me Mike if you want, Colonel."

"Good!" He didn't offer Farraday his own first name. "So - it looks like you two are adjusting to one another." Dodge had a nearly-faded southern accent; maybe Arkansan.

"Sure," Farraday said. "Anyway I'm comfortable with Jaron." It was almost true, all things being relative.

"I always think of that story -" Dodge said, leaning back in his chair, fingers locked behind his head, " - don't know if it's true or not, like so many stories - about the Indians who first saw Columbus and his men, and how the Indians, supposedly, wouldn't acknowledge that the sailors existed, the Europeans were so alien the Indians couldn't fit them into their mindsets. So the natives just wouldn't look at 'em. Some people can't adjust to the alien quickly - but in the end we're just Indians meeting explorers around here, only we're getting along a lot better than the Indians did. Luckily for us, the Zetans are not Conquistadores."

He smiled and winked.

There was something about Dodge that made Farraday think about the Disney animatronics of his youth.

Dodge unlocked his hands and stretched in his chair. "The Zetans're interested in sharing some of our minerals - things that are less important to us but rare on their world, like, say, boron -"

Boron? Seriously? Farraday thought.

" - and certain genetic resources," Dodge went on, "but -"

Genetic resources? What's that mean exactly?

" - but they aren't interested in taking anything or anybody over."

"Ultimately, taking over is not an efficient way of taking part in a world," Jaron said, in Dodge's voice.

Not an efficient way of taking?

But Farraday just kept nodding and smiling.

After that Dodge eased the subject to something neutral; was everything okay with Farraday, had he been able to talk to his wife, would he like her to come for a conjugal visit in a month or so.

They weren't going to let him leave for at least that long? And "conjugal visit"? Wasn't that a penal term?

And how did he like the food and were there any magazines he needed, had he been over to the rec room, and the corners of the room filled with meaningless phrases until he woke Farraday up a little by saying,

"- And I understand you've been taking care of our dear old 'prairie squid' for us -"

Prairie squid? Does he mean Ceph?

" - which is great, you're a flexible guy, relating to both Ceph and Jaron - and to the Military! That's exactly what we need. The psyche test gives you a good chameleon adaptability ratio without any residue of negative unpredictability, and that's a great quality - Would you like a Diet Coke? No? Jaron, some chocolate? I have some chocolate milk...oh that's right, actual milk products upset you..."

Good chameleon adaptability ratio...without any residue...?

"Upset us? Not exactly," Jaron was saying. "But the idea of removing a nutritional fluid from one animal for the use of a different species - somewhat repugnant, yes. And despite homogenization I am not sure it is microbiologically sound. I prefer non-dairy hot chocolate..."

Dodge laughed. "Boy you sure make it sound repugnant! My doctor's been telling me to give up dairy and now by God I think I will!"

Farraday laughed politely. He felt like he wasn't getting enough air in this little office.

Suddenly Dodge went quiet and looked thoughtfully at one of the seascapes like a man used to looking out a window when he was thinking.

"Mr. Farraday...Mike...You've been briefed about the Meta, I think...Would you like to see one?"

Without waiting for answer, Dodge tapped the PC keyboard - the computer screen lifted up from the desk, and swiveled silently to face Farraday. And an image expanded to fill the screen: a moving, color video of something that hovered against a blue sky. It seemed very definitely shaped and then again had no certain definition, no sharp edges. And then it seemed to be a sort of hatbox shape, metallic-iridescent. The video image zoomed in; detail brought out a quivering surface of both crystal and metal and a sense of *watching* from it.

"That's a Meta," Dodge was saying, popping a Diet Coke can. "...a creature that is itself a spacecraft, so we're told, *and* a living creature. A creature that lives in more than one universe at a time, perhaps. As you can almost see. Some kind of pain in the neck to look at, isn't it? Always gives me a headache if I look at it long."

"What uh - what's it made out of?"

"Well when we get a spectrographic reading, it appears to be some form of complicated silicon...but then again it's not."

"You are right to say 'appears to be'" Jaron remarked, in Dodge's voice.

"And these things," Farraday asked, staring in fascination at the image. "They are - hostile to us? We're sure of that?"

Jaron turned to look at him, then at Dodge.

Dodge swilled Diet Coke and looked at a seascape. "Put it this way - is an ant colony in the yard 'hostile' to you? But if it invades your house you got to spray it, right? A bunch of crows, say, eating all your grain - are they hostile? No, they don't give a damn about you, they just want your grain. They're just a damn problem is all. Practically speaking, the crows're hostile to... your interests."

Farraday nodded slowly. Dodge was not looking directly at him, but he felt sure that Dodge was, somehow, scrutinizing him closely. Listening for his reaction.

"Okay then. The Meta are a problem." He wanted to ask just exactly what *grain* they were getting into. But he found that he was afraid to. Some instinct - and Ceph's counsel - told him to play it cagey with Dodge.

"Now you're used to working in the standard media formats, Mike - you do TV commercials, you do PR campaigns for the internet, you set up interviews for celebrities, publicize new shows, all that. Am I right?"

"Sure, along those lines."

"Well - you'll be doing some of that for us too, even down to writing press releases, scripts for public education videos. But we also would like you to participate in a Staged Event."

"A what?"

"Derrick didn't brief you on that? Staged Events - ah, things that appear to happen in the real world but didn't? Gulf of Tonkin incident, going back to the last century, alien autopsy film, more recently the attack on the vice president at the United Nations -"

"You mean disinformation?"

"That's a term I don't like - and it would encompass, at any rate, only part of what I'm talking about. It's more like comfort-customized information. How can I explain this...bluntly, I guess. We take a holographic model of a Meta, and we project this 'apparent object' for the public to see, in a context that's valuable to us. We can even make it appear on radar." He looked at Farraday, then at his Coke can. "We will be using the holograph to stage what will *appear* to be a hostile attack on a military hospital. No one will genuinely be hurt - the only people who will 'die' you see are going to be already dead. Of natural causes, of course -"

- the only people who will 'die' are going to be already dead?

" - and what we'll be doing is dramatizing with an apparent event in the real world what the Meta will be doing anyway if we allow them to do it, later."

Farraday's mouth was paper dry. He was nodding, keeping a neutral half smile on his face. "I see. Could I maybe have a Diet Coke after all?"

"Surely...Here you go. Ice?"

"No, no thanks, it's already cold." He popped the top of the can, slowly and carefully, sipped, stalling. "You know - this sounds like a fascinating project but uh - I mean, you seem to have it all sussed out. What would I, ah, do? I'd be, you know, sort of redundant..."

"You'd handle the public relations around the event, as it came down. There was some debate as to whether you needed to know about its...staged quality. Know that it wasn't entirely 'real'. But we thought we'd want you in on the planning for future staged events so...you get your cherry busted on this one!" He winked.

Cherry? Busted?

"I see - Only I wonder...I mean, this isn't really my specialty. I'm not trained for, uh, staged events..."

"Aren't you? I think you underestimate the scope of what goes on in PR and advertising." Dodge smiled crookedly. "You see my father worked in PR...people like him...*you* people...are constantly planting newspaper articles through your contacts and your press releases, making them look like spontaneous reporting..." He leaned back, cheerfully checked it all off on his fingers, smiling gently at the ceiling: "...setting up celeb interviews and news spots that appear to be a function of 'news' but which are in fact just advertising contained in a news format...You people design junk mail that looks like an official document or a check and we open it and find out it's just an ad...You make cigarettes and alcohol seem safe and sexy...You arrange for articles to appear in the newspaper touting pharmaceutical drugs - drugs that do more harm than good... 'Do people care? People do.' When they don't at all - they're just polluters with good PR. Aren't all those things just around the corner from staged events?"

"I wasn't raising ethical issues with you, Colonel."

"Weren't you?"

"No, no. I was just thinking that I've honed my abilities for certain areas of media and uh - this staged event thing, uh - it's really not my forte..."

"A good liar is a good liar in any medium, Mike," Dodge said, rising from his chair and extending his hand. "You'll do. The

computer's got your number, pal. You'll do..."
A good liar is a good liar in any medium, Mike...

• • •

Sullivan wouldn't stop until they ran out of gas. When they did it was under sunset-lit clouds streaming from the East.

They were in the dusty grip of the desert, on a dirt road, with almost no water, no gas, and there was no human edifice in sight.

"We'll make a camp," Sullivan said, "until I figure out what to do."

The first thing he did was make a bed of an unzipped sleeping bag for Lila in the shade of a sandstone outcropping. He sat by her a while, frowning, saying nothing, dabbing water on her forehead, making her drink a little. She seemed to see him, sometimes, but couldn't speak. The water dribbled from the corners of her cracked lips.

The others sat in the thin shade of the car. Kian was stretched out on the sand, under the car, apparently sleeping.

Darkness crept up on them like the fear of death in the old. Mahler and Zizz built a campfire from crooked, termite-tunneled deadwood.

Quinn tried to think of some way to be useful; to be proactive, think ahead. Nothing at all came to mind.

Sullivan took a .25 calibre pistol from the car. "Don't want a loud bang," he said, as he started off toward the hills. "Anatole - you sit with Lila, keep any...keep the ants off her. Whatever. Just watch her."

"Sure, Dad." Anatole went to sit beside her, his back to the outcropping. Sullivan strode through the pooling shadows toward a bouldery hilltop.

"Where you going, Jack?" Zizz asked.

Something about the way she said it, and the way her eyes lingered on him, struck a pang through Quinn.

Whoa, am I jealous of this dysfunctional little mediabrat and Sullivan?

"Reconnoiter. Get to the top of that hill, look around, maybe shoot antelope or a rabbit or two."

"Shoot an antelope with that little pistol?" Quinn muttered.

"If anyone could, he could," Zizz said. Quinn looked at

her. *"What?"* she said.

He shrugged and went to gather wood.

The shadows thickened like a morbid certainty as Quinn walked past Lila and Anatole; the boy's body wrapped in shadow. "Hey Anatole, you okay, man?"

Anatole didn't reply. He seemed almost asleep, as he gazed into the sky. He blinked. He blinked again. He stared.

Quinn walked on, shrugging. But following Anatole's gaze.

There were lights in the dimming sky over there, due South. Distant aircraft he supposed, or early stars, oscillating in the waves of heat given off by the desert. Just lights. They're just lights.

Quinn began to break a crooked branch from a dead tree. In the crookedness of the dried-out wood he seemed to see the birth-labors of emerging events. A man screaming in epileptic frenzy; *Ataska*...and, on the horizon, black choppers.

He shook off the vision, the disorientation. He didn't want the intuition, just now. He was afraid of it. He bent to pick up another piece of wood.

Behind him, Anatole gazed...into Seeking One's scintillating heart.

Anatole...

Anatole was floating with her, hovering just below a slow-billowing, translucent ceiling of cloud. To the West the sun filtered the redder end of its spectrum through a long strata of atmosphere. Seeking One seemed to absorb the dull-ruby light and toy with it, internally.

"I'm afraid for Lila," Anatole was saying.

"If she were away from the others, I might help, if it's not too late."

"Then come, come and help her! We have to hurry!"

"Relative to that continuum, Anatole, you and I are moving very slowly. It takes more energy to create a pocket outside of time, but let's be rash, let's splurge, let's spend it today."

"I don't get it."

"Time is passing very slowly for us, relatively - you will only be gone from the camp for a minute, even if it seems like hours, here. Would you like to watch a little TV?"

"What? I must be hallucinating this, if you're offering to watch TV with me. That's too stupid."

She laughed. When she laughed she was all female sex, and he saw a beautiful, alluring, electrically naked woman floating in the center of the crystalline saucer that was Seeking One.

"This is the deal, Anatole: I can pick up anything transmitted through the atmosphere, and I can translate the signal into a picture, a sound. Television is important to this world; it is, as someone said, the modern hearth, the place where families gather, the tribal storyteller in electronic form. And it reveals all your secrets, especially when it thinks it's being discreet. Of course, this tribal storyteller is often full of shit, but there are some shows I like. Of the new stuff I like *Suburban Fortress* - even if it's a soap opera - and the Sci-Fi Irony Wave films based on the big Marc Laidlaw revival. Science Fiction, see, is humanity's way of warning, readying itself; it's what goes on under the racial Rapid Eye Movement; and when it comes to ETs like, I suppose, yours truly, why, it's humanity's way of breaking the truth to itself: humanity knows it's not alone, unconsciously. It knows we're here. Even the most hidebound skeptics know it unconsciously. So they make their Steven Spielberg movies and their *Forbidden Planets* -"

"Are you telling me you're an alien who's a science fiction fan? Come on now. Bullshit."

"Science fiction fan? I do have better taste than *that* - " As they spoke, she came more and more into focus as a human female. An ideal human female, from Anatole's point of view. He thought about her with clothes on, because she was easier to deal with that way, and *voila*, she had clothes on: jeans and white t-shirt. OK, it was a very tight t-shirt. Sitting legs crossed Indian-fashion in midair, she went on, "But I'm...what you might call an interworld sociologist. Only we don't believe in the 'Prime Directive' - much as I have enjoyed Star Trek. I like that one where Spock's in heat and he turns the spaceship around just so he can fulfill his *primal Vulcanic urges* - I guess that's before your time. Anyway, when we interfere with your people, it's usually subtle, like by introducing threads into your creative faculty...Sometimes we send a powerful current down that thread - like we did with William Blake. Sometimes a faint pulse, here or there: a sublime idea translated into Star Trek pablum - but it's a very nutritious pablum, you see. We talk to you through certain works of science fiction. *Close Encounters of the Third Kind* was my idea, personally. Of course, the writers thought it was *their* idea..."

"No shit, that was yours? I loved that one!"

"Thank you. Some of it we don't have to induce - it's all there buried in the ancestral memories, you see, the faintest nudge releases it. Humanity knows it's to some degree alien itself -"

"So you like *X Files*? Or did you guys create that?"

"Certain episodes. But the creators were already primed. Of the old TV, I think *Deep Space Nine* is my favorite. I sort of identify with Odo. And I love all the facially scarred humans they call aliens. The restraints of budget I guess."

"I saw one of those, my Dad had it on disk. Pretty dumb if you ask me. I'm so *sure* aliens would be like that. I mean, look at you."

"Oh but what does it mean to be human? It doesn't mean to be a talking monkey, a hairless ape. It has nothing much to do with your physical form. It has to do with a pattern inside; a longing; an inner map of the universe; a capacity for evolution, a struggle with one's animality..."

"So you're human?"

"Yes."

"But like a human...angel?"

"Mmmm...no. There's so much confusion about angels. Angels aren't really individual entities; they're a constructive idea personified in a movement of energy. I'm rather more complex than that. I am an organism. I must eat, and rest and propagate and I must dream, too, though I strive to rise through a thousand thousand gradations of waking...All must dream as they struggle to wake..."

"Oh come on. You're not human the way I understand what human is. I mean, do you crap? No."

"Of course I crap! How could you imply I'm not corporeal enough to excrete waste! I do my part, I assure you!"

That response puzzled Anatole so thoroughly he decided not to pursue it. "But - were you once a human being on Earth? I mean...how can you enjoy a TV show if you were never part of our culture and all that?"

"I can enjoy your culture without being a part of it. But

also...I have created a Working Model Earth Human Being within myself which interprets your television and film and theatre and music and literature and painting for me."

"A...Working Model Human?"

"A Working Model *Earth* Human. A 'person-construct' that can experience those things on the proper level of subjectivity...just as you have created one, really, on a smaller, less-controlled scale."

"What do you mean, 'as I have created one'?"

"You don't really suppose that the 'you' that you use to react to the world around you is the real you, do you?"

"It's not? You mean - it's not my soul?"

"Soul? A soul is hard work to make. You're born with spirit; not necessarily with a soul, depending on your definition. Unless you're James Brown."

"Who's James Brown?"

"I'll play some for you later." When she explained things to him it was always casual, offhanded, mildly facetious. "There are Anatoles within Anatoles within Anatoles. The outer ones are temporary constructions, defensive devices with which you have become identified. You've glued your attention to them. But they're not the real you. The real you is a faint, flickering light which can become a star, if it's nurtured. It can become free; free to choose which influence it will fall under..." She paused, and made a Fourth-of-July incandescence drip from between her fingers. "Would you like to watch an episode of *X-Files*? I bet I have some you don't have - there was the suppressed episode that got Chris Carter in so much trouble -"

"No shit? You have that?"

"No shit."

In short order, Anatole found himself apparently sitting in an easy chair, apparently watching a television, certainly a quartermile over the surface of the planet.

It was a brand new Wangchen TV set from the Republic of Pan Pacifica, the best TV around, wafer-thin with a ten-year battery. Seeking One was curled up beside him in her own easy chair, a lounge chair made of UFO-stuff. She was, then, the beautiful woman he had glimpsed inside the coruscating saucer. As she watched TV she painted her toenails onyx black, from a little toenail polish bottle.

They watched the first part of the show. He could see why it had been suppressed by the Feds.

Then a commercial came on. Anatole grimaced. "You keep the commercials?"

"If you don't mind...they interest me. The psychomechanics of desire..." She studied him for a moment. "Is something wrong?"

He was gaping at her. "No. I just..." He looked back at the TV. Then at her legs, her breasts, then back at the TV.

"Do you like my Working Model construct?" she asked. "The body I've picked?"

"Yes. Uh - it was a little different when I saw it before..."

"I didn't have clothes on before." She pretended to be surprised. "You prefer me without clothes?"

He swallowed. She knew the answer, of course, since she could read his mind.

But he made up his mind differently. "You look great in clothes." It was more respectful that way. His dad had taught him to respect women.

"Your Dad's a good guy, in a lot of pain," she said.

"You mean the wounds? He's had a lot worse."

"I mean psychologically. Self induced. He thinks he let your mother down by not being there to save her. He thinks he let you down by getting stuck where you were stuck..."

"Oh."

He felt an inordinate hurt go through him, then; something beyond empathy and ordinary remorse. Something he couldn't normally feel. It hurt but it also felt good, like stress on a muscle that had ached for exercise. As if he were feeling some hitherto numb part of himself.

"I don't think I can watch TV now..." He looked at his ghostly hands. They were there and then they weren't and then they were. "My Dad...if Lila dies...he'll blame himself...I know we're in a slow time stream, but..."

She nodded. The TV vanished. "Let's see what we can do...in your home-stream of time. But there are risks. We may attract the wrong sort of attention."

They spiraled into the arms of the Earth together.

• • •

Quinn was carrying an armload of wood back to the

campfire; the wood-smoke was so resinous he could taste the sage and manzanita in his mouth. He glanced at the sandstone outcropping, and saw that Anatole and Lila were gone.

He dumped the wood by the fire. "Where's Lila and the kid? You move 'em into the car?"

Mahler and Zizz turned to look at the sandy ground where she'd lain.

Zizz sprang to her feet. "Shit! Where is she?"

Sullivan strode into the firelight just then, tossing two jackrabbits at Zizz's feet. (An unconscious gesture Quinn didn't like.)

"Where's Lila?" Sullivan asked, staring at the spot she'd been in. "Where's my son?"

He plucked a piece of wood from the fire, ran to the outcropping, streaming flame, held the burning end like a torch over the ground where Lila had lain.

They all saw it at the same time: the marks in the sand where someone had dragged Lila, on her sleeping bag, away into the darkness.

• • •

The underground base. Nevada. The American military; the grey aliens, who said they were from Zeta Reticuli. The ordinary ochre-painted metal door.

"Just remember, Farraday," Colonel Derrick said, "whatever happens in there, *it's an honor*. No matter what. Understand?"

"Um...sure. You really can't come in with me?"

Derrick chuckled. "No. You'll be all right. Go ahead..." He opened the door for Farraday.

Farraday went through the ochre door into the alien's quarters; Derrick shut the door behind him. Was that a lock turning he heard? He wasn't sure.

Farraday looked around. Part of the dimly lit sixty-by-forty foot room was the stuff the inside of the saucers was made of, now quiescent, shapeless. It could become, he supposed, whatever the little humanoid used for a resting couch, or a desk. The mockingly-blank control consoles edged the walls. The other end of the room was standard bathroom tile; on one side was a short cloudy-glass rectangular stall; across from it was an old fashioned bathtub steaming with hot water.

Jaron came from a doorway behind the stall. He was nude, but in the dim room Farraday could make out no biological details. Jaron stepped into the stall, closed the door. Said, in Farraday's voice, "The bath there is for you."

Farraday didn't know what else to do: He crossed to the bath, took off his clothes, and got in. He eased down into the water as Jaron got into the stall. He could see the alien's silhouette in the stall; its eyes peeking over the top at him.

Its' eyes. His eyes. Her eyes.

The bath-water had a faint chemical smell Farraday couldn't identify. He tried not to be paranoid about it.

The stall began to fill up with a dark, thick fluid, rising up to engulf the alien's silhouette, cancel it out. The room swam with a rich smell of crushed ants. And, in the background, a *soupçon* of decay.

"I am, you know, taking a bath, just as you are," Jaron said, still using Farraday's borrowed voice. His oversized black eyes regarded Farraday gravely. "Cleansing myself deeply with a concentrated solution of engineered micro organisms. They will eat away everything inappropriate. Expired dermal cells, toxins, unwanted germs, the whole...shebang. I hope you don't mind my asking you here...But it is an honor, in my world, this bonding ritual: bath with bath."

"We have ritualistic communal bathing too, in some countries. But I don't know about the...the micro organisms thing." He was beginning to sweat from the hot water.

"Your humanity has always used micro-organisms," Jaron was saying, in Farraday's borrowed voice, "for various things. For example, yogurt, cheeses, alcohol, and lately for the creation of special pharmaceuticals. So many uses. And of course you are interdependent with intestinal micro organisms. In my culture, we - wait! This is a pun, right? In my *culture*? Ha, ha?"

"Right, yeah." Farraday wanted to be anywhere else, right now. He was exquisitely uncomfortable; the bath was too hot but more bothersome was the situation; it made him writhe inwardly. He had a sudden, anomalous desire to go bowling at the Lakeside Lanes in Chicago. He hadn't been bowling in years. Just him and his wife and a bunch of overweight, half drunk bowlers playing the best and stupidest game in the world, over and over.

"Yes - in my culture - ha, ha - we have a very delicately attuned relationship to micro-organisms. This made close contact between our species difficult. We can *see* your micro-organisms, see the energy perturbances they produce, we can smell even those your blood-hounds could not smell. You have controlled them to some extent but we have a sort of horror of having the Wrong Micro-organisms. A correct-relationship to micro-organisms is a correct relationship to the biological continuum. One should apply and manage one's bodily micro organisms as one selects...what would be an Earth-human analogy...as one selects make-up and clothing and jewelry. But this goes for one's interior as well as one's exterior. By degrees they will become more and more detectable to you, as you evolve."

"So...how do you keep, uh, the local bugs from getting on you and spoiling your...your..."

"Micro patina."

"...and spoiling your micro patina?"

"The genetically engineered micro organisms we employ are very effective predatory microphages. They eat the other...bugs as you call them. We do not think of them as 'bugs'... even non-preferred micro-organisms are part of the microscopic Pattern of Organization. Our greatest art-form involves the gestation and life-patterning of micro organisms...How do you feel, by the way?"

"Oh, I'm fine, I'm -" He broke off, staring at the water between his feet. It was strangely cloudy. There was a deepening smell of crushed ants.

His skin was itching.

"Uh - Jaron?"

"Do not be alarmed. There is some communication between my cleanser and yours. Part of this bonding ritual involves a sharing of my micro-organisms with yours. It's a one-way sharing, as it happens."

The expression *Shit runs downhill* insisted on popping into Farraday's head. Hastily he said, "I trust this isn't an...experiment. I mean, other humans have -?"

"Oh yes! Not to worry. There is no danger to your health. My micro organisms are not hostile to you, nor will they...damage you in any sense."

The bath water was cooling; thickening; turning squid-inky. He thought of Ceph.

This is more than some kind of ritual, he thought. This is a test: to see if I panic.

So he sat in the water and let it thicken around him. It thickened quickly, like fast-action Jell-o. Crushed-ants-flavored Jell-o.

"So uh...our...our micro-organisms are hard to get used to...we have, I take it, *vulgar* micro organisms?"

"Vulgar yes - but worse, they are more or less randomly accepted onto your person, except that you try to reduce their number by bathing. It is like dressing in random clothing. We have fully as many bacteria and viruses as you do. But every single - yes each *individual* bacterium or virus is *selected* - or instantly eliminated."

"Are there other things about us that repulse you?"

"We are a traveled people and have seen many variations of life; we are not easily repulsed. And we have been observing you for a long time. But there is one thing that always makes me...it gives me a *twinge* inside."

"Don't keep me in suspense, man," Farraday said, trying to keep the atmosphere light. The tub goo was heavy around him; sucking at him.

"It's when you people touch the tops of your heads. With your...fingers. Combing, scratching in thought, absent minded gestures..."

"Why does that bother you?"

"It would be...vulgar to discuss it any further."

He thought he saw Jaron shudder.

The gelatin congealing around him felt warm...a feeling began to rise in him which didn't identify itself as terror until the gelatin was nearly blisteringly hot. "Hey Jaron...?"

"It is all right," Jaron told him soothingly in his own voice.

And suddenly the gel disintegrated, became water again. In half a second. The excessive heat ebbed away. He felt a wave of sensation pass through him. Later he would try to describe, to himself, what the sensation had been like. An *almost* familiar sensation. Familiar unfamiliarity?

The level of the glutinous medium in Jaron's stall had fallen; light strobed in the stall, and a chemical steam hissed up to hide the alien entirely. When the steam cleared away Jaron had gone, like a stage magician, and the water was draining from the tub.

Feeling mildly feverish and weak, Farraday got out of the tub, found some towels, toweled off, and dressed.

He hurried to his own quarters and showered for almost an hour and a half.

. . .

No Lila. The drag-marks ended abruptly in the midst of a clearing in the cacti. It looked as if the cacti had been crushed, in a perfect circle...The sleeping bag was there, open, empty, and so were Lila's clothes. But no Lila. There were no footprints.

Sullivan looked around, shouting for her, his voice taking on an edge that the others had never heard.

Quinn felt one of his intuitions moving inexorably up his spine; meeting, halfway up, sensory patterns signifying probability. Knowing his hunches left him disoriented, he tried to fight it off...but found himself leading the others into the darkness...

...toward a lowering star. They couldn't remember, later, how they'd decided to move in that direction. (But it had come through Quinn; and there was more to come).

Nor did they did find out how Anatole got Lila from the crushed circle of cacti, to the hummock of earth and horizontal slabs of sandstone, half a mile away.

After a stumbling tramp through the dark, they saw her, there: Lila laid out on her back like the Bride of Frankenstein on the slab, against the starry sky. The stars seemed to gather themselves together over her; and then it was as if the sky shrugged the stars free and they swirled together into a miniature galaxy that thickened into a disk, maybe only thirty feet across. Whirling in the sky over Lila.

Sullivan ran toward her...

Zizz and Quinn and Mahler tried to keep up with him...

(Where was Kian? Where was Anatole?)

Sullivan was shouting, "Anatole! Lila!"

The thing in the sky lowered itself over Lila - and then engulfed her. As it got closer to the ground its ring of light expanded like a pond-ripple over the rock and reflected blue-white-violet over Anatole's face.

Anatole was watching from a crevice between the

boulders, just below Lila. He seemed to be talking to himself. Or to the iridescent, radiant crystal swallowing Lila.

They couldn't hear what he was saying. They could see Lila, faintly outlined inside the pulsing light as it immersed her.

Sullivan was almost there...

For Quinn, Mahler, Zizz, Sullivan: time slowed, nearly stopped. It was as if, on approaching the light, they stepped into a tar-pit of slow-motion. Anatole's mouth was moving normally, as he spoke to the light, up ahead; but around Quinn and the others time had taken a breather, and every step seemed to take twenty seconds, though they strove to run.

Lila's nude body inside the crystalline light became indistinct, like a vibrating tuning fork. There came a pulse of radiance that lit her up quite clearly so that Quinn saw her wounds - opening like crying mouths, gushing blood.

Blood, and metal; the metal fragments of shrapnel fell away from her, and struck the stone with faint but crystal-clear sounds. It looked to Quinn as if the shrapnel in her was *vibrating its way* from her wounds.

And a final pulse of light - light rippling out forever -

And then the floating thing lifted away from Lila, and hovered for a moment, and the flow of time returned to normal.

(Was it the flow of time? Or his perception of time? Quinn wasn't sure).

Sullivan ran to Lila, knelt beside her. "Lila!"

Quinn stopped where he was, watching the shining thing overhead; he could feel it returning his regard. Then he felt its attention shift.

He turned that way, too, following its eyeless gaze, and saw something else in the sky. Several clustered lights, in the distance, were rushing closer, probing through dust clouds with searchlights: black helicopters skimming the desert.

Something more. From almost overhead.

An aluminum-colored disk, its luminosity interiorized; big as a house, it dropped slowly from the sky, turning. It was solid; it showed signs of *engineering*: quite different from the thing that had engulfed Lila which had seemed to engineer itself over and over again, from one moment to the next.

(The choppers were thudding close; dust huffed and rushed.)

He felt the poised gray metal disk watching him, too.

Lila's disk, the lens of sparkling light, fell away into the sky. That's what it looked like to Quinn: as if it were falling, but straight up. And in a second it was gone.

The other disk rose in pursuit and was lost in the night sky. He thought the choppers would pursue them both - but they didn't.

The choppers were landing, all around them. Dust billowed and whirled in searchlight beams. Men leapt free and deployed. Flashlights probed their eyes, their hands.

Lila sat up, looking around curiously, completely unafraid. "Whose helicopters are these, Jack?" she asked, in a loud, clear voice.

Quinn stared at her.

Her bleeding had stopped; her eyes were clear, her color was good.

"I don't know," Sullivan admitted. He could barely be heard over the rotors still slapping the air.

Lights from the choppers spot-lit Quinn and Mahler and Zizz and Sullivan and Lila and Anatole on the piled slabs of stone. Anatole ran to his father; Sullivan put his arms around the boy.

Men in unmarked military uniforms came toward them, M18s in their hands. The red beams of aiming lasers danced on Quinn's chest.

"Put your hands on your head, and get down on your knees!" thundered a voice from the nearest chopper.

Quinn and Zizz looked at one another. What else could they do?

(Where was Kian?)

CHAPTER SEVEN

THE LEAGUE OF MICROBIAL FRIENDSHIP

Farraday decided not to worry about where they were taking him. He was just glad to be outside.

He was riding in the front seat of a school bus with tinted windows; the school bus was painted flat black, on the outside. There were no official markings. The windows were opaque from outside but he could see out, easily enough, as they pulled out of the camouflaged entrance to the base in the Nevada hillside. The sun was shining, out here, and large birds turned like dark wheels in the sky. Were they crows or vultures or hawks? He couldn't tell, at this distance, so for him they were all three.

Farraday suddenly yearned to have his wife beside him. But only Jaron sat beside him, eyes as opaqued as the windows. The alien wore a clean white mechanic's cover-alls, and "Timothy Leary Memorial" pattern-changing tennis shoes.

Derrick sat across the aisle. There were two Marines with dark glasses sitting a few seats back, M18s across their laps. The Marines looked melancholy, when Farraday glanced back at them; they were leaving the base, but not on leave. They must ache to get out as much as he did.

As the bus drove out of the compound, past the gates,

another vehicle was coming in: an unmarked towtruck, same color as the bus, towing a dusty 20th Century Volvo. The Volvo windshield, or rear window. Bullet holes in the trunk.

"Even the tow trucks are black?" Farraday couldn't help observing.

Derrick chuckled. Jaron 'chuckled' in Derrick's voice.

Farraday turned to watch the towtruck pull the battered Volvo into the compound. "Whose, uh - ?"

"Forget that one, Mike," Derrick said, casually but firmly.

They left the underground base behind, trundled down a dusty dirt road through wasteland and past fenced-off dumpsites. Eight bumpy miles on, they swung onto a sun-cracked highway. The cracks had been patched with tar that stuck to the wheels. Farraday could hear it rhythmically sticking and ripping.

A few miles and they swung onto another dirt road and Farraday began to fear for his life.

Why haven't they blindfolded me, if this place is so damn secret? he wondered. *Unless they plan to get rid of me out here...*

Jaron turned a flat-black gaze on him. "It is all right. All is well. You are safe."

"Am I that obvious?"

"It is only natural."

"Your command of English is really very impressive, have I ever told you that?"

"You are very kind."

They came to what appeared to be an abandoned resort. A cracked fiberglass sign almost said, 'ALE-E-INN PRESENTS *PALM SPRINGS EAST'*. The main building was derelict but still standing; a row of tourist cabins had some time ago burned to the foundations. There was a dried, debris-strewn swimming pool, and what might have been a cactus garden, now willfully overgrown.

Driving off the road onto a rutted track they circled the building and came upon a scene of anomalous activity. Four flat-black freight trucks were lined up, backed toward this side of the building. Three of the trucks had been emptied; silent Marines unloaded crates from the fourth one.

"Running behind schedule," Derrick noted, as the bus pulled up.

Dodge came out of the door-shaped hole in the back wall

of the derelict building, drinking a Diet Coke, waving to them.

As they got out of the bus, into heat palpable even in the shade of the walls, Farraday saw a tarp-covered saucer shape, about forty feet across, beyond the three trucks. He ducked to peer under it: it was suspended two yards over the ground, floating but utterly immobile.

A saucer, the real thing.

Jaron went immediately to the tarp-covered saucer and slipped into its shadow.

• • •

"I don't know, Anatole. I don't know why they're holding Kian separately," Sullivan said, and said it softly though every word fairly creaked with contained rage.

Sullivan sat on the lower bunk on one side of the locked military cell, somewhere in the underground base, with his back to the wall, one arm around Lila, one arm around Anatole. Lila was wearing oversized cammie trousers and shirt given her by a silent, glumfaced Filipino military nurse; the same taciturn nurse had treated their wounds, given them antibiotics and rebandaged them.

Sullivan had asked the nurse and the soldiers about Kian, of course. Received only shrugs for reply.

The sentries and the other soldiers they'd seen in the base wore service-designated uniforms - both Air Force and Marines - unlike the men who'd taken them prisoner. What little they'd seen of the place was in some sense reassuring: it was clean, orderly, businesslike. On the other hand...it had no windows.

No one had answered their questions; no one spoke to them except to say, "Are you armed? Hands on top of your head. OK, let's go."

Quinn sat on the bunk opposite Sullivan's; Zizz sprawled on the top bunk, scraping a design into her forearm with a fingernail. Mahler was just getting up from the toilet, in the next room, muttering to himself. The toilet flushed.

There was just the cell with two racks of bunks, the bathroom, and nothing more, not even a wall decoration. The concrete walls were painted ochre.

"Maybe these Army guys don't have Kian," Anatole ventured. His voice was hoarse.

"I hope they do. I don't want to think about him being out

in the desert alone," Zizz said.

There was more that went unsaid: If the military were holding Kian separately...*Why?*

And more than that: if he wasn't alone out in the desert somewhere, and he wasn't a prisoner here - then maybe he had been *taken by someone else.*

The word *Abducted* came into Quinn's mind.

He glanced at Anatole, wondering how he was taking all this. There was something strange between Lila and Anatole; some kind of mutual knowledge, like the unspoken secrets shared by lovers, but way past sex. A chance word would make them exchange knowing glances, knowing, resigned smiles.

Hours inched by. Bit by bit they talked about what had happened after Zizz and Quinn and Mahler had come to the condoplex; and some of what had happened since they'd left it. Yamahira. Metzger. The remote controlled lunatic with metal in his grey matter. The burning Winnebago and its suicidal owner; the lights, the lights...the living lights and Lila's healing; the choppers and the guns and the base...

Anything they said about the living light, the alien, Lila's healing...had a way of tapering off, unfinished, never completely said...murmurs becoming silence.

There were long periods of silence, in the cell; all that had happened was too fucking much to process.

All that Mahler would say about the saucers was: "They weren't aliens; had to be some kind of...of hologram or disinformation scam. Capitalism's bully-boys hiding their Black Budget mis-use of public money with some...some kind of camouflage..."

Sometimes, Quinn thought, when things reached a certain emotional flashpoint of intensity and bizarrity, you just kind of shut down. You just kind of...turned inward. You processed it any way you could.

And they all knew that more was coming.

Anatole had surprised everyone by saying nothing about the saucer that had pursued the living light into the sky, nothing at all, though they knew him to be a flying saucer enthusiast.

You don't have anything to say about what happened out there? Sullivan had asked his son, as they'd eaten breakfast.

No, Anatole had said distantly. *Lila will explain, when she can.*

But aren't you wondering what happened, son?

Anatole had simply shaken his head. *I know what happened. Most of it. I know what happened to Lila, except I don't know how to explain it; but I don't know what happened to Kian. That's all I can think about...About Kian...Kian...*

And he'd begun to cry, softly, so no one had wanted to push him further.

Lila had said only, *A creature who comes from two worlds at once: she came and healed me, and she gave me some knowledge. But I can't give it to you yet. It hasn't crystalized in my head. I didn't earn this knowledge...and I must digest it the best way I can...I'll tell you when the time comes...*

She still felt like Lila, to them; she still looked like Lila. Something deep in her eyes told them: *Yes, it's me, it's Lila. It's all right.*

But when she talked - it wasn't quite the way Lila had talked. And she didn't ask about her father. It was as if she'd already grieved for him and gone beyond grief; as if it were somehow resolved. Was that possible?

When the time comes...

So they'd decided not to push her further. They had to share their cell with the uncertainty, and that was all right. There was hope in uncertainty; the walls around them, now, and the locked door, those things were certain enough.

They had eaten pretty well, that was something. Quinn felt almost cheerful, after eating breakfast. At least, he assumed it was breakfast time. The sentries had silently taken away their watches and in the underground base time was marked by clocks or not at all.

The situation, Quinn thought, was enigmatically two-faced. On the plus side, they were in US Government hands, which meant they were in the Sovereign United States, in Nevada, and that's what they wanted. And they were fed and sheltered and, miraculously - there was no other word for it - Lila was healed.

On the minus side, Kian was missing. And they were prisoners, disarmed and helpless.

Sullivan's face was grim, pale. Quinn could see, past the affected impassivity, that Sullivan blamed himself for losing Kian.

"You know what?" Zizz said, suddenly. "We heard Black

Betty might've been taken prisoner by the Feds, right? Wouldn't it be weird if she were right here - maybe in the cell next door?"

Anatole looked at her. "Black Betty? The media terrorist?"

"She is a great symbol of resistance," Mahler said, coming in to lie on a bunk. He seemed confused, depressed. "Black Betty...she was...The terrorist label is unfair - even if she uses it sometimes."

"It's sort of a joke, her calling herself that," Zizz said.

"She's not likely to be here," Sullivan said, his voice distant; his tone saying he didn't care where Black Betty was. "If she's a Federal prisoner for anything like terrorism or media piracy she's in a penitentiary, probably in New York. That's where they put them now."

Zizz lifted her head. "New York? Fuck! We *came* from the East coast looking for her!"

Sullivan shrugged. "Just a guess. This is a military facility. Probably some connection to Area 51. Not a penal institution. But high security."

"So these bozos think we're - what?" Quinn asked. "Spies?"

"Probably. Or Freemen types."

"Shit!" He flopped back on the bunk. "And these are the Authorities who are supposed to be taking care of us..."

Thinking: What's that joke they have in Mexico? *If you're mugged, don't scream - you might attract the police.*

• • •

Movie-set lighting splintered the desert darkness.

The adapted resort-shell - the rehearsal space they'd selected for the staged event - reminded Farraday of a movie set he'd visited in L.A. Big, oddly-angled lights were set up, and cameras, and light-reflection umbrellas, and there were "extras" - volunteer soldiers dressed as hospital patients - and there was sound equipment and arcane special effects gear and a generator van trailing black cables. The cables snaked everywhere, criss crossing the ground and then reconverging in metal switchboxes.

And they had catering. In one downstairs room of the derelict resort, where once had been a Club Med type cafeteria, the base cooks had set up plastic tubs of cold chicken pastas, mixed vegetables, trays of deserts, coffee and juice urns.

They sat at fold-out picnic tables, Derrick and Dodge and Farraday, away from the other men, eating dinner.

"What happened to the resort?" Farraday asked.

"Toxic waste from the base," Derrick said. "Got in the water. Lot of people turned up with..."

He broke off at a censorious look from Dodge.

"Derrick - shit."

"It's not as if he hasn't got clearance for more than that, Dodge," Derrick muttered.

"Use your common sense, Derrick," Dodge said, plastic fork squealing as he chased the last of his pasta salad across a styrofoam plate.

Farraday was looking nervously at his coffee cup. "Uh - toxic waste? Ex-*cuse* me?"

"You see what I mean, Derrick?" Dodge said, shaking his head. He turned to Farraday. "The water we're drinking is trucked from the base, Mike, and it's as clean as it comes. Don't worry about it. I wouldn't be here if it weren't safe."

Not long ago Derrick was warning me about making inquiries past my clearance, Farraday thought. *Now Dodge is warning Derrick about need-to-know. Knowledge is part of the food chain here...And we chase each other around and around, constantly warning one another; Derrick warning me, Jaron warning Derrick, Dodge warning Derrick and Jaron and Me. Eventually I'll be warning someone.*

This is my new life...

Corporal Collins called to them from the door. "I think Jaron's ready for you, sir, if you're finished...?"

Dodge nodded. "Let's do it."

Half an hour later they stood on a hastily erected control platform near the corner of the building. From here they couldn't see most of the staging equipment.

The trucks and the bus had been driven out of sight; everything they wanted kept intact had been taken from the building.

The saucer was gone. Jaron was nowhere to be seen.

"Lights, cameras, action," Dodge muttered.

Lasers flickered through a rising pall of white mist sprayed from concealed nozzles...

Farraday remembered his childhood. An outdoor laser

spectacular in...Disneyland. *Fantasmic.*

He'd have laughed out loud, if not for the horror.

Then the Meta appeared - or appeared to appear - in the rising shroud of mist, above the shell of the resort.

Farraday felt a strange clutching in his throat, looking at the Meta. He wanted...he wanted it to be...

He didn't know. He wanted...he yearned...

There was a certain longing. There was a...

...Didn't know, didn't know...

The coruscation solidified, and changed its aspect, became sinister, heavy as a thundercloud.

"Extras" and actors in medical costume ran from the building, pointing at the glittering UFO - shouting in bad-acting simulations of terror. A guy in Priest costume held up a hand for the others. "Wait! Let me try to make contact!"

The "priest" walked toward the sinister cynosure, his face bathed in its alien, cast-off light, and raised a Bible in one hand. "My friend!" the faux priest shouted. "Let us put aside our enmity! In the name of the great God of my world and of yours - the God of all worlds! Let us reach out -!"

A scintillating ray of violet light reached out from the hovering "Meta" and stuck the "priest", changing his color to its color. He threw up his hands in despair and screamed, quaked in agony, and fell back..."dead".

"Where have I seen that before?" Farraday muttered to himself.

"*War of the Worlds*, old George Pal movie, mid twentieth century," Dodge said. "Only, in the movie the minister gets disintegrated. Don't have the special effects for that for this practice taping and anyway the story...well, you'll see..."

"What weapons *do* the aliens have, in real life? The Zetans and the Meta?"

"Hmmm? The Zetans have *all* weapons. Don't like to use them - not thrifty. The Metas...we don't know. But our not knowing is not for public consumption...oh, hey - watch this part."

The Meta was firing its ray into the building. Upper portions of the building, away from the extras, exploded dramatically with the shaped special effects charges.

"Of course," Derrick said, "in the actual staged event -"

"*Actual*" staged event? Wasn't that an oxymoron?

" - the devastation will be much more pronounced. Bigger explosions, dead bodies flying, what have you."

Extras screamed and ran; "death rays" seared them and the actors fell, "dying". Smoke gushed and flames fluttered.

The Meta seemed to quiver with malicious glee in the sky. Then it lowered itself, almost to ground level - where Farraday could make out the lasers projecting the illusion more clearly - and seemed to engulf three "victims" who were lying on the ground.

Energy sizzled within it, light pulsed, and when it lifted away the three were miraculously healed - only now they marched like robots to pick up fallen weapons from the " hospital security guards"; the body-snatched, erstwhile humans began to fire blanks at the surviving, cowering humans, coldly executing them.

Suddenly - a new presence in the sky. The shining aluminum-colored Zetan saucer hove over the rooftop, rising like a huge metallic moon above the Meta and its hapless human slaves.

Bolts of angel-white energy flashed from the Zetan spacecraft - an actual Zetan craft - and blazed into the "Meta", making it shiver and withdraw, trailing smoke, into the sky.

The three robotic humans collapsed, like puppets with their strings cut.

An amplified voice that was not quite from the saucer, but was designed to seem as if it were, echoed over them, in the sweetly mellifluous tones of...the land octopus. "Brothers and sisters of Earth..."

"That's Ceph!" Farraday burst out.

Dodge nodded. "Yep - his voice is perfect. Our li'l Prairie Squid seemed happy to cooperate at the recording session. Something of a ham, I think. He'll be wanting an agent next."

"We of the star system Zeta Reticuli," the amplified voice continued, "have long observed your world and sought opportunities to give you our help. Now we need your help...to stop this hostile invasion of your world...We will be in touch with the civil authorities of the United States of America - who will let you and all the world know how you can help! Until then - peace be unto you!"

And with that the saucer whirled away, into the sky - and

then came back, and landed on the other side of the building, in the parking lot.

"That's about all we've got so far," Derrick said. "Eventually it's going to be a hospital - a real one, a hospice where people are dying. The Zetans will save the survivors of the attack from execution....It doesn't quite feel right yet - that's what we need your help for, Mike."

Farraday nodded. He felt a hollow, aching laughter wanting to rise up out of him. But he controlled it.

Oh God I'm in deep shit...

"Sure," he said brightly. "Whatever I can do..."

"Right now," Dodge said, "Let's just get us some coffee and go look at the dailies. Jaron'll be there. He loves watching dailies."

. . .

About six hours after dinner had been brought to the cell, the Marines came, and escorted them to a smaller holding cell, and then one by one to a series of separate interrogation rooms. *"Should we try to fight this?"* Quinn had whispered to Sullivan, as they waited in the holding cell. Deferring to Sullivan since he seemed to have a feel for this place.

Sullivan had simply shaken his head resignedly.

Then they'd taken Quinn, alone, to a little blank box of a room, nothing there but a chair facing a desk, and told him to wait.

Then the black Colonel had come in, smiling faintly, shaking Quinn's hand, assuring him that his friends were all right, they were right near by, this was all just routine, relax.

Care for some hot chocolate? Cigarette?

Derrick sat on the edge of a desk; Quinn sat in a chair across from him. The room was otherwise blank, empty but for the Marine stationed at the door, who might almost been a piece of furniture himself.

"You know," Derrick said, "...we know." He said this after the preliminaries, and a few questions about Quinn's background. Which Quinn answered honestly.

"'I know you know?' Say what?"

"Well, my man. We took videofootage from those choppers - we saw you with the alien."

"Is that what it was? I kind of thought it might be. Was it

from that other saucer that came?"

A moment's pause, the kind of pause that speaks volumes. Then he said, "I love old movies. We're big fans of 'em here. You ever watch old movies, son?"

"Sure."

"Then you know the expression, *I'll ask the questions.*"

"Okay, fine. But look - I *have* to ask about the kid. I mean we've been asking but nobody's saying a word to us. The younger kid - he looks kind of Asian-Hispanic? Kian? Do you know what happened to him?"

"I can honestly tell you, I haven't seen the kid you're talking about."

Quinn thought about that little boy dying of thirst out there. Dehydrated, hallucinatory from the terror of abandonment. It could be that by now he was dead and the desert's beaks and mandibles were reducing his body to sand and dust.

"Whoa there, my man," Derrick said. "Don't go crying on me. We've been looking for the kid since this guy who goes by 'Sullivan' told us about him."

"What do you mean, 'goes by Sullivan'? You dess mothers don't really think we're fucking *spies* do you?"

"The real Jack Sullivan is a mythical person. He's 'the Specialist' - an idealized macho dynamo of murder that never existed and never could. You can't be all-good and a killing-machine at the same time. But that's the name he's giving us along with certain information that only interfaces with the mythology. Now, his fingerprints match those of a special forces vet by the name of Osterberg. And that's who he is: Jack Osterberg. Guy lost his wife in the first famine riots...Whoa, now you got me forgetting the I'll Ask The Questions rule here..."

"You didn't forget anything, you're just trying to get me to relax and if you guys are monitoring my signs close enough you'd know I'm *not lying.*"

"OK. Your name, anyway *is* Quinn Helden, like you told us. We confirmed that."

"I'm so relieved."

"Sarcasm is not an attractive quality, son. Anyway we also confirmed you've been involved in partisan fighting, which is against Federal law and FedControl emergency provisions. You've been working for the Alternative Media Channel which doesn't exactly endear you to us and you have apparently been looking for the Federal Crimes convict Black Betty -"

"She's in prison?"

Derrick winced. "I hate it when I over-estimate the other side's information."

"'The other side'? Colonel - We are not spies."

"*Spies* is not the word I'd use, son. But it seemed to us that you were in collaboration with a Meta, a hostile alien being, the declared enemy of the Sovereign United States and the United Nations of the planet Earth. You know about the Treason Laws?"

Quinn stared at him. "You're telling me...That thing was a hostile alien from...from another galaxy?"

"*Why* do people always say 'from a galaxy far far away' and all that? We've got plenty of hostile aliens right here in this galaxy. The term is *solar system*, son. Another solar system."

"Look...I figure all this is bullshit. But I'm telling you one thing for sure; before that thing came, Lila was almost dead. After it came, she was fine. She's better than ever. How hostile is that, man?"

"So she's changed, this Lila? I mean - since this healing, this...miracle?"

"I just met her recently, I don't know...Well sure, she's changed some, sort of, but - what are you asking me exactly, man?"

"I got a visual aid that might explain, Quinn. Got something I wanta show ya...Just check this out..."

• • •

Two rooms. Observation room, interrogation room. Observation room watches the interrogation room. Walls between them. Cameras. Two sets of people. Right?

In the observation room, Farraday and Dodge sipped coffee, watching Quinn and Derrick in the interrogation room on closed circuit fiberoptic thread-cam TV.

Dodge dumped creamer into his coffee and stirred it with a pencil.

"Wish we weren't outta Diet Coke. Kinda hard to get out here. And I wish to God we could get real cream instead of creamer," Dodge said. Adding with an unconvincing social piousness: "But I guess we shouldn't complain, long as we got food and drink of any kind, considering the condition the west coast is in..."

In the interrogation room, a screen was rising from the desk, swiveling toward Quinn. It was one of the "dailies". Tape of the staged-event rehearsal footage from this afternoon: on the monitor screen the "Meta" was dropping down, engulfing its victims; the "victims" rising up, moving robotically to kill and...

Cut.

"Looks pretty seamless, that footage," Dodge murmured. He glanced sidelong at Farraday.

"Yeah. Yeah it does."

"You know, Mike - Derrick didn't want to bring you in on this. But we just stumbled on these people, on Quinn here and his pals, and we're thinking on our feet. I mean here we've got these people in custody, and they had a known contact with the hostile aliens right under our noses - we just lucked into it when our people spotted the EMP flux and the lights. And we got good film of some of it...till now all that's only been hearsay: This stuff about the Meta 'merging' with people. Contactee bullshit. But now we've got proof, and we've got the people it happened to...and you know, this guy Osterberg - calls himself Sullivan - evil looking bastard, isn't he? He could fit into some kind of 'Collaborating with the Aliens' scenario. He's a loose cannon, even in a prison cell, that one...I mean, this has fallen into our laps and I took it to the General and he says, Hell Yes, it's the will o' God, man, go for it. So since you're going to be our PR point man, Mike, I figure you got to be in on this end of the staging...After the Quinn kid, we'll look in on the interrogation of the others too...That Osterberg guy, though - he's a waste of time. Real hard ass. Way beyond cooperating. I mean, we could put some pressure on him by maybe, you know, holding a gun to his son's head, this Anatole kid, but then he'd just wait for his fucking chance and he'd kill at least some of us, later...I swear to God I know his type...So, we'll use him in a 'takeover' scenario...you'll see..."

"Good, good." Farraday pretended to take a note on his pad.

Farraday was very quiet and very scared. *They're going to realize how I feel about this whole thing...*

And I'm. In.

Deep. Deep. Shit.

Farraday managed to say, "Can't see any cables or lights or anything in that footage...angle's real good..."

What are they going to do to this Quinn kid and his friends?

"Level with me now, Mike," Dodge was saying, "or forever hold your piece - you going to deal with all this all right?"

"Sure...sure...You really think this...this Osterberg guy's a, you know, a *problem*?"

"I know guys like this, like I said. There are only a few...they stand out. They have Being, see. Real essence, the power to concentrate yourself...Anyway, yeah, he's a problem. We're going to have to use him up."

"Use him up?"

"Make him into something useful - a staged event..."

"You mean kill him. On camera. But for real."

"He'll end up dead, yeah. *We* won't do it - but we'll set it up so it gets done." He sipped his coffee. "You've got that 'I can't cross that line' look in your eyes, Farraday. Let me tell you something - you crossed it long ago. You and your wife both. You know what I mean? We need you committed - *committed all the way*. You know? By the way, I've got some good news for you and some bad news. The good news is, your wife bought a vibrator and she's been spending her nights alone - except for the vibrator. The bad news is, she's not alone, even when she thinks she is. More coffee?"

• • •

"Look," Quinn was saying, "I want to see Zizz. I wanta know she's okay. And I wanta goddamn lawyer."

"A lawyer!" Derrick laughed at that one. Real laughter. "What I can do for you is, you can see your lady friend. Just tell me first - doesn't this look like what you saw in the desert?" And Derrick ran the tapeloop over again.

Quinn sighed and watched the screen as again the "Meta" seemed to re-animate and manipulate those it had just killed.

"Up to a point, yes. But it never harmed anyone out in the desert that night...it's not like Lila's been walkin' around like a brainstim addict since she got healed. She hasn't turned into a zombie. She sure hasn't *hurt* anyone."

"Maybe she just hasn't received those orders yet...Say you did want to get out of here alive, you and your girlfriend, right, my man? I mean, can we assume you'd like to do that?"

Quinn looked at the screen and, gnawing a knuckle, said, "Could you run it again?"

• • •

Farraday sat alone in his room, waiting for the land octopus.

He came through the ventilation chute, as they'd arranged, popping the grate out, which he caught before it hit the floor. Ceph oozed from the vent and dropped onto the bed, landing neatly as a cat. Some of his movements were surprisingly graceful.

"They really don't know you get around that way?" Farraday asked.

"Nope. Shaft's too small for humans. There's sensors in it for electronic gear, like an RPV probe, but I'm not electronic. Speaking of electronics..." Ceph handed him a little portaphone. "I got your secure frequency wired."

He looked at Ceph. How did you read sincerity in a cephaloped? "I can trust you, can't I, Ceph? My life depends on this, and my wife's."

"You can trust me, Mike. I work for the Higher."

"The what?"

"The finer energies. The evolved. The awakened. The right hand path."

"Oh. Right. If you say so."

"Mike - are you definitely committed? If you turn against these people, there's no turning back."

"Yeah. I'm committed. They threatened me. Threatened my wife...They're planning to murder someone...I just can't go that far. Although maybe murder for convenience is the logical extension of the public relations industry..." He took a deep breath, and punched his wife's carphone number. It rang and rang some more. "You really sure you got it set up so they can't eavesdrop even if they're listening in on her car phone?"

"Right. They'll hear static." The land octopus added: "Trust me on this."

Lyn answered, on the phone. "Yes?"

"Baby - it's me."

"Mike! Oh *God* I'm so glad you called - are you okay?"

"Yeah, yeah I am."

"Mike - I'm being followed. I think they want me to know

it, though they're not being so obvious I could call a cop on them. But they can't be trying all that hard not to be seen..."

"Who?"

"I don't know. Federal types in black suits and sunglasses. Just...men in black, Mike."

"Okay, listen...I want you to go to the roof of the apartment building. Just - wait there. Someone...Someone will pick you up."

"From the roof?"

"Yeah."

"Seriously?"

"Yeah. Do it..." He looked at Ceph. "When, Ceph?"

"Tonight, two a.m."

"Who's that?" she asked. "He has a lovely voice."

"You wouldn't believe me, if I told you who that was. But yeah he has a...never mind. You heard: two a.m. Okay?"

"Okay . What's going on, Mike?"

"I'm finding out as I go, hon. But I can tell you this: I have to get out of here. I'm in deep shit. So I'll see you soon. In person. Okay?"

"Mike, I'm scared I mean seriously, really scared."

He thought: *You have reason, Lyn; these people are in their own little world - with its own little rationales.*

But aloud he said, "It's gonna be all right, baby. See you soon." And he hung up.

"Great, Mike. This is an act of faith. People abuse faith and they don't really know what it is. But you do, instinctively. There's hope for you."

"How come, Ceph, you talk like someone who hasn't spent their whole life as a...well, here, as you are."

"I've had a lot of exposure to media..."

"I don't mean that. I mean - how have you come out of the life you've had here so...balanced? So healthy and cheerful and...I mean, if was me, in the kind of life you must have led...the only one of your kind, a lab experiment, to these people...I mean, I hope I'm not offending you but...Since we're friends, I thought maybe we could be honest..."

"I'm not offended. I'm touched you can be honest, in asking about these things, Mike. I've survived intact in this life...Because I haven't had only this life. The inner world, the spiritual world, is an infinite world, Mike. I used to be...more or less as you'd think I'd be. Neurotic, self hating, boiling with anger, scared, suicidal. Oh yes. But then I found out what life really is...There is life, and then there is Life. I have a way of being in touch with the wider, higher Life; besides the media, I've lived through many others, in the ground of Being; and through other people I've...interfaced with, temporarily."

He didn't like the ring of that term. Interfaced. "What do you mean, interfaced?"

"I have another talent...I won't be using it on you, don't worry. I'll show you another time, at the right moment. It's not something I can do lightly, or often..."

He decided that was another one to *not* ask about. "So Ceph - you can really do this? You can arrange for someone to pick up my wife...from the roof? How?"

"I can really do this, yes - as for how...Tell you a story. I tried to kill myself several times, when I was younger. Five years back I almost succeeded; I got hold of some pure benzene, drank it, and, basically, died. My spirit left my body. Something got in touch with me. I thought it was a dream - but I woke up healed. You can't be healed by a dream alone, Mike. Now, the something that contacted me in that dying dream, it gave me directions. I remembered the dream and I followed the Something's directions...Did you ever see *THX-1138*? Wonderful old George Lucas film. It was like that: I found my way out of the base. I went into the vents, and up, and around, and up some more, climbing till I thought my tentacles'd fall off, and finally came out the vents, to the surface: the roof of this place, the landing pads for the choppers. The Marines guarding the choppers had all gone to sleep. The Meta had put them to sleep: Three of them were up there." His pattern of colors changed, as he remembered; rainbow colors spread from a place between his strange, sad eyes. "The Meta showed me myself as I really am, Mike. They came to me and healed me in another way and showed me how to find transformation and salvation, and self discovery. And for that I'll always serve them...You wanta play some chess later?"

• • •

They were all back in the cell. Quinn and friends. It was late morning. They were all tired, sitting or sprawling on the bunks; and they were all scared.

Although Sullivan, Quinn thought, was scared in a different way.

Sullivan's face was ashen. He was thinking about Kian, again, Quinn guessed. The frustration came off him like heat from a radiator.

Quinn made up his mind. Began scraping something into the skin of his arm, with his finger, just a red mark that would soon fade; marking himself as he'd seen Zizz do, but his wasn't a design. He was making words. Acting like it was something he was doing idly, out of the tension of confinement. There were no obvious cameras, but he knew about micro camera-fibers, and he was sure they were watching him.

"You know what," he was telling the others, "we got no choice but to play along here. And anyway I think we oughta trust these guys. We thought they were going to torture us or something - but none of us were tortured. Not a hair on anybody's head harmed. Lila just kept saying, 'I don't know what happened, I was unconscious' and they just accepted that. They hassled us, but they didn't torture us."

"Not *yet*, you mean," Mahler said.

"What I *mean* is: *something* happened out in the desert, and *we* sure as hell don't know what it was - but these guys, they've been studying this thing for a long time - like, decades, probably since Roswell, and they know what's going down and we just have to trust that."

Mahler turned him the look he reserved for the treacherously politically incorrect. The look that said you'd fallen from ideological grace. "You can't be serious. They want us to act out some kind of government-sponsored propaganda scenario. Who knows how they'll use it?"

Zizz was looking at him in shock, too.

Sullivan - Osterberg? - shrugged and said, "Better cooperate. We've seen too much. That saucer. That...creature. Direct contact with it...the choppers and the saucer...the base and the choppers and the saucer and the creature - put it all together, they're gonna to kill us unless we're useful to them."

"Would they do that, really?" Lila wondered aloud, not seeming to care.

"This isn't the government," Sullivan said. "This is the satellite government. The shadow government. This is where the

Black Budget goes. It's something...more or less autonomous. I've heard of it; even worked for some of it. I always thought the alien stuff was a cover for some other shit they were pulling. Sometimes it was, I guess, but..." He shrugged, again.

"I don't care," Zizz was saying, "I can't be used like that..."

"I'm convinced it's really for the best for us to cooperate completely," Quinn said. "Seriously."

He got up from the bunk, and began to pace, slowly, stretching. He'd worked out the angle he was pretty sure the camera fibers would have to be watching from, and he kept his back to that angle, and showed them the marks on his arm, one at a time. Five words in fading red.

CO-OP NOW BUST LATER

After a minute Zizz nodded almost imperceptibly. Then she looked at Mahler. "Yeah well...maybe he's right, Mahler."

Mahler glanced at Quinn's arm. Hesitated. Then he nodded. "I guess so. Let's trust 'em this time...What choice do we have..."

Lila squeezed Sullivan's hand and smiled; that was all. Anatole didn't seem to be listening; he was gazing at his Dad - as if he were trying to impress him into his memory. As if he sensed he might lose him.

. . .

Farraday was standing behind Dodge in the "mixing room", as Dodge called it. It was one of the interrogation observation rooms, now bigger than an office, fitted with video editing equipment and computer imaging equipment Farraday recognized from TV-commercial production.

Farraday looked over Dodge's shoulder as Dodge worked at four screens representing camera angles in two arenas, one indoor, one outdoor; he was playing with the zoom on an outdoor scene, where a man in chains linking his wrists and ankles sat in the shade of the truck he was chained to; the man looked half black, was skinny as a rail, his hair explosively dreadlocked, his black eyes sunken, pitted skin glossy with sweat. Dreadlocks sat there, rocking back and forth, hugging himself, staring into the ground as if he could see through it to the center of the Earth; now and then grinning, muttering.

"Jeezus - who's that?" Farraday asked.

153

"You don't recognize him? He was all over the news a year or two back...that's Ataska."

"The cult guy? You mean - an actor playing Ataska?"

"No. I mean Ataska, himself," Dodge said, chuckling.

"I thought he was roaming around in the desert or something."

"Was until yesterday; I had him picked up. I figured he'd be useful, because he professed a lot of UFO stuff. Of course, *his* alien-contact stuff was all fantasy. Most of it usually is. But sometimes the fantasy version can be used...He's always been useful to us, here. We'd let him wander around with his tribe, near the base, because they kept people away. They were a kind of extra buffer."

"You let them....Dodge, those people were *cannibals*."

"Well yeah. That was the problem, finally: they started eating our sentries. Anyway...you'll see...he's going to execute someone for us and we'll make it part of our scenario...We've drugged the cult-leader there with some major steroids just to make sure he gets violent when we want him to...See, we're gonna make it look like Ataska's been 'Meta-stized' all along; like all along he's been the Meta's boy...I'm going to cut it together with some stuff in the Interplanetary Council room we've got tricked up - have you seen that set, the Council room?" He chortled at himself. "Guess I've always been a frustrated director..."

Farraday decided now was the time. He didn't want to know anymore. "Dodge -"

Jaron came into the room at that moment, and sat down, watching Farraday. "Please do not let me interrupt you," he said in Dodge's voice.

The presence of the alien made Farraday hesitate. But it was now or never.

"Colonel - Jaron - I admire what you guys are trying to do, your longterm goals. But I can't be privy to all this. It's just not my...my forte. I mean - someone's going to *die* here...And Derrick tells me there's no way it can be an acted-out death. The guy has to actually die..."

"Sure, well - Sullivan's dangerous, we want him out of the picture, no longer a problem, and uh -"

"I think *dead* is the word you're looking for," Farraday

said, almost whispering.

"Okay," Dodge said, shrugging. "Dead."

"And these people...the ones you make it look as if they're 'puppet mastered' by the Meta...You create that myth, it could be misused - CIAD, whoever, they could use it as an excuse to kill anyone they want. 'We had definite information he was a slave of the Meta so we had to kill him'. Whether he was or not."

"Is that misuse? Sounds damned useful to me..." Dodge turned to look at Jaron, raising his eyebrows.

"Yes," Jaron said.

"I just...I can't be a part of this," Farraday said. Feeling feverish and clammy, dizzy. His stomach lurched. "You can trust me to keep my mouth shut - because yes, before you tell me for the fiftieth time, I *know* what I'm risking with you guys, with...with all this...what with my wife and all...but..."

A sudden heat rose up in Farraday then. A wave of weakness. A sense of being gripped, invisibly, by a million tiny clamps.

He tried to speak but all that would come out was a squeaking sound.

His throat was closing up.

"You don't look well, Mike," Jaron said, in Farraday's own voice. "You'd better sit down."

Farraday almost fell into a chair.

His head whirled faster and faster. His temples pounded. Sweat poured down back.

"*Man* that's fast," Dodge remarked. "I am not believing how fast it hit him! Just like that?"

Jaron nodded. "The microbes we introduced into him respond to my bioelectric signals instantaneously; they begin to reproduce and do their work within seconds. They are specially engineered for this rapidity. A beautiful microbiological construction..."

Jaron's digits fluttered with pride.

Farraday began to choke. His throat had closed off completely now.

He couldn't breathe -

"But it's not communicable, right?" Dodge asked, looking a little pale himself as he watched Farraday dying. "I mean - you're sure *I'm* not in any danger, here?"

"No, you're quite safe. It is communicable only by the exactly-prepared medium," Jaron said, soothingly, in Dodge's voice. "You haven't had a tub treatment."

Couldn't breathe -

"Well that's a relief. He sure started looking like shit in a hurry. Wouldn't want to feel that way."

Farraday was making desperate hand gestures. *Please...*

Jaron stood up and approached Farraday.

"Mike," Jaron said, "the microbes I introduced into you, in the bath...they are very responsive to me. Psychically responsive, if you like, though that's not quite what it is. It is a particular wavelength we employ...At will, I can make them attack you...or release you. And what I'll have to do Mike is...*not* kill you. I'll just set them on a course of consuming you over ten years or so. Ten years of how you feel, right now. I'll tell them to let you breathe for a second or two, every couple of minutes...This I do with real regret, Mike. But there are worlds at stake here. We must have your complete loyalty, you see...Mike?...*Do* you see?"

Farraday nodded, desperately. The room was darkening...

Jaron looked at him silently for a few moments - and suddenly the fever, the choking, the terror began to recede. In under a minute, aside from some weakness, he was well again.

"Damn that's impressive!" Dodge said. "You got to teach us how to do that!"

Jaron seemed to genuinely laugh at that.

"You'll cooperate hereafter?" Jaron asked Farraday.

"Count on it," Farraday said hoarsely. But with conviction.

"Good. Welcome to the League of Microbial Friendship."

• • •

Just before dawn, they were all awakened by the clicking of the lock in the door. All except Mahler, who slept deeply.

Eight Marine MPs, heavily armed, had come to the cell; four came in, weapons at ready, and put handcuffs on Sullivan's wrists, chained to cuffs around his ankles.

Mahler at last woke and stared gloomily at the shiny steel chains, the shiny steel eyes of the guards.

"History is inexorable," he muttered.

"You don't have to do that stuff to my Dad," Anatole said angrily.

The MPs ignored him. They were flat-gazed white guys, highly trained thugs, and there wasn't much left of them except training. Nothing you could see.

"It's okay, son," Sullivan said gently.

Anatole rushed to him; Sullivan put his arms around him; whispered something to him. Sullivan's eyes were moist; Anatole's were pouring tears.

Lila gently pulled Anatole back but let her hand linger on Sullivan; mouthed something silently to him.

He nodded. Looked quickly away from her.

"Quinn?" Zizz asked. "What's going to happen?"

Quinn shook his head. "I don't know."

Sullivan and Anatole looked at one another, then a Few Good Men, a few highly trained thugs, dragged Sullivan away.

• • •

The darkness in their cell rotated around an axis of light coming aslant through the door-grate.

Quinn felt dizzy, exhausted, but he couldn't sleep. He kept seeing that look between Anatole and Sullivan. And feeling the strange vibe from Lila, the combination of distance and...what? The phrase *infinite compassion* came to mind, a quote from he wasn't sure where.

Lila was on the bottom bunk, lying with her back to them; she was cupping Anatole with her body, one arm around him. Every so often Anatole shook silently and her grip tightened and she whispered something inaudible. Mahler was on the top bunk above Lila and Anatole, dozing, looking heavy as a petrified log.

Quinn sat opposite, with Zizz, who was mostly undressed, just brassiere and underwear, and seemed to be picking at herself in the darkness. Was she hurting herself?

Then he heard soft clink, clink sounds - it reminded him of the sounds of the shrapnel from Lila's wounds falling onto stone - and he knew that Zizz was plucking out her piercings, extracting the rings from her labia, her nipples, and tossing them onto the floor and crying softly to herself as she did it.

"You okay?" Quinn whispered. Stupid. Of course she wasn't okay.

"I don't think we're going to see him anymore, are we..."

she whispered back.

"Sullivan? I don't know." Something hurt, in him, something that surprised him.

After a moment he asked her outright, "Were you in love with the guy?"

"What? No...Why? I just...I mean, we didn't know him that long but we did know him, in a way. I felt...the way you feel about people when you go through that kind of intensity with them. And...and the way they took him, it just had this feel about it like..." She lowered her voice even more to make sure Anatole couldn't hear. "...like *finality*... and Anatole, he's going to be so hurt. Isn't that enough to make me care what happens to his dad?"

"Yeah. It is. I just wondered..."

"And...I got so I....I don't know...I mean Sullivan was scarred up and he could be ruthless and sometimes I was as scared of him as I was of the guys trying to kill us at the condoplex and he had just about *no* sense of humor, but..."

"But you liked him?" Quinn suggested.

"Yeah."

"I guess I did too."

"And it makes you wonder...what are they gonna do to us?"

Yeah. It made you wonder.

He drew her close, nestled her face close to his. Instinct moved to instinct. He felt her tears on his cheek, mingling with his own. His kissed her once, on the cheek, to comfort her. She raised her lips to him; they kissed, and held one another. They stretched out, moved softly against one another; she shook as she returned his kisses; he stroked her hair.

They didn't quite have sex; but the intimacy was deeper than any Quinn had ever felt before.

They slept a little, Zizz first. The darkness rotated around the shaft of light.

CHAPTER EIGHT

MAGIC AND LOSS

A hangar converted to a stage set: The Interplanetary Council chamber. Quinn and Anatole and Zizz and Mahler. Dodge.

"Helden," Dodge said, leaning back and popping a Diet Coke, "you're one of these political science types. You ever read any history of 1960s politics?"

"Sure."

"You ever hear of a guy named Carlos Marcello? Louisiana Mafioso?"

"I think so. We had a chapter on the Mafia involvement in the assassination of President Kennedy, in Assassination 101. Marcello's the one supposedly ordered Kennedy killed."

"Very good - he was the team leader on that side of the project fence, yeah. You ever hear of the motto Marcello had on his door?"

"Nope."

"It was on the inside of the door of his office so you'd see it when you go out: *Three can keep a secret if two are dead.* And you know what? You won't see that motto around here - but every single employee, every enlisted man here...They all know that saying. I see to it they do. You understand what I'm telling you?"

"Uh huh."

"Good. You want some Diet Coke?"

"Nope."

"Don't blame you. It's not the classic Diet Coke. I dunno *what* they put in this shit now."

"Where's Lila?" Anatole asked.

"She's just talking to some of our scientists about her...experience. No one's hurting her, son," Dodge added, gently.

"I don't believe you. I want to see her. I want to see her and my father."

Quinn admired the way the kid spoke up; flatly, without a squeak in his voice, like a judge in court.

"One thing at a time. Now - Look...What do you guys think of our little set, here?"

He paused, looking around at the set for the "Zetan-Earth Interplanetary Council Chamber". The set looking relatively small in the converted, echoingly big hangar.

Zizz had been ogling the set all this time. Mahler blinking confusedly.

Zizz asked, without irony: "Didn't I see this set on an episode of *Star Trek Reborn*?"

"We may have borrowed an element or too," Dodge admitted.

There was a white backdrop with the "United Nations of Earth" - a modified UN insignia - side by side with the "Zetan symbol", the one Dodge had devised for them: A simplified smiling Zetan - although they couldn't really smile - raising a hand in friendship, against a galactic field. The colors were New Age bright and friendly.

A long desk curved in front of the backdrop, on foot-high risers, like a talk show host's desk, and across from it were a circle of empty seats. Between the seats and the desk rose a glimmering, enticing, TV-land-futuristic console that seemed to offer up on its altar the promise of a glittering and glorious forthcoming technology; it hinted of gifts to come from the Zetans.

And of course, to one side was a "viewscreen".

Dodge stood just out of the glow of the set lights, near Quinn and Zizz and Mahler and Anatole, who stood in an outwardly intimidated group under the watchful eye of four submachinegun-armed thugs in USMC MP uniform.

Farraday came in, then, with Derrick. Introductions all round. Farraday's smile was dead, his handshake limp.

Quinn could see immediately that Farraday didn't belong with these guys. No one was guarding him, but he looked "captured" somehow, anyway. It was in his pallor; it was in his eyes.

Farraday's voice was hoarse as he said, "If you folks would please take a seat..."

They sat in the chairs facing the desk. Minicameras drifted around in the shadows, taping them.

They were each given a script held together by brads. On Quinn's script, a few pages long, was a title page reading:

QUINN HELDEN
DESIGNED INFORMATION SUMMARY
MJ15 - Eyes Only

"If you would, please," Farraday was saying, "study the scripts. We'll have some read-throughs, which we'll tape, but you'll be required to know this material by heart for the final...take."

"And if we do all this - you'll let us go?" Anatole asked, as if only mildly interested.

"I'm...not in charge of all that," Farraday said. "But I believe..." He looked a question at Dodge.

"Well of course you'll be given your freedom," Dodge said, "But, also, of course, you'll be under electronic surveillance. The implants won't hurt, but you will be monitored, so - if you discuss certain things publicly, or even privately, we'll know. *We'll be listening to everything you say, everywhere; everything you write, everything you communicate.* Because we'll be listening from inside you. Talk about something you've been warned not to talk about, and we'll activate the enzymes in the implant node, they'll disintegrate in you, and you'll die, apparently of 'drug overdoses'." He smiled, adding, "And, of course, no one will give a shit about the deaths of a few more drug addicts."

"You're sweet," Zizz said, "you know that?"

"The discrete charm of the bourgeoisie," Mahler observed.

Dodge chuckled modestly.

Farraday smiled wearily and said, "Shall we get to our scripts?"

They had a run-through. Quinn was first; he read aloud, from his script:

"*I first became aware that these creatures the Meta were hostile to the human race when I saw them kill someone I knew. Or to be more accurate, they took control of a human being and used that human being to kill someone I knew. But there was no doubt in my mind that murder was what was going on...*"

Quinn broke off and looked at Derrick. "What someone is that going to be?"

"Nobody." Derrick glanced at Dodge. "You really should've briefed them about this."

Dodge nodded. "Can't think of everything. Quinn, we've got a volunteer Federal prisoner, he's condemned to death anyway. Someone you don't know. We're providing some money to his family. It'll be a real death but the circumstances'll be faked. Taking lemons, making lemonade. Sorta like recycling - recycling an execution, you see."

Quinn knew he was lying, knew it for sure. The desert, above the underground base, was trying to tell him: *he's lying*. The stale base air itself was trying to tell him. *The man is lying to you...* One of those hunches; one of those feelings; one of those intuitions; one of those voiceless voices that -

He shook the feeling off. The priority right now was survival. He went back to reading aloud.

"*What I realize now, is -*" He broke off with a sigh. "I don't talk like this, you know, it'll come off like bullshit."

"Now that's being helpful," Dodge said. "I appreciate that. Mike? What can we do about that?"

"It's irrelevant because I don't expect him to use our language - it's the...the 'information' we want. Once he gets that, and the sequence, he can put it in his own words."

Quinn nodded. He made an effort of will, to go on with the run-through. The realest part of him wanted to jump up on the chair and scream at them...to shout at them:

I DON'T BELIEVE THIS IS HAPPENING! YOU FUCKERS ARE NOT REAL AND I WANT YOU TO LET ME GO AND LEAVE ME ALONE! EVERYTHING I WAS PROMISED ABOUT THIS COUNTRY WAS A FUCKING LIE! *FUCK YOU!*

But instead...he read...

"...to realize that you could feel how evil these Meta creatures were. I met someone who tried to make them seem friendly, and I think we may all meet people like that, but it's a lie, the Meta are dangerous...I believe that, if the Zetans had not intervened, we'd all be dead now..."

Quinn stopped reading. End of script.

"What the hell is a 'Zetan'?"

"My normal response," Derrick said, "would be to remind you of that 'I'll Ask the Questions' movie, Quinn, but in fact you'll be meeting a Zetan or two for the taping..."

"Let's just get on with this," Farraday said. He was sitting, half slumped, in a metal folding chair to one side, reading along in a master script. "Mr. Mahler? Your turn."

His voice shaking, Mahler began to read, "*I really feel that it doesn't matter what your politics are - Separatist, Sovereign, Anarchist, Communist, Libertarian, what have you. The important thing is that we're united against the Meta, and we understand the necessity of working close with the Zetans. Over time I've learned that the Zetans can be trusted...We can trust them with our lives and our future...*"

Mahler paused, and swallowed. He looked as if he wanted to cry.

Anatole looked dazed. Zizz like she wanted to break into hysterical laughter.

"Go on," Farraday said.

Mahler cleared his throat, twice. "*...and that the Metas can't be trusted. And that the hope for the future is interplanetary alignment, and a trust in the people who have been working to make this alignment happen. All this came clear to me when I saw the changes in Lila, and I saw what the Metas had done to her...*" He stopped reading as if he'd come to a brick wall. "What?" He shook his head in disbelief. "What?"

"Mr. Mahler," Farraday began. "Umm...Just...just..."

Mahler glowered up at Farraday, then at Derrick and Dodge. "You know what? Fuck you. *Fuck you.*"

Derrick made some kind of hand signal, and a Marine corporal named Collins stepped in and clipped Mahler across the back of his head with the butt of his gun, in a measured, exact sort of way. Hard enough to knock him off his chair, hard enough to hurt, not hard enough to knock him out.

Collins went down on one knee beside Mahler and jammed the muzzle of his gun into Mahler's ear.

And said: "I can get a mop, and some soap, and I had enough KP in my time I sure as hell know how to use it. Won't bother me none to blow your brains out, Trotsky-boy."

He said it, too, as if reading off a script. Face expressionless. His voice sharp.

Dodge nodded approvingly.

Quinn wanted to do something. But he sat there, feeling trapped within a trap within a trap.

(Where was Lila? Where was Kian? Where was Sullivan?)

"Get up, Mahler, please," Quinn said, at last, moving to help Mahler up. "Just take it easy, and get up. Sit down. Read the stupid fucking thing."

Mahler slowly got up, and sat down, looked uncomprehendingly at the script lying on the floor at his feet.

"Pick it up," Collins said. Mahler listlessly picked the script up.

Derrick glanced at his watch. "Dodge? I'm gonna get those two together, in the other arena. It can't wait. The stuff in subject one oughta be kickin' in..."

"He was already nuts," Dodge said, "I don't think he' needed 'em. Might go past control."

"We'll see."

Dodge nodded and Derrick hurried off; as his heavy footsteps receded, other, lighter footsteps came echoingly from the opposite doorway of the hangar: two sets of quick little echoing footsteps that made Quinn think of the expression *the pitter patter of little feet*. He turned to see Kian coming onto the set, and with him was another child, a strange looking child, about the same height, wearing a polo shirt and jeans and tennis shoes...

"Oh shit..." It wasn't a child.

"I'd like to introduce, now," Dodge was saying, "our home-base Zetan contact, Jaron. Please don't be alarmed for your adopted brother, Anatole...Kian is fine. Our Zetan friends have been taking care of him. He's in great shape, better than ever..."

Quinn, Mahler, Anatole, Zizz...Their mouths dropped open as they watched Kian and Jaron mount the risers and sit at the desk together, on elevated chairs.

Jaron put a fatherly arm around Kian. Who snuggled into the alien's gentle grip.

Kian's face was exactly as it had been when Quinn had seen him last: more or less empty. If there was anything else there, it was a kind of bovine contentment.

"Now that..." Zizz whispered, looking at Jaron, "is how an alien should look."

Mahler licked his lips and shook his head. Then winced; his head still hurt. "That's gotta be...gotta be a little guy in a suit...Prosthetics...costume..."

"I don't think so," Zizz murmured.

Quinn could feel it: *that thing was genuinely not-of-this-world - or...not only of this world...*

"Do you have something to say?" the alien asked Kian, *in Sullivan's voice.*

"I want..." Kian's voice was soft. He hesitated, then spoke more loudly, so everyone, and the microphones, could hear. "I want to thank Jaron and my Zetan friends for taking care of me...I thank God they are here, to help us. I was so frightened when I saw the Meta...I know it'll be all right now."

He smiled and leaned against the alien.

"Jesus," Farraday muttered. He hadn't been expecting this either. "Dodge...This is a public relations disaster. You can't have them messing with kids -"

"He has no family. The Zetans have adopted him. He's got no parents, see. They haven't hurt him - a few skin samples."

"Kid looks like a zombie - you don't think that's going to come across when we show even the edited version on network TV?"

"You should have seen him before - he was already messed up. They... They've...recruited him, psychologically, is all. And they took a little gene-breeding seed material -"

"What's that mean?"

"No big thing. The Zetans took a few skin samples - one

of his kidneys, a very small amount of cerebral tissue...nothing damaging, some testicular tissue. That part doesn't have to be public anyway."

Got no parents? Quinn thought. What about Sullivan?

Maybe Sullivan was dead already...

Farraday was saying, "You have to be very careful about how kids are treated in this..." He turned to look at Anatole. "What's wrong with the older kid?" Farraday asked, suddenly.

Everyone turned. Anatole was leaning over in his chair, like a nodding junkie, his eyes fluttering. Zizz had to catch him to keep him from falling on his face.

"Like the Lila girl," Dodge muttered.

Farraday looked inquiringly at him.

Dodge shrugged. "She's been like that all morning. We tried..." He broke off, made a *Tell you later* gesture.

Zizz gently shook Anatole. Called his name.

No response.

. . .

"Seeking One..."

"Anatole."

"I've been waiting for you. I thought you would come down and help us. They took my father and Lila and they've given Kian to the Zetans."

"I see that. I'm sorry. I couldn't come. And I see how deeply all this hurts you: you can even feel it here, away from your normal attachments."

"You can tell me, again, it's all illusion, suffering is identification and it's...it's...temporary and the 'normal' world isn't real, it's all like a dream, and I'll know what you mean, fine, Seeking One, *but where we are, we suffer* and the suffering is real to us and it matters to us, it has to."

"I know. I know that. And the Archons are making it worse."

"Who?"

"The Zetans. They are the Archons, in one of your older religious traditions; the servants of the Demiurge, the false face of God; the God who is to the real God as your ego-identified personality is to the real Anatole. Their demiurge is their Group Mind...an ancient thing that -"

"I don't get that and I don't care, I just want to know...Can you help my Dad?"

"The capacity for suffering among your people is so remarkable..."

"Can't you come down and get us out of that place...? Or bring us all up where you are?"

"You are 'up here' because you have a special capacity to be. But the strange thing is, what enabled me to contact you in the first place was the proximity of a stranger to you."

"Who?"

"Quinn Helden. Because he came to your house, I was able to come to you. Quinn has the necessary genetic imprint, and the cerebral inter-framework, that conjures, and calls - there are many orders of Being he can call upon, if only he knew it. If he knew how, he might be able to call me...a little closer. But I cannot come down there as I was able to come to Lila in the desert..."

"Why?"

A hawk swam past through the sunwashed sky; it gave them a wide berth, sensing them more than seeing them, then squawked, startled, when a third Someone abruptly appeared in the sky, along with Anatole and Seeking One.

"Hello, Anatole."

"Lila!"

"I'm glad you made it, Lila," Seeking One said.

"It took me all morning to find you..."

"But you're here. We have a good connection, now."

"I'm afraid for Jack," Lila said.

"Yes," Seeking One said. "Look."

They saw him; it was as if they were there with Sullivan, and in the sky, at once.

"Can he hear me?" Anatole asked.

"No, he is unaware of us," Seeking One said.

Anatole floated over to nestle against Lila. She put her imagined arm around him. Together, they watched Sullivan walk across the dusty open ground, toward Ataska.

• • •

Sullivan rubbed his wrists where the metal cuffs had pinched him. He had seen the cameras and from across the open ground; the open area like the space of a small arena between the high, chainlink, razor-wired fences. He had seen the Marines uncuff the lunatic leaning against the truck. He knew this lunatic's face.

"You're Ataska..." Sullivan said, coming nearer the lunatic.

He stopped, twenty paces distant, seeing the wall-eyed rapacity in Ataska's wandering stare; and the new surgery scar on his temple. Some sort of implant.

"The aliens," Ataska said, "they...you with 'em?"

"No," Sullivan said.

"They..." He made a noise that was close to a giggle, but shriller, uglier. "You ever fuck any alien pussy? I often wondered, man. I've seen it. Seen it in my visions. Some of them aliens they make ya fuck, to get the samples, they got the bifurcated pussy; other ones, they got the *tri-*furcated pussy. Now, *tri* furcated pussy, in one direction it feels like pussy unless you push it in far enough and then it's...it grabs you and shoves a kinda like a tube in and sucks the semen out...but if you pull back before it gets you in there that far, see, ya shove in again kinda to the right, another angle, you go into the other pussy tube on that side, that one, it's got *wooden kitchen matches in there* and you fuck against them match heads and they flare up and burn your johnson or you pull back and shove in to the *other* side, the left side o' that tri-furcated pussy, and in there it's all garbage disposal blades that -"

"Hey," Sullivan said.

"That trifurcated alien pussy -"

"*Hey!*" Sullivan said.

"What?"

"You don't have to go along with anything they've got you set up to do here, Ataska. You could still break out."

Ataska stared at him, mouth drooping.

That's when the mist began to issue from beneath the unmarked flatblack military truck - from a distance, it would probably look as they had intended it to look: that the mist was coming from the air itself, simply appearing. Then from inside the cab of the parked, driverless truck, came a pale-red rapier of laser light, barely visible in the bright sun, and the mist sparkled with a coalescing image: a glittering flying saucer, a thing of living silicon. An illusion, he knew, designed to look like the...

The whatever it was...

...that had settled over Lila, in the desert, and healed her.

Now it was settling over Ataska - as if to take him over.

"Bullshit!" Sullivan shouted. "That's not what was out there! That's a fucking hologram!"

But he knew that they'd erase whatever he said, replace it with some scripted fake-up of his voice. They'd edit him, they'd edit Ataska. He knew a staged disinformation scenario when he saw one.

Ataska was feeling around under the truck...

And bringing out an M18 machine-rifle. Left there for him to find.

"The voices told me about you..." Ataska babbled, the words emphasized by a wagging string of drool. "You work for those things and you're...a son of the devil, a devil ghost, you...servant of the trifurcated alien pussy, you...devil from the hell between the stars, you..."

Sullivan looked around, and saw that he had no time to run for cover. He could lie down and die or he could charge Ataska.

• • •

"Lila? Seeking One? There must be something...?"

"No, I'm sorry, Anatole," Seeking One said. "The Zetan's force fields keep me away, bar the door against me, unless someone unlocks it - Ceph came to me outside the fields: he has not the power, until he transfigures through death, to bring me in, through them; nor have you. Only Quinn..."

• • •

And as Sullivan charged Ataska, the "Meta" settled around the lunatic...and Sullivan knew it was supposed to look as if the Meta were *making* him kill Sullivan - and the first bullets hit him, Sullivan felt them like fists of ice -

But he kept moving - He felt a nasty, strobing juxtaposition in his mind between himself and Anja's stimslave Sol, moving upstream against the current of bullets; he was Sullivan, he was Osterberg, and he was Sol and though he was really Osterberg he was programmed too, in his way -

• • •

"Seeking One..."

"I'm very sad," Lila was saying, "that I can feel so little about this, from up here...Jack is getting shot..."

"Seeking One...!"

Seeking One said: "The part of you that feels

authentically is still half asleep, Lila...Here you are only authentic."

Anatole made himself grow to the size of a dirigible to get their attention.

"Seeking One! Help him!"

Seeking One assumed the girlish representation that he liked, in jeans and t-shirt, and looked up at him.

Lila took shape beside her, modestly clothed out of respect for his puberty.

"It's too late," Lila said.

"Yes, it's too late," Seeking One said.

The words echoed through all the tender places in Anatole. Too late, late, late...

"He's too badly hurt. But I might be able to help you and the others if you can go back to Quinn..."

• • •

Dodge was just joining Derrick and the technician working the remote cameras: the military techy in his white coat was a slender blue-eyed Iowan, so young he still had his pimples. Dodge elbowed the techy aside and zoomed in to get the action more intensely...

Always wanted to be a director.

Derrick burst out, "Shit! He's still walkin' - this isn't in the scenario..."

"It might work out quite well, friend Derrick," Dodge was muttering, digitalizing the image for enhancement.

"But he's - Sullivan...Osterberg, he..."

They could see it clearly on the monitor: Sullivan had six bullets in gut and chest and a seventh wedged in a cheekbone - but Sullivan was still standing and he...

"Holy shit...."

Sullivan was jerking the M18 from Ataska's hands and turning it, moving with *chi* directedness, shoving the barrel of the gun -

"Right through his pants!" Derrick blurted. "Ow! He shoved it up the fucker's ass!"

"Sure did, didn't he? And look at that, there was one round left in the gun and there goes Ataska's brains all mixed up with his entrails - now what could be more apt for Ataska, I ask you -?"

The technician sprinted for a waste basket and threw up.

"But - " Derrick snorted with exasperation. "Ataska was supposed to kill Sullivan - "

"Osterberg."

"- Whatever you want to call him, you know who I mean. And then The Zetans were supposed to come and kill Ataska in revenge for the Meta-slave's murder of the American hero..."

"Well, we'll cut something together...Oh, hell - Sullivan's still moving! He's pulled out the gun...he's found the other clip!"

"How the fuck can he stay on his feet?"

"He can't last much longer, he's sure to - fuck! *He's coming this way!*"

They heard the sound of a door breaking down.

Gunshots. More gunshots and the shouts of Marines outside the observation room door.

Dodge threw himself to the floor - Derrick and the technician were too slow, they stood there staring, frozen like deer in the headlights as -

The door burst inward. A gun-muzzle dripping with blood, shit and torn entrails blazed in the doorway; there was a glimpse of Sullivan's blood-masked, snarling face, and -

That was the last thing Derrick ever saw. In this life.

. . .

Sirens were going off. And were those...gunshots?

Anatole was sitting up, shaking Quinn's arm. "Ignore the sirens...Quinn, listen - I have a message - you have to 'get into an altered state', she said...get into a...a frenzy!"

"What? What are you talking about? Who said?"

"The shining one, the Seeking One...the one who helped Lila...I communicate with her - and she says *you* can bring her close enough to help us -"

The guards were arguing, confused, calling on three phones at once; the alien was standing, looking around. Kian looked bemused.

Farraday had a look on his face that was a felicitous blend of scared and relieved.

"Look...get into the sirens...they're a rhythm...she says you, the way you're made, to contact her you need a rhythm..."

"Kid all this stuff with the aliens has glitched your little mind -"

Zizz was looking oddly at Quinn. The Marines were rushing toward the door - then they seemed to remember Quinn and friends and began to argue about who should stay to keep them under wraps.

Quinn thought of his silent-movie class in film school. Take away the familiar stimuli and even trained men turn into Keystone Cops.

"Quinn!" Zizz said. "Those hunch feelings you told me about...Try to find them - the way Anatole says -"

A pregnancy of possibility suffused the air: Quinn could feel it. Maybe, then...

Anatole began banging on a chair; rhythmically. Then Zizz. The sirens rose and fell, rose and fell.

"What'd she say, exactly, Anatole?"

"She said for you to get into the rage you feel, work with how pissed off you are, get into the rhythm...She can't get very close but maybe enough..."

Quinn looked at them. Then at the ceiling.

"It's stupid," Mahler said. "But what does it matter now?" Then he began to pound rhythmically...

And someone was banging rhythmically on the door.

And gunshots -

The door burst open and three Marines fell, screaming - others ran for cover and fired as they went -

Quinn felt himself unable to bear this world any longer; the rhythm promised another world -

He closed his eyes - he began to pound rhythmically on a chair...

He saw a glittering behind his eyelids; a coruscation that was ovoid and was other shapes too, all at once, that was like a shining silicon eye opening, looking back at him...

Hello, Quinn. Hold me here long enough, I can turn off the -

Then he lost it. The gunshots brought him out of the tremulous trance he'd been in.

He opened his eyes -

The lights flickered, flashed - and went out.

That was his answer, that was the response. A massive power surge: and the sirens died. All power, all over the base. The power and the auxiliary power too. Darkness. There was a strobing of gunshots...

Gunshot, darkness, gunshot, darkness...

Quinn and Mahler and Zizz threw themselves flat. Anatole ran toward his father -

Sullivan moved lurchingly but steadily toward Kian, in one hand the M18 propped against his side, the other a newly-appropriated submachinegun. Sullivan fired a burst. Another Marine went down, wailing with pain.

Bullets shattered the Interplanetary Council insignia; cracked and broke the fake control console. Inside, it was hollow, empty.

Farraday was flattened on the floor by the console - he seemed to be laughing like a lunatic - then crying - then laughing -

Anatole ran past Farraday - steel-jacketed bullets sparked the floor near Anatole and Farraday reached out, tripped him, pulled him yowling in protest ("Kid, get down, flatten!") to safety behind a table as -

Jaron was moving, fast, with the boy in tow, heading toward an exit door -

Darkness. Quinn waited for another gunshot strobe.

A muzzleflash and suddenly Sullivan was there, blocking Jaron's way.

Sullivan swept Kian up in one arm and with the other -

Darkness. Quinn couldn't see.

Then another strobe of light from another Marine firing another gun...

In the strobe of gunshots from the edges of the movie set Quinn saw...

Sullivan lifting Jaron off the ground with one hand, wringing the alien's neck.

A tight group of Marines burst in the nearest door, firing as they came, and Sullivan's body jerked and jerked and spun and Kian seemed to dance grotesquely with him and the two of them were riddled with bullets, bullets passing through Kian and lodging in Sullivan; through Sullivan and lodging in Kian.

"Dad -!" Anatole screamed. *"Daddy! Kian!"*

Long after, Quinn tried to forget what the bullets did to Kian. He remembered Qarma's death, someone shouting *His head, his head* - And Kian...

Someone shouted, "Hold your fire Crow Team!"

The gunshots ended. Sullivan fell. Really dead now; the dead, smaller child in his arms.

Anatole sobbed. The room went completely dark, except for a couple of stabbing flashlight beams, almost quiet, men speaking in hushed tones as if the darkness were mumbling to itself.

Then Quinn heard a voice from the floor nearby. A rather sweet voice. "I'm a friend! Seeking One has sent me, and Lila! Come with me. Quinn, Mahler, Zizz! Mike Farraday! Anatole! Follow the sound of my voice! This way...this way..."

It was a voice you believed. They needed to believe someone.

They scrambled up and followed it through the darkness. "This way....that's it..."

The Marines shouted at one another. Quinn and Zizz and Mahler found Anatole and Farraday, together at the exit door, barely visible as their eyes adjusted to the light. They didn't see whoever it was who had led them here.

"My Dad, Kian," Anatole was saying, "I want to check them, to be sure..."

"I have checked them," said the sweet voice, from the darkness overhead now. "They are dead to this world. We have to go help Lila now..."

Anatole numbly let them lead him through the door, into a dark hallway.

"This way, come on!" Farraday said, happily. "Ha ha you little bug-assed son of a bitch! He wrung your damn neck, Jaron! This way, I know where they're keeping Lila, this way...Watch your step...ha ha you little vermin-carrying vermin, he twisted your damn bug-eyed head right off your goddamn..."

Through pitch darkness, they ran down the hallway. Farraday stopped at a door which popped open, its electronic lock nonfunctional, and they heard Lila's voice inside.

"Jack?"

. . .

Down a hall, another, a third, up an echoing back stairway. Darkness, cold metal of bannister under Quinn's hand; his other holding Zizz's arm, guiding her; Zizz holding Lila's hand; Lila holding Mahler's hand; Mahler holding Farraday's; Farraday holding Anatole's.

Quinn, following the patient, musical little voice, and the sound of someone shuffling, a flapping sound up ahead of him, now and then calling to them.

"Right this way...up here...."

Up the stairs, banging shins, up, tripping, falling, getting up, up flight after flight - a doorway - push the door open - a rooftop! Sunlight on a rooftop!

Dazzling sunlight. This, too, was another world.

They were out on a roof, which was also a landing pad of some kind, on a terrace cut into a hillside. They'd come through a doorway in an outbuilding, almost the only built-in feature on this side of the three-acre landing pad. But there were four large black military choppers armed with 9 mm cannons, windows opaqued like a limo's, lined up to one side.

Marine guards were running about at the other end of the landing pad, firing at something hovering above them: something that glittered and took the sun's light and radiated it outward in a thousand arms of Shiva, arms of Vishnu...

"Thanks," Anatole said, to the shining apparition.

Anatole, thought Quinn, seemed dazed but surprisingly centered, somehow, considering what he'd just seen: his adopted brother and his father, shot dead. Something to do with Lila; with the Meta; some unseen nourishment from that source...

Farraday was grinning. "I knew it, I *knew* it! Come on, into the chopper - ha ha ha ha! Little bug eyed bastards!"

Mahler squinted at Farraday. "'Into the chopper'? Why should we trust this son of a bitch, this Farraday?" Mahler asked. "This is all some kind of staged scenario...this asshole was part of the last one!"

"You can trust him," the sweet voice said, from the doorway they'd taken to the roof. "He's free, now that Jaron is dead."

They turned to see, in the doorway...

"Oh *SHIT* -!" Zizz shrieked. "KILL IT! WHAT IS IT? KILL IT KILL IT *KILL IT!*"

"No no no no....! Don't hurt him!" Farraday was saying, "that's a land octopus, he was an alien-human-octopus hybrid experiment...they did lots of them but he's the only one who survived. His name is Ceph."

"Oh God KILL IT, *it's horrible* -!"

"Everything's horrible," Anatole whispered. "It doesn't matter. It has to be okay, after this. There isn't anything else..."

"KILL IT - !"

"No, hey, calm down - " Quinn said, shaking her. "It helped us get out!"

"*He*," Farraday said, keeping an eye on the distracted Marines. "*He* helped us. That's my man, Ceph. Or my prairie squid, Ceph, whatever. He's a great guy, trust me. Hey Ceph, Sullivan killed that little bug eyed fucker! I'm free! Ha HAAAAAA."

"I know. An amazing feat of conscious, one-pointed attention against the current of suffering; a great feat of the spiritual capacity to *Do*. Jaron's dead, yes."

"Little bug eyed bastards -! He choked me, Ceph, he tried to kill me! But he's not fucking with me now, 'cause we wrung his neck!"

"I know. Calm down, Mike."

"You calm down too, Zizz," Quinn said. "The little guy's on our side."

Zizz took several deep breaths. She looked at Ceph; at Quinn; back at the land octopus. She swallowed. "I...okay, I'm okay - I've been acting like my mother...I don't usually, I just...all that shooting...everything we went through...I've been so close to freaking out...and..."

"I quite understand," the land octopus said.

"Yeah I...I'm sorry...octopus dude, uh, thing..."

"That's quite all right. Your tattoos gave me quite a start when I first saw *you*..."

The land octopus had clung to the frame of the door, was climbing up it, as he spoke, like a snail up a wall. In a moment he was just above the doorframe. "Someone is coming," he explained sweetly.

"That chopper there, that one's open!" Farraday said.

"Nah, uh uh, not for you," Dodge said, coming out of the door, onto the roof. He had a machinegun in his hand trained on Farraday waist-high; he swiveled the gun to show them he could turn it on any one of them.

Anatole took a step closer to Dodge. "You one of the brain-dead fuckers who killed my father?"

Anatole's voice was even, almost soft.

Dodge replied without even looking at Anatole. Not taking him seriously. "Your father was killed by so many people, son, I lost count. I don't think I got more than one or two bullets in him. He was some balls-out sumbitch. I'll give him that. All right now..."

Dodge's eyes were flicking over them and to the apparition, the wheel of fire turning in the sky, on the other side of the landing area. Not sure what to do with all that information. Deciding to focus on the problem in front of him, on Quinn and friends. Hardly noticing when Anatole edged around the side of the door...

"OK," Dodge said, "Holiday excursion's over, let's go. Get your asses face down on the -"

Then Anatole grabbed the gun barrel and jerked it to one side - Dodge pulled it easily away from him, turned to shoot him...

The land octopus jumped directly *onto Dodge's head;* Ceph's body covering Dodge's eyes. "Peekaboo, Colonel. It's me!"

"Dammit, get this calamari abomination off my -"

He fired one burst of the gun - no one was hit, though Zizz was cut by flecks of concrete spat up by the bullets.

Then he went stiff, his voice getting shrill and parrotlike.

"Get it off my - my - my...my. My. My. My. My...."

Dodge dropped the gun. Farraday grinned.

They could only see his mouth under the land octopus - which had engulfed the top of his head all 'round. Like a living helmet.

"I'm sorry, young lady," the land octopus said, to Zizz. "I hope you're not hurt badly...I didn't get my fibers into his brain sooner..."

"Your...fibers?" she asked, turning to look at the Marines running from the disk of scintillating light, as the Meta chivvied the Marines back and forth, and back again.

"Yes," the land octopus was saying, "My external neurofibers, for cerebral interface...I've got complete control of the Colonel now...very distasteful, having to participate in Colonel Dodge. Couldn't bear this sort of thing for long, and never tried it on one of the Big Shots here...tested it on the occasional Marine sergeant who thought he'd 'lost time' from drinking rubbing alcohol...but I'll have to get used to it - we'll need the Colonel's skills and his knowledge, his authority, you see...I think you know more or less all you need to know about me, apart from that - except what should be obvious, by now: I'm an agent of the Meta. Until now, I was undercover in Area 51/S-4. I found my way to the Meta psychically, and they recruited me, and that has been my liberation...We'd best get underway, now, don't you think?"

The Marines ran...the shimmering saucer seemed to pursue the soldiers - but hurt none of them.

Then it lost interest, rose into the sky. And Quinn seemed to hear:

I'm sorry, Quinn, they're getting their electrical power back on. I was only able to stop it temporarily. The Zetans' field uses the same power source. The field effectively keeps my kind away. And the other Zetans are coming. They are dangerous to me...Best you and your friends get in the chopper soon so that they mis-identify you...Oh and Quinn...about New York, you should...the Middle Man...find the Shaman who...Middle Man...Fetish broker...find the...

He lost the rest as the voice faded.

Quinn hoped he wouldn't hear it again anytime soon. Hearing voices in your head was a bad symptom.

Dodge was walking with a wobbly stride toward the nearest open chopper, now and then skipping like a small child and saying, "Tum te rum! Tum te rum and hot fucking DAMN!"

The others followed and found seats in the helicopter. In one minute, just as the Zetan saucers appeared on the horizon, the chopper lifted into the air.

With Dodge piloting - or Dodge's skills piloting, guided by Ceph's eyes - they flew south.

"I can get you to the edge of Las Vegas," the land octopus shouted, even its shouts sounding lovely, "and you're on your own from there...Can't take you with me to where we're going to hide out...You have something else to do...but you can have Colonel Dodge's credit cards..."

"What about me?" Farraday asked. "And - you know - what about Lyn?"

"She's waiting for us," the land octopus said. "You'll see! She's waiting...We arranged a transport that wouldn't freak her out. She *thought* it was a helicopter. We had to affect her perceptions a little, she wouldn't have been ready...You and Anatole and Lila will come with me, to Campbell's place in the hills -"

"Who's Campbell?" Farraday asked.

"A friend. You'll see. I've been talking to him via Modem for years, giving him tidbits. And he works with a secret society that has Meta contacts. I told him what I am - I'm not sure he believes me...he lives a ways outside Vegas..."

"Where do we go after this?" Mahler wondered dazedly, barely audible over the rotor noise though he sat close by Quinn.

Zizz was looking out the window at the saucers, hovering near the base, behind them, in as much confusion as the Marines.

"New York!" Quinn said, suddenly. Without knowing definitely and for certain why, he was sure of it: they had to go to New York.

"That's it," Anatole said, his eyes drooping, the trance coming on him. "You have to go to New York...and find Black Betty. We need her...Go to the Middle Man and through him..."

They couldn't get him to say anymore after that, or Lila either. She just smiled. Sphinx or Mona Lisa?

Lila.

PART LEZ TREZ

For as soon as the intellect attains the place of the heart, at once it sees a thing of which it previously knew nothing. It sees the open space within the heart and it beholds itself entirely luminous and full of discrimination...God asks only this of us, that our heart be purified through watchfulness.
 —from THE PHILOKALIA
 compiled by St. Nikodimos
 of the Holy Mountain
 and St. Makarios of Corinth

CHAPTER NINE

SHAMAN

It was funny, the things you could get used to, as life went on. The ideas, the changes, the revolutions, the inversions of values, the shattering of paradigms. The prospects of chaos. Sometimes you could make them part of you.

Shattered paradigms, broken frames, snapped locks, Quinn thought, as he got out of the chopper. *Sometimes damage is the only omen of hope.*

"I really regret not being able to go to Vegas, this time around," Ceph said, gazing at the architectural caricatures, the grow-your-own-crystals spires and lights of Vegas just visible on the skyline.

As he let Zizz and Mahler and Quinn out of the chopper, on the cracked, empty highway, just outside the Las Vegas city limits, Ceph shifted his position on Dodge's head, a little, still looking wistfully at the horizon. "The Living Wayne Newton exhibit...the Win-a-Kidney Tables...The Vegas 'Old Mafia Days' Parade..." Ceph sighed. The blades of the idling helicopter made slow, mournful slices into the air overhead. "I always wanted to go on the Las Vegas amusement rides I saw on TV, especially that old one before it's gone, the tower with the roller coaster on top...but they're tearing that down, it's going too...Old Las Vegas is going...Ah, well..."

Ceph waved with one of his baby's hands goodbye; he made one of Dodge's hands wave too. The effect was nauseatingly grotesque but they waved back. "See you sometime soon," Ceph called, as the chopper began to rise. "If you aren't killed, of course!"

"See you later, instigators!" Farraday called nonsensically, waving, as he closed the chopper door.

And the chopper - piloted by Dodge's body and some of Dodge's brain - lifted away, carrying Lila and Anatole and Farraday with it.

As they watched the chopper recede into the distance, Mahler muttered: "We're on the outskirts of Las Vegas. Where do we go from here? I mean...*Now* what?"

"Now I'm exhausted," Quinn said, looking around, one hand shading his eyes against the sunlight.

"Me too," Zizz said.

"So tired I could sleep for ten or twelve hours anywhere, even on a bus. And I hate long bus rides. And there's a bus station right there...Let's buy some bus tickets to Chicago, what do you say."

He pointed to where a quartermile down they could just make out a truckstop and a bus station, with an interstate bus standing next to it; one of the new Amtrak satellite-driven propane-lines.

"And from there?" Mahler said dully, as if he didn't really care.

"New York."

"Quinn...I'm going to try not to think about what happened in the last few days...I just...I'm not sure what was real, anyway. I mean - maybe it wasn't real, maybe it was all...induced somehow. You ever read Philip K. Dick?"

"He was a contemporary of Charles Dickens, wasn't he?" Zizz asked sleepily, as they trudged to the bus station.

"The point is," Mahler was saying, "I just don't want to talk about any of this for a long, long time...OK, Quinn? Please?"

"It's okay, Mahler. It's okay."

• • •

Quinn and Mahler and Zizz in the bus station.

"What if they come and look for us here?" Zizz asked, as they sat down on the old plastic benches.

"Who?" Quinn said.

"What do you mean, who?" Mahler snorted. "The cryptonazis with the secrecy fetish back at the fucking base, obviously."

Zizz nodded. "Yeah. Men in Black or whatever."

Quinn shook his head. "Ceph's got that covered. He's got Dodge issuing orders to cover us..."

"I guess. I can't stop worrying about it..."

Quinn found himself worrying, instead, about Anatole, and Lila. Hadn't known them very well - but how could you not feel for someone, when you saw their loved ones shot to pieces, almost within their reach?

Ceph - Ceph/Dodge? - would take care of them. Quinn imagined telling someone here, the pimply kid at the snack bar, the Pakistani guy repairing the coke machine, what had happened. Or just about Ceph. *Genetic experiment?* the guy says, *I heard of that. There was an episode about that on Star Trek Reborn...*

No, man, Quinn would say, *This was for real and the experiment was carried out by human beings collaborating with aliens from the star system Zeta Reticuli.*

You have a good one, man, I got some work to do.

But then, Mahler didn't quite believe in the aliens either.

"Do I read you right, Mr. Postmodern Commie?" Quinn asked, not even looking at Mahler as he asked it. "That you don't think there were real aliens from, you know where, involved?"

"You read me right, 'Mr. Postmodern Politically Unfocused'..." BIGTIME bitterness, in that sarcastic return. Mahler dug fingers into his beard hard enough to rip some of it out by the roots. "Yeah: No aliens. Holograms, costumes, maybe some PSYSOP scam. It's well known U.S. intelligence PSYSOP pulled off some fake UFO abductions..."

"That doesn't prove they're all fake. You're suffering from major denial, man. Did you talk to Farraday? Was it human science that made Ceph? Come on, man. Get on the channel."

"Just don't talk to me for awhile..."

Fuck him, Quinn thought. I know what's real. This bus station: This bus station is real.

What could be more ordinary, more everyday, than a bus station? But after all that had happened, the place seemed strange, even otherworldly; a waiting room between worlds. Vagrants drifted through, burbling to themselves, footsteps echoing, each in his own world; her own world. A microwave oven at the snack bar whined warningly and then chimed in mockery: *Tried to warn you! Too late! Ding! Too late!*

Every so often an arcade game in the corner spoke up; it was some thirty years old, a game that had been sold and resold seven times. There was a picture of an old time movie actor on it: Keanu Reeves. *"Can you face it, Johnny Mnemonic? Can you play a game with your own brain?! I dare you! Enter virtual reality...and enter the HELL OF YOUR OWN MIND!"*

Who the fuck was Johnny Mnemonic?

An old woman with a face like a collapsed purse, toothless, one eye patched with a taped-on bandage, came and sat down next to Quinn, though there were dozens of empty seats. She coughed the cough of the dying. Poor old girl smelled like she was dead already. She turned to Quinn...

Uh oh, Quinn thought.

The old lady nodded.

Quinn looked at her. Her head drooped onto her chest. Then it lifted up, abruptly, and she turned to Quinn, and Lila's voice came out of her mouth.

"Quinn. Hi. It's Lila," the old lady said; her voice was a creaky old lady's but it was also a lot like Lila's.

Quinn was too tired and mentally burnt to argue the reality of the event. He turned to Zizz and Mahler - and saw they'd gone to the snack bar.

"How can you be Lila?" he asked, not knowing what else to say.

"I'm in a trance on the helicopter. We're getting close to landing. I promised to tell you guys some things. I've processed some of it - what the Meta told me, taught me, showed me. That's how I'm doing what I'm doing. They gave me the gift of willed altered states. You...you have the gift already."

"I do?"

"Those 'hunches' of yours are just the beginning, kiddo."

"What'd you find out about the Meta?"

"Things I can't describe.'

"But you just said -"

"And things I can try to describe. They come from another world - which is in another dimension, which is metaphysically linked to this world. They call themselves the..."

A series of pictures came into his mind then. Later he'd try to describe them to Zizz - but now they seemed like a series of energy flashes, lightning routed into symmetry.

That's...what they called themselves.

"...They can only help us for a time. Most of it's up to us. Willed effort toward the higher, toward more Presence, toward more Being, is what we're here for, and is the ladder of our evolution. So they can't do everything for us."

"Are you *possessing* this old lady, or what?"

"This woman died about five minutes ago, outside. I stepped in and borrowed her body."

"I read that comic book."

"It's funny you should say that - I learned from the Meta how much that is fantasy is real, and how much that is real is fantasy. We superimpose our models on the universe around us, and we mistake our models for the universe. On the other hand, the majority of what people suppose to be transcendant - psychics, channelers, most so-called gurus, the Elizabeth Clare Prophets, the Aleister Crowleys and Rajneeshes and Blavatskys, basically anyone who makes money from 'cosmic consciousness' - they're either frauds or self deluded or...A few, like Blavatsky, knew some of the truth, but they buried it a mile under all the claptrap..."

"So - the supernatural is real, and isn't real? Spirituality is real and isn't real? Cosmic consciousness is real and isn't real?"

"It's all 'yes and no'. But if you can incorporate both yes and no, can encompass both of them with the Living Question, then you can meet that Third Thing: the thing, 'the Force, Luke', that is produced at the interface of yes and no, positive and negative: the Higher."

"But why is there so much...bullshit? About...all the New Age vibratory color-healing flying saucer horseshit and all the..."

"Yes? The...?" She smiled crookedly; only one side of her mouth worked.

He made an all-inclusive sweeping gesture; there was so much to include. "You know. Channeled messages from Sirius and the Pleides, a thousand Uri Gellers and ten thousand psychic hotlines. Armies of fake gurus, legions of therapy frauds...Why?"

"Because the truth protects itself." She paused, as if she wanted that to sink in. "You don't get the truth unless you earn it - except sometimes, for the Higher's own reasons, when it's time, there is a kind of Grace...A kind of gift." She paused, picked up a MacDonald's Burger King Division sack lying crumpled and greasy under the bench, and spat phlegm into it.

"And that," she went on, "is what happened to me - And now I'm not what I was. I *did die*, on that boulder in the desert, just as dead as this old lady you're talking to...You have to die, before you can be reborn. You have to die to that part of yourself that -"

"Quinn?" Zizz said, coming up to him with a donut in each hand. "Uh...ask the lady...I'll ask her. Lady you want a donut?"

The old lady smiled toothlessly at her - and keeled over, muttering only, "The chopper's landing..." And that particular human body never ever said another word.

• • •

A journey through an aluminum-and-neoprene limbo: a bus ride to Chicago. Quinn had ridden a bus interstate with his older sister when he was six. He remembered it vividly. But now he was in the future, relative to that six year old kid. Buses in the future are like...

...buses. They are the same except they have their own peculiar fumes; the old buses had strong gasoline fumes, chemical toilet fumes, and the odors of the poor and the forgotten; the new buses have a faint natural-gas reek, chemical toilet fumes and the odors of the poor and the forgotten. The old ones were crowded, uncomfortable, jangling, and they had a taciturn human driver; the new buses are crowded, uncomfortable, jangling, and they have a taciturn non-human driver. The gum chewing driver of the old buses said only, "Naw, we don't stop there. Siddown if ya gettin' on." The satellite-directed, traffic-sensing mechanism says nothing but "Please insert ticket and take your seat. Please remain seated unless you have a bathroom chit issued by the permissions box on the back of the seat in front of you." Somewhere, a security guard watches the new bus on closed circuit camera.

Quinn slept a lot of the way to Chicago, anyhow. He had strange dreams, and hypnogogic visions of his mother's diamond wedding ring encircling the sun, the diamond on the ring talking to him in his mother's voice...

Chicago. A jet-shuttle to New York City; four anti-terrorism inspection delays later: JFK airport.

As per the phone calls, Cisco was at JFK waiting for Quinn at the gate...

"Quinn you crazy bot-fucker!" Cisco was half-Puerto Rican, half-Israeli. He was short, stocky; big brown lady-killer eyes with thick black lashes, mouth a little too wide, lips a little too thick, curly black hair, off-white East Indian shirt and rope-belt pants and sandals. He didn't bathe often enough but his sweat smelled like chicken soup so no one complained till it accumulated for a few weeks. He was twenty-four, a neo-beat poet, a self-styled mystic – a pain in the ass about it, too.

"Good to see you too, man. Don't ask me where I've been. Got to introduce my friends..."

"Hey bro I heard some rumors about Black Betty –"

"Cisco, whoa! Not here, ya fuckin' blip, jeezus...Anyway. Cisco: This is Mahler, this is Zizz –"

• • •

Burning choppers at dusk.

Farraday really enjoyed using the old Ford truck to push the precariously-balanced chopper into the gorge. "There's your black chopper, you bastards!" he chortled, as it rolled and bounced and then...it didn't disappoint him. "Yes Virginia," he said, almost dancing on the edge of the abyss, "there *is* a fireball. Look at 'er burn, Ceph!"

"Yes - spectacular." Still attached to Dodge's head, like a Medusa's mask made by a Dadaist, Ceph looked over the cliff's edge at the chopper burning below. "But we'd best leave before the explosion attracts attention...Campbell left the truck for us here this morning, it might have been noticed...We'll have to drive without lights..."

"MJ15 doesn't know this place we're going?" Farraday asked, walking back to the truck. Anatole and Lila sat in the shade of a rusting, wheel-less, target-shooting-pocked car-hulk someone had abandoned there decades before; they were both gazing at the same spot on the blank horizon, as if in silent communion.

"I don't *think* so..." Ceph said, steering Dodge around a scorpion. "Judging from my online contact with him, Campbell believes - or pretends he believes - that MJ15 doesn't know he's there. He thinks he's got them convinced he's left the State. These oldtime UFO researchers like Campbell keep their sanity by believing they've outsmarted the 'Men In Black'. It may be that MJ15 is holding off on doing anything more about Campbell because they think he may be of further disinformation value...Not that he knew how he was being used before...Yes, that's it - I see it, now, in Dodge's memories: MJ15 was waiting till Campbell should become useful again...what an awful taste Colonel Dodge's memories have: like bile and amphetamine, mixed together..."

• • •

Lyn was there. She was there!

Farraday's wife was a short, plump, pale woman with curly brown hair and a little nose and big eyes and a wide, impish mouth. She wore shorts, and a tank top. It looked like she'd lost a little weight.

She was smiling, crying, on the porch of the two-story adobe style house, which stood in the shade of a cliff of red sandstone: Campbell's place, since he'd had to move out of Vegas, after the raids: so Ceph told Farraday.

They got out of the bus and hurried up to the house.

The house looked like an old Mexican-Indian Ranchero, but that was on the outside. Inside it was a 'smart house', precision air conditioned and watchful, with its own well, an expensive ground-water purification system, and a full fledging of security surveillance fibers.

"Ah - you've brought my truck back intact. God bless you for it, and welcome," Campbell said from the front door.

The grand old man of Area-51 gadflies and UFO researchers, Campbell came out to greet them as Lyn ran to her husband. Campbell was a thin little old bachelor with a small white mustache and a distracted air about him.

Ceph remained in the truck for a moment, talking into a sat-uplink phone, trying to cover their tracks, Farraday supposed.

Campbell wore khaki shorts, an old, fading Dreamland t-shirt, and sandals. He had a cocktail in each hand, with little paper umbrellas.

"Just call me Campbell," he said. "You'd be Mike Farraday..."

The others introduced themselves. "Lovely. Who's drinking with me, if you please?" he asked. "Oh, those two are in their own quite enviable world..."

Farraday and Lyn were deep in embrace, seemed almost to have melted into one another.

"Mike..."

"Oh Lord, Lyn, you feel good..."

"*I'll* have a cocktail," Lila said.

"Have four or five," Campbell said, winking at Anatole. "And come in."

Then Ceph came out of the car and Campbell stared at him...took a step back...

"That...that's not an alien, is it? I mean - it's a man with some sort of....some sort of rubber *prosthetic costume thing* on his head -"

"Excuse me?" Ceph said, pretending offense, voice betraying humor. "You're describing me as a rubber costume thing?"

Campbell was now looking closer, seeing the way the "thing" on Dodge's head moved and how it regarded him. He could sense its aliveness. He drank down, in one long gulp, all of one of his cocktails.

"Squid...ventriloquism?" he ventured, gasping after the long drink.

Farraday laughed, turned to him, keeping an arm around Lyn. "'Squid ventriloquism!' Mr. Campbell, this is Ceph. His name is taken from 'cephaloped'. Physically he's a creation of the Zetans collaborating with human scientists...a squid-human-alien hybrid with some innovations like the neural interface tendrils he's using on Dodge here...This other individual he's riding about used to be Colonel Dodge. Dodge was an asshole. I mean, figuratively. I don't think Ceph literally uses him that way. Dodge, anyway, is effectively dead, now..."

"Ceph? I communicated with an entity who called himself 'Ceph' by modem...on-line...he claimed he was sending from inside S-4, with some kind of secure secret line...He told me a great deal..."

"That was Yours Truly," Ceph said. "Nice to meet you at last."

"Well...yes. You're really him, uh...it?"

"Yes. Him."

"I see." Still trying to absorb the Ceph concept, and then the Ceph-Dodge fusion reality, Campbell sucked down the other drink. His voice became only slightly slurred. "I've heard about Dodge. He's supposed to have various ranks, various secret-society hieratic functions. Looks to me like a bit of a come-down for him...You sure that...I mean, Ceph here, he's not...not some sort of put-up job? Some kind of...staged event illusion?"

"Would you like to examine my beak, my neural tendrils, my private parts?" Ceph offered. "I'll submit to an x-ray. I can offer you that, but I have to draw the line at vivisection..."

"No no, I'll just, ah, observe from afar...a safe distance..." He turned to Farraday. "Mike, did you say: 'physically' he's a hybrid creation? Why that qualifier...?"

"I happen to think that Ceph is *spiritually* way beyond the reach of the Zetans or the military."

Campbell nodded, now trying not to stare at Ceph but turning to look at him every few seconds anyway. "Well, do come in, all...I'm sorry...I'm trying not to eye-pop at...at Ceph but...but God, I need another drink..."

"Another?!" Anatole blurted, impressed.

• • •

Quinn in a dank, steamy, *un*airconditioned New York apartment; a rent-controlled flat sublet AltMed at the usual wildly inflated New York "rent"; cluttered with sagging furniture; the walls jittery with half-burnt-out video paintings, looping fuzzily through their sequnces; a noisy refrigerator; odds and ends of garage-made VR equipment in wiry tangles; a twenty year old Sony TV, the bulky kind; on its built-in VCR ran video clips of Black Betty...

Quinn drank ersatz iced tea, waiting for Mahler and Zizz to come back from their contacts with the Middle Man's middle men; and waiting for the amino/endocrine cap he'd taken to wash away his jet lag. Hoping that with his jet lag would go his depression, his doubts.

Maybe Mahler was right; maybe it had all been - what? - *appearances*, in Nevada...

If not, maybe he should try to do an altmed report for the channel and WWW, try to describe what he'd seen at Area 51, tell them all that'd happened. But he had zero proof; he didn't have so much as a snapshot. And it all sounded pulp fantastic to him now. He was in the classic sumphole that the few genuine close-encounterists had found themselves in: no one would believe you. Dorothy returned to Kansas: "And you were there, and you, and the Wicked Witch of the West and..."

Shit.

A documentarist's dream, and it was stuck in Dreamland...

Maybe what bothered him most, he realized, was that it didn't bother him: that is, he didn't care all that much about exposing the Alien Presence. He *should* - but somehow it was secondary to something he couldn't put his finger on. Something to do with the Meta; with the flashes of intuition; with the moment of voudounesque contact he'd felt in the base, when he'd opened the door for the Meta, made it possible for the Meta to cut the lights, the alarms...

All that seemed so much more important; taking part in the communion with the Meta seemed more important than *exposing* it. Something in him yearned to return to the heights, the perspectives of those moments. That most-peculiar connectedness.

He watched the videotape, the few seconds of a former President yammering with a good approximation of sincerity in his State of the Union address - and then Black Betty stepping into the shot; stepping her video-persona into the former President's restricted public space; taking public space back from authority, giving it back to the public, the Public personified by Betty. Tall and lean and smiling from a crystalized inner confidence, black robe sewn with silver multicultural symbols, she seemed to lean on the Bully Pulpit and stare at the president from within his Personal Space: a rudeness, a solecism become a political statement. The President was of course oblivious to her as she was a "media-terrorist" transmit-interruption, transmitted from one of her uplink vans; she could only be seen by the masses watching in 21st Century TV Land.

She raised a hand to the President's mouth and drew an imaginary line across it with her fingertip. A zipper appeared there, on the president's mouth, following her fingertip, and as it appeared she *zipped his mouth shut*, muffling his voice. Then

Black Betty turned to address millions of outraged, delighted, bemused, puzzled Americans...

"It's your turn to talk." She reached into empty space and plucked a sheaf of papers from it. *"Letters,"* she said, *"Printed out from the SubNet...* The SubNet: the quasilegal alternative to the FedControlled Internet. Microwave-transmitted bursts of data alternating with coded signals passed through the fiberoptic modem system as apparent "conversations"; constant changing of de-scrambling codes to confound the government. She read the letters aloud, *"'Black Betty, I don't know what to do or who else to write to. I'm a woman living in Atlanta but I have to travel a lot, and I have this job overseeing shipments from subcontractors overseas for a big company that makes sneakers and soccer balls, and I had to go out to the factories overseas to check on some shipments and there were all these kids in the sweatshops...they were making our kid's toys, and tennis shoes...and these little kids, some of them only six years old, are fed once a day and they're beaten if they slow down and they are given no holidays and they are not given any schooling and they die from malnutrition eventually and I don't know what to do because I was almost homeless myself, I couldn't get a job, because the ChrisFuns put pressure on people not to hire Muslims and I married a Muslim guy and he was a wonderful guy but he shot himself so I had to take it all on myself and if I quit my job who knows where I'll find another and my kids and I will be homeless but how can I work for these people who pretend they don't know their products are made by children who are sold into slavery and beaten and starved...'"*

Black Betty turned to the President. She unzipped his mouth which was saying: "...the economic stimulation necessary to provide a job base that will help re-unite the country necessitates a removal of outdated workplace health regulations..."

"Mr. Prez," Betty asked him, as he rattled on, *"Can you answer this woman's question? What can she do about this dilemma?"*

"...deep-seated economic necessity calls for a stimulation of the supply side of ..."

Quinn laughed.

Betty turned to the audience. *"He doesn't seem to hear*

me. Let's try another letter..." She zipped the President's mouth and read another printout. "'Black Betty, my family and I were forced out of our house in Northern California by FedControl shock troops who said they were "relocating probable refugees" - I guess it was some kind of evacuation because there was a Separatist force coming and they said we'd be out of this refugee camp after a week but it's been three and a half months and they just cut our rations in half...I have to go, my laptop battery is going down again because the uplink transmission drains it...there are seven of us in our tent and the others have to use it before I -' Well, the letter ends there."

She turned to the President and unzipped his mouth. "Mr. President? Can you help this person?"

" - re-allocation of Federal resources towards the more realistic goals of preparing for a military solution to the Separatist problem. This in turn will provide jobs through the sector that services military needs..."

"I guess not," Betty said.

Quinn shook his head, laughing, and turned off the VCR.

A subway rumbled by; he could feel it through the walls. Some of them still ran, it seemed.

Hopeless. This whole undertaking was hopeless. He was wasting his time. He needed to rest, after all he'd been through. He should go back to Florida. He shouldn't risk his ass for this woman, Black Betty. Her voice had been stilled months before, except for 're-runs'; but there would be others to take her place. It was a stupidly quixotic mission. Grow up, he told himself. Don't do it.

A rattling of keys and locks at the door. Zizz came in, then, with Mahler.

"We have a place to begin," she chattered, looking wired, half-dancing from foot to foot. "The Middle Man knows about the Fridge! Lot of people think that's where Betty is! You want to try it, Quinny, Quinnickle, Quinnsickle?"

Mahler looked at her. "'Quinnsickle'?"

Zizz hadn't wanted to go on looking for Black Betty, at first. She'd wanted Quinn to come and stay with her at her parents place and "get drunk for about three or four months."

"I thought," he said, "You wanted to go get drunk at your parents' house, Zizz, and blow this off?"

"Changed my mind, I'm psyched up now, *toh*-tuh-ly psyched. We can get her out! I feel it, I *feel* it!"

"Feeling's got nothing to do with it," Mahler said. "It's a calculated risk. It's not a risk we need you to take, Zizz. You can wait here, be our back-up, arrange a back way out of the town for us if we need it...You were going to blow if off anyway, so - "

"I wasn't very serious about blowing it off, I'm coming with you!"

Part of Quinn argued for giving up. But a deeper part of him felt, inexplicably, even more momentum to find Black Betty, now - as if in crossing some mystical interval he'd been propelled onward...

Hopeless, Quinn thought. Quixotic.

But the city called to him; the traffic noise hummed to him. The synchronicities had been piling up; someone walking by the apartment whistling the Black Betty themesong; Black Betty's picture left by a former tenant on the apartment fridge; a 'special' on *Media Terrorism: What You Can Do About It* on TV, earlier. (General Electric still owned NBC).

No, he told himself, it's time to grow up. Don't listen to all that fuzzy logic. It's fantasy. Your imagination. Rorschach inkblot effect. Don't do it. Hopeless. Quixotic.

"Sure," he said.

• • •

Quinn and Cisco and Zizz emerged from the subway station, laughing over some inane joke. They were laughing to cover being scared, because this was sniper territory.

Coming out behind them, Mahler wasn't laughing. Mahler was grim as a granite crag; wearing an olive drab T-shirt and olive-drab fatigues and colorless boots, he radiated disapproval of any departure from the Two-tone seriousness of Radical Purpose. He was far more comfortable here than in Nevada or California. This sort of place, this sort of mission, these sorts of risks, this city's *particular* bizarrities: they were more familiar to him. Or so he thought, at this stage. He had regained some of his confidence. The search for Betty gave Mahler purpose, returned definition to his worldview...

And Zizz...*I wasn't very serious about blowing it off. I'm coming with you.*

Mahler had argued all through the subway ride for her to

go back. But she'd insisted. *I've got special instructions...I've got something for Quinn...I have to come!* She wouldn't explain what she meant by special instructions; she enjoyed being mysterious when she could.

Cisco had been flirting with her since they'd met. He was their guide, tonight, to the Middle Man...

Zizz had changed her look for New York. Now her hair was bleached bone-white, blown out like some hungry tidal pool creature; her eyesockets were blacked with kohl. She could've co-starred in an episode of *Vampire Girls*. The Walkman capsule plugged into her right ear was gradually destroying auditory nerve-ends with one of the Shaped Static bands, *Fucked-Up Heaven*. The left ear clustered with rings and screws twisted right through the cartilage. Dangling from her left wrist was a sort of doll, four inches long, a primitive thing cunningly wrought of brightly colored electric wires and bits of circuitry; it had a little silver wire like a tongue sticking out of its mouth . . .

When Quinn looked at the little wrist doll, he thought of Seeking One and the saucers. He didn't know why.

Under a transparent plastic skirt Zizz wore a clinging grey body stocking woven with micro signal-sensitive image reactants that reproduced the imagery in TV signals randomly across her body; a news flash about the black-out in lower Manhattan was TV-imaged across her torso, the newscaster, his head warped to the contours of her belly, was mouthing soundlessly while above him a sex-com's nude actress did a comic double-take as her father came on to her.

Quinn looked again at the pendulum swinging doll on Zizz's wrist.

The saucers...Seeking One... Somehow the fetish on her arm made him think of Dodge, of Ceph, of Sullivan's death and the alien with his arm around Kian and...

Mahler argued that in a concrete, objective sense, it had never happened. Except maybe Ceph, Mahler admitted that Ceph had been real - but he'd been the result of military experiments, not aliens.

Quinn had given up arguing.

And Zizz - she'd been trying to forget what had happened in her own way: She was getting loaded. She'd been hiding it, because she knew Quinn didn't approve of drugs: his

Dad, the singer Izzy, had been a recovering drug addict, every so often blundering into relapse.

Trying not to wonder where the crosshairs were centered, they climbed gratefully from the rancid, moldering underground into the sloppy heat of the night.

"Didn't use to be this warm here, this time of year," Cisco remarked.

"Global warming," Mahler said.

They'd walked through a pedestrian tunnel that led from the Sixth Street station to this one. The blue emergency lighting system for the subway tunnels was running, so there was light down there, but it was infused with another kind of darkness: the clammy darkness of screwed-down, bridled fear.

Quinn thought about the Fridge: the prison where Black Betty was supposed to be 'on ice'. It had to be worse for her...

They stood around in a small, worn-out park, sixty square feet of packed dirt, expiring grass, graffiti'd benches, young trees shriveled like burnt matches from acid rain.

The park was in the triangle between several intersecting streets. It wasn't completely dark here; a web of light stretched from the lit-up part of the city, north of Houston Street. And there was a little illumination from two light-storage billboards–during the day their pigment soaked up sun-power, gave it out at night with the brash glow of commerce – advertising the Panam low-orbit shuttle *(Ninety minutes to Paris!)* and, across the square from the Panam billboard: *Protect your health with Palmer Vreedeez's Intravenous Sex: Makes partners obsolete!*

The shopfronts were dark. Quinn could make out a People's Republic of China Chinese-food franchise, with its cartoon of a jolly Mao in a chef's hat; discount boutiques, shops selling remaindered consumer junk; and the double-padlocked entrances to the big underground malls.

On the outer walls of the locked down public restroom overlapping partisan posters demanded support for various sides of the Civil War.

Quinn and friends paused to lean on the rusting iron frames of children's swings, the swing-chains missing. Nearby stood metal-mesh trashcans crimped like cigarette butts, overflowing with plastic and tin and scrap-paper: the shed skins of slithery junk food.

In the distance, the sirens: rising and falling.

How long before the Feds checked out Funs territory? Quinn wondered. Or before one of the blackout riots spread to this neighborhood?

Maybe it depended on who had attacked the power station this time. Which Faction: Christian Funs, Muslim Funs, anesthets, Movement, Media Thugs, whomever . . . there were conflicting rumors.

Quinn turned to Mahler, and turned his own question back on him: "What now?"

Mahler rumbled, "We have to wait here. This is the edge of the Funs territory." He nodded toward a luminous-blue Muslim Fundamentalist slogan sprayed in Arab script across the asphalt park path. "They'll contact us. Or they'll decide . . ." He let it trail off, and they knew he meant the snipers.

Looking around, Quinn spotted more of the Funs tags, fresh-looking, overlaid on the other graffiti, and rain-spotted posters of the boyish, spectacled Ayatollah Daseheimi slapped up with static-stick guns on walls, benches.

He wondered where the crosshairs were now . . . on the back of his neck, on his forehead, the base of his spine?

Maybe the rescue pact Cisco had arranged was a mistake; maybe it was childish and arrogant and unrealistic, even with the video key-cassette Cisco's Fridge contact had stolen (thinking that, he absently touched the bulge of the little cassette in his shirt pocket). Even if it worked, it was just *fried* to think they could break Black Betty out of the Fridge.

But it was something else: it was following through. It was commitment. Fuck Dodge and his ilk anyway.

New York always made Quinn think about his father; Dad had loved the town. "Show where you're going with your clothes," Quinn's Dad had told him. "Start outside, work inward." One of his Dad's non-adhesive platitudes. His Dad, now, had been dressed by professional designers before he hit the stage; had a superstitious faith in costuming.

Tonight, Quinn kept the faith. He wore all black: a black T-shirt, black guerrilla baggies tucked into black skinhead boots. The color of commitment.

Because it was Black Betty who'd first made him really look at himself. It was Black Betty who had shown him what commitment could be . . .

So he stayed, and waited to see if the snipers would kill him.

Zizz, whistling and talking to herself in a sing-song whisper, swinging on the postage-stamp playground's monkey bars now, seemed to have forgotten all about the snipers, and the fact that this was Muslim territory.

"What do we gotta hang he-errrre for huh, Mahl-errr?" Zizz asked, pouting, snorting a hit of designer meth from her thumbnail-implanted stashbox.

"Stopped pretending you're not getting fucked up, Zizz?" Quinn asked.

"Was I pretending...? *Sorrrr*-reeee."

"I hate the way she talks when she gets like this," Mahler muttered. "Sounds like a ten year old. She could get us killed, loaded like this."

"I don't know -" Cisco said, musingly. He was admiring the way she filled out her bodystocking. He wanted her around. Can't get into pussy that's not on the premises "Maybe there's something sorta, like, disarming about it. Might be safer if the local tribes-types don't take us *too* seriously...."

"Yeah-eah! Might be safer!" Getting off, Zizz did a few listless dance steps to something on her ear-tape. "But you know what? We can't find Black Betty like this, this is bullll-*shii*-iiit."

Mahler glared at her. "You think we're going to a concert? This is *Funs* territory. We can't go through it till they check us out."

"Maybe," Cisco said, turning a frozen smile at the rooftops, wondering where the Funs were, "this isn't the time. Maybe it's, like, not the right vibe." He turned to Quinn. "Could be predicated on whatever, like, vibe-patterns you guys brought with you from out west. You going to ever tell me what happened out there?"

"Oooooohhhhhhhhh," Zizz said, "what hap-pened...If you even *halfway* knew...." Her pupils dilating and shrinking just as her mouth opened and closed. "You'd...you'd *plotz*...you'd-"

"Well - what *did*?" Cisco asked.

"We're not sure, so we can't really say," Quinn said.

Mahler nodded. "Definitely." He changed the subject. "The time to get Black Betty out is now. We have the in at the

HopeScope tonight, isn't that right, Cisco?" Mahler glanced around, trying not to look directly at the rooftops.

"Big mother risks, man," Cisco said, looking round, licking his substantial lips.

"We don't risk anything more than Black Betty risked for all of us," Mahler said, with radical piousness. "She knew what would happen eventually if she kept blowing the whistle on FedControl, Cisco. Media terrorism - what bullshit. Media truth for once -"

"I know, man," Cisco said, trying to forestall a political diatribe. "It's not that I don't think we owe it to her, it's just, I don't know, the aspects, the omens, they're not–"

Quinn couldn't stand any more. "*Will* you shut the fuck up, Cisco?" he hissed. "If you didn't wanna risk it, you shouldn't have come."

"Who you mad at, *Quii*-iiinnn?" Zizz asked, grinning at him. "You're mad at Cisco because you're scared too huh, don't want him to talk about it *huhhhh?*" She put her hand on his arm. "Me too." With those two words, her vocal affectation vanished.

She irritated him. But he liked the way she made the effort, at least, to see into him. Maybe she'd understand him, if they got more involved.

Involved? Sure. Like they were going to survive this. Breaking into the Fridge . . .

At first, Quinn and the others actually, honestly, really believed they could break Black Betty out of the country's most impregnable prison. The incandescence of their outrage at what had happened to their heroine blotted out sweet reason with its glare. Now, though . . . now, taking the first step of Mahler's plan, they began to think about it, to turn it over and over, fingering it like a blind man with a 3-D puzzle; and they knew it was insane, there was no getting into the Fridge, except for the One Way entry that Black Betty had.

But no one wanted to be the first to say, Let's blow it off, this is impossible, this is the wrong way on a one-way street, Black Betty can't ask this of us . . .

There was something more: Quinn's feeling of unreasonable optimism. Something he'd picked up when that chopper had lifted him away from the base near Area 51.

Zizz said, "I'm tired of waiting. Can't we contact them or

something?" She'd sensed she was irritating the others with the dope-girl persona, and she'd dropped it. Magic.

Mahler was peering into the shadows of the storefronts across the street. "We're doing that. We *are* contacting them. You're supposed to stand here, in this spot, if you want to talk to them, and then their *Mufti* comes out. Or they snipe you."

"Or both, in proper sequence," someone said, behind them.

They turned, half expecting to be shot before they got a good look at whoever it was. But the H&K laserscope equipped carbine hung on its strap over the little man's left shoulder, casual as a carrybag, pointed at the ground. He could afford to be casual, because of the snipers.

They were *his* snipers.

The Funs guerrilla was about five foot six, slender; there were sharply defined veins on his hands and forearms; he wasn't as dark as Quinn had expected. He wore a white short sleeve shirt, neatly creased black trousers. Only the boots were military. He looked like the manager of a Middle Eastern restaurant. Maybe he was that, too. He had whitemetal wire rim glasses, like the boy Ayatollah–the Ayatollah didn't approve of eye implants: he believed they could be used by the implanters for mind control. The boy Ayatollah had a tradition of paranoia to live up to.

The Fun said, matter-of-factly: "I'm Sadiq. We were told you were coming. We were not told why. You are the children of our enemies."

He looked at Zizz. A television PAV chasing a lawbreaker wound its way over her hip and across her belly; the climactic genital-slashing scene from *Realm of the Senses* played on her thigh. "Ah. Charming. You are decadents."

He left the implication hanging, swaying, kicking.

Before their journey had begun together, Zizz might have enjoyed being called a 'decadent'. Fin de Siecle cool. But not now; now, Quinn could see, it bothered her, and not because of the danger here: she was growing. She wore the drugs she'd taken badly: they no longer suited her...

"Why I should trust you, I wonder," Sadiq said musingly. "Maybe I have had brain damage recently? No." He tapped his head. "Still there."

Sadiq, Quinn thought. It didn't feel like an Iranian name. Maybe it was true: that the boy Ayatollah had united the Arabs and Persians...

"We want to help Black Betty," Zizz said, serious now. "She said a lot of things, in her media break-ins, that were, you know, supportive of your cause."

"The Middle Man agreed to help us," Mahler said.

"And tonight all the transport's fucked up, like," Cisco said. "We can't get through to HopeScope, where the Middle Man is, without going through your piece of things."

They were all in a hurry to explain. They could feel the crosshairs.

Sadiq made a cone of his lips. "Black Betty. You are friends of hers?"

Mahler nodded. "We work with her. For everyone in this area, against FedControl. We're Alternative Channel."

"You might be CIAD." Meaning CIA Domestic.

Mahler shook his head. "Alternative Channel. When we get her out, we'll put her on the air."

"Anyone could say this," Sadiq pointed out.

"Black Betty used to say..." Quinn hesitated, not sure if he were saying the right thing. "...used to say about Islamic, um, activists: `Terrorism is easy to condemn when you've got other avenues open to you.' She was trying to help you."

Sadiq nodded, a flicker of amusement at the corners of his mouth.

He said, "The Fedayeen know this saying. We know Black Betty. We don't know you. We almost shot you. You were standing in the correct place, but you did not have your hands on your head. That is the rest of the signal, and this rest of signal states that you are unarmed."

Instantly, Mahler, Cisco, Quinn, and Zizz put their hands on their heads.

Quinn's mouth went dry. They'd agreed to come with Cisco because he was the guy in the Black Betty Movement who was supposed to know all the ins and outs over here. Only, it looked like he didn't.

Quinn said, "Sorry. Didn't know. Sorry."

"Did we mention we were sorry?" Zizz said.

"Shut up, Zizz," Mahler growled.

Sadiq motioned with his gun, "You'll come with me."

• • •

They were at Campbell's ranchero two days before Farraday noticed that Dodge was dying.

It was an hour after sunset; the night wasn't yet as dark as it soon would be. There was a hooked moon, up above, that looked sharp as a razor.

Dodge/Ceph was in the bathroom. Ceph was having increasing difficulty making what was left of Dodge use the facilities. The others sat in comfortable canvas chairs on the back terrace, drinking cocktails, listening to desert creatures call to one another with rattles and coughs and trills; breathing in the spice of the desert's austere perfumes.

Farraday held his wife's hand. They felt the night air on their skin like diaphanous silk.

They'd had a moment of tension a few hours earlier. Campbell's beeper had gone off; his surveillance equipment warning him. They'd taken refuge inside and indeed a black helicopter had flown past - but it hadn't changed course to inspect the ranchero, hadn't shown any interest in them.

"I'm well out of their territory," Campbell had said, giving the all-clear. "But I see them once in a while. They have another base out there in the desert somewhere, I think..."

Now, Campbell serenely sipped a martini and watched the starry sky with the air of a generous proprietor. They were his stars, but you were welcome to them too.

Anatole sipped a virgin Margarita. He hadn't said much, since they'd arrived. He spent all his time with Lila. Sometimes she whispered to him; sometimes he whispered...to things that weren't there.

Dodge/Ceph joined them, walking like a drunk. Ceph gave the appearance of an amateur stilt-walker, sometimes, with Dodge's body his stilts.

Ceph eased Dodge down in a chair. The skin on Dodge's right arm seemed to be peeling away; his pallid hands twitched.

Was that something rotting, Farraday smelled, coming from Dodge?

"Hope so," he muttered.

"What, hon?" Lyn asked.

"Nothing. Ceph - how long you planning to stay on your

mount, there?"

"Why until he dies. Which will be..."

"Soon, I'm guessing, right?"

"Quite right. Tonight, or tomorrow night. Soon. I kept him in case I needed him to issue some orders...and I did have him issue a few, from 'a safe house in Las Vegas', through source-coded modem. I do believe he's kept Majestic's 'Men In Black' off our trail..."

"Does...did...Dodge have that much authority?" Lila asked.

"He did and does. You see, he's not a Colonel. He's a four star General."

"You mean he was busted?" Campbell asked.

"No. He's been a General all along. But his real rank is secret. He is one of three *human* directors of MJ15; there are others who are Zetan. The other two humans are scientists. Ostensibly civilian. But no one in MJ15 is really civilian..."

"The time has come, the walrus said..." Campbell said. It was a sort of question, directed at Ceph.

"Yes the time has come. It's time I told you as much of the story as I know. A lot of it I learned from what MJ15 calls the Meta; much I learned by probing 'Colonel' Dodge...I'll start by telling you this: that MJ15 is an arm of an ancient organization, a branch of which is in some places known as the Priory of Scion..."

"You mean the Illuminati?" Campbell asked, eyebrows raised.

"Oh no - nothing so mundane as that," the land octopus replied.

• • •

Quinn was crossing the street in southeastern Manhattan on that warm, humid night, hands on his head, with a terrorist submachine gun at his back–when he saw the luminous skullhead of the vinyl batwinged cop-car banshee.

First he saw the PAV, the Police Assault Van, on its way to a blackout riot; it was pushing a double pool of headlight glow ahead of it as it screamed by on Delancey.

Glimpsed flashing past, the armored cop-car was a grey blur, mohawked with a streak of red glow; its cherrytop a con trail of hellish shine against the dirty darkness of the sweltering, blacked-out inner city.

And then came the hallucination, vision, or whatever it was, rising above the building the PAV had passed behind...

Weightless, but big as an armored car, the banshee spread its vinyl batwings and lifted its fiery head over the roof-rim; a UFO in pop cultural drag, it pulled itself into the sky, and Quinn saw that its head was, quite literally, as follows:

A translucent-red human skull shining with the whirling electric lights that were its brains, its mouth a sirening bullhorn, its body a bulked-out pterodactyl of studded grey metal.

Quinn gaped, and looked at the others... but their eyes were focused entirely on survival, on getting across the street. He suspected they couldn't see it even if they looked.

I'm over the edge, he thought. All that stuff I saw in Nevada. I'm hallucinating. Shit. This was triggered off by getting involved with that *thing* that healed Lila...But the batwing thing - That's no UFO. That's...

I'm seeing my own fucking mind....

The terrorist jabbed the gun-muzzle into Quinn's back, and he looked away from the thing in the sky, which faded because he looked away. Under the gun, Quinn lurched on, crossed the street.

In a store-front opposite, one of Sadiq's men stood in the doorway with an auto-shotgun in his hands.

Quinn thought: *An auto-shotgun. God, what that'd do to you–* Sadiq prodded him. They entered the old storefront.

The windows of the storefront had been boarded over; its entrance was choked with trash. Inside, in the dim, waxy light of a chem-lantern, Quinn saw stacks of cardboard boxes against the flaking plaster walls; a few on the floor were open, and he saw that they contained racks of import-banned silicon wafers, chips, AI brain-units, cartons of untaxed cigarettes and syntharettes and liquors. The black market paid for the Muslim Funs' weaponry.

Sadiq picked up the lantern and led the way; two other men came behind, herding them into a crowded back room that contained a desk, a dead computer terminal, two phones, and the accumulated reek of unfiltered cigarettes and strong coffee. The two dark men stood in the doorway, smoking.

The vision of the banshee had left Quinn shaken - he had never had a vision of that vividness before.

But as he looked around...

Being trapped in a small room with hostile guerrillas armed to the teeth somehow put everything else out of his mind.

Sadiq hung the lantern from a hook in the corner of a ceiling. The lantern swung slightly on its hook, making the shadows in the room leap and yaw.

In the same corner, Sadiq bent to fish through a heap of posters and Arab-lettered newspapers; he drew out a flat cardboard box. He carried it to the desk and opened it, laid the contents on the desk.

It was a video painting, switched off. A rectangular chunk of glass and plastic, two feet by three feet by one inch. "Black Betty's sister was Movement, and we knew her," Sadiq said, looking up at them. "She gave us this painting. She said everyone in the Movement knew it by heart. If you are Movement, you know it."

Quinn looked at Mahler and Zizz and Cisco.

Cisco shrugged.

Quinn thought: *We didn't say we were Movement...we said we were Alternative Channel and he assumed the rest from the context...But maybe if I say I'm not Movement I'm fucked...*

Breathless, Quinn stared at the painting as Sadiq switched it on. There were many Movement video paintings. But there was one he knew by heart, because he'd made it himself, at NYU. And Black Betty had been a bit vain about it . . .

The painting flickered through a series of street-shots (Quinn knew immediately: it was his) outside the squat slums; high contrast images of weirdly well-dressed kids who lived in the squats gathered at oil-barrel fires; of Smoky "the Ghost" Casparino–his face hidden, but Quinn knew Smoky's spray-painted flightjacket–buying a gun from D'Angelo, whose face was white from heavy chipping on china synth; a skateboard gang showing off their moves for the camera; old Mrs. Pesca with her sawed-off shotgun and collapsed grin. And paced through the loop, images of Black Betty: tall, angular, jet-black skin, cheek punctured with a stud imprinted *NFC*–No Federal Control–in red on black. Black Betty ministering to the kids, the black marketeers, the beleaguered old ladies, talking till she was hoarse, telling them that FedControl wasn't all powerful, it was going to fail in its drive to move them out of Manhattan and into the little security-cop police states they called Highrise

Relocation . . . Telling them that Federal Control had promised their boros to the wealthy development barons . . . Telling them it was just plain stupid to trade home and something like freedom for a cop-haunted high rise that would slide into a slum in two years.

Flick flick flick, three moving images just that fast, and every fourth one was of Black Betty.

Sadiq stabbed a button on the frame, freezing the painting on an image of Black Betty setting up a corner video re-education booth, vidding the slums the truth about FedControl's part in the Brazilian War and what happened to anyone who joined the Army and what went down in the refugee camps in San Francisco ...

"What comes after this?" Sadiq asked.

"There are lots of Movement paintings," Mahler said desperately. "We can't–"

"It'll be a shot of a kid watching a TV-graffiti pattern with Black Betty's name in it," Quinn interrupted. He turned to Mahler. "I oughta know. I shot it myself."

Sadiq hit the button. The painting moved on, and a small child with his back to the camera sat watching as video-animated words snaked in superimposition over the President's face: *Black Betty says only fools listen to liars . . .*

Sadiq nodded. "Okay." He pointed the gun at Quinn. "Now tell me with complete truth, what is it you are to do, eh? What? Because I know you've lied to me. You are Movement, but you are lying."

Quinn looked at the muzzle of the gun. He could hear his heart hammering far away somewhere, like a distant construction site noise. "Uhhh . . . We told you. We're going to get Black Betty out."

"Black Betty is in the Fridge," Sadiq said, an impatient adult with a dense child. The flickering light from the video painting lit his face from below, shifting its planes in eerie dislocation. "No one can be broken out from there. If you say that is what you do then you are stupid or liars."

Quinn looked at Mahler, eyebrows lifted. Mahler chose to tell the truth, as he saw it. "We're going to see the Shaman. The Middle Man. But not because I think there's anything to his, you know, ah, claims about the Spirits of the Urban Wilderness, any of it. I think they've got some kind of hardware or wetware access to the FedControl grid. Whatever they've got," Mahler went on, talking fast, "it seems to work. Black Betty herself swore it worked for her once. Only, the Middle Man is probably a schizophrenic so he interprets things . . . you know, mystically."

Quinn thought about the banshee. *Spirits of the Urban Wilderness* . . . but all he said was, "Mahler made arrangements to go to the Middle Man because he thinks the Middle Man could get Black Betty out of the Fridge. We got to get there at a certain time. And the blackouts brought the riot squads down, they've sealed off the other ways through. The only way left to get through is . . . here. Through your territory. We need an escort so your people don't shoot us."

"A way to get into the Fridge." Sadiq's nostrils flared, his eyes hardened. "If it's true, then you will take our people out, too. We have four in the Fridge." He fingered the gun meaningfully.

"I told you, Mahler," Cisco muttered. "The vibes were–"

"No, this is *great!*" Zizz broke in, doing a little spastic dance that made two of the guerrillas look at each other and snort. "We could get them out, too! We could–"

Mahler shook his head. "One will be hard enough. We have a video key for her cell. We need the Middle Man to get us past the guards and failsafes and cameras. We only have one video key."

"A bomb!" Zizz suggested gleefully. "We could get in, then blow up their com-pu-uuu-ter! Then maybe all the cells would open up and–"

Quinn groaned. He felt the sweat sticking his shirt to his back. The room seemed chokingly close. "Zizz," Quinn hissed, "stop trying to help before you help us into even deeper shit."

"No, it's not a bad idea," Sadiq said, looking at Zizz with a new respect. "A bomb in their master computer."

Mahler shook his head so hard you could hear his beard rustle. "No! Listen–"

"No, *you* listen–if you are going to break out your people," Sadiq said, grinding the words between his teeth, "and you want our help, then you will break out our people, too! We will provide the explosive."

He had lifted the SMG, was pointing its muzzle at Mahler's face.

Zizz's expression shifted radically in a split second, from glee to a grim *uh-oh.* She saw that she'd blown it.

She moved closer to Quinn. Out of the corner of his eye he saw her take the little wire-doll dangling from her wrist . . .

She jabbed its tongue-wire into Quinn's forearm. Quinn jerked his arm away, sucked in his breath, and felt . . .

A flash of white light; a wave of white heat.

Quinn went rigid. Electrified within. Paralyzed. He felt a Presence. Someone . . .

Click. Suddenly he was standing outside himself. He was tethered but detached, off in a dark corner, unseen, apart from the others, watching himself, seeing an expression on his face that had never been there before.

He couldn't smell or hear anything—except he heard his own voice. It was talking nonsense. No, it was talking in Arabic, to Sadiq. He, Quinn, was speaking Arabic. He had no idea *how* to speak Arabic. Not one lesson. But he was doing it. And he knew what the words meant in English:

"Sadiq! The Fridge is wall-to-wall biomonitoring. The prisoners are all in restraints, on IV medifeeds and spinebox. They can't move unless the spinebox moves them. The cyberguards watch them, they never sleep, they never take a break, they're always there—if you destroy the master computer the subsystems might not shut down, they might feed the prisoners overdoses of medication, the guards might get confused and kill them - the bottom line is, if you destroy that computer the system will break down and the people plugged into it will die. Including your men." Cisco and Mahler were staring at him; at the physical part of him, the part that was talking. Outright amazed.

Sadiq got over his surprise and replied in Arabic, "Why should we help you if it does not release our people? If we're involved and the Feds find out, they'll push us even harder. Already they fabricate this blackout to harass us, to try to drive us out. Already they raid us twice a month, when they can find us. To provoke them further would not advance our cause, not now. It would be too much pressure. In our position, we have learned how much trouble we can make and still survive. We're not fools."

"Black Betty struggles for your cause. She spoke up against the anti-Muslim INS rulings. She spoke up and said that you were being harassed, driven to urban war, because the Christian Fundamentalists are beginning to take over government; she said you were being framed and prosecuted and jailed and deported only because of the prejudice against Muslims. She spoke up so many times they had to get rid of her. So they planted illegal chemicals in her house, bomb-making equipment. The irony is unspeakable. Black Betty, a bomber! Countless were the times at the Movement meetings when she argued against bombs. She said bombs couldn't discriminate civilians. But FedControl framed her, they said she was a terrorist bomber, and that gave them the authority to put her in the Fridge, to sentence her to conditioning. She spoke up for you, for all of us–and they kidnapped her! Superficially legal–but kidnapping, Sadiq! Surely Allah tells you now what you must do . . ."

Sadiq gaped at him.

Then Quinn–the watching, detached part of Quinn–drained into a red tube, and passed through a wall of pain. Through white light, a wave of heat . . .

Click.

He was back in himself, bathed in sweat, shaking, but alone in his body now.

Everyone was staring at him.

"This one," Sadiq said, slowly, in English, "has cared enough to learn our language. And he has spoken good sense. He has moved me. I am the Mufti and that is my judgment."

• • •

"...The aliens, you see, the Zetans, have, as many have guessed, been interfering with humanity since before humanity was humanity..."

As Ceph spoke in the dimness, his beautiful voice was like something called up at a seance, coming from the dark Rorschach-splash shadow of his silhouette where Dodge's head should be.

Farraday, too, was thinking that it was surprising what you could get used to...

Overhead, three falling stars scratched white streaks on the celestial sphere, as Ceph went on:

"...They imprinted some of their own blueprint onto the first primates whom they supposed would otherwise have died out. They have a blind spot, these stick-sketches of men from

Zeta Reticuli.

"They could not see the hand of God at work. They were, and are, the consummate scientists. Yet they were aware of the power of religion...and they were aware of certain metaphysically potent genetic phenomena: phenomena the Zetans themselves took to be mere accident..."

"What kind of 'metaphysical genetic phenomena'?" Campbell asked.

"Only this: a gene that makes it possible for a man to be partly a God..."

CHAPTER TEN

BLACK BETTY BLAM BUH LAM

A sloppy breeze, moldy-damp from the East River, oozed between the ruined tenements, and carried some heat away from Quinn and Mahler and Zizz and Cisco and the Mufti as they trudged down the middle of the rubbled street.

Quinn felt strange. Still a little dislocated; like he was here and not here. Zizz did this to him, somehow. The doll. Its wire tongue . . .

Quinn dropped back and whispered to Zizz, "What did you do to me back there? You fucking inject me or *what?*"

Zizz bit her lip. "I got the thing from Cisco's friends, the ones who told us where to find the HopeScope - they said they got it from a woman called the Fetish Broker..."

"Who?"

"The Fetish Broker...she works for the Middle Man...I just did what the Fetish Broker told them I should do. They said if there was an emergency, I...well, see, the Fetish Broker sent the doll around when Cisco made the deal but they asked me not to talk about it unless we had to *use* it–"

The Mufti turned and hissed, "No talk!" He gestured toward the rooftops.

The buildings were picked out with a little starlight, and with the soft edges of firelight from clearings in the rubble: smudges of red on the black-pocked wall of night.

Faint fragments of Arabic and Farsi reached them from the rooftops as they moved through Lower East Manhattan. They were still in Muslim Funs territory but only barely.

The precarious cease fire had crystallized the Muslim and Christian zones on their respective sides of Clinton Street. National Guard barriers and checkpoints stood a block West; nearer were the stripped, wheelless chassis of military trucks and the burned shells of blasted cars, humped in shadow like desiccated carcasses.

Quinn stiffened every time they came to a cross-street. Intersections exposed them to the strong possibility of sniper fire from the Christian sectors. Tonight of all nights, with the cops and soldiers massively occupied by the black-out riots, would be a great night to start something, to pick off a few Allah-Kazams, in the ChrisFun vernacular...

And the Christian snipers wouldn't know at this distance that Quinn and friends didn't belong in their gunsights.

Come to think of it, even if they knew who they were, they'd probably shoot anyway: Quinn's bunch came from the Registered Socialist boro.

Quinn almost wished someone would open fire. Something to break up the flow of events, the current that tugged him deeper into this thing.

He was so scared he didn't recognize the sensation at first. He'd never been *that* scared before. It was a ball of shaking tautness in his gut, like a rabbit having a heart attack.

Something had taken him over, back there. It was gone now, but... he felt its footprints on his nervous system. And that scared him more than bullets or bombs or even the Fridge.

Get real, he told himself, you're liable to get a fucking bullet in the brain, any second now...

But no one fired at them. Ten minutes later, Mahler said, "Here's the HopeScope."

It was a bank. A derelict bank.

"This is it," the Mufti said. "Now I go." He told them, in Arabic, to go with God, and then he was gone himself, around a corner.

"Mahler - this is the HopeScope? It's a busted up old bank!" Quinn said.

"Here," Mahler said, handing him a plastic card. "Put it in the Instanteller slot."

"What? That thing's trashed–"

"Just do it. You're going in."

"Why me?"

"I don't know, Quinn . . . They said it had to be you." Mahler was looking at him strangely. A little angrily. "What did you do back there? Babbling in . . . I mean, you didn't tell me that you could speak Arabic, or Farsi, or whatever it was..."

"*I can't*. I don't know what happened."

Mahler shifted his weight and looked at the bank, frowning. "I don't like this mumbojumbo. Occultism is perverted religion and religion is social paralysis; first the flying saucer flimflam artists, and now this. Urban myths with teeth. I thought the Middle Man was . . ." He shook his head. He reached out and closed Quinn's hand around the slip of paper and the card. "Fuck. Just do it."

"Tell you the truth, I'm kind of–"

"We're all scared, Quinn. But do it for Black Betty."

Quinn took a deep breath. He looked at Zizz. Saw her swallow; saw her skull-eye makeup was streaked. He found himself wanting to take her in his arms, and just lie down with her somewhere, and hold her, and then hold her some more.

Now? Are you kidding?

But the feeling lingered.

He reached into his shirt pocket, took out the video key-cassette, and handed it to her. Some instinct told him: *Give it to her and not Mahler.*

Their hands touched for a moment and he found himself giving her fingers a dry, shaky squeeze.

He remembered their intimacy in the cell, in Nevada. They hadn't shared another such moment. Maybe they were too dazed. Or maybe he wasn't sure how real it had been.

Quinn turned and made himself walk up to the grime-streaked face of the old ATM. He looked at it dubiously, not expecting it to be functional in any way at all.

The ATM was in a bank whose roof had collapsed; whose windows were blind with graffiti, walls streaked with burn-marks.

But he inserted the card, the teller lit up, and he looked at the piece of paper.

Numbers. Random numbers.

He felt a ripple go through him, heard a sort of buzzing, and smelled something burning. There was a faint vibration at the top of his head.

That's all: then all the doors of his perception silently closed.

"Quinn!" someone shouted, nearby. Was it Zizz? "You...are you..." The voice faded, the way Seeking One's had, and he fell through the street as if it had become a cloud, a cloud of atoms, which is what it was, and he fetched up in a river of darkness...and drifted...drifted on the river of darkness...It carried him into tunnels that had never known light, tunnels carved into a substance that was hardened blackness itself...

Light. From somewhere -

From - the other side of his eyelids. So he opened them.

A buzzing fluorescent light. A moth thumping itself on the light.

His head ached, and he didn't know where he was. A fluorescent light overhead, and another along the ceiling a little ways, blinking and going *Zzt-zzt-zzt.*

He sat up and looked around. Long rectangular room, forgotten grey-green lockers against the far wall; rusty pipes overhead and rust-flecked puddles of water on the floor. Wooden benches, like the one he was sitting up on. A locker room, for sure. What did a locker room have to do with a bank?

No Mahler or Cisco or Zizz. Quinn had fallen asleep standing up, never felt himself hit the ground, and then he was here, sitting against the wall, all alone. How? Some kind of hypodermic dart? Had be been drugged?

There was someone there. Someone sitting a little ways from him.

The guy hadn't been there a second before. But that couldn't be right, his brain was probably fogged from the whatever-it-was. The guy must've come in while he was spacing out.

He was just another guy. Street sleeper, looked like. Matted hair, matted beard, so grimy he shared a grey-black skin with the city. Long horny yellow nails. No shoes, clothes unrecognizable from sleeping in them; you couldn't tell the shirt from the coat. For sure he probably smelled bad, if you got any closer: the guy sat slumped against the wall just out of the direct light, about eight feet away.

Must be another devotee, another supplicant to the HopeScope. Supposedly the Middle Man helped anybody he chose, and he chose almost at random.

"You okay now?" the guy asked.

"I guess."

"What you going to get?" The guy asked.

"Help a friend. Shit, my head hurts. Uh - how about you?"

"Kinda obvious isn't it? Someplace to rest my butt and maybe a grade D credit rating. That ain't much to ask the fuckin' Wizard of Oz here for."

"You could've applied to move into the Socialist boro, they'll give you-"

"I look like a fucking Red to you?"

"Guess not. Me neither. But they got good rent control there . . . How'd we get in here anyway?"

"With a headache. That's all I know."

"I don't even know if I'm awake. Or if this place is-"

"It's not a hallucination. Even the thing you saw tonight, in the sky, that wasn't hallucination, that hallucination. That was the Higher Reality of the events you were caught up in, taking shape as an 'object'. You're not hallucinating. You're here. I'm here."

"How'd you know I saw anything?"

The tramp rattled on, "The vision wore off in you, but it's the reason you're gonna work so well. It put your brain into the right frequency, for a while. Visions isn't just hallucinations, man. It shows you things. The Conceptual Dimension of a thing. And things you don't even know're there."

He's a loon, hasn't been taking his medication, Quinn thought. It's not *enough* drugs, that's why he's a Street Sleeper.

"So," Quinn said. "What do we do now?"

"We wait. You're in a waiting room, man."

"You know all about it, huh?" Quinn said. "Then explain this place to me. Explain who the Middle Man is." Thinking that the guy probably had it all wrong. But Quinn was scared. He wanted to hear someone talking.

"The Middle Man works for the Spirits of the Urban Wilderness, to use a bullshit terminology for lack of any other, and the Fetish Broker works for the Middle Man. You got a cigarette?"

"Uh uh."

"Then I'll smoke one of my own." From some foul wen in his clothing he took a crooked, dirty cigarette and pushed its end into his tube lighter. The smoke smelled like real tobacco. He'd bummed somebody generous.

The tramp leaned back against the wall, blew smoke out through his nose and said, "The Middle Man is a Wetware Medium. He . . . how much do you want to know?"

"All of it, if I can get it."

"You'll be sorry you said that . . . "

The Street Sleeper blew smoke out in a belch, and went on: "OK, lemme see: There's a subatomic particle called the IAMton. Physicists, they speculate about it, but the Middle Man knows. He was a cutting-edge hot shot at Stanford. He isolated the IAMton, using a Wetware subatomic scanner that re-created the thing in his natural cerebral imaging equipment, and when he did, *it spoke to him.* It spoke to him! Can you fade that? A subatomic particle that tells you, *Yeah! You found me!"* The street sleeper laughed.

"It spoke to him in English?"

"No but he *heard it* in English. Actually, see, it was *all the IAMtons on the fucking planet* that spoke to him, in the local macro-octave. Spoke to him *through* the group of 'em he had contained in the tokomak field and scanned with the electron microscope interfaced with his wetware. You know?"

"No, not really. Sort of." *Electron microscope interfaced with his wetware?* Okay, so this Street Sleeper was one of those glib paranoids who grew up reading Neil Stephenson or something.

"Anyway, the Middle Man, he changed bigtime after that, and now, *now,* he wants other people to know what the IAMton can give you, which is why he lets people spout off all about it like this, like I am, because he wants to empower people, the ones who have the capacity, like you, see, he wants 'em to use the knowledge–to find their own way to use it–but so far almost no one has. Not everybody's the shaman the Middle Man is, you see. And the Middle Man, he's sorta stuck where he is... And he lost the way to where he is, 'cause, see...it's like biting your own teeth or licking your own tongue, once you're there, you're too inside to...to...well, he's gotta find people on the outside...people maybe like you, see and . . . But it's hard, it's all so hidden and...and there's a reason for that. It's designed that way. The truth protects itself, see; absolute objectivity on the full-spectrum level, it hides from us, because it wants us to struggle to get to it. Everything's designed, see - even chaos. From the Higher it's designed; from here it looks like - and it *is* - random misery. The Law of Accident. You following me?"

"No."

"Good, good..." He took a drag, coughed, blew smoke. "The IAMton, now, it's a subatomic particle that's present anytime there's awareness. It's necessary for *any* degree of consciousness. The body is electric, right, like that oldtime patriotic fag said, what's his name..."

"Whitman."

"Right. The body has its own electromagnetic field, right?" He turned, spat something nasty in a corner. Cleared his throat, spat again. "This IAMton, it's a ubiquitous particle but not necessarily a *participating* particle in *your* particular system - but when an organism has the right sort of magnetic field, magnetic center, some of these particles–more for the higher organisms– are attracted to that system, that organism, and incorporated into the organism's *holographic seat of consciousness*. Which is tucked away, see, in the brain. It's the *I*, the '*I Am*', the thing that is capable of acting beyond reaction; the movement beyond reflex. Essence o' free-will, sorta. We all have a *certain amount* of this particle; the Meta have a lot more of it, because they're part of the hypersphere..."

"The 'hypersphere'? Man you're making my headache worse -"

"No pain, no gain. Hypersphere, or Ruckersphere, is the dimension that incorporates our dimensions and two higher dimensions...Rucker didn't entirely get it...Now when a tribe of people are in psychological alignment they generate an external collective electromagnetic field–"

"Whoa, hold on - you mentioned the Meta about two minutes of gibberish ago. What do you know about the Meta?"

"Stories, rumors. The Meta! Ha! Fiction! Myth! You got anything to eat, on you?"

"No I don't. Tell me something - What were you before you were a Street Sleeper?"

"A jerk. A different kinda jerk. Anyway–the IAMtons..."

"I mean, you're talking different, some of the time," Quinn pointed out. "Some of the time you talk like a Street Sleeper and some times like a paranoid on a verbal buzz, sometimes like...I don't know, a -"

"You want to know about the Middle Man or not?"

Shaken for new reasons, Quinn said, "Go ahead."

"Anyhoo, this tribal field generates entities, or attracts entities–the Middle Man is still not sure which it is–and the entities, so-called Spirits of the Urban Wilderness, appear to us as expressions of our consensual interpretation of our environment."

"Whoa - hold it - do these 'spirits' exist for real or not? Are they some kind of holographic illusion or are they...spirits?"

"They exist for real - But what have demons and angels and nature spirits and the like always been? The IAMton field's response, the Great Mind's response, to the models men create in their minds...They are real but they are man-created...But they are often more powerful than ordinary man...A man created a fighter jet, but one man cannot fight a fighter jet: it is more powerful than a man alone..."

"But the Meta -"

"The Meta, they're on a whole higher level, but they use this level too at will." He spat in the corner again. "Now your so-called 'primitive' Shaman, your aborigine, your 'priest' sometimes he can talk to the IAMton entities - he maybe calls them Voudoun Loa, whatever - and, sometimes see, he can get results and sometimes not. But ya see we have a whole new set of entities nowadays...pay attention to that part, son: *a whole new set of entities*...Especially now that the Middle Man has made some solid contacts - Are you listening?"

Staring at the tramp, Quinn had seen him flicker. "You're part of the HopeScope. Some kind of . . . image. Image behind the image...You're the Middle Man."

"Well *duh*. I mean: So? Ignore the little man behind the curtain."

"I am *so* sick of Wizard of Oz references -"

"Can't get too many. You ever see Sean Connery in *Zardoz*? Hey, I had to check you out, didn't I? I mean, you're so fucking ridiculous, you and your friends . . . getting P.O.'d and walking around with a fantasy about cracking the Fridge. And you, your old man's Izzy Dose. Progeny of a popstar? Gotta be a flake! Spoiled little rich kids. In short: What a bunch of jerk-offs. I had to see how serious you were. Engaged your top mind so I could look in the lower mind . . ."

"You're reading my mind?"

"No, you're exhibiting some of it to me. We're not really here, you understand. This room doesn't exist. It's a virtual room. You're actually lying on a table under the old bank in a cerebral hack-helmet."

"The fuck you say!"

"Turn the gain down, homes, the helmet won't hurt you. You're hooked in, socketed with the DataBase that I use to talk to the Spirits."

"Mahler doesn't buy the Spirit part. He says you've just got good hackers."

"He's a right-brain-limp left-brain-hard-on Stalinist ignoramus."

"Look–"

"You want to know what we want from you in return for opening the Fridge. If it was anybody but Black Betty, or if you didn't have the key–which you can bet your ass isn't enough by itself–we'd tell you to cruise on. There's a thousand people who want to get somebody out of the Fridge. That's *hard*. I think I'd tell you to fuck off anyway - except you've got something else with you...A vibe, a kind of scent on you: the burnt-silicon scent of the Meta is on you, Quinn. The grace of the Meta's on you. And the Meta...them I trust. And then too: it's Black Betty, she's part of the reason we want to help. Maybe she's one of the puzzle pieces we've been looking for and *maybe* you can actually get her out...The other reason is our usual fee, which is worship. You pay us in worship. I mean real worship, I don't mean ego pumping."

"You want us to worship the, uh, Spirits? The Spirits of the 'Urban Wilderness...'"

Another flicker, and then the street sleeper wasn't exactly *there* anymore. The guy had gone two-dimensional, was a geometrically emblematic figure on a screen, like a product insignia.

Quinn was sunken into a sweet numbness, from within which he could hear the emblem talk, could see the hieroglyphic's mouth move, knowing he was seeing this on the back of his closed eyelids . . . while the Middle Man, the transformed tramp, his voice now ringing out like a clarion call, said:

"It's a sweet thing, Quinn, our worship. It's not submission, not really: it's vanity. The spirits: *They're us*. It's a rush, Quinn. To sing of the Spirits, and bleed a little for them, and give them offerings, and ergs.

"I'm talking Floures, who exhales electrons.
"And issuing from Floures, I'm talking Network and Grid –
"Network and Grid, the messengers of the gods, one for back and the other for forth, sexing with their mistress Wavelength.

"I'm talking TeeVee the Belly-stroker, who eats everything and consumes nothing, the Buddha who lies.

"I'm talking One-Oh-One–of whom you, Quinn, are a halfling–the Spirit whose sword is Input and whose shield is Output, whose recollections are the ice-melt flowing between the arid banks of every computer online; whose silicon embrace will finally carry you beyond all computers.

"I'm talking Pixel, the video queen–your true mother, Quinn–who awaits you in the on-screen demimonde.

"I'm talking Fractal, the living gateway to the Fifth Dimension, whom you met in a lamp post and a drainpipe, who unites the dimension of the human senses with the dimension perceived by the electronic.

"I'm talking Pharmus-Hormona, whose translucent flesh swells voluptuously or shrinks to sinewy sweetness; who has made Fertility and Fashion indistinguishable.

"I'm talking MaxBux, the energy that is money, the money that is energy, the living flow chart of ease and power.

"I'm talking Score, Lord of the Stash, Mister Gooddrugs, whose teeth are needles; plead, beg to be sacrificed to him, beg him to take your throat in his jaws. He will destroy you if you beg hard enough; or he'll make you wish yourself destroyed.

"I'm talking Androgyna the Disco Queen, who is the shortcut to the Spirits, who is the hip-hop voodoo and the Womb of the Urban Primitive, who is also the Trickster.

"I'm talking Vehicle, on whose crown is the Mack Bulldog and in whose heart is the GM slogan.

"I'm talking Court, the Liar, the speaker with two tongues, both of them brown.

"I'm talking Bust, the Cop, the Destroyer, whose face is chrome stamped with all numbers, and whose arms end in a gun and a stunstick; Bust, to whom sacrifices must be made.

"I'm talking our relatives, Quinn. Because sometimes Zeus becomes a swan..."

"I'm...I'm uhh..."

"I know you're scared. But you're gonna be okay. When One-Oh-One took control of you to talk to the Mufti in Arabic–"

"Yeah–what *was* that?"

"*That* was One-Oh-One, using your tongue to talk to Sadiq, in Arabic taken from its linguistics database, which is *all linguistic databases everywhere;* tapping heavily on its rhetoric database and working in my own contribution... What matters is, afterwards you were a little shaken up yes...*But you were okay,* you were remarkably all right, considering. That tells us something, that means you're suited for this. You've got one of the key genes, kid. You were born to be a shaman. Which is what all those hunches were about; all those visions of patterns, trying to warn you, back in California and Nevada. You're a shaman. So have confidence, Quinn. You've found your wavelength."

"But I don't know how to use it even if I've got it–"

"I do. I'll guide you. Now: Let's see if the Fridge is crackable. It has a kind of unseeable Spirit of its own protecting it, Quinn, and it is Terrible."

"I'm–"

A circuit closed.

Quinn watched with the Middle Man's eyes. They were eyes that seemed to float over a scene, unwatched themselves. They might have been electronic, they might have been human, they might have been both. They were . . . apart from Quinn.

...Quinn, who was still locked away under the bank, on a table, heavily into an unusual pattern of R.E.M.s.

Physically asleep but more awake than he'd ever been before, Quinn watched the outside world.

Quinn was watching remotely; he wasn't sure if it was remote viewing, a psychic watching, or if it was something electronic. With the Middle Man, the two were blurred.

He realized, thinking about it, that one led to the other: a *kind* of electronics that led to psychic connection, through the IAMton field.

You'll be here right here, as the hours pass; you'll be physically right here, Quinn, the Middle Man said, *while your friends go to try to get Black Betty out of the 'Fridge'. But you'll be with them in something more than spirit: you'll be helping, tilting the quantum plane of probability; the ball-bearing of time rolls this way, it rolls that. Concentrate, and you can influence its roll, Quinn. With my help: with your talent...*

• • •

"I'm worried about Quinn," Zizz was saying. " I mean - what happened? He was there, putting that card in the machine, then there was, like, a *big black blot* that came from the machine and blotted him out - and it went away and he was gone too..."

"Stage magic," Mahler said, "to dazzle the believers. Something we've got to put up with."

"I'd like to know what's up with him myself though," Cisco said.

Mahler's earlier confidence had slipped away. Quinn speaking in tongues - or anyway in Arabic - had freaked him out.

That's when the tramp appeared, levitating above the ruins.

He appeared like somebody's wiseguy joke on a visitation by the Holy Ghost. Cisco and Zizz and Mahler stared up at him; all three of them saw him manifesting in the air above them, a holy wino, a levitated tramp with an aureole the color of a monitor screen's glow in a dark room.

Mahler shrank away, and turned his back on the apparition, shaking his head. "Holographic projection. Stage magic bullshit..."

The vision spoke to Cisco and Zizz: "Quinn is all right - he's working with me, on our end. We can shift some things for you...we can add some English to the spin of the ball of time in space, you see...But there are some things you have to do yourselves, in this world: what you think is the ordinary world. You have to get some other circuits closed for us, in the hypersphere, and you'll do that through the Fetish Broker..."

"What's the Hypersphere...?" Zizz murmured.

The Middle Man fluttered gawdy silver metal-flake wings, scratched a louse from his armpit, and drew on an ethereal cigarette; he blew a smoke ring that shaped itself into a swastika. Then he blew a stream that shattered the swastika and, with suave detachment, said: "There is an old pornography theater in the next block south. The place is derelict now, and looks blocked off, but climb over the rubble and you'll see the way in. The Fetish Broker is there. She will equip you. She is real, in your world. She'll give you what you need to open the Fridge. Or else," he added philosophically, "It won't work, and you'll get shot dead. That could happen too..." The voice had just the faintest telltale of electronic filtering.

The apparition faded, the details first and then the outline, the way projected holos do.

Zizz and Cisco looked at one another.

Cisco gave a long, slow exhalation, then said: "I don't know what else to do...Do you?"

Zizz shook her head.

"I don't trust that...thing, whatever it was," Mahler said, shivering. "I'm going to wait here for Quinn."

"Meet you back *heee*-errre, Mahler," Zizz said, "since you're gonna be a *butt*-hole about it."

And they went to meet the Fetish Broker.

Mahler waited behind, alone in the ruins, unarmed,

sulking in a fog of ideology.

    . . .

On the next block, in the so-called material world, Cisco and Zizz clambered over fallen masonry and into the shattered Adult Sensurround Theater across the rubbled street, and there met the Broker.

The Broker was an emaciated woman, lying in a bed of smut.

The photographic imagery on the twentieth century porn magazines had been transferred onto pseudoskin–High Silk, the expensive brand–so that the Broker lounged on a wallowy pillow configured with hundreds of small interlocked nudes, a cloth-print pattern of languid faces, of canted buttocks and flowing breasts and the intersection of genitalia.

The Fetish Broker herself was sunken-eyed, dagger-haired, and almost skeletal-skinny. A tattoo of prettied-up nervous system lines, embroidered with curlicues and fleurs-de-lis and blossoming vines, was etched across her torso and legs in sullen colors.

She was outfitted with an alumitech spine: a long grey metal millipede down her naked back, a millipede equipped with implant wires instead of legs.

It was a signal transformer for the nerve-ends, hyping impulses from the erogenous receptors, from every sort of pleasure-sensitive nerve. It was state-of-the art, but it was a new art, and her movements were sometimes erratic, when incoming somatic pleasure signals interfered with motor coordination transmissions. A porcelain mechanism beside the bed blew warm, therapeutic mists onto her, jets that strategically probed her enhanced erogenous receptors; the pillow undulated slowly beneath her, its hidden servos massaging, falling slack, massaging again . . .

Zizz and Cisco stood before the Broker's bed like courtiers at a royal audience. And Quinn, tranced and jacked-in, watched remotely, from his hiding place under the old bank.

Watching from another place, Quinn noticed the flesh-colored plastic box of the drug-doler implanted into her calf.

Zizz noticed it too. "Ooooh, a doler, those are expensive, what you got in it, what's the dosage?"

"That's a rude question," the Broker said. Voice like an

annoyed Siamese cat. "People don't ask people that."

Quinn assumed the Broker was getting low doses of amphetamines trickled out to her, cut with maybe demerol, the occasional wash of beta endorphins.

The room was a concrete cave, with its edges lost in red shadow, and the Broker's electronic fetishes were its stalactites.

Cisco was staring up in fascination at them. They hung from the ceiling, hundreds of them, each about six inches long. Made with tiny pliers and tweezers and the Broker's teeth, sculpted intricately from color-coded wires, bandsaw-cut pieces of circuit board, microprocessors, semiconductors, condensers, and . . . bone. Hanks of hair. Strips of blue velvet, green satin. All of it twined into little almost-people, and shapes suggesting animals no one had ever seen. None of the figures were definite, but all were clearly defined.

The Fetish Broker grinned, lips skinning from teeth that showed the tops of their roots in receding blue gums.

On a solder-spattered wooden worktable next to the bed, four fetishes were strung together on a black wire. They were figures of brightly colored rubber and copper and alloy.

She moved a hand toward the table and it looked like she was moving it through strobeflashes; the movement had no flow to it. Jerk-jerk-jerk.

Annoyed, she reached behind her with her other hand and made an adjustment on her spine. The hand moved more fluidly now as she picked up the ring of fetishes. "For you, Middle Man says, for Black Betty."

Cisco reached for the fetish-hoop, and tugged on it–but the Broker wouldn't let go of it. Her lips skinned back from her death's head teeth again.

"A price." She moved jerkily into a robotic parody of a seductive pose. "He says I can't charge bux this time. But I can ask for something else." She looked at Cisco's crotch. "You, for a while. The other can watch."

Cisco swallowed, visibly. Muttered, "Mahler's getting off easy."

The Broker put a new tube in her doler, and lay back on the bed. She spread her legs, and said, "Don't waste time."

They had to wait for the Broker to finish with Cisco.

"She's a pain in the ass," the Middle Man said. "She's going to throw off my timing if she takes too long."

Quinn couldn't see himself, or the Middle Man. He saw Cisco and the Fetish Broker on the bed, from some objective nonplace. But he and the Middle Man could hear each other.

"Hey," Quinn said. "How do the fetishes work? I mean, are they just a psychological trick or–"

"They're attuned to an IAMton transmission, and channel it. What matters is *why* they work, Quinn. The human world has reached a psychological critical mass..."

• • •

The Nevada night was wearing on. But Ceph had captured them: they were hearing the secret history of History. For once and all.

"...the Zetans gave humanity certain Zetan genetic components, and they helped early Man over some evolutionary humps - but they saw too late that the majority of the race retained a great many primate impulses they had thought expunged - impulses that would lead from little wars to bigger wars and which would end as another ancient Zetan experiment had, in another world: in world-wide devastation. They couldn't genetically redesign the whole race at that point, so they decided they had to influence it in other ways, so it would survive. So they decided - or they thought they decided - to introduce the concept of Higher Religious Ethics to keep humanity from self destructing before the experiment was done.

"They had already observed Earth humanity's tendency to contrive cosmological explanations for life and nature and death...They themselves, in the distant past, had once had such a tendency, until they'd expunged it, thousands of centuries earlier...

"They were aware of an order of creature we have called the Meta. These creatures had a way of infusing harmonious direction into the races they visited. Why? The Zetans did not know. They assumed the Meta were caught up in some sort of megalomaniacal cultural outreach obsession - they decided they could use this obsession for their own purposes.

"So they captured a powerful Meta in something like an enormous Tokomak generator field, and introduced it to Earth. And a variation on this same field, by the way, is the 'force field' that keeps the Meta out of the Zetan's way, most of the time..."

"The planetary IAMton field responded to the captured Meta, and crystalized a 'deity' around the Meta in a form the local sentient lifeform, humanity, could understand. The One God. The Great Spirit. Aton. Yahweh. G'Broagh Fram. Many names in many places. The Meta's influence on the IAMton field was especially direct in certain places - as for example the Middle East in the time of Moses. Eventually - the captured Meta escaped the Zetans, and departed Earth. But its influence lingered. It had left something behind that hung in the air, and that connected the IAMton field with humanity. And there was another factor at work - the Higher Itself...The Third Force. And the Zetans, like so many humans, are Third Force Blind..."

"Enough!" Lyn Farraday burst out, overwhelmed. "I mean, Jesus!"

"Yes," Ceph said. "*About* Jesus...Well..."

• • •

The Fridge looked like an office building.

"Why should prisons be ugly if the new technology can make them internally secure?" the designers had asked, thinking themselves stunningly innovative. Why not make them so that the locals would be less likely to object to having them nearby?

Out-of-towners seeing the Federal Control Penitentiary, rising austere but unthreatening from the artificial island that forked the Hudson, took it for the headquarters of a security conscious multinational corporation.

But when you saw it from Shacktown, it looked different. Shacktown was the towering personification of the housing crisis: The roof-slums, the intricate, interconnected, precariously-bridged maze of fiberboard shacks precariously piled on tenement roofs, warehouse roofs, any open space they could stake out, up above.

From up there, the Shacktowners could see the Fridge's octagonal polarized-glass skyscraper, and know it for a prison. A seventy-story prison without roving spotlights, without outer containment walls or electric antipersonnel wire. It had a stylish notch up one side and sprawling green lawns and a topiary garden and floodlit fountain.

The Shacktowners knew what it was, though. It made them shiver because it was so *confident*.

But it was guarded, all right.

As Cisco and Zizz climbed out of the boat, up the concrete embankment, and onto the lawn–they stopped cold. They listened. They heard the muted whir of the hover-cams approaching through the darkness.

• • •

Quinn was still lying on a table, snugged in a helmet, in a pristine basement under a filthy ruins. He was still in trance; electronic and psychic. A low-grade silicon embrace.

Watching and listening through the Middle Man's own remote systems, Quinn too heard the hover-cams approaching Zizz and Cisco.

The Middle Man switched to infra-red scan, and Quinn saw the hovercams as two abstracted birdshapes glowing red with motor heat as they hovered on either side of Cisco and Zizz, thirty feet up: the hover-cams looking down at Cisco and Zizz, evaluating them, classifying them as intruders, alerting the cyberguards in their niches around the base of the building.

"That's it," Quinn told the Middle Man. "They're fucked." He couldn't see the Middle Man, but he was *There*. He was the unseen but ubiquitous background. "The last time someone tried to break somebody out of there, the cyberguards came down on 'em, there was twenty of those little fuckers rolling up all at once, blazing away. There was choppers, everything–all in about one minute. They're screwed."

"Not if we intervene."

"We don't have time."

"We do. You and I are talking in dreamtime now. Braintime, which is anything you want it to be. Ask your friend Anatole about that. You ever have a dream where everything that happens takes days and days–only when you wake the whole dream took place in three minutes realtime? It's like that. We're ten times faster. Twenty. Thirty. Okay?"

OH BLACK BETTY BLAM BUH LAM

"I hear music," Quinn said. "A hip-hop beat. House music. But bluesey. Singing about Black Betty..."

"Yes, it's a sort of remix of the old Leadbelly song she took her *nom de guerre* from, cut with some Nick Cave."

LOOKEE LOOKEE YONDER THE SUN DONE GONE
OH BLACK BETTY BLAM BUH LAM

YEAH BAM BAM Buh-BAM
BLACK BETTY HAD A BABY BLAM BUH LAM
BABY WAS BLIND BLAM BUH LAM
BETTY DIDN'T MIND BLAM BUH LAM

"You got to have the confidence, and the focus for this, man. You can do it: You have the talent to be intelligently empty. To be a channel. To be a zero in the right place in the equation. You and me channel the Spirits to intervene. To do that, you got to empty your mind. You got to . . . come on and DANCE."

"Say what?"

"DANCE!" A woman's voice now, singing.

OH BLACK BETTY BLAM BUH LAM

"DANCE!" A twenty-first century Motown singer. "Come on and DANCE!" Chanted in the rhythmic pocket. BAM BUH BLAM

"Are you serious?"

The beat, a ubiquitous Linn drum detonation, went on into infinity as she (for the moment, a she) sang:

Come on and DANCE
Bam Bam Buh-BAM
OH BLACK BETTY BAM BUH LAM
DANCE YO WAY
 to another place
Come on and DANCE
Bam Bam Buh-BAM
internalize space
Come on and--

The beat radiated out from the marrow of Quinn's bones. Its Linn drum was programmed in the genetic core of his cells.

OH BLACK BETTY BLAM BUH LAM

Suddenly Quinn was in another place: Androgyna's womb, a mirror-walled Disco suffused in crystal blue; he was embodied, dancing free, dancing with himself, one of the Broker's fetishes hanging around his neck on a cord, whipping with his movements, each movement sloughing off doubts, all uncertainties falling away; only Life in This Moment remaining.

OH BLACK BETTY BAM BUH LAM

There were neon strokes of light in the ceiling and he knew from their patterning that they were impulses firing through

his neurons. *That he was dancing in his own skull.*
OH BLACK BETTY

And his spinal cord radiated somatic impulses in the center of the ceiling: a split-laser, spitting streaks of laser light to the beat, and that was the campfire he danced around, in the dance of the urban primitive . . .

BAM BUH LAM
OH BLACK BETTY
Come on and DANCE

(In the Amazon, in an *oca*, in a village of the Topajo, the *Feiticeiro* danced around a fire; the men of his tribe squatted around him, gifting him with rhythms. They twanged the *birinbal* and thumped hollow trunks. He was naked but for the sacred marks in green pigment, and the shining sheath of his sweat. The hut baked with the heat of the campfire, of bodies; the shaman was trembling like a leaf in a wind of a drug American medical shamans called Ibogaine, the powdering of a holy plant. The shaman danced in the groove, to the beat that radiated out from his marrow, programmed in the genetic core of him: that's what his body did. His mind had another body that eased through the World, the jungle, searching for the black jaguar, the bamboo blowgun in his right hand; humming deep in his throat to the distant plangency of the Birinbal as he called to the Spirits . . .)

Quinn felt himself dancing physically, in this dream that was more than a dream: sweating, aching, short on breath, heart banging, but getting his groove, going into the trance that made it seem possible to dance forever, realizing that the gateway to the other continuum had a corridor and this corridor was the infinite dance; letting your own bodyheat melt you down and sweep you along, moving your hips into the pocket of the beat, completely lost in it. So the pain of exertion seemed far away, a distant smear of color . . . And it seemed to him, as he danced (COME ON AND DANCE BLACK BETTY BAM BUH LAM), danced in this dream-place, in the suit of lights that was his perspiration, that he was on his way somewhere . . .

He touched the fetish at his neck. A circuit closed.
Something clicked.

CHAPTER ELEVEN

DANCE IN THAT WORLD IF YOU CAN'T IN THIS ONE

Earlier that night. Ok? Earlier.
"There were two factions of Earth-Monitoring Zetans, you see," Ceph was saying. "One was the Microbiological Team: their interest in humanity was to create a species that was itself an ideal microbe farm for their micro-organism-breeding experiments. The usual laboratory was just not enough for their purposes: they wanted a full, living world for their laboratory and they wanted to use intelligent Zetan-primate hybrids as their breeding ground. Humanity was enough like them to be the breeding ground for micro-organisms that could be useful to the Zetans. And that way, humanity ran all the risks of exposure to micro-organisms that weren't quite working out. Ultimately the Micro-biological Team wanted to create what they thought of as exquisitely tooled free-range microbes...The black plague was of course one of their miscalculations, and then there was HIV: some viruses, you see, were not intended to be 'farmed' on human beings. They'd been developing certain organisms amongst the African primates, certain monkeys, and HIV was actually not intended to come into contact with people, but humanity nosed into the wilderness faster than the Zetans had

predicted and certain green monkeys bit certain human beings...and there was AIDS." Ceph changed colors sadly.

"We're just a *microbe farm*?" Lyn asked, horrified.

"Not just a microbe farm. Only partly. Now, the other faction of Zetans was the Macrobiological Team: they had noticed that humanity's tendency to create 'spiritual systems' and cosmological philosophies, had interesting side-effects: *miracles*."

"Miracle-type miracles?" Campbell asked, eyebrows raised.

"Yes. Miracles even to the Zetans; miracles which could not be explained, with the Metas absent. Only the Meta were supposed to be capable of that sort of thing, somewhat unevenly...

"And the Metas *are* usually absent: the Archons - the Zetans - block them from the planet where-ever possible, first by means of the force fields and second...Well, there is a way that humanity can contact those creatures who are at one with the Higher. This means is *within* man. The Zetans were aware of this, and puzzled by it. But rather than explore it too deeply - it frightens them, you see - they chose to try to suppress it. So, the Zetans genetically programmed us to hide from our deeper selves, our inner links to the Higher, the self knowledge which they regarded as volatile; they programmed humanity to turn outward, to numb self-knowledge, to identify with desire, with striving, with competition, with the building of empires, as this increased probability of sheer *reproduction*, of long-term propagation of the DNA they wanted, and the survival of their 'microbe farms'...At the same time the Macrobiological Team wanted to produce in certain *controlled* specimens of humanity what they failed to produce in the laboratory: the gene that seemed to make miracles possible. They wanted *pet* miracle makers. They wanted spiritual power, from a controlled group of humanity but no real spiritual growth - the Zetans, in their own way, are as confused as the rest of us, you see..."

"Miracles..." Lyn said softly, eyes wide. "Miracles?"

"Miracles. Miracles which seemed, to the Zetans, to be only manipulations of the quantum probability fields underlying reality itself. Which was of course merely the medium for the miracle: not the *real* cause of it. They couldn't see the Third Force component of the miracles...

"Certain strains of humanity developed, apparently spontaneously, a gene that made them unusually interactive with the ambient IAMton continuum: with the Sea of Mind that intertwines quantum probability, and which can manipulate quantum probability...and improbability. They communed with this continuum and called it God.

"The Zetans had no natural capacity for this communing, this manipulation, this 'magic', this 'grace'. But the Macro Team thought that humanity could be used to develop this capacity in a form that would allow them to manipulate reality itself through humanity's 'realized prophets'...If you manipulate the prophets who manipulate the quantum-fabric of reality, you by extension manipulate reality...

"Only, every experiment of this sort seemed to go wrong. The Zetans helped create Moses, and stayed in touch with him...but they lost control of him. They helped create Jesus, and got in touch with him...but could not control him. He seemed to pass beyond the range of their control in some way they didn't understand.

"They tried to reduce this power of the miraculous to calculatable, weighable, fixed and definable elements. They failed. They tried to create this 'prayer and grace' effect in the laboratory; they tried to infuse themselves with human genes taken from the likes of Jesus so as to give them this power...but they failed at that too. The power seemed to exist only for humanity, or for mad creatures like the Meta...and strangely enough, it sometimes manifested for human beings who were *not* carriers of the 'gene of divinity'. How could this be? The Zetans didn't understand it. More research was called for."

"Why can't the Zetans manifest this...this miracle gene in themselves?" Campbell asked.

"They could - but the thing that activates it is beyond them, because they refuse to let the Higher take part in them. They of course deny that it exists, except as something like a blind force - but it's a force they're blind to..."

"The Zetans have been controlling everything the human race does, like, in history?" Anatole asked. "All through history?"

"The Zetans have not controlled humanity in every particular," said Ceph. "Nor wanted to. Chance is always a necessary part of any longterm evolutionary experiment. For centuries at a time the Zetans would merely sit back and watch...

"However...Certain humans are telepathically sensitive, and from time to time the Zetans influenced these certain humans through telepathic signals sent from a transmitter which is hidden in space, past the orbit of the moon; a transmitter corresponding, in position, to the star Sirius...A small, hidden 'moon' of Earth...

"They influenced men to seek out those who carried this gene in human blood-lines, this inherited proclivity for the apparently Divine, and to refine it, develop it into a form they could exploit; they did this through, among other places, certain royal families in Europe descended from Joseph of Arimathea and Mary Magdalene and Jesus himself, who fathered Magdalene's children, after he escaped from Jerusalem."

"Escaped?" Campbell asked. "He wasn't crucified?"

"He was but he didn't actually die on the cross. Jesus was active, under other names, in Rome and the far East afterwards...The Zetans tried to keep these 'sacred' families in power so as to protect this 'holy' DNA through a variety of human organizations, for example the Priory of Scion: An ancient and secret organization of which General Dodge was a member. In fact, Dodge was an initiated member of a series of interlinked secret orders, culminating in a certain Arch Masonic cult wherein he was an initiate of the 23rd degree of the Order which underlay all orders, and which formed MJ15 at the behest of the Zetans..."

"I'm getting a headache," Campbell said. "I need espresso. I need a drink. I need amphetamines. Something."

"And in fact," Ceph chuckled, ignoring Campbell, "many organizations which supposed they worked for their own purposes - like P2, and the true Knights of Malta and of course MJ15 and even the Chinese Tong - all these were in fact working for agents of the Zetans: it was always easier to use human resources for research and experimentation and the building of bases than it was to import resources from Zetan Reticuli. And it was easier to buy these resources here than to endlessly have to commandeer them. So money was needed; secret bank accounts and deals with drug dealers and the CIA and the Vatican were needed. P2 was needed...

"But humanity has always shaken off its manipulation; it

has always struggled to be free. The Ecclesia Gnostica, the Cathars, the Sarmoung, the mystics of Mount Athos, certain hermetic societies, certain esoteric Buddhist schools, especially in Tibet - these arcane groups worked in secret against the interests of those the Zetans controlled. There never was only one conspiracy. There was much opposition to the Priory, and the other 'ambient conspiracies' - was it Robert Anton Wilson who said that if there was only one conspiracy behind it all, the world would make sense?"

"What about the Meta, all this time?" Anatole asked.

"Ah, the Meta...The Meta were now interested in this world, and they influenced it in their own ways.

"The Zetans have only lately begun to suspect that there is yet another factor interfering with their cultivations, something they haven't seen: a power outside the scope of their normal investigative apparatus, and above the Meta...They believed that the Meta were somehow preventing them from seeing what this hidden factor was...This 'Third Force'...

"They decided that in order to see the experiment through they must now take a more direct part in humanity: they plan to..." He hesitated, as if wondering if he should reveal what came next. After a moment he said, softly, "If they succeed...it might be better if you don't know..."

Campbell leaned forward, sweat on his forehead. "Say it. I've been waiting so long for the truth. *Say it!*"

Ceph considered, and the Dodge-body "nodded" the squid-capped head. "They plan to mate with humanity via genetic engineering, *and to do it on a vast scale which requires the involvement of millions of people*. And so they must reveal themselves to humanity, make humanity dependent on them, and thus master humanity."

"They'll co-opt us by 'helping' us?" Campbell asked, agitating a martini shaker. "And from there - enslave us?"

"Exactly. They have decided to fuse with humanity more and more completely, *to meld the two races* and take this miraculous power that shows itself from time to time for their own. Of course, they're going about it all wrong, and they've been told that, but they don't believe any but their own models of reality. So: this cumbersome mass-merging will go on. And to do it they must come out in the open...and they have been preparing for that for many decades now...Partly in a crash-course of genetic fusing experiments - I am the result of one of those - and partly through preparing humanity for them, with their deliberate waves of 'UFO activity' - showing themselves little by little as part of what Vallee called their 'Control System' manipulation of human events...Preparing humanity for the Embrace...

"But they once more underestimated humanity. Certain of the wiser humans - particularly a group in Tibet working with another group in the Middle East - used their inexplicable spiritual gifts to contact the Meta: to open the way for them, into our world; to open gateways, here and there, for the Meta. And the Meta have been interfering with the Zetan plans wherever they could. The Meta have been entering holes in the anti-Meta force field opened by the human Spiritual Masters. There *is* an invasion of Meta - but it is an Invited Invasion, and there is no harm in it...The Meta help when they can: For example, by bringing Anatole and Quinn together. Anatole and Quinn are each specially gifted - though Quinn has had only glimpses of that gift till now - and *together* they are even more powerful..."

"But once and for all," Farraday asked, "what *are* the Meta?"

"Well - as for that..."

• • •

Quinn was somewhere on the IAMton plane...

There was an amoebic grid, a rubbery lattice of light, that rippled in three dimensions with sine waves. If you kind of squinted, it was man-shaped, too. It was forming around the fetish that Zizz had thrown on the ground, as the Fetish Broker had told her to.

Quinn felt the rippling lattice thing quiver in his hands. It was two things, two Spirits, and he felt them in his hands like there was a mild electric charge going through them . . . That buzzing feeling . . .

Like the buzzing, the vibration he'd felt just after he'd inserted the card.

Now he had the intertwined IAMton spirits in his hands like small animals that would respond to his will, trained beasts, hungry and curious . . .

Go to the cameras.

The rippling grid stretched itself out, with hunger and interest, to the two hovering metal birdshapes each with its camera-lens head–and seemed to split into an electrical amoeba and drain into the lenses . . .

"Network and Grid: inseparable," the Middle Man said. "One thing going to two places at once."

(In some far place, Quinn was still dancing.)

Quinn saw a man looking at a bank of monitors.

On one of them was a view of the lawn by the riverbank, where Zizz and Cisco had stood. But (PUSH IN on the monitor) they aren't Zizz and Cisco; through the intercession of the spirits Network and Grid, sent by Quinn, Zizz and Cisco are now - on the monitor - two guards out for the evening patrol of the island. Normally no one would have to go patrol the island in person but what with the blackout riots in the city and all . . .

The two guards were at the front door and the man at the monitor, "recognizing" them, hit the keyboard sequence that opened the gate and let them in.

In the antechamber, the guard looked up to see Zizz and Cisco come in, instead of the sentry images that had appeared on his surveillance monitor, and almost pissed his pants.

(Quinn and the Middle Man, each dancing in his own skull, in shamanistic ecstasy, invoked Pharmus-Hormona, and MaxBux.)

The guard at the TV monitors was named Krutzmeyer. He was stubby and he had a donkeyish face and bristly black hair on his knuckles. He was reaching for the alarm button when the spiky girl touched him with a little doll made out of wires.

Suddenly she wasn't there anymore. In her place was a sex-swollen thing from the guard's fantasies, impossibly voluptuous. The sight of her was an electric shock. It was instant hard-on.

The feeling that rose up in Krutzmeyer was not sexual attraction. It was sexual consummation, ongoing. It was like being hit by a freight train made of soft, warm, sticky ladyflesh, and the train had hit him from the inside, had come charging out of the base of his skull down into his spine, down to the groin chakra and IMPACT. There was no resisting it.

(To Cisco it seemed that the guard looked at ordinary Zizz and–bafflingly–gave out a wail of ecstasy and monstrous fulfillment and fell onto the floor, convulsing.)

Krutzmeyer was watched by other guards on a second bank of monitors. One of these wanted to raise the alarm but Floures of the Electrons poured through him, holding him rigid, till Cisco figured out how to open the door into the second checkpoint.

This guard's name was Wolfeton, he was sixty-two, emphysemic, and sick of his job, easy as it was. And when Floures could no longer hold him, when he saw the two weirdos walk in, and he reached for the alarm button . . .

Cisco touched him with a fetish.

For Wolfeton, Cisco was someone else. Cisco was Darrel "Ducky" Barker, grandson of Bob Barker and host of *Bux, Boy, Bux!!,* TV's most popular game show, routinely giving away $NB100,000 a show. Transmuted from lead into gold by MaxBux, Cisco was the apotheosis of Easy Money and Instant Luxury, he was a ticket dispenser for a non-stop to that island in the Florida Keys Wolfeton had dreamed about, and with the money Darrel was transferring to his account Wolfeton could buy a place on the island–Hell, he could *buy the island!* And he and Gertie could . . .

The hell with Gertie, he could afford a pricey divorce, he could dump Gertie and buy the best mistress bux could buy–hell, make it *three* mistresses, and while you're at it . . .

What happened to Wolfeton went beyond pushing his greed buttons. His rational mind would never have believed Ducky Parks had come here. MaxBux reached into the part of Wolfeton that yearned for infantile gratification. Something buried beneath the foundations of the personality; wired into the nervous system itself. Gratify that place, where a personality interfaces with a nervous system, and the rest of the mind will follow. MaxBux was quickfix; the Big Release; Mama and Papa in one. And Wolfeton had been waiting years for him.

To Zizz it looked like the guard was staring at Cisco and grinning a sort of rictus grin and hyperventilating, turning bright red . . . But nodding frantically, muttering "You goddit, Darrel, anything you say, Darrel–" as he punched the code to open the door to the control room.

She shrugged and went into the computer-control room.

• • •

Brandis Danville was anorexic, anal, and–in the words of his coworkers–"a suck-up." He thought of himself as "ambitious and diplomatic." He looked up and saw the strangest woman he'd ever seen walk unaccompanied into the control room. She wasn't even wearing an antidust suit to protect the computers. He reached for his console and she touched him with a faceless doll made of wires.

The girl wasn't there anymore; instead, a man in the uniform of the Federal Control High Command stood there, his eyes in mirror shades, his uniform crawling with braid and brass; he was *big*, and Brandis could no more defy him than a straw could stand up to a hurricane. He had five-hundred-mile-per-hour authority.

For Zizz...Zizz had been visually transfigured by Bust, the Destroyer. Bust, for whom even a fractional defiance means death.

Bust, The Compleat Officer, said, "Black Betty Meriweather, FP87041, in unit 4577BB, is to be released and remanded to me."

"Absolutely, right away." Not a thought of all the orders, the papers, the various failsafe checks and countersignings and video authorizations. Except one. "If you'll give me the key, sir. Keys are kept in FedControl Central and transmitted in emergency or–"

Zizz handed him the cassette.

• • •

"How did you get the image code?" the Middle Man asked a part of Quinn's mind.

"When she was locked in, her lawyer was there, he recorded it off a screen with a lapel cam. Fuzzy image, couldn't use it for the key, but I figured it out, video animated a dupe. Took me four months."

"You got an eye. You were born to it. Cause it's working."

• • •

Black Betty was entering the third part of the cycle. In that part, the voices ceased for a while, and the small electric shocks ceased, and the rehab computer held back on the nausea drug. Giving her system a rest before the conditioning started again.

She felt her arms and legs twitch in their restraints as the impulsers exercised her inside the capsule.

Calendar pictures of idyllic countryside were flashed in front of her eyes for "psyche refreshment." She had the option of talking to the Friend, if she wanted. But the computer that was the Friend always gently steered her back to the subject of rehabilitation, and it could not be induced to break down or to do anything extraordinary, so she didn't talk to it anymore. She couldn't think about the Movement, of course, the resistance to FedControl, not overtly, because the biomonitors knew what her body and bloodstream did when she thought about the work she'd undertaken before the incarceration. The little glandular hints, the involuntary reactions . . . and when it sensed those things, it punished her.

But she tried to think of something that would–

A ripping sound. A deep, sickening disorientation. A burst of light.

Oh no, she thought, *it's happened: I've gone crazy*. The thing she was most afraid of, since coming here.

She was hallucinating that the cyberguards were taking her out of the mesh, wrapping her in a rubber sheet, carrying her between them for a long whirring time. Her mind had snapped into a fantasy of escape, she decided, like *Occurrence at Owl Creek Bridge*. She'd gone pathetically insane.

And when she heard Cisco's voice she was sure of it.

"Oh Black Betty..."

BLAM BUH LAM

• • •

"The Meta," Ceph said, "...they incorporate more of themselves into themselves than we do..."

"What's that mean?" Anatole asked. He didn't look sleepy at all.

Lila smiled. Lyn had fallen asleep in her chair; Farraday was nodding, near sleep. Campbell listened blearily, sagging in his seat.

"There are levels of Self few in this world ever awaken to," Ceph said. "So the Meta tell me. These other levels exist in wider and wider octaves of sheer Being, incorporating more and more, finer and finer energies, until they begin to exist in the hypersphere at the same time as they exist here; an interlocked mirror existence. This is what the Meta are. They are 'aliens' - some of them. Aliens from other worlds who achieved the

Higher. But some are human beings who achieved the Higher. They are from our world; they are from other worlds. They transcended their native worlds and became Meta, and forgot, for millenia, their origins...But sometimes they can hear our calls for help, and they come to convey what they can of the energy of the Absolute, the Mind beyond Mind, the Being beyond the Ground of Being...One of them, even now, helps me to explain all this to you: and I learn all this as it speaks through me."

"You're *channeling*?" Farraday asked, surprised.

"No. Channelers are generally liars and frauds and self deceived people," Ceph said, using the terms of insult with a voice that was infinitely compassionate. "No, it is closer to what the poets called 'inspiration'. Much subtler than the channeling idea..."

Farraday noticed something; something he found disturbing:

Dodge's right arm was falling off.

"Dodge seems to be...really dead."

"Yes, he's been dead for a few hours, I've been holding him together. He's decaying with a strange rapidity...Now I must shed him, and prepare to go to something better, and you can make that into a parable, if you want..."

With a sigh of relief, Ceph slithered away from Dodge. What remained of Dodge's face was mostly skull, though the eyes remained, lidless.

Anatole choked.

Lila looked away, grimacing.

Campbell gagged. "*God*, Ceph, you might have warned us!"

"Oh - sorry. Would you mind very much dragging the body into the desert, Mike?"

"My pleasure, actually," Farraday said. "I'm glad Lyn's asleep..."

He and Campbell slung the fallen-away limbs onto Dodge's torso, and lugged him by the remaining limbs to a dry wash in the desert. Intrigued, coyotes snuffled in the brush.

They dumped General Dodge, Grand High Poobah of the 23rd degree of Initiation, into the gully, and went back to wash their hands.

"Shouldn't we feel bad about him?" Anatole asked, when

they returned to the terrace.

"Do you?" Lila asked him.

"No."

"Why not?"

"Because he was an asshole who would have killed us and he ordered my Dad killed and that got Kian killed. Aaaaannnnd...I don't know. Something about karma."

"Right."

"But...you work for the Meta. And you let him die. And...*do the Meta kill?*"

Lila turned to look questioningly at Ceph.

"Even among those who serve the Higher," Ceph said, from the tree he was perched in, "there is no agreement on that issue. The great Bodhisattvas of Buddhism are opposed to taking life. Other Masters shrug and say, it doesn't matter, you are only liberating them. Still others reply, 'But that is not for us to do'. That's how it goes. Around and around. The Meta will create conditions which allow the vehicles, the dark momentum, of their enemies to carry those enemies into death...Not all spiritual powers are pacifists. There are angels, even in the sacred books, who bear swords..."

Ceph paused, and then added:

"Remind me to tell you about Atlantis later..."

"*Much* later," Farraday said wearily.

• • •

Quinn had come to himself walking down the street, with the Mufti and another Islamic Funs guerrilla he hadn't seen before; they were on either side of him, supporting him as if he were a drunk. And they'd laughed at him the way they'd laugh at a drunk. He'd looked around, and found the world dull, grey, bloodless. An enormous rock pit where humanity quarried mediocrity like gravel. He had lost the Urban Spirits and lost touch with his own spirit.

He knew by the dust and the gravitas of that mediocrity, by the mocking weight of it, that he was most definitely back in the 'material' world...

Quinn had gone to the apartment Mahler kept here, and there found Mahler and Zizz and Black Betty and Cisco waiting for him. They'd rested, and before dawn they'd gone to meet Mahler's contacts.

• • •

"It's going to be a long time before Betty's... before she's all right," Mahler said, his voice cracking. "I don't know if she'll ever be. But at least they haven't got her in that place anymore."

It was dawn, and the smoggy light washed everything dirty blue. They were in an alley between a warehouse and a subcontractor's superconductor plant, near the Brooklyn Bridge, waiting for the van that would take them out of Manhattan.

Mahler was going to take Black Betty to a place in Maine, a house in the mountains where there were people learning how to use automatic weapons for something Mahler wouldn't talk about. "They're good people. They'll take care of her," is all he'd say.

They were all supposed to go with him.

Quinn felt hollow, detached, like everything was happening to someone else. Disorientation? Despair? He wasn't sure. But he knew he was wrenched.

Zizz was talking in a dry, cracked voice to no one in particular. "I feel like shit...why did I take that stuff...I feel like shit...I'll never take it again..."

"I told you, you shouldn't be taking that shit," Cisco said. "Herbs, ginseng, and meditation, that'll get you just as high."

"I don't want to be just as high. I don't even know what happened...I just feel so burnt out today...No more drugs, no more drugs. Oh God, give me a tranquilizer somebody."

Quinn had to laugh at that. But he put his arm around her. Today she wore jeans and boots and black t-shirt and no makeup. She had stopped caring who looked at her.

Quinn looked at her, and felt a little better.

"We take you to your friends," the Mufti had said. "And so you should not be weeping."

But he had wept.

Now, Black Betty was sitting on someone's grimy back steps, dosed on tranquilizers, holding her knees, swaying, now and then her head making a chicken-pecking motion, her tongue protruding, some kind of hideous motor twitch . . .

Quinn looked away. He couldn't stand seeing her like that. The conditioning had broken something in her. Maybe not forever. But she was forever altered in Quinn's mind.

Everything was altered. Black Betty was no longer frozen

in the Fridge but she could not stay in New York. She had to run; her fight here was over. She could only run, and hide, and try to heal.

And Quinn could no longer believe in the usual models of revolution.

Because in his trance he'd had a vision, he'd seen FedControl: the vast and growing stainless steel matrix of it, binding them with economics into a societal "Fridge Unit," the macroscopic mother of the one that had held Black Betty.

Meaning well, was FedControl, saving them from themselves, saving them from their own impulses to anarchy. It was too big, now, too technologically coordinated, to fight with guns, with bombs.

The Middle Man had shown them how to fight it. It had to be fought on a plane that transcended technological superiority.

Cisco was chattering, "I mean, it was so *fantastic*, the guards just sort of turned into babbling idiots and I could, like, feel the spirit workin' through me–"

No, Quinn thought, it worked around you. At most used you to prop up the scarecrows.

There were other things he wanted to say to Cisco, and couldn't.

Wanted to tell him that the only reason the manifestations took the form of spirits was because guys like Cisco could comprehend them no other way.

That it was because there were a thousand million people using all of civilization's technology without understanding it; the children of the new illiteracy. Using electronics the way a Cro-Magnon had used fire: assuming it was magic. Using a computer as if it was a medium to the spirits.

And so it became: the IAMton field had given them back their own interpretation of the new wilderness, the technological wilderness . . .

Quinn wanted to tell Cisco that he really didn't understand at all. That Spirit was real but it wasn't what he thought it was.

That what it *really* was couldn't be seen from here, but could only be lived.

Quinn shrugged, and looked at Zizz.

She was different, too, he saw. She was ill; but beyond that, something glittered in her eyes...

She wasn't looking at him through the subpersonalities she'd used for years. She was looking at him from the core of her self.

"I was there, too," she said, suddenly.

"Where?"

"In the dancing place. Just watching. I felt . . . I was halfway in . . ."

Quinn nodded. She could make the connection, too,

"I don't think we should talk about it," Mahler said. "Generates misunderstandings. Struggle to align with the necessity of focusing on issues the Masses can relate to. Mysticism is decadent, elitist."

"You're too predictable, Mahler," Quinn said. "And I got news for you. I'm not a fucking Communist. Like I told you six hundred and twenty seven times."

The van was coming down the alley, jouncing with potholes and trash.

"I don't wanna go," Zizz said, looking at the van.

"You have to," Mahler said.

I'm supposed to go with them, Quinn thought.

"You aren't going," said a wet voice.

It was behind him. Quinn turned, took a shaky step back.

A mercurial thing, a balloon-face in silver. It was just inside a grime-caked, broken window, extending from something he couldn't see. From an empty light socket, probably. It spoke again, and its two-dimensional lips moved.

"You were made for us," it said. Its voice sounded synthetic, but not electronic. It was a mathematical model of a voice, made audible. "We let you come back to these others, so you could choose fairly. To let you choose without fear. Choose: Come home and learn, Quinn."

Mahler was tugging on Quinn's wrist. "Come on," he said. "The van." He was careful to pretend he didn't see the thing.

"Mahler, look at this thing, this *means* something, man. Look and then tell me it's not–"

"I don't see your hallucinations. And I don't want to see any more holo-projections. Hypnosis, whatever they used, it worked–but it was tricks, man. Gimmicks. Mirrors and hidden compartments."

A shadow fell over them, then. They looked up, and saw something blotting out the sky over the alley, lowering itself massively between the buildings, only just fitting (or did Quinn see it compress itself to fit?), and Mahler ran to Black Betty, pulling her toward the van, shouting, "Feds! Come on, it's a bust, let's go!"

But Quinn shook his head. "It's not a bust. It's from the Middle Man." He knew it, looking at the thing. A kind of mechanistic semiotics informed him. The vehicle's identity spelled out in dancing chrome and glass; its heraldic styling.

None of them made the thing out clearly. It had a style, but its specific lineaments seemed to shift. Was it a sphere? A saucer, a teardrop, a swept-wing jet? It was constantly redefining itself like an animation drawn with a shaky hand. Quinn had an impression of the design essence of the sleekest helicopters; the design symmetry of a Japanese Magnetic Induction train; the design elegance of the new, slim orbital shuttles; the compactness and *attitude* of an Italian sports car. All these affects shifting, warring to assert themselves. Here was no vehicle: here was a Spirit, personifying vehicles.

It was a Meta, adapting itself to human expectation.

It settled onto the pavement between Quinn and Mahler. A section of the shimmering, nervous hull shimmered faster yet, and dissolved. A door yawned. An invitation.

Strength and hope returned to Quinn; faith was already there: he'd never lost his faith, not really.

"Stay away from that thing!" Mahler said hoarsely, his eyes wild.

Zizz said, "Quinn . . ." She took his arm. Quinn was amazed: her touch felt so good. It felt like a completion.

Black Betty stood up then. Twitching, she said, "Thank you..."

And walked toward the saucer, the vehicle that was all vehicles, the Meta.

Mahler went to stop her. The van held back - watching, probably the driver was scared.

Cisco was going, "Uhhhh.....whoa...Hey...I can't...Quinn? I mean, what if it's...they might ram something up us or..."

"That's not who this is," Quinn said. "Come on with us, Cisco."

"I can't, man - I'm scared."

That's what stops most people at the edge of freedom, came the voice in their heads.

Mahler clapped his hands to his ears. "Mind control...!"

Cisco was backing away from the saucer. Mahler was pushing Betty back, away from the Meta.

"Mahler?" Quinn said. "Bro?"

He put his hand on Mahler's shoulder. "I'm takin' her on with me. You wanta come?"

Mahler took a big ugly antique Russian pistol from under his jacket. He'd picked it up from a safety deposit box, in the still-functional uptown Manhattan, after Zizz and Cisco had returned to him with Black Betty. The pistol was his pride and joy. Very old, quite operational and he made the bullets himself. Probably something of the sort had been used to execute the children of the last Czar.

"No. She's not coming either." He pointed the pistol at Quinn.

Black Betty moaned, and twitched. Zizz said, "Mahler? You suck. Did I ever tell you that?"

Quinn just looked at him. "So - shoot us, man. After all we've been through together. Shoot us."

Quinn looked into Mahler's eyes. Mahler looked away, and lowered the gun.

Quinn patted Mahler on the shoulder again. Mahler shook off his touch and backed away, then turned and walked lurchingly toward the van.

Muttering, "Imbeciles...tools...Fools...."

Shivering with relief, Quinn followed his instincts.

Sirens. Choppers approaching.

It's time, Quinn.

Quinn and Zizz each put an arm around Black Betty and helped her walk into the vehicle.

The Meta; the living flying saucer. It rose into the sky, and it went somewhere else.

Cisco watched it go - and then burst into tears.

CHAPTER TWELVE

THE WEDDING OF PROBABILITY AND IMPROBABILITY

Nevada. Quinn back in Nevada. He couldn't fuckin' believe it.

"Hot day, isn't it?" Campbell said, as Quinn walked up. Campbell fanned himself with his straw hat as he pottered among the little rose bushes edging his terrace.

Campbell wore dark glasses, a white short sleeve shirt, white shorts and sandals. He glanced at Quinn, then looked back at the potted rosebush he was watering.

The ground around the canvas chairs was littered with last night's plastic glassware. Wasps darted at the sugaring remains of cocktails.

Campbell replaced his hat on his head, turned off the water and coiled the hose as they spoke.

"Yeah," Quinn said, walking into his backyard, pausing in the shade of an ornamental tree. "You don't seem surprised to see me, man. I mean - I don't think we know each other, for one thing."

Quinn hoped he hadn't made a mistake, walking up on this guy's back yard like this. He didn't know anything about Campbell, except he was a UFO researcher and some kind of

Area 51 gadfly. And he'd heard about UFO researchers: they were unpredictable, flaming eccentrics. Some were more or less sane - others barely concealed a quivering psychosis. Maybe, despite his aplomb, Campbell was about to whip out a .44 magnum and start blazing away.

But Campbell smiled and extended his hand and they shook. "You're Quinn, right? You were described to me. Ceph said you were coming. My name's Campbell."

"I recognized you. I bought one of your books once. *Unseen Invasion*."

"Ah. That old thing. Feckless speculation. Well, thanks. It was a royalty, anyway."

Campbell turned to look at Zizz and Black Betty, as they came up the path behind Quinn.

Zizz was holding Betty's hand, guiding her. She was a little less twitchy now; whispered to herself from time to time, inaudibly.

Zizz giggled, looking at the expression on Campbell's face. "He looks like he's trying to decide which of us is weirder..."

Campbell shrugged. "After Ceph I can get used to anyone."

"I'll take that as a compliment," Ceph said, suddenly lowering himself from the branches of a plum tree. He hung there from a couple of tentacles like a fire-melted Christmas tree ornament.

Everyone took a slightly startled step back.

Ceph laughed gently.

"Ceph," Campbell was saying, "I didn't mean anything uncomplimentary."

"I know you didn't. Welcome back Quinn. Young lady. I didn't catch your name before."

"I'm Zizz. This is Betty."

"*Black* Betty!" Campbell blurted. "I *thought* she looked familiar..."

Betty looked into the middle distance. Her head jerked on her neck and she said, *Shush-ush-ush-sussss.*

"She's been hurt," Zizz said, holding one of Betty's hands between hers. "I'm staying with her..." Zizz turned to look at Ceph, bracing herself. "Ceph - I didn't thank you before for helping us. I just...I wanted to thank you. And say I'm sorry if I hurt your feelings or...I mean, screaming 'kill it, kill it' when you meet someone, that could make a bad impression I guess..."

"Not at all!" Ceph mischievously extended a tentacle to her. She made herself shake it, between her thumb and forefinger; then she smiled. Happy to have healed something.

Quinn had seen that healing impulse in Zizz before; with Lila, when she was hurt, with Betty now. And he remembered she'd studied nursing. Zizz was a healer; maybe born to be a physician, and didn't know it yet.

"Betty...She's a...a part of the Meta's plan?" Campbell asked, evidently not sure how to put it.

"Yeah," Quinn said. "She's part of the chemistry, the Meta say. She's...a necessary part."

"She is part of the true alchemy," Ceph said.

"All this occult intrigue gives me a headache," Campbell said raspily. "...a worse headache. I was prepared for interplanetary stuff, Secret Science and cover-ups, something wild but rational...but this metaphysical component..." Campbell raised a hand to rub his temples.

"Hangover, huh, Mr. Campbell?" Zizz said. "I've got a recipe for that."

"How far did you have to walk, Quinn?" Ceph asked.

"From the ship?" Quinn shrugged. "Mile and a half maybe. Most of it was in the shade, around the base of a cliff..."

Campbell gazed past him, along the edge of the overhanging cliff, into the desert. "A...ship? A spaceship? *Dammit*! I missed it!"

"What's the matter?" Ceph asked sweetly.

"I hate to admit this..." Campbell sighed. "Famous UFO expert - but my dirty little secret is we're well into the 21st century and I still haven't seen a UFO. I've seen aircraft I'm pretty sure were Air Force copies of flying saucers. I've seen some anomalous lights that could have been lots of things. I've seen videotapes of UFOs. Heard ten thousand descriptions...Just missed seeing half a dozen alleged interplanetary spacecraft...Watched Area 51 for years but...they always seemed to be there when I wasn't. If not for...certain evidences, certain contacts, I wouldn't have believed..." He looked at Quinn. "What was it like? I mean, actually being *on* one?"

Quinn had been asking himself the same question.

"There are flying saucers," he said slowly, "and there're flying saucers. I don't think these are anything like the ones the Zetans use...I mean - I don't think these are spaceships exactly though I'm pretty sure they can travel through space ...and they do. They're more like living beings that - they sort of extend their own bodies outward in some way to become craft they themselves can ride in - and they carry other living beings sometimes...It was like..."

How could he describe it? The sense of a delicious danger and the simultaneous certainty of complete safety; of being in the center of the universe no matter where you journeyed. It had been like a dream, that brief ride through the skies in a living flying saucer: but it had been as real as pain or orgasm.

"It was like...riding in light. A room made out of light. Floating in it but not in free fall. It felt solid but it reminded you that nothing is really solid, somehow."

"It spoke to you?"

"Yeah. In my head. Told me some things...Tell you the truth, I can't describe it without getting it wrong."

Campbell shook his head enviously. He looked ruefully up at the blue sky, the faint streamers of clouds, began to sing, campily: "*Que sera, sera whatever will be, will be...*" He looked at Zizz. "That was my Doris Day impression."

"Who?"

"Never mind. You've had a long hot walk. Come in and have a drink, rest. The others are sleeping in..."

"Let them sleep," Quinn said, as they followed him inside. "But not for long. We're expected soon, on Roeser Ridge. There are things that have to be done..."

"Are you hungry? Come to think of it, I need to take some vitamins, maybe with some tomato juice. Maybe some hot sauce in the tomato juice. Maybe some vodka in the hot sauce..."

• • •

The sun had dimmed behind a slate of clouds. Campbell was setting up an old Minolta camera on a tripod.

The underground base was not precisely in Area 51. It was an adjoining property.

They stood just beneath the highest point of Roeser Ridge, overlooking the dusty bowl of land that lay between them and the hills hiding the base.

They were well within the remote-surveillance perimeters of the Restricted Access land the government had appropriated in the 1990s, so it was inevitable that the choppers and the flat-black jeeps should come.

Quinn, Farraday, Black Betty, Lyn, Anatole, Lila, Campbell and Zizz: in the shade of a single big upthrusting dolmen-like boulder, gazing out over the flatlands below Roeser Ridge, overlooking S4, Area 51. Waiting for the Cammo Dudes. Black Betty sat on the ground, hugging her knees, whispering, her shoulders twitching.

Every so often Anatole looked at Betty, and blinked back tears.

She seemed to notice him, tried to smile at him, as if distantly aware that he was one of her fans, and she was disappointing him, in some way. He smiled back, as if to say: *It's okay, I don't expect anything from you, I know what you've been through.* But still, she was Black Betty. Wasn't she? Maybe she wasn't anymore.

Lila sat on one side of Black Betty; Anatole on the other side of her, comforting wordlessly. Lila sang some sort of song to her, sotto, in Japanese.

Ceph was on the top of the boulder, in the shade of a little hollow of stone. He didn't like to be conspicuous.

A jeep approached. Dusty, flat black. Two of the Cammo Dudes in it; they wore camouflage outfits, without insignia, and pistols on their hips.

"Quinn?" Zizz said. "Are you sure this isn't stupid, being here? I mean - this is scaring me...I never wanted to go anywhere near this place again and now...Now we're climbing back into the viper pit."

"Amen to that," Farraday said. Lyn Farraday moved a little closer to her husband as he went on, "We shouldn't be here. This is nuts. If they drag me back down into their goddamn little termite colony again..."

"We'll be okay," Quinn said, with a confidence he knew was utterly unreasonable.

Unreasonable - but it *felt* right, to be here; he could feel the patterns converging...

All the synchronicity signals had been there; the

coincidences in the television news had spoken to him; the cawing of crows; twentythree minutes of monitoring fluctuations in the Dow Jones: all this had spoken to him through Grid; and Floures, even now, crackled in the air and said, *It comes, it comes...*

He would need the Middle Man no more; he was becoming increasingly sensitive to the signs, the significations. The time for the trance would come, too.

"You rode inside a Meta," Zizz," Quinn said. "You were carried in the arms of a god. How can you doubt?"

Zizz nodded distantly. Quinn knew she was remembering the walls of energy within the Meta.

The Area 51 patrol jeep pulled up a few yards away. One of the Cammo Dudes was a pot-bellied middle aged guy with receding gray hair and a lipless mouth; the other a thin, flat-topped rooster of a man. Hands on their pistols, they got out of the jeep and approached, swaggering just a little.

The MJ15 chopper circled the hilltop, making its presence felt, a statement in hardware.

"Campbell," said the older Cammo Dude wearily, "how many fucking years have I been asking you not to do this?"

"Twenty years, Jerry. Maybe twentyfive."

"Hey - I do not acknowledge any names you may think I have -"

Campbell turned to the others in his group and introduced the older Cammo Dude. "This is Jerry Niven, my very very good friend of many years, who has actually only held me in so-called citizen's arrest three times..."

"And I'm gonna have to do it again, Campbell, if you don't get the hell off this ridge."

The hair was standing up on Quinn's arms; it had nothing to do with the Cammo dudes. *Something was imminent.*

"Let's just cuff 'em and call the Sheriff," the skinny one said.

Six desert birds fluttered down, around them, unnaturally close. Zizz stared at them. "Those birds..."

"Campbell and his gawkin' buddies here are right inside restricted," the skinny one went on. He ached to arrest someone.

More than a dozen lizards rushed out from under the nearby rocks, and crowded round them. A squadron of tarantula-hawks, with their black bodies and red wings, circled them, alternating with carpenter bees, as if by pre-arrangement. A spontaneous menagerie was gathering with unnatural mutual-tolerance.

"Campbell here loves to be arrested, he loves the publicity, Joel," Niven was saying.

Campbell smiled and shook his head.

Electricity jumped between Zizz's fingertips. Coyotes moved restlessly in the brush. Three of them. Four. They whimpered and began to howl softly. Scores of walking-stick bugs crowded the shrubs. Grey foxes and bobcats climbed the ridge to prowl near them, strangely fearless.

Quinn thought: I should be afraid of all these animals converging on us; but none of us are afraid. We're too stoned: stoned by the energy in the air...

"Mr. Niven here," Campbell was explaining to Farraday with a kind of suave sarcasm, "is one of the lower-level guardian angels who watches over the restricted access borders of Area 51, along with a lot of other hale-fellows-well-met, for Wackenbush Security, which works for the CIA and CIAD and the NSA and the DIA and finally for MJ15, if only they knew it.."

Joel was looking around. "Weird lot of animals in the brush here...you see that? Was that a bobcat? *Two* bobcats? Now that's something you don't never see. Look, damn, there's a fox, I ain't never seen so many...what the fuck..."

A whirlwind was kicking up around them, Quinn noticed....

From the chopper?

But the chopper was nowhere to be seen...

They heard a metallic thud and a groaning of metal, and turned to see the black chopper crash-landing on the dirt road down the ridge from them, its rotors snapping off against a rocky outcropping. Its engine had simply switched off in midair.

"Shit!" Joel burst out. "What happened to them!"

They saw two USMC pilots scrambling to get out of the chopper. The pilots stared up at them from about five hundred yards away, conferred briefly, then turned and began trudging down the ridge away from them.

"Where they going, Jerry?" Joel said.

"Look kind of spooked...I guess they weren't hurt by the

crash...Jeez, that chopper just kinda...sagged right outta the air. Shit."

"The helicopter fellows look like they'll be all right," came Ceph's voice, chirping merrily from above.

"Who the fuck said that!" Nivens asked nervously, squinting at the big boulder leaning over them. "Joel, there's somebody else up there!"

The wind picked up - it seemed weirdly localized, and almost *visible*, though no dust rose into it - which was also strange. Wasps and a swarm of red flying insects Quinn had never seen before buzzed around the whirlwind, as if accompanying it; nighthawks, normally out only at dusk and dawn, fluttered near and away. Scorpions danced on the rocks, scuttled amongst impossibly-fearless road-runners, both species weirdly amicable.

Electricity crackled between Quinn's fillings.

"I feel...strange..." Lyn said.

"I feel it too," Farraday said.

In the sunwashed flatland below the ridge, gigantic shapes were forming in relief, coming into view in what had seemed the random patterning of cacti stone and scrub: the shapes of a dancing shaman, and a cougar. The two figures were hundreds of yards long and wide; shapes which hadn't been there a moment before.

"What the hell are those?" Joel said, pointing.

"It's those big Indian markings you can only see from up high," Niven said. "Only...we don't *have* any around here..."

"You hear something like...a beat, music in the air?" Joel was saying. "Sounds like...like an old country rock song..."

"No," Zizz said, "it's angst rock."

"No," Lyn said. "It's an old Rolling Stones song..."

"No, it's disco," Niven said.

"No, it's some kind of old bebop thing," Campbell said. "Where's it coming from? I can't...I can't locate the source...It's like...it's almost like it's in the boulder here...like the boulder's a big crystal radio, but...no, no it's... "

Quinn himself heard a dance song by Jerome-X. A song Black Betty had once used in a maddening tapeloop to jam FedControl transmissions for seven hours. *"The Power Underneath Despair..."*

The hilltops across the flatland from them...

...The hilltops were opening up. They were disgorging grey metal saucers, rimmed with sullen light, which rose to zigzag through the sky.

"It's now, Lila!" Quinn yelled over the rising wind.

Lila was already pulling Betty to her feet. Betty seemed afraid; a small girl in a tall grown-woman's body, whimpering, eyes flicking fearfully.

"It's okay, Betty," Anatole was saying. He and Lila hadn't left her side since she'd arrived. "This's gonna heal you. All you have to do is be part of the circuit..."

"I'm gonna get the fuck out of here, Jerry!" Joel was yelling.

But he didn't move; he and the other Cammo dude seemed frozen in place with fear, their eyes rolling like cattle smelling blood.

The Marines from the chopper were running down the road, helterskelter away from the ridgetop.

Campbell's camera exploded for no good reason at all. "Shit!" Campbell yelled. "My camera!"

Three Zetan saucers approached like flat rocks skipping a pond...

Lila took Quinn's hand; Quinn took Betty's hand and Anatole's; he took Betty's free hand and Lila's. They made a circle, clasping hands as they'd been instructed, but facing outward, their backs to one another. An irreverent joy rose up in Quinn as the circuit was completed.

The music thudded louder; the electricity crackled blue and white around them; the wind roared. The music was many songs that merged into one. Quinn picked out threads of this song and that...

> Well I'm beginning to see the light
> Some people work very hard,
> but still they never get it right
> Aw baby I'm beginning to see the light...

Zizz and Farraday and Lyn and Campbell huddled together on the ground in the shelter of a mound of rocks.

Diamondbacks writhed and rattled in the bushes, gila monsters hissed, tortoises crept up and raised their heads to the sky.

Campbell grinned at the flying saucers hovering fifty

yards above and, though he was grinning, sobbed, "My camera, my fucking camera!"

"What's *happening!*" Lyn yelled. "Please, Mike! What's happening!"

"I don't know -" Farraday told her. "Ceph said it was something to do with bringing them together here - there's some kind of geomagnetic power-spot here, at this boulder, and Quinn and Black Betty and Lila and Anatole, they're like...like elements of a chemical reaction - or - shit, I don't know!"

"But you were quite right!" Ceph shouted happily, lowering himself down the boulder and dropping into the circle made by Anatole and Lila and Betty and Quinn. "They have four of the 'chemical' components and I have the fifth!"

The saucers wobbled overhead; they were beginning to pulse with angry-red inner lights; heat throbbed from them.

The Zetan surveillance was done: they were about to strike, Quinn could feel it.

The Zetans were about to destroy them all.

What weapons do they have? Farraday had asked.

They have all weapons...

"Bringing Betty and Anatole and Lila together with Quinn..." Ceph yelled, turning and turning, dancing on his awkward and graceful limbs in the circle of his friends. "The most powerful gene is divided between them - together we have the complete gene, the five facets of the gem - and we have the faith to activate it - !"

The Zetan saucers were coming down and the air throbbed with heat and impending murder.

The sky opened, as the hills had. The sky...

...the bluewhite sheet of the sky seemed to rip, shedding thunder and showing red-edged blackness glistening with stars, night showing through a crack in the day, and through this crack came seven living-galaxy shapes, spiraling and coruscating, throwing off spears of light like mirror balls. And under that dancehall mirrorball Quinn and the others danced, simple one-two steps in rhythm, Indian steps, backs to one another but linking hands...

Quinn was conscious of Now as a state of Being; he was immured in Now; there was change, there was time, but it was whirling around the quiet center of the hurricane: NOW.

Gazing upward into this Now he could see aspects of the Meta he'd never seen before; intricate skeins of geometrical forms, facets reflecting facets infinitely, the universe reflected in each Meta, in microcosm.

The Meta surrounded the metallic saucers that seemed to quiver like cymbals - and then began to unravel, disintegrating, the Zetan saucers coming apart in midair, and for a few moments...

For a few moments it rained Zetans.

Alien bodies crashed around them wailing in despair. Three of them fell from a great height - onto Jerry Niven, crushing him.

All but one; this Zetan was held suspended in space, and was lowered gently and unhurt to the ground by some unseen giant's hand.

Then the Figures of Earth, the giant pictoglyphs of the shaman and the cougar, grew in relief, in the flatlands below the ridge, and thickened, *and rose up*, golems high as the hills, Titans made of dirt and stone, frilled with cacti and sage. The giants of stone and earth and sand - no vision, no hallucination, but there in physical fact, as real as a Manhattan skyscraper - towered up over the underground base, and reached into the hangar opening whence the saucers had come, and pulled the entire base up from underneath -

And turned it inside out. Quinn had once seen a termite colony exposed with a crowbar applied to the side of a house; from here, on the ridge, it was something like that.

The ridge shuddered and quivered; a thousand screams of terror rose up as one; lights flared in the cracks in the earth and the metal infrastructure below ground - and then went out. Coughing explosions and smoke; men fell crying through metallic cracks and into forgotten shafts that led down to ossified radioactive caves...Then the giants fell onto the squirming metal-edged wound in the hillside, two living avalanches, with a noise that made thunder slink away, and the giants were gone, and so was everyone in the base...

Quinn looked away; he could no longer watch.

A light settled round him. He felt them before he saw them: the Meta were landing, all around him; were coming down to enclose him and the others.

He heard Black Betty cry out in a kind of rapture.

He turned to look at her and she was smiling, her eyes full of light. The Meta had healed her.

"Am I in some kind of drug-state in the Fridge?" she asked.

"No, you're really not. This is real. We got you out."

"I remember, I think - some of it. I just..." Her eyes filled with tears. "Thank you."

"That's all right - we needed you."

"Is this...voodoo?"

"No - and yes."

"But this has got to be a dream...Those giants!"

"To that I'd have to say...No, and yes, too."

She nodded happily. "One thing I understand is 'no, and yes'. Everything always said no to me and I always said yes right back. Lord I'm glad to be here...These lights...these lights...! This energy!"

Then she became aware of the devastation in the flatlands. The erupted base; the distant shouts; the smoke rising, the muted explosions from down there.

"Did we do that?" There was horror in the question.

"I'm afraid so..."

"I never...I never got into violence, never. I always acted through images. Ideas on screen. Attacks on mindsets. I never...I can't believe it..."

Helicopters from the surface buildings of Area 51, a few miles away, arrived and hovered round the ruins of S4 like angry birds around their overturned nests. Soon trucks and ambulances sped to the site; rescue workers prepared to search through the wreckage...

"We should go down there," Zizz said. "We should help..."

"All that can be done for those people will be done," Ceph said. "The Meta will cull out the surviving innocents; the ones who haven't survived physically have survived after all."

"But there's so much death down there..." Betty said. And Zizz nodded. And Quinn felt sick, contemplating it.

"And at other bases," Ceph said. "We cannot interfere. We have only let their dark momentum arc back upon them..."

Suddenly a hush fell. An uneasy quiet; the winds had calmed; the light shimmered and grew -

There came a gunshot.

Quinn turned and saw that Joel, the younger Cammo Dude, sobbing hysterically, had fired his pistol - directly into Ceph's head, three times. Quinn felt, empathetically, as if he'd been shot himself.

"You *moron!*" Farraday yelled, leaping up and snatching the gun away, pistol whipping Joel with it. Joel fell to this knees and crawled away, babbling.

Farraday ran to Ceph...who was already dead.

But as the light - coming in more and more frequent waves of blue-white, picked out with iridescence - grew into effulgence around them, it seemed to draw something from Ceph's twitching, grotesque corpse, like an infant bird from its eggshell: a phantom of glimmer, there and not there, only visible as the waves of light passed over it, then coming into focus, coming increasingly into Being.

Something hovered over Ceph's body. It was a figure of violet light, with veins of fire and thoughts that were skeins of electricity. Only the eyes were the same...The rest was the outline of a man, a man they'd never seen before but who seemed almost familiar...A stranger who was familiar; who was no stranger. Who was...

"Ceph!" Farraday and Quinn said, at once.

"Yes. *Free at last, free at last. Yes. Yes call me Ceph, call me Ishmael if you want, call me Yeshua, call me home, just don't call me late for dinner. Free at last!"*

The figure of light whirled and danced with joy.

Then other figures descended from the Meta...

And the figure that had been trapped in Ceph hurried to them: men in robes, men with beards, men with eyes of light and shining mouths and fingers that beamed illumination...

Moses. Elijah. And Ceph was...

"Jesus!" Quinn burst out. Crucified, this time, in disfigurement; in the dislocated shape of a land octopus. Jesus in a prairie squid. Christ in a cephaloped.

It's good to see you again, said Ceph, said Yeshua, said Jesus of Nazareth, to Moses and Elijah. *The Zetans, the poor Zetans...*

You always were a bleeding heart, Elijah said, laughing.

Then Peter was there too, laughing, smiling at the humans gazing at him in a combination of awe and confusion.

"Should we build a tabernacle?" Lila said.

Not necessary, as it turns out, Peter said.

"You hear them too?" Quinn asked Farraday.

"Yeah. Yeah I do."

Peter and Elija took Ceph, who was Jesus, also called Yeshua - took him by the hand; and with him was Moses, and with Moses, now, was a bald, Greek-looking man with piercing eyes and a black mustache, someone Quinn didn't recognize. He heard Moses call him "George Ivanovitch".

We go now, who is called Ceph here, said George Ivanovitch, smiling ironically. *Others are waiting...Clive Staples Lewis, a long time he has waited to meet you...*

He is here? Ceph exclaimed. *Lewis is here! Draw the pints and call him to me!*

Ceph and these other radiant figures rose into the air...

"Wait, Ceph!" Farraday said. "Wait!"

"I'll be around - 'Where three gather in my name, there also I am...Split a piece of wood and I am there; lift up the stone and you will find me.'"

"Ceph -"

"'The body of the bodiless, the face of the invisible, the word of the unutterable -'"

"Ceph -"

"'The mind of the inconceivable -'"

"Ceph!"

"Yes, Mike?"

"Don't gimme that *E.T. will be here in your heart* crap, Ceph! Don't blow us off!"

"I'll be here..."

"Ceph - dammit - !"

Ceph, the astral Ceph, the perfected Ceph, also called Yeshua, rose up with those who had come here to fetch him: ascended: to join more of the Meta moving overhead...

Farraday sighed and went to his wife.

They began to slow-dance, like a couple of teenagers at a sock-hop, on the dirt of the ridge; rattlesnakes cruised by their ankles. They ignored the rattlers, inexplicably unafraid of them, and the rattlers reciprocated. Lila and Anatole held hands and swayed; Anatole's face was a piquant mesh of joy and profound sadness.

In the flatlands below, in eternal night in the midst of sunlight, men coughed their last and others wept and there was gnashing of teeth, there was beating of breasts.

But here, on Roeser Ridge...

An energy prevailed. This particular wavelength, *Das Energi*, made its dominion felt over them all. In the shelter, in the cupping of this energy, there was no grief for those who'd died. All was revealed as pageant, all was passion play, all was tragicomedy, the play was the thing, and they watched the play, and swayed to the music and were somehow in that moment outside of Time and Consequences.

Helicopters approached them and hovered nearby, expressionlessly expressing puzzlement. Jeeps approached them but stopped outside some unspoken perimeter. They were, for now, under the umbrella of this energy, this particular energy: untouchable. They accepted their own culpability; they accepted choice and inevitability. They were stoned on this energy; it did not permit them fear or grief or regret. It was possible to dance, on the ridge, while the base burned on the flatlands below, and the choppers hovered out of reach.

The Meta re-shaped themselves to form a living temple of incandescent stained glass overhead; colors quivered in the air. The bodies of the Zetans sank into the earth, which rose up to claim them; the Earth made graves for them, closed over them.

The animals that had gathered around backed away, as if in obeisance, out of the light.

Black Betty and the others danced to the beat that still hung in the air. All but Zizz.

"I'm a fucking murderer," Zizz said.

"You really know how to mess with a guy's sense of *awe*," Quinn said.

Betty stopped dancing, hearing Zizz, and came to listen, to ask:

"Don't you feel...above it, sort of? Or to one side of it? Stoned on something that makes you feel..."

"I do - but *I question it,* Betty. It's like we've been drugged...And - all those people who died in the base...we killed them! We helped, anyway..."

Betty nodded admiringly. "You make it seem like you got no depth to you because you've got so much depth you don't know how to deal with it."

Quinn nodded, surprised. Betty had sussed Zizz, alright.

"I know how you feel, Zizz," Betty went on. "But we haven't been drugged - it just hasn't got that quality. It's like we're set free to feel something that was always there..." She looked around happily. "I always knew this freedom was there...it was what I was trying to say to the world all this time but...but I didn't know how to say it..."

"I know the feeling you mean," Zizz said. "But I'm fighting that feeling because...I didn't want to kill all those people, Betty...I helped get you out of the Fridge and bringing you here was like bringing a piece of a bomb and then all those people blew up with the bomb...I mean maybe a lot of them were assholes but *so what* - I even feel bad about all the Zetans..."

"It's all right," the Zetan said, walking up to them.

He spoke not in their voices, like Jaron, but in a slightly mechanical sounding voice from a small metal sphere he held in his digits. He wore a dull-silvery jumpsuit. To Quinn's eye he looked more or less like Jaron, but Quinn was somehow sure this was not Jaron.

And the alien was speaking to them through a device, instead of with the Zetan mimicry faculty, and Quinn was certain there was significance to that, but he didn't know what it could be.

"You can call me Bill," The Zetan said. "That's what Dodge used to call me...Poor old Dodge...Said I reminded him of a lizard named Bill in *Alice in Wonderland*...."

"Well uh...Bill..." Quinn said. "How the hell are you?"

"Very well, considering all the sadness I feel," The Zetan said. "It's hard to feel sadness in this...atmosphere. But I manage it, it's my nature. I was a prisoner on one of the Zetan ships. They were going to take me back to Zeta Reticuli for consumption by the microphages. I am a traitor, you see. I have been, as they see it, conspiring with the Meta, for a good long time. I was living in a cave in Tibet for much of that time, almost a hundred years...it's good to be out of the cave...

"I have come to tell you, young lady: do not feel distress for those killed here today. The shamans, and with them the Meta - all they have done is channeled the destructive impulses already generated by my people, and by MJ15, into the quantum-probability region, and allowed its refraction and echoing there to return to its origin. A sort of massive spiritual judo. The men in the base called the giants down upon themselves. The Zetans too summoned their own dissolution. You have no culpability."

"I have to ask, Bill," Quinn said. "What are you going to do now?"

Farraday and Lyn approached, and then Campbell and Lila and Anatole, and all began to listen. The Meta-become-cathedral arched overhead; they didn't have to watch or listen: they *were* watching and listening personified.

"I will arrange a meeting with your president, soon. I've heard she's actually a nice lady, caught in everyone else's cross purposes. I have to explain a few things to her. The time has come; the truth was out there and now it has come in from the cold."

"You're...an ally of the Meta?" Lyn asked.

"I am," Bill said. "I am a follower of the Way, and the Meta are the living embodiment, a beacon for that Way. There are a few others: a friend of mine, another Zetan, was hidden for years in a grotto in Mt Athos, protected by the monks. All the Traditions are the same, finally, in the Ground of Being. Some of us saw the truth; that what the Macrobiological Team tried to create was always created, was only quickened a little, now and then, by those with the special seed. It is always there for everyone who struggles hard enough to find it..."

"I'm relieved to meet you," Farraday said. "I didn't want to think the Zetans were..."

"No. We aren't 'all bad' - but neither are your people all good, to say the least," the alien said. "We did not create Pol Pot, or Stalin, or Mao, or Joe McCarthy or any of your serial killers. They were all yours. Nor was Hitler our man. He distorted some ideas taken from one of our secret societies - but we did not create him or his works. He was all yours...."

"Point taken," Farraday said. He reached out and took the alien's boneless digits and held them for a moment.

Zizz smiled. Betty put her arms around Zizz. "You okay, Zizz?"

Quinn could see Zizz visibly relax; see her accept the gift that hummed in the air, in the Earth around them.

"Yes. Yes."

Campbell had walked off to examine something that was emerging from the sand, thrust up by a living earth: A section of Zetan flying saucer that had fallen, driven itself into the ground. It was a broken segment of curved aluminum-colored stuff that was metal and was something else too. "Look!" Campbell burst out, pointing. "Something's..."

The hull was peeling back, exposing a compartment - within which were two human bodies.

Anatole ran to them, crying out.

Ceph was there, between the two bodies, touching them, hovering like a flame over a candle wick, speaking in some forgotten language of benediction, as Anatole and Lila ran to kneel beside the twisted, limb-skewed figures of Sullivan and Kian.

Anatole wept, for a time, as the others drew the bodies out, and laid them in a shallow grave, placed a cairn of stones over them.

Then a light thickened about the cairn, and a young woman seemed to materialize, to hover, as if levitating, over the grave. She wore nothing at all but her shine was such you could see little of her body.

"Seeking One!" Anatole yelled hoarsely, running toward her. Lila ran after him. "Anatole, wait!"

Seeking One put out her hand - and Anatole fell to his knees, a few paces from her, and sank into his familiar trance. Lila knelt with him, and bent her head, seeming to pray.

Quinn gazed up in awe at Seeking One...She gave him a glance, only, then seemed to fold inward upon herself, and vanish.

• • •

He knew he once had a name; he knew that the smaller one with him once had a name. He knew more or less what a name was. There were names here, with him:

Sullivan. Kian.

It didn't matter, much, really.

They were all right, without names or with them.

They were two patterns, interlocked, on the face of a wave that moved eternally through darkness. But he knew it was moving toward light. It had been, since...

Since what?

He couldn't remember how it had happened exactly. He and the little one had experienced it together: Death.

So this was Death.

But another current intersected with theirs; another more powerful wave drew their patterns another direction; down a drain, in a way, inside out and back to the pain and the strange compression, the compartmentalization, the separation...

So this was Life. Big deal.

He found himself and Kian embodied, hovering in a between place, where the sky was blue if you thought of blue and green if you thought of green. Out of this suggestive void came two shapes, then a third, approaching from neither up nor down.

• • •

When he recognized them, Sullivan felt a deep, nurturing warmth; a profound satisfaction shared by the sea of Being on which he was a wave: his embodiment was only on one level; he existed on several. "Kian - it's your brother! And Lila!"

"Is the other Lady an angel, Dad?"

"She must be...Words feel sort of strange, don't they?"

"Yeah. I don't mind them, though...Hi, Anatole!"

"Kian! Lila, he's alright! Dad, Kian!"

Sullivan took Anatole and Lila and Kian, all three, into his arms.

If you or I think a loved one lost, and find them miraculously safe, we are joyful. But it's a shadow of the real joy, the experience possible to someone set free; someone outside life, outside death.

We can try. We can try to imagine it.

• • •

When Anatole and Lila stood up again, Quinn felt relaxed, centered, just looking at them: they radiated serenity.

"They're in the shining sea by now, aren't they?" Anatole asked Lila.

Lila nodded. "I know they are - because I can feel them near us. Seeking One said we'd feel them near us when they entered the shining sea...."

Quinn thought that someday he would ask them what had happened, in their trance, but he never did.

The effulgence washed over all of them in impossible

colors. They spoke to Quinn, those energies.

He closed his eyes, and the altered state was just a flicker away. He saw...

...He saw the remaining Zetan saucers, everywhere, withdrawing, pulling back to their base on the far side of the moon and their artificial moon aligned with the star Sirius. He saw the Meta, here in force now as they'd never been before, patrolling the world, protecting it from the Zetans, a vast sentrying by living jewelry of unthinkable power. He saw that he and his friends, with the strange alchemy of their essences, genetic and spiritual, had opened the way for the Meta, breaking the Zetan field that held them back.

But he heard a voice, then, and thought it was the Meta that Anatole had known: Seeking One.

"You were only the medium; we are only the medium; the Zeta are only instruments; the Higher cannot reach us directly, but by degrees, it reaches out to us: through serendipity, and one to another: you to me, me to you. The Higher has opened the gate for the Meta, to redress the imbalance. Bill will give you the means to hold the Zetans at bay - but then we will withdraw..."

"No!" Quinn said, aloud. Zizz looked at him, wondering who he spoke to. "No - don't leave us."

"We go to wait for you. We have given gifts. But you have reached that interval in the octave of your evolution that you must pass on your own, with your own willingness, with watchfulness, with consciousness. With slow and steady work..."

"I want to ask...there's a lot I want to ask..."

"You like the Rolling Stones?"

"What? They were a polka band or something, weren't they?"

"'You can't always get what you want, but sometimes you get what you need, Quinn...'"

"Seeking One -"

But she said nothing more to him, after that.

"You okay, Quinn?" Zizz asked, touching his face.

He opened his eyes and looked at her; enfolded her in his arms, and kissed her. "Yeah."

"Well, Bill," Campbell said. "I've got a cooler in my truck...I badly need a libation... Would you care for a drink?"

"Do you have any chocolate?" Bill asked. "Or perhaps a

cigarette?"

Under the over-arching Meta; under stained glass that shifted and reflected their thoughts; beneath the Meta, beneath the Higher: The music began again, each hearing a different song, but all of it to the same beat, even those songs that weren't in the same beat; which is, of course, quite impossible and which is, in fact, exactly what happened.

The party went on far into the night.

• • •

Joel, the Cammo Dude, still moving like a dog on his hands and knees, reached the bottom of the ridge about dawn. Leaving a trail in the dust behind him, he crawled into the desert.

There were sightings of him for years afterward. He was always seen on his hands and knees, babbling to himself.

EPILOGUE

Quinn gave the twins breakfast; a boy and a girl, Bette and Mikey. Then he kissed them and got them off to school. They had to leave a little early as they were going on a field trip to the new antigravity testflight center.

It was a fine autumn day in Montana, twelve years after that day on the ridge.

Quinn and Zizz went to the grove of maples behind their house, and into the meditation hut. Zizz rang a small bell, and the two of them sat in meditation, and silence, for one hour.

Then they got up, kissed, and went to breakfast. After breakfast together, they each went about their business. Zizz went to work at the hospital where she was an intern; in another two years she would have her residency, in obstetrics.

Quinn worked for four hours editing the documentary he was making about the use of Zetan technology in cleaning up Nevada toxic waste sites. He let his computer answer the phone, which kept ringing, and ringing. He rarely answered the phone. He wrote a letter, answering an inquiry from a journalist wanting to know if it was true that he'd been at the destruction of one of the ill-fated underground bases and did he believe, as most people apparently did, that the bases were destroyed as a result of a concerted effort of unknown human saboteurs, using explosives. He answered by suggesting the journalist read certain ostensibly unrelated books; otherwise he gave no opinion, or testimony.

He also wrote a letter to Mike and Lyn Farraday, in New York, and congratulated them on their newest baby, Jason, and thanked them for the photos of the New York United festival; photos of Muslims line-dancing with Christians; blacks with Jews. *"Too good to be true?"* Farraday had written, on the back of one of the photos. *"But seems like it'll take hold - maybe because we dissolved FC."* With FedControl gone, the pressure had been off: the country had been free to heal. And only a small part of California had, in the end, seceded, with the armistice signed, and one entire state. The country could live without Orange County and Louisiana, if it had to.

Quinn thought about asking them if they were going to vote for the performance artist and perennial candidate, Betty "Black Betty" Meriwether, for Mayor of New York, even though she didn't have much chance of winning. But there was no point in asking; of course they'd vote for Betty.

He did ask them if they'd heard from Anatole and Lila, who had been married a year, and were supposed to be somewhere in Tibet.

Screw the age difference, Quinn wrote. *They're happy.*

Writing the letter made him think about Mahler and Cisco. Mahler had died in the police-riots, in Brooklyn, gut-shot by a cop. Cisco had tried to find his missed opportunity in cyberspace; thought he could reach higher consciousness there; he became an addict, and starved to death in a virtual reality helmet illegally rigged for pleasure-stim.

Zizz...Zinnia was her real name. Zinnia had had most of her tattoos removed. "I always liked your tattoos," Quinn had told her. "Don't do it for me."

"It's for me. I've got nothing against tattoos," she'd said. "But I don't want my ideas of my Self to be...fixed."

After lunch, Quinn went outside and began to rake the yard. He raked it consciously, and with unbroken attention, thinking of nothing but raking, and watching within, and raking.

After that, he watered the flowers, and fed the chickens, and then he went to make dinner for the kids and Zizz. He did these things consciously and with seamless attention.

271

Once, when he looked at the sky, he saw a message in the proximity of an airplane to a peculiarly shaped cloud; he felt the intuition come, and pass through him, and he shrugged. The entities came to him, sometimes, and told him things, and sometimes he gave readings to people who needed the help badly enough. But he rarely deliberately summoned the Urban Spirits. It was just more phenomena; he had other Work now.

After they had dinner, Zizz and Quinn sat in meditation for about one hour. Then they played with the kids, and talked to them about what they had seen that day on the field trip.

The kids went to bed, and to sleep. Quinn and Zizz went to bed, and made love, and went to sleep.

The next morning, Quinn fed the twins and got them off to school. Then Quinn and Zizz sat in meditation for one hour.

After that they had breakfast and Zizz went to her internship.

That afternoon, Quinn did some weeding, and then he harvested the carrots from the garden.

The novel? The end.

APPENDICES
Optional Reading

THE READER

Optional reading? Hey, Shirley, listen - the *whole book* is optional, you know? I don't *have* to read anything.

THE AUTHOR
(hastily)

Oh I know! I just assumed that if you got *that* far you might feel a sense that you were obliged to read the -

THE READER
(interrupting)

Listen, dweeb, I am not *obliged* to do anything. Like I said, the whole book is optional.

THE AUTHOR

You could not be more correct. In fact, if you want, supposing that you had the book but you were not sure you wanted to read all of it, you could read *everything third word only*. For example, the first line of the book, reading every third word, would come out: *Peter and Jesus whom Yeshua mountain into dusk*...Like that. The whole book, if you wanted. Who knows? Maybe it's secretly coded to be read for arcane meaning, that way?

THE READER

Is it?

THE AUTHOR

No.
(beat)

At least...not as far as *I* know...

APPENDIX A

The following text is many hundreds of years old. I did not make it up. The Emerald Tablet has been very influential, over the centuries, amongst certain mystics, particularly alchemists. This particular text is a new translation by Richard Smoley, from the Latin, and first appeared in *Gnosis Magazine*. Other versions exist in Arabic. All known versions are assumed to have their origins in a more ancient, oral source.

THE EMERALD TABLET
of Hermes Trismegistus

Newly translated from the Latin by Richard Smoley

1. True it is, without deceit, certain, and most true:
2. What is below is like what is above, and what is above is like what is below, to accomplish the wonders of the one thing.
3. And just as all things have been from the one, by the design of the one, so all things have been born from this one thing, adaptation.
4. Its father is the sun; its mother is the moon. The wind carried it in its belly; its nurse is the earth.
5. This is the father of all consecration of the whole world.

6. Its power is intact, if it shall have been turned toward the earth.
7. You will separate earth from fire, the subtle from the dense, sweetly, with great ingenuity.
8. It ascends from earth to heaven, descends again toward earth, and receives the force of the things above and below. Thus you will have the glory of the whole world. Therefore all darkness will flee from you.
9. This is the strong strength of all strength, because it will conquer everything subtle and penetrate everything solid.
10. Thus was the world created.
11. Hence will be wondrous adaptations, of which this is the method.
12. And so I have been called Hermes Thrice-Greatest, having the three parts of the philosophy of the whole world.
13. What I have said about the working of the sun is complete.

APPENDIX B

Further remarks from Ceph with respect to the Zetans:

"Man was designed to have two eyes that look outward and an eye that looks inward; the Zetans, through their telepathic influence and genetic manipulation, blinded the inward-turning eye. Some human beings learned to restore this inner eye's sight; most died third-force blind, blind to themselves, slaves to their automatism, having sleep-walked all their lives, knowing only a small portion of themselves, a small portion of their world: the inward is a world to itself.

"The Zetan encouragement of man's outward-turning, man's identification with the ephemeral, the superficial world outside himself, was the original fracture that led to a series of fractures and a greatly magnified suffering for the human race...

"Of course, this fracturing, this relentless outward-turning, gave man a sense of being dualistically separate from the universe from which he sprang: hence the identification of the Zetans - the Archons - as the servants of the Demiurge, the mythical deceiver, the false God, who separated us from paradise in some ancient traditions..."

APPENDIX C

Ceph's further remarks with respect to Jesus of Nazareth and the early Christian church:

"Jesus, of course, never intended to establish a new religion - in this, he defied the Zetans. He wanted only to clarify the mystical roots of the fundamental, existing religions; the insights of the Judaic mystics, and the Essenes and, yes, the early Buddhists, with whom he was in touch.

"Certain select disciples, under the influence of the Meta, rescued Yeshua, also called Jesus, from the cross, giving him a narcotic which made it look as if he'd died there: he did not die, and was later escorted from the tomb; yet he did indeed appear miraculously to certain Disciples, in an incident of 'bilocation'...St Paul, heavily under the telepathic influence of the Zetans, created his own version of Jesus' teaching, larding on the Messianic stuff, the hellfire business, the original-sin connection, and fabricating a lot of things Jesus never really said. A religion mostly designed to create obedient followers, Paul's version was a vector which led to the Holy Roman church, and which was oriented to the protection of the Zetans' pet secret lodges and the suppression of any advancement which the Zetans considered to be dangerous; they wanted civilization, of a sort, but not the 'Enlightenment'. Still, they tolerated a great deal, including many cross currents in the Roman church, Catholic individuals who worked for the Higher in opposition to the agenda of the Zetans: that tolerance too was part of the experiment...Obviously the Vatican proscription against birth control, detrimental though it might be to an overpopulated world, was useful to the Zetans and their genetic experimentation...There was much involvement in the agenda of the Zetans in the Vatican but this involvement fluctuated...

"Once the Zetans realized Jesus had spread his seed in Europe, they organized the Priory of Sion; the seed of Jesus was unusual, special; they were never again able to produce precisely its like...They were blind to the forces that manipulated them even as they supposed themselves manipulating the human world...

"The Zetans were themselves used by the Higher, the finer energies that emanate from the Absolute: from God;

gradually, and by exquisitely slow degrees, these emanations subtly lend their Good Orderly Direction, the 'English' on the spinning ball, to all the concatenations of chaos, to the peregrinations of randomness, and from a macroscopic perspective they slowly draw consciousness into Being, as dew is drawn by evaporation to become sky. The process is slow; the process involves suffering; there is no other way.

"There are only two things in the universe: Mind and Chaos.

"'Him who has ears, let him hear.'"

APPENDIX D

OFFICIAL NOTIFICATION:
HIS EXCREMENCE, THE GRAND HIGH INQUISITOR
SURREAL NEOPRENE IPSISSIMUS
DOKTOR OF DEJECTION: JOHN SHIRLEY
INFORMS YOU THAT:
THE HYPOTHESIS has been CONFIRMED: YOU ARE IN DEEP SHIT.

HYPOTHESIS 788857A predicts that the Implicitly Privileged Secret SubGenius Research Team, exactingly employing its improbable 74 MILLION DOLLAR BUDGET, will, through extensive laboratory research and field testing, and through exquisitely, precisely, immaculately conducted experimentation, confirm that this world is at the dog-shit end of the intergalactic spectrum, is in fact a forgotten alien experiment, a petri dish gone bad through having been left in a refrigerator whose plug was accidentally pulled, and in a generally hopeless mire of existential toxification and psychophysical fugue. After many years of ceaseless and pointless research the SubGenius 788857A Confirmation team has definitely concluded the following: YES YOU ARE IN DEEP SHIT*.

YOU HAVE BEEN NOTIFIED.
/////////////////////////////

* The story going around is this: there is a way out which is the way in.

APPENDIX E

There are no Zetans. I'm not saying there are no extraterrestrials; there just might be a few saucer-pilots checking us out.

There are no "grey alien" abductions. There are no implants. Unless these events are staged by - as some have suggested - government intelligence services.

I have seen the enemy and he is us.

• • •

In real life, and not just in this book, American intelligence services had - and some say, still have - a Black Project devoted to mind control, to some extent using mass media, called MK Ultra. This program experimented with direct control of human behavior through the transmission of microwave impulses (every paranoid schizophrenic's fantasy), through the (much documented) use of LSD and other drugs on unwitting, non-voluntary subjects, and, some claim, through such devices as the Warren Commission, which "investigated" the assassination of John F. Kennedy, and the subsequent selling of the Commission's "Oswald was a lone nut" conclusion to the public by means of a pliable media.

There are also numerous rumors - some of which have percolated into mass media via the "X Files" TV series - that MK Ultra was involved in *creating* the "alien abduction" stories, in fabricating the tales of UFO abductions to cover up other nefarious intelligence activities, or, as yet another rumor goes, as a test of mind control methodology.

After all, if you can make someone believe they've been abducted by creatures from outer space, alien beings who've poked probes into their asses and stolen some of their "time", you can make them believe anything.

Researcher and writer Jacques Vallee reported that an investigation into an apparent UFO abduction in France turned up evidence that the whole thing had been staged by human beings: a man was drugged, and then found himself swallowed up in a luminous fog; he woke up days later with a vague memory of alien abduction. Certain agents of French Intelligence admitted to Vallee, in Paris, that they had staged this entire event as an experiment in mind control.

There are indications that a "UFO close encounter" at an American air-base in England, widely reported in the press, may have been staged by American military Intelligence. The medium here is the Staged Event. It is theatre disguised as reality - and the theatre extends even into the news media reporting the Staged Event. The same may apply to the notorious "alien autopsy" film which is likely a fabrication involving certain notorious crop-circle hoaxers collaborating with an American CIA agent - perhaps working for MK Ultra - with some arcane mind control agenda.

The USSR, during a time when the SALT treaty was newly in force, reported a rash of UFO sightings in Siberia. Their media interviewed bemused country folk who spoke in awed tones of the strange lights in the sky. Post-USSR revelations of KGB documents revealed that the "lights" were in fact night time missile tests carried out by the Soviets under the camouflage of a "rash of 'flying saucer' sightings", in order to avoid exposing their violation of the SALT treaty. The KGB, too, is the likely source of the notorious UMMO letters supposedly from "extraterrestrials" circulated a few years back.

Rael. Solar Temple. Look for cults to arise who use UFO imagery to seduce the lost and rootless into their agendas. Trust in God but tie your camel down.

APPENDIX F

Something more about Anatole.

...Anatole, very tired, came home from his work at the school, and wrote a letter to Farraday's son Jason, before going for his walk on the beach. There was a long PS. The PS was longer than the letter.

PS: Jason, you asked about Soul Making, as your father called it; and you asked about the Meta. That term, Soul Making, is a bit deceptive, though there's a sense in which it is literally true. I refer you to the list of books I gave you last time, including the Moses Maimonides and the Boris Mouravieff, and the Gospel of Thomas (the Gnostic version of the gospels, from the Nag Hammadhi Library). Eg, from the Gospel According to Thomas: "...These are the secret words which the Living Jesus spoke and Didymos Judas Thomas wrote: And He said: Whoever finds the explanation of these words will not taste death. Jesus said; Let him who seeks, not cease seeking until he finds, and when he finds, he will be troubled, and when he has been troubled, he will marvel, and he will reign over the All. Jesus said: If those who lead you say to you: 'See, the Kingdom is in Heaven', then the birds of the Heavens will precede you. If they say to you: 'It is in the sea', then the fish will precede you. But the Kingdom is within you and it is without you. If you will know yourselves, then you will be known, and you will know that you are the sons of the Living Father. But if you do not know yourselves then you are in poverty and you are poverty."

This 'knowing yourself' is not so easy. There is a story (several extant versions) of a Zen monk who went to his Master and said, "Master I want to be like you, and soon, how will this be accomplished?" And the Master said, "It can be accomplished like this: go for just seven days watching everything you do and everything you feel, and do not let your attention lapse at all for those seven days." The Monk said: "Piece of cake!" He went and tried to do this, and after just a few minutes found he was thinking, instead, of dinner, and ceasing to be vigilant within himself. He tried again and again but could not be completely vigilant for more than a few minutes at a time. And he had been asked to be vigilant *continually* for seven days! So he returned to his Master and said, "It is too difficult to learn to do this in seven days - can you give me more time?" The Master said, "Yes. Take seventy years."

The time of the gifts given by the Meta is past. The Meta have removed to their own vibratory home-base, as it were. We can go to them, and they can give us, through that Higher thing, a sort of help; but they - and Ceph, who is with them now - can no longer come here and take us into their substance, as they did with Lila and me, and as Ceph did, after his transfiguration, and offer an immediate exposure to the energies of transformation.

Now they have moved up, beyond our immediate reach, and they call to us and we must strive to rise to them; strive to burn with a consciousness that is like a fire in wood, and release the sparks that rise: that slow burning, that slow striving, that is how the process works. And even that which they gave us, in those days, is not permanent; it is an open window but it is not an open door. Lila is now, once more, in Tibet, working to open that door (my work with children keeps me here this time). Even Enlightenment, you see, can be trod down under the usual identification with life. So we have to work. And work and work, second by second, year after year, with the methods given to us by the various traditions which are at root one tradition; we have to walk the Way ourselves, step by trudging step. We cannot be carried.

• • •

    Having written this, Anatole Osterberg, aka Anatole Sullivan, went for his walk on the beach, near his house.
    ...Dusk on the sea. Fine energies moved in keenly attenuated waves through the hard and soft places of the world. Anatole felt the gentle tug of apocalypse; of mass epiphany; another cycle of change coming.
    He smiled wearily and shrugged.
    He was more interested in this moment, on the beach, on San Francisco Bay. There were machinations in the sea. Walking near the lacy fringe of the water, Anatole could see machinery just under the surface. DuChamp's pistons and vents and, vaster than that, a subaquatic architecture of chrome, made of vast pipe organ arrays locked into chromium dynamos, like some flooded Fritz Lang set (remembering the Fritz Lang videos cinema-obsessed Quinn had lent him); part of it moving in machine-precise patterns; part of it stationary as a mountain of iron. Inflexible laws improbably seen in the purely chaotic. Machines of the sea. Impossible, paradoxical, and glisteningly evident.
    An orbital shuttle rising from the Zetan airbase thudded through the sound barrier; the only sound the nullgrav vehicle made. Several small black children in cutoffs were thrashing through the surf, playing Good Zetan and Bad Zetan, and they waded right through his visioned machinery, up to their knees in steel, and yet Anatole knew it was there; knew he was not hallucinating. A vision is not a hallucination. A vision is a disclosure.

Why the sea? he wondered. What inexorable function is prefigured here?

Breeze-blown sidewinders of sand skirled the beach, struck at his ankles, between his socks and cuffs, with a pleasant grainy stinging; the sky roiled with sullen power, and at the horizon small angels in dull neon were strung like children's paper dolls, refolding into crystalline orbs.

Gazing at the horizon, Anatole thought of time and loss...magic and loss...and of course thought of Lila. The separation from her hurt like a son of a bitch.

Looking at this suffering as a thing-in-itself, Anatole thought of the place at the cusp of Being, just beneath the Absolute, at the juncture of the Pleroma; the place where plus and minus meet, where positive and negative, active and passive neutralize; where two needles meet point to point, their infinitely sharp points exactly poised one on the other; the needles (widening past the junctured points to infinitely expanding cones) turning each in the direction opposite the other.

And pinned between these infinitely sharp points is consciousness, present tense: the first circle of consciousness, the stone dropped in the pond; between these point-on-point spikes is crucified this: the unspeakable suffering of God.

The unspeakable suffering of God.

And radiating from this suffering: The ineffable mercy of God.

He felt Lila, nearby. Close: Only on the other side of the planet. Close as a heartbeat.